Sci-fi
£

MARIK'S WAY

NICK BROWN

Copyright © 2018 by Nick Brown.
All rights reserved.

This is a work of fiction. All of the characters, organizations, and events portrayed in this novel are either products of the author's imagination or are used fictitiously.

ISBN-13: 978-1725079359
ISBN-10: 1725079356

Printed in the United States of America.

CONTENTS

Chapter One 1
Chapter Two 11
Chapter Three 23
Chapter Four 31
Chapter Five 39
Chapter Six 49
Chapter Seven 58
Chapter Eight 68
Chapter Nine 79
Chapter Ten 89
Chapter Eleven 99
Chapter Twelve 108
Chapter Thirteen 116
Chapter Fourteen 126
Chapter Fifteen 134
Chapter Sixteen 144
Chapter Seventeen 154
Chapter Eighteen 165
Chapter Nineteen 174
Chapter Twenty 187
Chapter Twenty-One 194
Chapter Twenty-Two 203
Chapter Twenty-Three 213
Chapter Twenty-Four 222
Chapter Twenty-Five 233

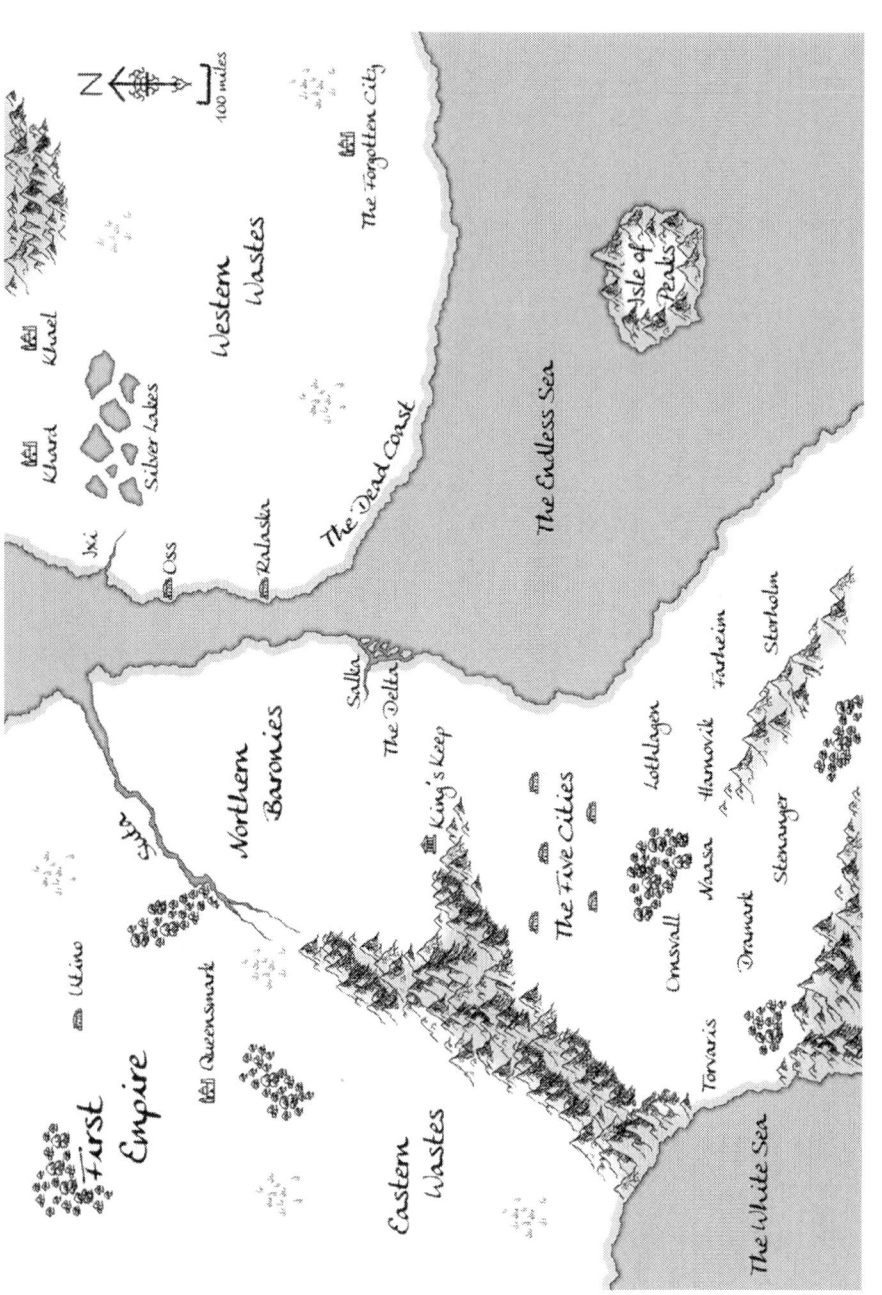

Chapter One

'Perhaps I'm being unduly harsh here but it's hard to consider you a swordsman when you don't actually have a sword.'

Marik had seen that one coming. 'Fair point. Entirely fair point. But you know what the Lukva road is like – my misfortune to encounter a bunch of bandits. It was six to one. If you give me a blade, I'll show you what I can do.'

The recruiter – narrow eyes, broad shoulders – gestured to the men lined up behind Marik. 'They all have their own swords.'

'Again, a fair point but you've got to look past the weapon - see the man. You can't buy experience. Or *quality*.'

The recruiter looked him over. 'If you're going to try that on, I suggest some better clothes. No offence.'

'None taken.' Marik shrugged. 'Bandits.'

'Sorry, friend, not today. Move along.'

Marik aimed a thumb over his shoulder. 'Youngsters – lacking the wisdom of age.'

'I'm thirty-nine,' said one of them.

The recruiter tapped his fingers against the hilt of his own sword. 'Move along.'

With a sigh, Marik stepped out of the line and strode back past the other hopefuls. Most were in fact younger than him, only a few older. A couple had a sharp look about them, the rest looked like amateurs who didn't know one end of a blade from the other.

At the edge of the courtyard was a low wall. Marik sat on it and idly watched the recruiter interrogate the next man. He told himself it didn't matter: who wanted to trek countless miles into the notorious Long Marches with a bunch of amateur warriors? No thanks.

And yet. He needed a job. Any job. A few weeks earlier he'd been hired as a bodyguard for a kindly widow who seemed very generous with her late husband's fortune. Nice, easy work. But a couple of ill-advised comments to her younger sister had been the end of that. Heading east from the port city of Lukva to the capital, Ralaska, he had encountered the bandits. Marik put three of them down before losing his sword and the larger of his two bags. Five hours of hide-and-seek in a cornfield had concluded the confrontation. So now here he was, a week later, with not a single coin to his name and only one change of clothes.

'You got a no, I suppose?'

He turned to see a small fellow standing beside him. The stranger had the dark colouring and narrow features of a local. Unlike most of them, however, he spoke Common and with only a slight accent. Hanging from his belt was what looked like a half-decent scabbard.

'You suppose correctly.'

'How much is he offering per day?'

'Four coppers.'

'By the eternal gods, Estrek is getting cheap.'

'Not going to bother then?' asked Marik.

'I can get six a day guarding warehouses in Lukva.' The stranger bobbed his head from side to side. 'Then again, it's bloody boring. The Long Marches could be more exciting.'

'If you go to Lukva, be careful. I got robbed on the road.'

'Will do.'

Marik aimed a thumb at his backpack. 'This is all I have left.'

The small man examined him. 'You as strong as you look?'

'Good question. I haven't eaten for two days.'

'How do you feel about crew work?'

'Today, wildly enthusiastic.'

'I might know of a job. Only three coppers a day but food's included.'

Marik stood. 'Where?'

'I can show you. Not too far.'

Marik hadn't experienced many acts of kindness recently. He examined the small fellow's face for a while. You could never really tell, of course, but he saw no malice in him. He offered his hand. 'Thanks, friend. I'm Marik.'

'Flyn. Pleased to meet you.'

On the whole, Marik was not fond of cities; and Ralaska had so far not done much to change his mind. He would not have gone to the capital at all were it not for the fact that it was the largest settlement for two hundred miles. Apparently, more than fifty thousand people lived here and where there were people there was work. And until he could earn enough to buy either a blade or a horse (ideally both), he was stuck.

Flyn clearly knew the city well. The merchant Estrek's building was close to the centre, and from there he charted a path through the crowded, noisy streets. It took them almost a quarter-hour just to negotiate the market. Marik's greedy eyes were drawn to cauldrons full of stew, plump loaves, glistening fruit. Even the dried fish impaled on skewers made him salivate. He noted a number of city guards there, every one armed with a spear. Their cloaks bore their monarch's colours - red and gold - but the hues were as thin as the material. Once beyond the market, there were no pleasant smells to mask the unpleasant ones. Marik didn't know a lot about sewage systems and it seemed that no one else in Ralaska did either.

It was the capital of Urlu, a once sprawling kingdom now limited to a narrow strip of coastline and kept alive by the trade that ran from Ralaska and the ports of Lukva and Ikk. The king – Elemer VII – had been in power for four decades. Having presided over the decline of his empire and his people, he was not overly popular.

As they entered a quieter street where women were emptying pots into a drain, Flyn finally slowed down.

'You a Souther?'

'How did you guess?'

They both smirked. Aside from his size, Marik possessed fair hair and ruddy skin; neither of which were common this far north.

'What brings you to Ralaska?'

Marik didn't particularly want to explain himself. 'I like to travel. Explore. See something of the world.'

'Ah, a restless fellow like myself. How long since you left the South?'

As they stepped carefully over a dense pile of horseshit, Marik realised he was dealing with yet another curious man. He rarely asked anyone about anything; why did others have to ask so many questions?

'About three years.'

'Things still bad down there?' enquired Flyn.

'Depends whose side you're on.'

'They say Baldar has five of the nine provinces in his grasp now.'

'At least.'

Flyn led the way around a corner. They had to wait for a heavily-laden cart to pass. 'You don't seem too happy about that.'

Marik didn't reply. Baldar the Bold was just about the last thing he wanted to talk about. In fact, it was a subject he would prefer to not even *think* about. This was yet another reason to find work; he had far too much time to think.

Once past the cart, they reached a wide avenue that came eventually to a broad, arched bridge across the river Kal, which reached the sea at Lukva. Here, dozens of hawkers plied their wares amid the hundreds within the bottleneck. Halfway across the bridge was a short, squat guard tower. Like Marik, the city guards stationed on top gazed down at the river, where dozens of barges, skiffs and the odd sailing vessel somehow avoided each other. Marik also cast an eye west towards the cranes and warehouses of the docks. He had little experience with ships and sailing but if Flyn's lead didn't work out, he knew he might have to search for employment there.

On the far side of the bridge, soldiers were scrubbing out some graffiti daubed on the bricks with white paint. Marik couldn't read in Common though he did know a few letters. The Urlu alphabet was a complete mystery.

'What does that say?'

'The usual crap – 'pox on the king', 'no more taxes' – that sort of thing.'

'Not very popular is he – old Elemer?'

'A fine leader, in his day,' replied Flyn gruffly.

Marik decided on another topic of conversation. 'Assuming I eventually get enough money together, where's the best place to buy a blade?'

'What would you be looking for?'

'I don't mind iron but it has to hold together.'

Flyn considered this as they picked their way through the crowds streaming towards the bridge. 'You could try Brownleaf Road – there are four weapon-smiths there I can think of.'

'And how much for a blade?'

'Three or four bronzes.'

Marik whistled.

'Nearest mine is a hundred miles away,' explained Flyn.

'Ah.'

Three streets later, they reached an area where most of the buildings were derelict and unoccupied. Flyn waved a hand around. 'This has all been bought up by some foreigner so it's one big clearance job. All these have got to come down.'

They reached a crossroads and looked out over an entire block that had been demolished, leaving only collapsed structures and rubble. A crew of eight were at work, smashing walls with hammers and dragging bricks away on sledges. Close to the road, the bricks formed a hillock where a cart was loading up.

Flyn pointed at an older man sitting on a barrel smoking a pipe. 'Carlis – this is his crew. I went to school with his son. He's tough but fair.'

The pair followed a narrow path surrounded by rubble. Where the men were labouring, clouds of red brick-dust filled the air. Marik could already taste it on his tongue. This would not be pleasant work.

'Good day, Master Carlis,' said Flyn.

Carlis plucked at his beard and peered up at the young man. 'Who are you? And why are you talking Common?'

'Flyn Rellun, a friend of your son. I'm talking Common for the benefit of this fellow.'

Carlis took a drag from his pipe and appraised Marik without meeting his gaze.

'I went to school with Simmyn,' added Flyn. 'You used to take us fishing.'

Carlis spat as he stood. 'Simmyn – don't even say that name.'

'Oh.'

Marik sighed. It had been a long walk and this was not going well.

Carlis continued: 'Little shirker won't get out of bed. Always got an ache somewhere. Little bloody shirker.'

'I haven't seen him for a while. You know my father though, I think – Drys Rellun.'

'Drys, eh? Rings a bell. What do you want anyway?'

'This is Marik. He's looking for work.' Flyn gestured to Marik, who did his best to appear strong and trustworthy.

'Mmm,' said Carlis. 'Where you from?'

'The South.'

'Mmm. Personally, I don't mind foreigners. But some of the lads aren't so keen. Don't need any trouble in my crew.'

'You won't get any from me,' said Marik. 'I've worked everywhere, never had any trouble.'

Not a complete lie, but not entirely true either.

'Mmm, well, you're a big lad.'

'Not afraid of a day's work either.'

'Dawn to dusk. Hour for lunch. Three coppers a day. You work until the sun sets today and impress me - I'll take you on. Should be about two weeks' work.'

'And if I do impress you, how much for the rest of today?'

'Nothing.'

'Maybe you'll just say no and I'll get nothing for half a day's work.'

Carlis drew in more smoke and inspected the long neck of his pipe. 'Maybe. But I need to see if you've got it in you. Hard going's not for everyone.'

Marik looked at Flyn, who shrugged.

'Well?' added Carlis. 'I reckon you'll be handy dragging a sled.' He nodded at the numerous smaller piles of bricks that needed moving to the big pile. Two men had straps around their middles which they used to haul the sleds across the uneven ground. Marik knew it would be tough going but if he really did get two weeks' pay, he would have enough for a sword. Then he could look for proper work. Sword work.

'In exchange for a day's pay, you can use the tent.' Carlis pointed at a shabby awning slung between two half-collapsed walls. 'Straw mattresses. I throw in food and water too.'

That settled it. Marik had been sleeping on a beach for three nights and – despite the cover of a wrecked boat – had been too cold to get much rest.

'Very well.'

Carlis offered his hand and Marik shook it. The foreman then gestured at a third sled. 'Off you go then.'

Marik nodded and turned to Flyn. 'Thank you. Really.'

'Happy to help. I know you appreciate it.'

An awkward pause. Marik knew he owed him and he wanted to pay him but what could he do?

'Master Carlis?'

The foreman was already heading for his crew. 'What?'

'I owe Flyn for bringing me here. Could you advance him one of my coppers for tomorrow? I give my oath I'll work hard and you'll hire me.'

Carlis considered this for a moment then reached into a money-bag tied to his belt. 'Must be getting soft in my old age. Here, as I know your father.' Carlis threw the coin at Flyn but it was Marik who snatched it out of the air.

'Gods, you're quick.'

'You should see me with a blade.' Marik handed Flyn the copper. 'Thanks again.'

Flyn smiled as he took the coin.

'Still heading to Lukva?' asked Marik.

'Maybe. I'll see what my mates are up to. Listen, whether I go or not, I'll be around for the Festival of Light. That's ten days' time and I'll probably end up in The Rampant Horse. Ask around, everyone knows it.'

'The Rampant Horse. Ten days.' Marik didn't have any other friends in Ralaska and reckoned he might need Flyn's help again.

'Farewell,' said the Urlun as they shook hands, 'and good luck with the job.'

'Farewell.'

*

The thin, itchy straps that cut into his skin were annoying; the never-ending supply of brick and rubble was infuriating; and the dust was worse than either. But when Marik set his mind to something, he was not one to baulk. So he worked on; even when the coughing became painful; even when the dust seemed to have coated his mouth, his throat and his guts. He stopped only momentarily when offered a gourd of water by Carlis and continued when the other workers drew their employer's attention to the fact that the sun had set. A quarter-hour after they had trooped off to the tent, Carlis ambled over and watched Marik pick up a spade and move yet another load off his sled.

'All right, hero. You've done enough. But don't forget to drink – I don't want you falling over and cracking your head.' Carlis pointed at the tent. 'The lads will cook up some grub. See you in the morning.'

Marik was relieved. Relieved and exhausted. He had been a soldier and he had been a labourer but he had not worked that hard for years. As Carlis walked away, he slapped his hands together, trying to get rid of the worst of the dust. He returned the spade to a pile of tools and recovered his pack, which he had hidden inside a barrel. There wasn't much in it but what little he had he wanted to keep. He found his clay flask and drank every drop of water.

The men were gathered around a fire not far from the tent; some sitting, some standing. Three small, well-oiled birds sizzled on a spit. The smell was wonderful but Marik affected indifference. Beside the fire, arranged on a cloth, was a pile of dried apple and nuts, apparently untouched. One man noted his approach with what might have been a slight smile. The others ignored him.

Marik was considering walking on to the tent with his pack when one of the seated men turned and looked up at him.

'You going to work that hard tomorrow?'

'Hope not,' replied Marik.

'Good. You're making us look bad.'

The worker's Common was clear enough but held a strong local accent.

'Understood. I'm Marik, by the way, for those I didn't already meet.'

The seated man leaned forward to turn the birds. Of the others, only one reacted: he walked over and offered his hand, palm high and facing Marik.

'Uvek.'

Marik knew the local custom and pressed his hand against the one offered to him. The man was short and well-built with a heavily-furrowed brow. Marik had noted that he didn't seem to have talked much throughout the afternoon.

'How long have you been working here?'

'Uvek.'

The cook and two others laughed.

'He don't speak Common.' The cook stood up. 'I'm Yaluv.' He pointed at the six others and named them in turn. To Marik they all seemed like local names. He would try his best to remember them.

Yaluv was the oldest; forty-five at least. He was of middling height but very wide without being overly fat. His thick, unkempt hair was the same pure black as the others. Marik couldn't help noticing his ears: one had a ring in it, the other looked to have had the lobe bitten off.

Yaluv aimed a thick finger at a younger man. 'Nyll here speaks a bit but none of the others do.'

Nyll gave a nod. He was distributing the nut and apple into bowls. 'Carlis buys food. Got bowl?'

Marik reached into his pack and took out his wooden plate. This – along with a spoon, a mug, a fire-starting kit, a needle and thread, two candles, a thin blanket and a change of clothes – constituted his worldly possessions.

He put the plate beside the bowls. 'Water?'

'There.' Nyll pointed to a barrel beside the tent.

'Thank you.' Marik set off but stopped when Yaluv spoke again.

'Very polite, Blue.'

'Blue? I told you my name.'

'That's what we call Southers – blue eyes. We don't have no blue eyes here.'

The birds turned out to be something called sandlark and though he reckoned his portion was a little smaller than the others, Marik enjoyed what he was given. Uvek continued to be the friendliest of his new companions but could say nothing in Common beyond his name and a few basics. After dinner, Marik made sure he contributed to the tidying up: he washed the metal spit, ensuring that every last bit of fat was removed before leaving it to dry. He wanted to get along with these fellows, earn his money and move on without any problems.

However, it seemed likely that Yaluv would constitute at least one. He insisted on calling Marik 'Blue' and – once all the work was done and they again sat around the fire – embarked on an interrogation. It didn't seem to bother him or his compatriots that most of them couldn't understand either questions or answers. Nyll did some translating but seemed to pick out only a few points he deemed worthy.

'What you doing up here on your own then?' asked Yaluv from the other side of the fire.

'Travelling.'

'What do you think of Ralaska?'

Marik was sitting on a chunk of rubble, elbows on his knees, hands together. 'Seems all right so far.'

'Not what it was,' replied Yaluv with a shake of his head. 'Not by a long way. Foreigners always putting us down; keeping us weak.'

Even with his limited knowledge, Marik knew that to be an inaccurate reading of recent history. He also knew it for bait and he had no intention of biting.

'Nothing to say?' pressed Yaluv.

'Got no opinion on it. Just looking to make my way.'

'And what way's that? How'd you get here?'

'Came across the Strait.'

'Any news from the baron's lands?'

Again, Marik had to be careful. He had heard some Urluns talk of their hatred for Baron Zanzarri: the nobleman dominated the territory on the other side of the Shivar Strait and had long eclipsed his cousin, King Elemer. Others, however, seemed to admire his aggressive, avaricious leadership.

'Towns were busy, shipyards too.'

'Another one who wants to see us on our knees,' observed Yaluv. 'Where you from in the South?'

'Ever heard of Three Rivers in Lothlagen?'

'Can't say I have.'

'Well, it's a long way away.'

'A thousand miles?' asked Yaluv.

'More, probably.'

'When did you leave?'

Marik's patience was wearing thin. 'When's my turn to ask a question?'

Yaluv gave a lop-sided grin. 'You're the stranger, Blue.'

Marik was also beginning to tire of all the eyes on him. Didn't this lot have anything else to talk about?

'You from the city?' he asked Yaluv.

'Born and bred.'

'Me too,' added Nyll.

Before Marik could ask any of the others, Yaluv fired another question at him.

'What about old Baldar then? Damn near unstoppable, isn't he? How many provinces is it now?'

'Not sure,' replied Marik evenly.

Nyll briefly spoke with two of the other men in their own language.

Yaluv said, 'six, apparently.'

Marik pretended not to be interested.

'Your people on his side or against him?'

Marik hesitated. Given Yaluv's determination to press him, either answer could cause him difficulty.

'Enough questions, eh? It's been a long day.'

Yaluv hesitated then nodded and crossed his arms. For a couple of minutes, the locals spoke amongst themselves in Urlun. Beyond the tent, a few townsfolk could be seen passing by, many carrying lanterns. Then came another lull in the conversation. Yaluv couldn't resist.

'Thousands dead down south, so they say. Whole villages and towns wiped out. Men burned alive, women and children enslaved. What is it, five, six, years of fighting? And you up here with us, Blue. Strange. Surely you must either be for Baldar or against him. Or maybe you just didn't want to fight?'

Stay out of trouble.

Marik glared at Yaluv for long enough to make his point then stood up and walked away.

Chapter Two

The first few days at the site were not pleasant. Carlis was a hard taskmaster and persisted in giving Marik the toughest jobs; either the sled or breaking up the largest pieces of rubble with a great hammer. Marik finished the days with a parched throat, bleeding hands and whatever sleep he got never seemed enough.

Yaluv only ceased his questioning when he realised he wasn't going to get anywhere. After a while, he ignored Marik completely, which was fine with Marik. The others – initially unfriendly but eventually cordial – clearly respected his work and contribution to the camp. And Uvek, who seemed similarly isolated from the others, became a friend. The two would usually eat their meals together and the Urlun introduced Marik to a simple game which could be played with small stones and a grid drawn in the dust.

Carlis would occasionally engage his new employee in conversation. He had travelled widely and they spoke of the lands between the Urlun Empire and the South: The Five Cities, the Northern Baronies and the Cloud Passes. As the days passed, Carlis became happier because *his* employer was happy; the crew had almost finished their work and would be done by the Festival of Light. They would be rewarded with a bonus to compensate them for fewer days' work.

Marik's spirits also improved. As the end of the second week approached, he had saved four bronzes (a bronze being worth five coppers) which he kept in a moneybag slung from his belt. He had enough to travel now; enough to survive while he sought his next job. Unfortunately for him and the rest of the crew, Carlis had nothing more for them; he was soon to leave on a long journey to visit an ailing relative.

A blade would probably have to wait. Marik couldn't afford to spend almost everything he had on one thing, even if it was the most important thing a man could own.

On the day of the Festival of Light, everyone in Ralaska finished work at midday. Though the clearance job was over, Carlis had said the crew could use the tent for a few more days. Four of the men said their farewells but the other five remained behind. Marik was relieved to have some time off; he could go and speak to Lena.

The previous week, he and Uvek had been sent to buy some fruit. While the vendor put their order together, a well-dressed young lady came to the store, accompanied by an older woman who looked like a servant. The young lady caught Marik's eye and asked him where he was from, confessing that she needed to practise her Common.

Lena was the daughter of a local moneylender. Their home was around the corner and apparently her father was annoyed that the demolition and clearance was taking so long. Lena had pointed out that the ensuing construction work would probably be even noisier. She was not only pretty but kind; taking the time to include the shy Uvek in the conversation. She laughed when she realised how little the unlikely pair could say to each other. When her order was ready, Marik offered to carry it for her. Despite the servant's protestations, he insisted and during the brief journey, Lena told him more about the Festival of Light, declaring it the best day in the Urlun calendar. They said farewell at the door of a large, red-brick house. She gave him a warm smile and said she hoped he enjoyed the festival.

So, when the day arrived, Marik donned his better trousers and tunic and spent half an hour cleaning his boots. Once at the house, he didn't dare knock for fear of facing the father but waited a while until a young servant came out. Marik tried the few words of Urlun he'd picked up but the girl just shrugged and hurried away.

Half an hour later, he got his first look at Lena's father. The moneylender exited his home alongside a very large bodyguard armed with a cudgel and a sword. The driver of the carriage awaiting him was similarly armed. The vehicle itself was the height of luxury; elaborate metalwork, reinforced wheels and plush curtains at the windows.

Before departing, the moneylender had secured the heavy front door with a padlock. Marik waited until he was out of sight then knocked twice – loudly – but no one answered. He even asked the jeweller in the store next door but the man ushered him out immediately with what sounded suspiciously like an insult.

Back at the camp, he found Yaluv, Nyll and their friend Aranydd quietly discussing something. When Marik laid out on his bed, Yaluv took his cohorts outside to continue the conversation.

Marik tried to focus on the coming days, telling himself that there was little point pursuing Lena. However friendly, moneylenders' daughters didn't court rough-looking foreign labourers like him. He wasn't sure of his next move but hoped that if good old Flyn kept his promise to be at The Rampant Horse, he might know of some opportunities.

Having dozed off, he was awoken by the return of Uvek, who had bought some pears and another type of fruit Marik didn't recognise. Ever generous, Uvek shared the food with his friend. As they ate, Marik tried to explain his plan to visit The Rampant Horse. He was eventually reduced to play-acting but Uvek just stared blankly back at him. When Yaluv returned to the tent, Marik asked him to translate. After muttering several curses, Yaluv did so. Once Uvek understood, Marik asked Yaluv what his plans were.

'What do you care, Blue?'

'For the festival, I mean.'

'Ah, it's a load of nonsense. Lanterns and flags – who can be bothered with all that?'

'So, you'll be staying here?'

'Yes. Why?'

'Someone should watch the camp. I don't know about here but back home, festivals are a dangerous time. Thieves can take advantage.'

Yaluv regarded him for a moment then grinned. 'Don't you worry yourself, Blue.'

Yaluv had so often tried to provoke Marik that he couldn't read the meaning of the expression on the Urlun's broad face. He wouldn't be leaving any coins at the camp, that was for sure.

'We'll be off at first light,' added Yaluv. 'I expect you'll miss me.'

'Terribly.'

'Still never really explained why you left the South, did you?'

'I suppose not.'

With a smirk, Yaluv returned to Nyll and Aranydd, a tall man who seemed as close to the older man as Nyll.

On a nearby street, a parade of youngsters had appeared, each dressed in a white tunic and carrying a white candle. At the head and tail of the procession were adults; they were also clad in tunics but theirs were decorated with some sort of insignia.

'Rampant Horse,' said Uvek suddenly with a grin.

'Rampant Horse.' Marik hoped Flyn would be there; otherwise it was going to be a very long night.

As they neared the centre, the crowds grew. Dusk was close and every other person seemed to be carrying a lantern of some description. Most were gathered in families or what seemed like religious groups similar to the one seen earlier. The atmosphere was cordial and relaxed and Marik enjoyed some of the songs he and Uvek heard as they negotiated the busy streets. One in particular seemed popular and reminded him of a tune his mother had liked.

He reckoned it took them an hour to reach The Rampant Horse – and several more minutes to squeeze their way to the bar. The inn was situated on the corner of two main streets and clearly favoured by working men. There wasn't a single woman in the place. Uvek bought the first round – a dark, spicy ale served in wooden mugs. While he was waiting, Marik looked around for Flyn. He couldn't help notice all the eyes upon him: most expressions were curious, a few hostile. It was no surprise; his big frame and fair hair stood out a mile. Unless Flyn turned up quickly, this didn't seem like a good place to hang around.

Marik and Uvek went to stand outside with their mugs, watching the parades and pedestrians filing past. Marik kept a close eye on a rough bunch of fellow drinkers; two of them had already cast unpleasant looks in his direction. Both had sheathed knives on their belts, which made Marik wish his dagger hadn't been stolen by the bandits along with his sword. As one of their friends came out with another round of ales, Marik ushered Uvek further away, using a group of youths as a barrier. Now feeling rather tense, he started when a hand slapped him on the back. He was ready to strike as he spun around.

Flyn was already grinning. 'Only me. You know, you're pretty easy to pick out in a crowd.'

'Good to see you.' Marik introduced Uvek and the two locals spoke briefly in their own language.

'So, what do you think of the festival?' asked Flyn.

'Er ... some good songs.'

Flyn inspected their mugs. 'Looks like you two are running low. Back soon.' With that he hurried off to the bar.

'Flyn,' said Uvek.

'Yes,' said Marik, relieved that the conversation was about to improve. 'Flyn.'

Soon he began to relax. The glaring thugs moved on and Flyn did an excellent job of exchanging news with Marik and befriending Uvek. His time guarding warehouses in Raska had passed without incident and he had travelled there and back with a large group to deter the robbers. He was pleased to hear Marik had done well with Carlis.

'I knew it would work out. So, what now?'

'Good question. I was going to ask if you have any ideas.'
'Actually, I might. Do you have enough money for a blade?'
'At a push. If I knew I had some more coins coming.'
'I might be able to loan you a bit. Remember Estrek was recruiting guards for his trade caravan across the Long Marches? There's another merchant named Yarlen; he's going a lot further – to Six Peaks. He has some trade deal with a baron – metal goods go that way, hides come back. Should be about a month. I have a friend who's already signed up. Yarlen is looking for around twenty men. The pay is good – a bronze a day and a hundredth of the profits.'
'Not bad. I take it this is a dangerous route?'
'Very. The marches can be unpleasant but-'
'-You mean the bog vipers?'
Flyn's eyes widened. 'Exactly. Twenty feet long with fangs that will go through a man's arm. They take horses and people … occasionally. But it's the second half of the route to Six Peaks we really need to worry about. There's a religious sect that live not far from the road – the Dark Cloaks. They follow the teachings of some long-dead holy man and consider anyone who enters their territory to be an enemy. There are dozens of them and they all carry these long, serrated knives. They call them the Teeth of the Lord.'
'And they attack traders?'
'They do – but for every party that gets hit, three or four get through. There are several routes to Six Peaks. Just depends on luck.'
Twenty-foot snakes and knife-wielding warrior monks. It sounded like a job to avoid, yet that pay rate couldn't be ignored. If Marik returned with all those coins, he'd have enough to travel as far as he wanted.
His original intention in crossing the Shivar Strait had been to head north and locate his old friend Sanni Dern in the city of Khard. Dern had lived there a while and was a man who somehow always seemed to make a success of things. It had been more than two years since they had last crossed paths but Dern had said Marik would always be welcome.
'So,' said Flyn. 'What do you think? You're wasted as a labourer. Anyone can see that.'
Marik let out a long breath. Uvek asked something and Flyn answered. While they spoke, Marik drank his ale. He really wasn't sure what to do. The risks were obvious but this was a rare opportunity with considerable reward.
'Well?' said Flyn.
'I'll think about it.'

'Don't take too long - I think they're leaving next week.'

'And you're definitely going?'

'Unless something better comes up. My mother won't like it but it should be quite an adventure.'

'Mmm.'

Uvek grabbed their empty mugs and headed for the bar with a grin. The sun had set long ago but there were still plenty of locals around. Marik noticed that the numerous lights in view were starting to swim a little. Apparently, this spiced ale was on the strong side.

'How's your Urlun coming along?' asked Flyn.

'It's not. I can say hello, goodbye, good morning, goodnight, water, food, tired, shovel, sled and hammer.'

'Ha! Life as a labourer.'

'Tell me, what does 'esdi' mean?'

'A curse. Quite strong.'

"Walla?"

'Dinner.'

'Ah. That makes sense.'

"Larris?"

Flyn frowned. 'Say again.'

Marik repeated himself.

'That's a name. Must be one of the crew.'

'I don't think so,' said Marik. 'Unless it's a family name.'

'Could be. Ah, what a fine sight.'

Flyn gazed admiringly at a passing group of young women, each carrying a lantern. They were arranged neatly in rows, walking in a slow, precise march. They wore long, pale robes and silver diadems on their heads. Though the women were hardly making a sound, every person in their way moved aside and turned to watch them respectfully.

'Followers of the goddess Esmyra,' explained Flyn. 'Virgins.'

'Is that right?' Marik found himself equally entranced – until Uvek returned with the next round.

Flyn exchanged a few words with his fellow Urlun then turned to Marik. 'That word – Larris – where did you hear it?'

'Mainly from Yaluv, I think – one of the crew. I slept close to him and he sometimes rambled in his sleep.'

Flyn's expression changed. 'It *is* a name – it's the name of the moneylender who lives near where you've been working.'

*

The streets were quieter but there were still so many lanterns and lamps alight that they could easily find their way. Marik knew he could not be sure of Yaluv's intentions and hoped to find him at the camp. And yet, Larris had clearly been on his mind; and he was planning to leave the next morning; and he, Nyll and Aranydd had seemed preoccupied. Marik could also not forget that odd moment when he'd mentioned how festivals offered an opportunity to criminals.

As they neared the camp, he broke into a run and arrived at the tent to find it unoccupied. Marik and Uvek's bags were as they'd left them. Uvek pointed at the gear Yaluv and his cohorts had left behind.

'Looks like they're coming back then,' observed Flyn. 'There may be an innocent explanation. Perhaps he knows the man?'

'Unlikely. Come on – we must at least check.'

Having evaded a large party of singing revellers, they ran along the adjoining street and around the corner to the moneylender's house. It was a three-storey structure, part of a long terrace including the jeweller and several other expensive stores. All the lower windows were protected by metal grilles. There were many visible lights on the higher floors of the adjacent buildings but the moneylender's house was quiet and dark.

Marik walked up to the door, surprised there was no guard. There wasn't enough light to see the door properly so he felt with his fingers. He found a knob made of glass or some other smooth material and two adjoining metal rings to accommodate the padlock. The lock itself was hefty, as wide as Marik's hand. But it was just hanging uselessly from the exterior metal ring. When he twisted the knob, the heavy door clicked open.

'Shit.'

'What?' asked Flyn.

'It's open. Something's wrong.'

'A mistake perhaps?'

'Moneylenders don't make mistakes like that.'

'Marik, if you go in there and anything's happened, it's you that will get blamed. You're a foreigner. Best we go and find some city guards – there are dozens out tonight.'

'What if something's happening *now*? People could be hurt.'

He didn't say so, but Marik was thinking of Lena.

Stay out trouble.

But what if she was in there - injured or in danger?

'Can I borrow your sword?'

Marik could see enough of Flyn to realise he was looking along the street.

'I'm really not sure that's-'

'-Fetch the guards if you wish. I'm going inside.'

Flyn muttered some curse as he drew his sword and offered Marik the handle. Marik weighed the weapon – it was light but well-balanced.

Flyn spoke to Uvek then translated. 'He'll go in with you.'

Marik clapped Uvek on the shoulder. 'Good. Tell him to stay behind me.'

As Flyn set off at a run, Marik turned and opened the door. Ahead was a long, shadowy corridor and an illuminated space perhaps fifteen feet ahead. He took the two steps up carefully and hoped that Uvek would follow his example as he moved quietly but steadily forward. He was halfway to the light when he heard the voices: not loud but urgent, talking in Urlun.

He slowed, took one step at a time. He passed an open doorway to a darkened room that seemed empty. As he neared the illuminated doorway ahead, he turned and gestured for Uvek to stay put. Despite the lock, Marik couldn't be sure. If the place was being robbed, why hadn't the criminals posted a sentry?

Wincing at a slight squeak from a floorboard, he halted. The doorway opened onto a large room that extended to the left. In the section he could see ahead was another dark doorway and a luxurious chest of drawers topped by a vase and a candelabra. Three thick candles were alight. The talking seemed to have stopped. Then he heard a voice: an angry, desperate voice that sounded familiar.

Marik took a final step and peered through the gap between the open door and the frame. He soon understood why the attackers hadn't posted a guard. Whatever had happened, the robbers had made a mess of it.

A broad knife in his hand, the back of his tunic visibly sodden with sweat, Yaluv was standing over three kneeling figures lined up against the far wall, about ten feet from the door. Master Larris' brow was also slick with sweat and his jaw was shaking. Yaluv jutted the knife towards him and repeated the same phrase again and again. Kneeling beside Larris was a middle-aged female servant, who was staring at the floor. Next to her was Lena. She was wearing a smart green dress, her red hair held up in a high tail decorated with flowers. Her gaze shifted from her father to Yaluv. Considering the situation, she looked quite composed.

To Marik's left, on the far side of the room, a big fellow - presumably one of the bodyguards - was lying on his side, groaning. Not far from his open hand was a cudgel. Leaning back against the wall nearby was Nyll, one hand shakily gripping a knife, the other holding his bloodied head. He touched the wound, grimaced, then wiped the hand on the wall, leaving a red smear. He was close to another doorway and in the adjoining room two sets of legs could be seen. Marik couldn't make out the rest of them but both figures were still. He guessed that one pair belonged to Aranydd and the other to a second bodyguard or employee of Master Larris. No wonder Yaluv and Nyll looked so desperate.

When Yaluv darted forward, Marik almost moved. He reckoned he could take out both men with the sword but he had a distance to cover and they were close to the hostages. Yaluv pulled two rings off Master Larris's fingers, pocketed them, then gripped the moneylender by the hair and put the blade to his throat. He persisted with the same question.

Marik felt a hand on his shoulder. Uvek came close and whispered. 'Want money. Yaluv want money ... moneybox.'

Marik nodded.

A fearful moan from Larris. Marik looked back to see that Yaluv had placed the point of the blade inside his nostril. Lena squealed and shuddered and put her hands over her eyes. Yaluv turned towards her. Marik readied himself.

But Yaluv was not the one who moved. Nyll hurried past him, grabbed Lena by the arm and lifted her up. He hauled her past the servant and positioned her in front of her father. Gripping her arm with his bloody hand, Nyll put his blade against her ear and yelled at Larris. When the moneylender's hands shot up in a gesture of panic, Yaluv grabbed his collar and put the knife against his face.

Marik knew he had to act. Nyll was turned away from him and had blocked Yaluv's view of the door but there were still those yards to cover and two blades only inches from Larris and Lena.

Marik turned and whispered to Uvek. 'You run. Straight through. It will confuse ... Just run. There. There.'

He jabbed a finger at the adjoining room where the dead men lay. Uvek nodded, eyes wide in the darkness. Marik moved aside so that Uvek could go first. His fingers were clammy on the sword. Yaluv shouted something at Nyll.

Marik hit Uvek on the back. The Urlun ran through the doorway and turned left, sprinting past both the robbers and into the next room. Nyll was still trying to work out what had happened when Marik clubbed the hilt of the sword into his head. The thudding impact sent the would-be robber flying across the room.

As he brought his hand back, Marik deliberately knocked Lena aside with his shoulder. She and the servant fell in a heap. Recognition flashed in Yaluv's eyes as he let go of Larris. This time, Marik didn't have the advantage of blindsiding his foe.

The men faced each other; blades at the ready. Hoping that the scuffle to his left was Uvek dealing with Nyll, Marik raised the sword. Yaluv didn't seem concerned that he had only a dagger. His hand twitched.

'Don't do it,' warned Marik.

'Should have stayed down south, Blue.'

Yaluv moved quickly for a big man, slicing at Marik's sword-hand. Marik saw it coming and twisted easily away, leaving his foe committed and overbalanced. Before Yaluv could recover himself, Marik's left elbow hammered into his hairless head. The Urlun staggered, then fell to his knees. Marik was about to grab his weapon when he heard a shout.

Spinning around, he saw Uvek totter backwards, one hand gripping his arm. Nyll's knife was low but he was already turning when Marik took three quick steps and heaved the sword downward. He had aimed at the knife but the blade caught Nyll's hand. The Urlun shrieked as his weapon spun away. Marik readied himself but when Nyll realised just how badly injured he was, his knees buckled and he collapsed onto the rug below. Blood leaked from the stumps of his severed fingers. The four digits lay close by.

Marik spun back to face Yaluv but the big man was still on his knees, hands pawing the ground as he tried to get up. Marik kicked the knife away then sunk his left boot into his side. Yaluv tipped over and began to retch.

The female servant crawled away from the combatants then used the chest of drawers to get up. Larris rushed to his daughter and embraced her. Marik found himself looking at Lena as she rested her head on her father's shoulder. Her earlier composure gone, she now let the tears come.

Marik was impressed to find Uvek still on his feet. The cut on his forearm was long and quite deep but there was not too much blood.

'You'll live.' Marik pulled a cloth from a small table and used it to wrap the wound. 'Outside. Take these three with you.'

Uvek did as he was asked. Unsurprisingly, Larris, Lena and the servant were quick to leave.

Marik was left alone with two dead men, the dazed Yaluv and the stunned Nyll. The former was now on his back, eyes rolling. The latter was on his knees, whimpering as he tried in vain to halt the issue of blood from his mutilated hand.

Stay out of trouble.

Somehow it just never ever seemed to happen.

Two hours later, he was still in the same room. The dead men had been taken to the city morgue; the injured bodyguard and Uvek had been taken to the hospital. Yaluv and Nyll had been arrested by the city guards, who didn't seem particularly concerned that Nyll had lost a bucket's worth of blood.

'Would you like another one?' Lena was holding a bottle of some local spirit. Marik had enjoyed the first glass so much that he eagerly held it up. As she poured, the female servant tutted. Like Lena and her master, she'd returned inside once the city guards arrived and was now busying herself by cleaning up the mess.

Marik was sitting on a fine chair in a corner. He had been questioned already by a sergeant of guards, who was now interrogating Flyn while another official spoke to Master Larris. This man wore robes and was not armed so Marik assumed he was ranked well above the sergeant. The official was listening attentively to Larris, who seemed more upset than either of the women.

'This isn't the first time, unfortunately,' said Lena as she returned the bottle to a nearby table. 'Three times men have got in here. None recently but Father has lost bodyguards before. All I can think about is poor Garek's wife. A blessing there are no children, I suppose. Taralis has two but at least he'll be all right. What about your friend?'

'Stitches should do it. It'll hurt awhile though. And you, miss?'

'I'm fine – just a couple of bruises where they manhandled me. We're so lucky you came.'

Marik stood. 'It was *all* luck. If I'd not met up with Flyn, I'd never have even worked out what they were up to.'

'I'm very grateful,' said Lena. 'And I know Father is too.'

Marik wondered just how grateful. He also couldn't help wondering if this turn of events might affect his chances with Lena. She really was pretty: those green eyes, those full lips.

'What's the name again?' The sergeant had finished with Flyn and now switched to Common.

'Marik.'

'Family name?'

'Where I'm from we don't really have them. I can give you my village's name.'

The sergeant frowned and fiddled with one of the buttons on his leather jerkin. 'Not necessary. No address here, I suppose?'

'I only arrived two weeks ago and I've been staying on the site.'

'Well, I don't see that we'll have any more need to speak with you until Magistrate Neryn here makes a decision. You may need to attend court but, if so, it won't be for a few weeks. We can't hold you in Ralaska against your will but if you're still here, you'll be expected to attend. In any case, we've got enough witnesses.'

The sergeant took a final look around. 'You did well, all things considered. Looks like you Southers don't deserve your reputation.'

After three years in the North, Marik had gathered that many there considered the South backward and uncivilised. Given recent events, he wasn't sure he disagreed.

The sergeant went to join Magistrate Neryn as the senior man concluded his discussion with Master Larris.

'Was that a compliment?'

'I think so,' said Flyn as he approached. 'Sorry, Marik. I should have come in here with you.'

'You probably did the right thing.'

Flyn glanced at Lena, clearly ashamed.

'What will happen to Yaluv and Nyll?' Marik asked.

'They'll hang,' said Lena in a whisper. 'Father will make sure of it. I expect he's already pressing for it with the magistrate.'

'They deserve nothing less,' said Flyn. 'The sergeant's going to leave three guards behind, miss. You'll be safe.'

'With a moneylender for a father? Never.' Though she'd kept her voice low, Marik was surprised by her frankness.

He felt weary; as if he'd done a full day's work for Carlis. He'd almost forgotten how it could be when your blood was up and time seemed to slow down. He needed to sleep but he wasn't sure he could.

Magistrate Neryn and the sergeant left. Master Larris came over and put a hand on his daughter's shoulder. 'I've already said it, I know, but sincere thanks to you, young man. I haven't yet decided how to repay you but I would be grateful if you would join us for dinner tomorrow. How does that sound?'

'Ah ... well, very kind.'

'Good. Shall we say the tenth hour?'

'Tenth it is. I suppose we better be going.'

'Goodnight, Marik,' said Lena. 'I'll see you tomorrow.'

Chapter Three

To his surprise, Marik slept well. He had Flyn to thank for this; the Urlun clearly still felt guilty about the evening's events and insisted on giving up his bed. Flyn shared a room with two friends at an inn close to the centre. The pair had arrived there to find the room thick with the smell of ale and the friends snoring loudly.

Waking to find himself alone, Marik was looking for a chamber pot when Flyn returned with some cured meat and bread. He explained that his friends had work with a crew clearing up after the festival; they would be out until the evening. After breakfast, Marik and Flyn made their way to the hospital, a sprawling building not far from the high towers of the palace and government.

The establishment was manned by surgeons and nurses from the Royal Institute of Medicine. The Urlun Empire's historical achievements in this field were clearly still a point of pride for King Elemer: the complex was spotless and Marik and Flyn passed dozens of well-equipped chambers where they saw many patients being attended to. Judging by several overheard conversations, the night's festivities had resulted in more than a few casualties.

When they eventually found the right room, a friendly nurse let them in. Marik was pleased to see Uvek looking well enough, his wound already stitched and bandaged. The nurse gave him a bottle of medicinal tonic and told him to return in a week to have his stitches removed. Marik was impressed with the treatment; he had never seen anything like this in the whole of the South.

It took the trio ten minutes to find their way out. Uvek confirmed that he felt fine so they embarked upon the long walk back to the site. Marik didn't particularly want to discuss the incident but Uvek spoke of nothing else and Flyn did an excellent job of translation once again. Marik soon realised that Uvek also felt rather embarrassed about his role – failing to successfully tackle Nyll. Marik assured him that he'd done well; he had been unarmed after all. As they spoke, Marik's eyes drifted to the sword hanging once more from Flyn's belt, now cleaned and sheathed. He supposed he should have been able to disarm Nyll without cutting him. Then again, why should he feel any guilt about it? He had no doubt the thieving bastard would have sliced off Lena's ear to force her father to give up his riches. He and Yaluv had got what they deserved.

The three of them had only been back at the site for a few minutes when Carlis arrived on a horse-drawn cart. Having heard of the night's events, he'd immediately cancelled his trip. As they spoke, the foreman shook his head and rubbed the back of his neck. He could clearly not believe his former employees capable of such a crime but was full of praise for Uvek and Marik. He gave both men another two bronzes for accommodation and together they packed up the tent. Once that and the remaining gear had been loaded onto the cart, Carlis disclosed that he was returning home to write a letter of apology to Master Larris and certain influential officials. He seemed concerned that by employing Yaluv and his cohorts he had harmed his business.

When offered a lift home, the weary Uvek gladly accepted. Marik helped him onto the cart and passed up his bag. He thanked him for his friendship and the Urlun returned the compliment. Carlis set his horse away and the cart rumbled across the flattened ground towards the road.

Midday had already passed. Flyn reckoned it was time for some refreshment so led the way to a nearby inn. His head still fuzzy from the spiced ale, Marik refused the offer of a beer but tucked into a bowl of thick soup. The two discussed the job with the trader Yarlen; and Flyn agreed it was wise to delay a decision until Marik knew what Larris might offer him.

'Think about it. You probably saved both he and his daughter – not to mention whatever money he had lying around.'

'I wonder how much longer he would have held out. Even when Nyll had his blade against Lena's ear, he didn't say a word.'

'I've no doubt he's a calculating fellow,' said Flyn as he wiped ale-froth from his mouth. 'You don't become successful in his line of work by being anything else. Anyway, it's worth going to dinner just to spend a bit of time with that Lena. I've always had a thing for red hair. You know what they say about redheads.'

'You do realise it's dyed?'

'Well, yes.'

Marik took his last mouthful of soup. 'The only real redheads come from down south.'

Flyn leaned forward. 'And is it true – what they say?'

'What do they say?'

'You know – fiery, a bit wild.'

'I've known a few. One was pretty fiery. She bit me.'

Flyn seemed impressed. 'Bet Lena will dress up for dinner too. Try not to stare – you don't want to annoy her father. And watch your manners at the table.' Flyn downed the remainder of his beer and belched.

'Thanks for the advice.'

Marik felt reasonably confident about the dinner until Larris' steward opened the door and looked him over with thinly-disguised disdain. He had done his best, donning freshly-cleaned clothes and daubing himself in perfume supplied by Flyn. His boots were so old and worn that polish had no effect but Flyn had lent him a decent belt with a bronze buckle. He had also visited a barber, who had trimmed the worst excesses of his shaggy blonde thatch.

'Please follow me, sir,' said the steward after his inspection. 'And do wipe your feet.'

Marik had met the man the previous night: the steward had returned to the house offering profuse apologies for his absence, even though Larris had given him the evening off.

There were still two city guards stationed at the door and the pair seemed somewhat amused by Marik's arrival. Following the steward along the same corridor he had crept along the previous evening, he gulped with unease. He was not used to money, manners and finery and hoped the evening would not be too formal; he didn't want to embarrass himself in front of Lena.

Passing through the lounge where he had foiled Nyll and Yaluv, he observed that the blood had already been cleaned from the walls and the rug replaced. They turned right through a dining room with a table set for three then entered a library. Marik had never seen so many books in his life – there must have been at least two hundred.

Master Larris was standing beside an unlit hearth, clad in the pale robes favoured by rich Urluns. He was small in stature, narrow-faced with a thinning V of black hair.

'Ah – the hero of the hour. Do come in, Marik. Derkis, tell Lena our guest is here.'

'Sir.' The steward departed with a bow.

Larris took a gleaming goblet from a gleaming tray upon a nearby table and handed it to Marik. 'Here, young man. How are you? I trust today was calmer than yesterday?'

Larris' Common was excellent and the precision of his delivery reminded Marik of some of the officers he had served with.

'Yes, thank you, sir.'

'And your friend? I seem to have forgotten his name.'

'Uvek. He's out of hospital and on the mend.'

'Good. Another brave fellow, though clearly not in your league. Tell me, what experience do you have?'

'I served with the People's Guard back home for ten years.'

'Ten? Really? I wouldn't have thought you were old enough.'

'Joined at seventeen, sir.'

'A type of militia, isn't it?'

'Yes.'

'And were you with or against Baldar?'

Marik knew he would have to be more open with this man in order to win his trust. 'Against.'

'I see. I'm afraid we've little grasp of the war's intricacies up here. We generally don't concern ourselves with affairs beyond the King's Keep. My father spoke of the days when the Crown's Road was thick with traffic but I doubt there's much at all now.'

'No, sir.'

'And what brought you up this way? I've met a few Southers during various trips but I've seldom met one on this side of the Strait.'

'Well, that is a long story.'

Fortunately for Marik, Lena chose that moment to arrive. She had selected another lovely gown – this one a shade of dark red similar to her hair. She also wore an immaculately cut jacket with triangular buttons that looked like purest gold.

'Sorry, Papa, Irikyl managed to lose one of my shoes. Hello, Marik.'

'Hello, miss.'

'You can call me Lena.'

'I think 'miss' is more appropriate,' said Larris.

Lena gave him a look but said nothing. She sniffed the air theatrically, wrinkling her nose. 'Ralaskan Chicken – you're in for a treat, Marik.'

'I hope you feel all right after yesterday, miss.'

'It's strange,' she said, clasping her hands together as she neared the hearth. 'There's a sort of elation that comes and goes; but a horrible feeling too – when I think of Garek.'

'I am so very sorry that you had to see such a thing, my dear.' Larris walked over to Lena but addressed Marik. 'It's true that I have many precious things but none are more important to me than my daughters.'

Marik couldn't think of anything to say to that.

'What are your plans now?' asked Lena. 'Your job has finished, hasn't it?'

'It has. I'm not sure, miss. Flyn may have found me something.'

'You're intending to stay in Ralaska?' asked Larris.

'I really haven't decided, sir. I was aiming to head north at some point – I have a friend I'd like to visit up in Khard.'

'Khard, eh?' replied Larris. 'That's a four or five-week trip at least.'

'I'll have to save up to pay my way. I shall just have to see what's available.'

He sipped what turned out to be a sweet wine, hoping for some clue in Larris' reaction. The moneylender made a neutral sound but commented no further.

'Papa, where is *my* wine?'

'You can have some with dinner, Lena. This is very strong, not for young ladies.'

'I'm twenty soon.'

Marik hadn't realised she was so young; there were ten years between them. She was not only out of his class; she was too young for him.

Still pouting, she gestured at a bookshelf. 'Are you interested in books, Marik?'

'Very much, though I'm afraid I cannot read.'

'Not even in Common?'

'Lena.' Larris rolled his eyes and sighed. 'How many times have I told you not to assume that everyone has enjoyed the benefits of education you have.'

Lena flushed slightly. 'Sorry. You can read a map though, can't you?'

'As long there isn't too much writing.'

'Come then. Papa, can you help us find the right volume? Marik can show us where he's from.'

An hour later, Marik was feeling relaxed - probably a little too relaxed. The Ralaskan chicken had been one of the best dishes he'd ever eaten. The first course, a selection of fish, and the last, an apple cake, were almost as good. He was thoroughly full, and the room had acquired a hazy quality, undoubtedly on account of two more goblets of wine. He poured himself some water and downed half of it to revive his wits.

Lena sat opposite him and she had continued in what was clearly her usual charming, spirited manner, offering her views on life in the Urlun Empire and beyond. It seemed to Marik that both she and her father were keen to try and forget the events of the previous night. Master Larris censored his daughter at times but overall Marik found him a warmer, more personable character than he'd expected. His comments suggested that he'd come from relatively humble stock and worked hard to better himself. Only one passing reference was made to his wife – Lena's mother – and it seemed that she lived some distance away. Marik also learned that Larris' older daughter was married to a high-ranking official in King Elemer's court and that Lena was rather contemptuous of the pair. When she made the latest of several critical comments, Larris instructed the steward to remove her goblet. Lena seemed to consider protesting but then turned her attention to Marik.

'So why did you leave the People's Army?'

'People's *Guard*,' corrected Master Larris.

Marik never felt comfortable answering that question, even though he had lied about it so often. 'I had done my time, miss. I wanted to see more of the world than the Nine Provinces.'

'No wife to go home to?'

Larris tutted. His daughter shrugged.

'No.'

'And you crossed into the North at the King's Keep?'

They had earlier identified this and several other locations on Larris' maps. The documents were some of the most impressive Marik had ever seen – precise, clear and colourful.

'I did. About three years ago now.'

'And then?'

Marik noted that Larris was happy to let his daughter do the questioning but was as interested as her in the answers. Fortunately, he had a 'respectable' version of his story ready for such occasions.

'Well, miss, it's very difficult to remember it all but I have done many things and met many interesting people. I have held simple jobs similar to what I've been doing here but I have also worked as a military instructor, a bodyguard, and a ranger. I even did a few months as a hired sword for the Queen of the First Empire.'

Larris nodded with approval.

'Did you meet her?' asked Lena. She was not alone in being curious about Queen Casarri. The First Empire was the oldest, richest domain in the world and its rulers were as secretive as they were influential. It still surprised Marik that he had spent time – however brief – at the heart of the empire.

'I cannot truthfully say that I met her, miss, though I did see her on three separate occasions.'

'They say she is very ugly.'

'No, no, I wouldn't say that. Plain, certainly, but not ugly.'

Larris sipped more wine before adding his view. 'I cannot claim that she is popular in these parts but to rule for so long – we must at least respect her.'

'Indeed, sir. I don't think anyone would claim she hasn't made mistakes but her empire is at least united and largely peaceful. I wish the Nine Provinces could find such a leader.'

'Isn't Baldar the Bold a great leader?' asked Lena.

'Great, perhaps,' said Marik. 'But not good.'

The three of them spoke for another hour. Marik eventually learned that Larris' wife lived on the other side of the Shivar Strait and that Lena's annual visit was imminent. The moneylender also revealed that he had plans to open another office in the port of Ikk. Apparently, there were good profits to be made by lending to shipping concerns. He also intended to move his residence to a safer neighbourhood, closer to the royal quarter. Marik was surprised by Lena's reluctance to leave. Despite the events of the previous night, she wanted to remain in the house – she had known no other home.

The conversation took a darker tone as they reflected on the dead bodyguard, Garek. He had been employed by Larris for six years and was considered by all to be reliable and honourable. When Lena mentioned the possibility of a replacement, her father did not comment. Marik reckoned he might be in with a chance.

When a household bell announced the third hour of night, Master Larris told his daughter it was time for her to retire. Lena seemed annoyed but politely bade both men goodnight. Marik was relieved that she hadn't been overly friendly and he thought he had managed the evening well.

'It's late,' said Larris when Lena had gone. 'And I have a busy day tomorrow. So, I shall get to the point.'

In fact, he then took a minute to light a long, expensive-looking pipe. Marik would have liked to join him but declined.

'With Garek gone and Taralis injured, I have only two men left I can rely on. The city guards will remain for a few days but after that I'll be on my own. Would you be interested in working for me, Marik?'

'I would, sir.'

'Of course, a reference would be ideal but there can be no doubt you have proved yourself. You seem a decent fellow and I am reassured by your experience.'

Marik drained his goblet. This was going well.

'I have one remaining question though. And I suggest you answer it truthfully. As you can imagine, I hear a lot of lies in my business.'

'Sir?'

'The usual term of service in the People's Guard is *twelve* years, correct?'

Most people this far north hadn't even heard of the Guard. Marik was surprised Larris knew that.

'Correct.'

'And yet you left after ten. You told my daughter you had 'done your time'. Is that the truth of the matter?'

Marik took his time and chose his words carefully. 'Not entirely. There was an incident during a battle. One of which I'm not proud.'

'Go on.'

'I would prefer not to go into the details, sir, but ... well, that is why I left the South.'

'I see.' Larris took two long draws on his pipe before continuing.

Marik watched the smoke drift and curl in the candlelight.

'Well, that is no great recommendation but I admire your honesty. For the last two years, Garek has accompanied Lena and her sister on visits to their mother. Unlike my other employees, he knew a good deal about life outside Ralaska – an essential qualification. In the next day or two I will consult that idiot who employed both you and the robbers. Assuming I hear nothing from him to alarm me, I will employ you as a bodyguard. The girls are departing for Alkari in six days and will return in no longer than four weeks. Assuming all goes well, I will pay you ten bronzes a week, forty in total – one quarter now, the rest when you come back. That should be more than enough to get you up to Khard. What do you say?'

Chapter Four

'Maybe? Why in the name of the gods would you say maybe?'

Marik wasn't entirely sure himself.

Flyn continued to frown at him. The day was only an hour old but he had demanded an immediate briefing on the evening's events.

'I don't know. I only just came across the Strait. I don't really like the sea.'

'But the money – that's way more than you'll make if you come with me for Yarlen.'

'You've decided then?'

Flyn exhaled a long breath. 'Rent's gone up – I don't have much choice. Marik, you should really think about it. It sounds like most of it will be a paid holiday. Don't tell me he's going to leave you alone with Lena?'

'No – his other daughter's coming too. I have to guard them both.'

'If it was me, I would have said yes straight away.'

Marik understood Flyn's view but he quite liked the idea of just being a sword-hand for this Yarlen – following orders, being part of a group. Lena and her sister were undoubtedly targets - if not for robbery then for kidnapping. He knew from some of his discussions with Carlis that, with the failing fortunes of Ralaska, many were turning to crime.

'Easy decision, if you ask me,' added Flyn as he sat on his bed.

Marik stood at the window, looking down at the street. The inn overlooked a market and two city guards were currently turning out the pockets of an urchin. He had managed to steal quite a bit.

'What do you know of this Alkari place?'

'It's a territory south of Baron Zanzarri's lands. Run by his cousin, Count … something. The coast is very pretty - too expensive for commoners. The count rents out plots and properties to the rich. So, does Larris keep her?'

'Not sure but the daughters go over every year.'

'A holiday from their tough lives here in Ralaska, I suppose. All right for some, isn't it? I'm telling you, if you can get in with these rich folk, you should do it.'

Marik turned away from the window. 'Well, one thing's for sure. Whatever I decide, I'm going to need a sword.'

*

Even with a loan from Flyn, he could only afford to choose from the iron blades. These were situated in a shadowy rack towards the rear of the weapon-smiths.

'These are all twenty,' said the owner in passable Common. He was a plump, greasy fellow whose foul stench filled his store. According to Flyn, this put off many customers – but it was the place to find a bargain.

'Except that one with the emerald in the handle, that's thirty.'

'You mean the one with the green glass,' said Marik, drawing only a shrug from the owner.

Marik took out two of the more promising blades. They were roughly-cast and rather top heavy but just about acceptable. He practised a couple of moves with both; there wasn't much to choose between them. Marik cursed to himself as he thought of the fine steel blade he had fought with as a soldier. He had lost that in a bog during a storm north of the King's Keep. In the South, no swordsman worth his salt would be seen dead with an iron blade. Marik reassured himself with the reflection that while steel was more durable and prestigious, such a weapon could do just as much damage.

'May I?' Flyn took them from him and did his own routine. 'Not bad. This one's a bit shaky.'

'They're both a bit shaky.'

'Wear and tear,' said the owner. 'They'll hold together.'

'But for how long?' said Marik.

He took out the blade with the square of green glass embedded in the hilt. It was about as good a weapon as you could expect an iron sword to be. The hilt was a mix of wood and horn and it was a couple of inches longer than the others. The mountings were solid and well-maintained. Marik tried out a few more swings and lunges and parries.

'You like it?' asked Flyn.

'That's a good blade,' interjected the owner.

Marik ushered Flyn away. 'I have only twenty. What more can you loan me now?'

'Two. But I doubt you'll get him down that far.'

'We'll see.' Marik walked up to the owner. 'I'll give you eighteen for it.'

'This isn't a market stall. The price is thirty.'

'It's not worth that and you know it. The glass weakens the handle.'

'Nonsense. But I'm a reasonable man. Let's say twenty-six.'

'That blade has dust all over it – no one's picked it up in weeks. I'll give you twenty.'

The owner sighed. 'Twenty-four. Final offer.'

Marik took the two coins from Flyn then counted them all out and placed them on a nearby table.

'Twenty-two. That's all I have.'

'I'd heard Southers were *mean*,' said the owner before shaking Marik's hand and scooping up his coins.

Marik winked at Flyn. 'I think the word is *astute*.'

Their route back to the inn took them through an area of cloth dyers. They passed numerous sprawling workshops where locals hunched over wide pots, colouring garments of every imaginable size and shape. Hundreds of freshly-dyed items hung from racks and lines – mainly oranges, yellows and reds.

'Nothing blue or green?'

'Green is associated with country folk,' replied Flyn. 'So not very popular in Ralaska. And blue is considered unlucky.'

'What about brown?' said Marik, gesturing to his tunic and trousers.

'That's just ugly.' Flyn smirked. 'Don't you want a few stripes or lozenges?'

Marik glanced at his companion's attire, which was similar in style to most he had seen in the capital. The tunic and trousers were a pale yellow but decorated with bands of black and white. It seemed that anyone in Ralaska with any money whatsoever spent it on clothes.

'Down south colour and bits and bobs are for women. You wouldn't last five minutes in that on the other side of the King's Keep.'

'*Real* men, eh?'

'Not necessarily.' Marik didn't want to make Flyn feel any worse about what had happened at Larris' place. Perhaps he'd been fearful; perhaps he'd genuinely thought it best to leave it to the city guards.

As they walked on, Marik realised how used he had become to the sunshine. 'Doesn't rain much here, does it?'

'Not in this season. It's called gold for a reason, you know.'

'So, gold for the sunny months; and the others?'

'White for what you call winter. Green for spring. Bronze for autumn and Iron is, well, a special time – dedicated to the gods and the king. It only lasts seven days.'

'I did not know that.'

'Not so much sun in the Nine Provinces?'

'Three Rivers is in Lothlagen – we get a lot of rain. In Torvaris and Drammar the ground is frozen almost the whole year round.'

'Must be a hard life down there.'

'Breeds hard people.'

'Torvaris – that's where Baldar's from, isn't it?'

Marik nodded though he really didn't want to discuss that topic again. And he didn't listen to what Flyn said next because another matter had occupied his attention. He moved a little ahead of the Urlun then stopped and turned. Forcing a smile, he clapped Flyn on the shoulder.

'What are you doing?'

Marik kept the smile on his face. 'Don't worry, it will make sense in a moment.' Having seen what he needed to, he manufactured a chuckle then continued.

'What are you playing at?'

'This street coming up on our right?'

Flyn was still frowning. 'Yes?'

'It connects to another running parallel?'

'It does.'

'Good. We're being followed. Might whoever it is be interested in you?'

'I can't see why they would.'

'Then that leaves me.'

The turn was about thirty feet ahead. 'Go right. When you reach the parallel street, make a square so you come up behind me – and him. He's about forty, heavily-built, bearded, pale orange tunic. How far does this street go?'

'Right into the centre but we turn off at the Silver Fountain.'

'I remember it. I'll wait there. Keep your wits about you.'

'Who do you think it is?'

'Not sure – but I intend to find out.'

They reached the corner. Marik stopped and they parted with a handshake. 'See you soon.'

Flyn did a rather poor job of appearing unconcerned and hurried away.

Marik continued on and glanced down at the sword he had owned for less than an hour. He hoped not to have to use it.

They met as agreed at the Silver Fountain. Marik guessed that twenty minutes had elapsed.

'You look tense,' he told Flyn. 'At least try to seem relaxed.'

'He's here. Still watching you.'

'I know. Do not – whatever you do – look at him.'

'Of course not.'

Marik leaned against the short stone wall that surrounded the fountain. The central plinth that had presumably once supported something silver was currently empty. A meagre flow trickled from the pipes set into the base and there was more rubbish than water.

'Anyone else with him?'

'Not that I saw.' Flyn was chewing his lip.

'Don't do that. It's a sign of nerves.'

Flyn tutted but stopped chewing his lip.

'Notice anything else about him?'

'Big bastard. Slight limp. No weapons on his belt but something heavy in his pack.'

'Mmm.'

Marik also found it hard not to look. But without staring directly, he established that the man had not moved. He was about fifty feet away, close to one of the four wide streets that met in the broad square.

'So now what?' asked Flyn.

'Anywhere quiet nearby?'

'Quiet?'

'Less people; somewhere we won't be disturbed.'

Flyn considered this for a moment. 'A couple of streets away is an old temple. A few vagrants hang around there but most of it's just a shell.'

'That'll do.'

'For what?'

'I want to talk to our bearded friend.'

'All right,' said Flyn warily. 'But there's definitely something in that bag of his.'

'I daresay. But we both have swords. And we know how to use them, right?'

'He really is a big bastard.'

'But there is only one of him,' said Marik. 'And two of us, right?'

'Er ... right.'

The temple was situated between a warehouse and a large stable. It had clearly once been an impressive building; with high, broad steps leading up to a colonnaded central structure with a dome on top. But the dark stone was now covered by weeds, dust and bird droppings. A man wrapped in shabby robes was drawing on the steps with chalk.

'What happened to the followers?' asked Marik.

'Some foreign cult, I think. Built many years ago but they had to leave.'

'And we can get out the other side?'

'Yes.'

Marik was pleased to note that there was no passable space between the temple's surrounding wall and the warehouse. There was an alley separating it from the stable but this was currently occupied by three tethered donkeys. If the bearded man wanted to follow them, he'd have to come through the temple.

Marik led the way up the steps. When the man with the chalk saw them, he grabbed his belongings and scuttled away past the stable. A man arriving there with a cart watched Marik and Flyn but was soon occupied by his horses – they'd become unsettled by a braying donkey.

'Don't look back, whatever you do.'

They reached the top step and passed through the doorway into the shadowy, cavernous space. The temple was at least a hundred feet long, perhaps forty across. Other than a few empty niches and two stone altars, the place was empty. There were several holes in the roof and the new arrivals disturbed some birds that fluttered around in a panic before escaping.

'Straight through.'

When the braying of the donkey ceased, the only noise came from the tap of their boots on the stone. As the sound reverberated around the temple, Marik glanced up at a faded, incomplete mural on one wall. It showed three naked female figures rising out of a volcano.

'Do exactly as I do,' he said as they neared the far doorway. He went through first and descended the steps. Running perpendicular to the entrance was another street, this one fairly quiet: mainly large townhouses with balconies adorned by hanging plants.

Marik abruptly stopped, trotted five paces to the right then ran back up the steps. He halted beside the temple wall and slid along it until he was beside the doorway. Flyn came up behind him and had the sense not to speak.

Marik only heard the footsteps when the follower accelerated. Having lost sight of his quarry, he was clearly keen to catch up. Marik placed his hand on the hilt of his new sword, now hanging in its sheath on his left side. The follower was close.

'You stay this side of him,' he whispered. 'Keep a distance between us.'

Flyn nodded but could not hide his nerves. Marik was beginning to wonder if the young man had ever done anything more demanding than guarding warehouses.

The bearded man came through at a jog, straight past them. He was almost at the top step when Marik spoke.

'Looking for me?' By then he had side-stepped to the left so the bearded man found himself facing two foes, both with their hands on their swords.

He was indeed a large man, broad-chested and powerful. His clothes told Marik nothing; the two scars on his face a little more. Across his shoulder was a roughly-made pack secured by a rope. He spoke in Urlun, his tone one of mock-innocence.

'Common,' instructed Marik.

The follower shook his head then spoke again in his own language.

Flyn translated. 'He says he's never seen you before.'

'He's a liar.' Marik drew his sword and advanced a step. The bearded man held up his hands and spoke again.

'He swears he doesn't know you.'

'Ask him why he's following me.'

Flyn continued to translate. 'He says he's on his way to work. Maybe we were wrong, Marik.'

'Tell him to open his pack.'

When Flyn gave the instruction, the man shook his head and descended onto the first step.

Marik tapped the tip of his sword against the stone. 'You tell him that if he runs, I'll cut his legs out from under him.'

At this, the bearded man yelled his response.

'He says you've no right to threaten him. He'll tell the city guards.'

'I doubt it. If he shows me what's in that pack, I'll let him go.'

Upon hearing this, the man shook his head vigorously.

'He says he won't. You can't make him. He-'

The man turned and set off towards the street at a sprint. Marik sped after him, taking the steps two at a time. By the time the man leaped off the final step, Marik was right behind him. There was no need to cut his legs away. A well-placed trip did the job and the big man hit the ground hard, sliding to a halt with his head in a gutter.

Thankfully there were only two young boys and an old woman watching. Marik placed the point of his sword at the base of the man's neck. The Urlun didn't need any translation to understand he would be unwise to move.

Flyn arrived, looking rather shocked.

'Open his pack.'

The man continued to utter what sounded like oaths but did not resist. Flyn opened the buckle on the pack and pulled out a hefty wooden club, a lump of bread, a flask of water and a scrap of paper.

'What's on it?'

'Er ... oh ... it's a description of us both and ... and my address.'

'Well, well.'

Marik prodded the man with his boot. The Urlun understood and rolled over. Marik now pressed the blade against his chin.

'This time the truth – or I'll give him the closest shave he's ever had.'

The man babbled something but then rubbed his brow for a moment and spoke a few sentences.

Flyn listened, registered surprise, then translated. 'He works for Master Larris. He was hired this morning – Larris wants to ensure you are who you say you are and have no connections to any criminals.'

Marik wasn't entirely surprised. 'Has he worked for him before?'

'A few times, yes.'

'Then he'll know the names of Larris' steward and daughter.'

The man knew both names. Marik kept his sword where it was, conscious that more than few people on the street were now watching. On balance, he reckoned the man was telling the truth.

'What's his name?'

'Riddek.'

Marik withdrew the blade and gestured for him to get to his feet. Flyn replaced his belongings in the pack.

'You can give that back. Tell him that if I see him again, he won't be so lucky. If he agrees to tell Larris that I am to be trusted, I will not disclose just how remarkably inept he is.'

Upon hearing this, Riddek nodded, dusted himself down and sloped away.

A small crowd had now gathered.

Marik sheathed his sword and set off back up the steps. 'Let's get out of here.'

Chapter Five

At Flyn's request, the pair spent an hour of the afternoon practising with their blades. Marik appreciated the distraction; it was hard to predict how the encounter with Riddek might affect his dealings with Larris. They found a quiet bit of waste ground not far from Flyn's room and covered the sword-tips and edges with sack cloth. Marik started by observing Flyn's technique. The young man seemed passable at first but when it came to facing an opponent, his confidence ebbed away. He was clearly alert and agile but there was a brittleness and naivety to the way he moved and fought. Marik discovered that he'd had no proper instruction at all. He spent the rest of the time taking him through several simple defensive moves that had served him well over the years.

By the end of the session, both men were sweating. Flyn collected a pail of water on their way back to the inn. And once they had cleaned themselves up, he went out for some wine. Later, they sat by the window, drinking and watching the world go by.

Twilight was near when the door burst open. Flyn dropped his mug, splashing both of them with wine. Marik (who had finished his) sprang up and was halfway to his sheathed sword when he realised he wouldn't need it. Standing there was Karyl, one of Flyn's roommates. He was breathing hard, eyes flicking between the two of them. He didn't speak Common, so Marik left the questioning to Flyn. As soon as Karyl replied, Flyn explained.

'It's Rukka, he's hurt. Come on.'

Rukka was Flyn's second roommate. The two Urluns hurried out and down the stairs. Marik grabbed his sword and ran after them; past the innkeeper – who yelled something – and out into the street.

'What happened?'

Marik got no reply from Flyn, who was close on the heels of Karyl. They zig-zagged between pedestrians then darted into an alley. Despite his longer stride, Marik had to work to keep up. Two streets and three alleys later, they reached a shabby house with boarded-up windows. Rukka ran to the side of it, to a staircase leading down towards a dim light. Flyn followed him down the steps.

Marik halted at the top. 'Ask him what happened,' he said, more insistent this time.

Rukka blurted something as he reached the bottom of the steps.

'They were attacked,' said Flyn. 'He's bleeding badly. We need to get him to a surgeon.'

Marik followed; descending the steps and turning into a passageway under the house. Lanterns hung outside doorways leading to two cellars. Flyn had just run into the one to the right.

The muffled cry and the silence that ensued halted Marik five feet from the doors. He knew with a grim, familiar certainty that this was a trap. He drew his blade and berated himself for not stopping the young men sooner.

'You coming in then, Souther?'

He didn't know the voice but whoever it belonged to spoke Common well.

Marik checked that there was no sign of anyone behind him. 'Why don't *you* come *out*?'

'We have three of your friends and knives at their throats. Don't make me ask again.'

Sword up, Marik first checked the cellar to the left. He saw nothing there, but kept his body at an angle as he turned to face the second doorway. At the rear of the cellar was another lantern. There stood three men, all hooded, all wearing wrappings to hide the lower part of their faces. Rukka, Karyl and Flyn were on their knees, a man behind each of them, hand-axes at their necks.

Marik thought of Riddek, the man who had followed him. Was this connected somehow? Then he realised there was a far more likely explanation.

'You want me, I suppose?'

'*Only* you.' The man behind Flyn was bulky, his eyes close-set and dark. Marik noted how well-honed his axe blade was.

'And if I stay, you'll let them go unharmed?'

'We will. Once you give up your sword.'

'I'm reasonable - not stupid.'

'You really want their blood on your hands, Souther?'

'No. But I don't particularly want mine on my hands either. They die, you die. Let them go and it's between us. Or is three to one still too much of a challenge for you?'

The leader's eyes smiled.

Marik wasn't finished. 'And don't forget, if you kill me, it's just a dead foreigner. These three are subjects of King Elemer – as are you.'

'We let them go, there'll be city guards here in five minutes.'

There was no denying that.

'No matter,' added the leader. 'Two of us should be enough.' He aimed his blade at the cellar behind Marik. 'We fight in there. If *you* come out, our friend here lets yours go. If *we* come out, well ... you won't be around to care.'

Marik didn't believe the pledge for a moment but he preferred to face two than three. 'Fair enough.'

Though they seemed nasty enough, these people at least had some honour; otherwise they would have slit their captives' throats one by one until he'd thrown down his sword. Marik withdrew to the doorway of the other cellar. Dank and dark, it was no place to die; and he could hardly believe that having been relaxing a quarter-hour earlier, he now faced a fight for his life. He watched as Flyn was sent with Rukka and Karyl to the back of the room and made to lay down, facing the far wall.

Marik retreated into the cellar. With a nod to the man left as guard, the leader and his compatriot advanced. They were both a lot broader than Marik, if not as tall. He also had the advantage of range with his sword. What he didn't have was much room to swing it. The axes were ideal for a confined space.

He felt a sudden need to confirm who he was facing. 'I heard Yaluv and Nyll will hang for what they did. This is revenge, I suppose?'

'You shouldn't have stuck your nose in,' said the leader.

'I feel obliged to point out that they were carrying out a robbery and holding two women as hostages.'

'I didn't know Southers talked this much.'

Marik found himself discouraged by the man's calm; and the unblinking eyes of his comrade. He needed to rile them if he could.

'We talk a *bit*, fight a *lot*. And if your friends are anything to go by, you two won't last long. Honestly, I reckon you Northers just haven't got it in you.'

'We'll see.'

'You're both going to die in a cellar. Embarrassing, really.'

The pair moved forward, side by side.

Marik addressed the other man. 'And what about you, can't you even talk Common? Can you even talk at all?'

The quiet man opened his stance, axe held loose and low. He murmured something to the leader. They moved apart, pressed Marik towards a corner. He swung at them: no more than a gesture, but it reminded them who had the range. He guessed the murky cellar was no more than ten feet by ten and he could see nothing he might use to help him.

The leader darted forward, feinted a chop with his axe but held back. Marik side-stepped like a boxer in a ring as they took turns to swing, deterring them with lunges and sweeps. As yet, none of the weapons had touched.

When he saw it, he cursed himself for not noticing sooner. The leader was right-handed, the quiet man left-handed. They had arranged themselves so that both weapons were on the outside, enabling them to swing freely. If he could find a way to swap their positions, they'd be at a disadvantage. He needed to engineer an opportunity.

But the leader was in no mood to wait. Axe high, he threw several blows at his foe. Raising his sword to block, Marik was now vulnerable to his right. The quiet man swiftly took advantage, shuffling closer and closer, axe at the ready. The leader kept Marik occupied, forcing him to parry. The blades met for the first time. The quiet man drew his axe back to strike. Marik saw his chance.

He took two steps forward and dived between them. Half-expecting an axe blade to strike an ankle, he tucked his sword-arm in and completed the roll. As he sprang to his feet, he saw that the men had turned inward towards him, their positions now reversed.

His attack was not subtle but it was swift. The quiet man was now to his right and Marik swung at his neck. The Urlun moved his axe to parry but Marik adjusted, dragging the blade below his enemy's elbows, then aiming up.

Encumbered by the proximity of the leader, the quiet man could not block. He did however throw his head back … but not quickly to avoid the tip of Marik's new sword, which sliced across his mouth and sent him spinning away.

Marik knew he was exposed and could not get the blade back in time. He let his own move pull him away and felt the second axe feather his side. Realising only his tunic had been cut, he struck back.

The leader was off-balance as Marik jabbed the sword-hilt between his eyes. Bones cracked and he staggered backwards. Sensing movement to his left, Marik launched a blind slash. He at first had no idea what he'd hit but when the quiet man dropped his axe and his arms shot up, warm blood splattered his face. Instinct had now taken over and he turned his attention back to the leader.

'No!' The Urlun had the presence of mind to speak in Common but it did not save him.

Both hands on the sword-hilt, Marik swept at him once, then again. At the third blow, the leader emitted a howl that quickly became a moan. He slumped to the floor.

Marik wiped blood off his brow and turned to see that the quiet man was lying close to the doorway, helplessly trying to stem the flow from his neck. From the sound of the liquid striking the floor, he didn't have long.

'Marik!' Flyn cried out.

The last man darted into the passageway. Eyes raging, the Urlun drew his arm back, ready to strike with his axe. But his anger had destroyed his judgement. The doorway protected Marik from a wide swing; but it did not protect the Urlun from the straight jab of Marik's sword. The blade slid easily into his gut and Marik drove it in deep. The axe fell from the man's hand, bounced harmlessly off Marik's arm and clattered to the floor. When he keeled over, Marik had to wedge a boot on him to heave his sword out. The last man hit the floor like a rag-doll, not a single breath left in him.

And then Marik stood there, blood dripping from his blade, body trembling. As Flyn and the others got to their feet and approached him, he fell back against the doorway.

He had tried very hard not to kill again. The last time had been more than a year ago and the memories of it had finally begun to fade. Now three more men were dead.

Whatever Flyn was saying, the words didn't reach him. Marik lurched along the corridor and up the stairs. He turned and sat down. His fingers let go of the sword and it clattered down the steps.

The headquarters of the city guards was an imposing, three-storey building close to the palace quarter. At its centre was a broad courtyard which incorporated a sizeable stable. As dawn broke, grooms began to arrive and guards took their mounts out on early patrols. Trotting towards the main gate, they crossed elongated shadows cast onto the pale earth by nearby towers.

Marik glanced up at one of those high structures: narrow and rounded with ivy covering most of it and a flag flying proudly at the top. He wondered who occupied it, and what they thought when they looked down upon Ralaska.

He, Flyn and Rukka were sitting on a bench beside one of the three arched doorways that led into the building. Karyl was lying on another, snoring. He and the other two Urluns had talked throughout the night, during breaks between individual interviews within the headquarters.

Marik had already spoken to three different officers, including the sergeant from the Larris robbery. The four were not to leave until Magistrate Neryn (who Marik had also previously met) arrived to review the night's events.

Even so, the last interview had eased Marik's mind. With the evidence given by the other three, there seemed to be little interest in charging him with anything. He was grateful that the Ralaskan authorities had been just on both occasions, knowing from bitter experience that this was not always the case when locals dealt with outsiders. He also knew that his cause had been assisted by the identities of the three he had slain. The leader was Nyll's brother; he and his two cohorts had been wanted for more than a year - for the murder of a merchant and his wife.

'Marik.' Flyn pointed to the main gate. Two men had just ridden in on fine-looking horses. As they were intercepted by several alert grooms, Marik realised one of the new arrivals was Magistrate Neryn.

'Thank the gods,' said Flyn. 'Hopefully not too long now. I wonder if they'll give your sword back.'

This had been confiscated at the scene when the city guards arrived. Marik was in no great hurry to reclaim it. His first job would be to clean the blood off.

Magistrate Neryn glanced at the waiting quartet then strode inside.

Karyl woke up. He and Rukka went to fetch some water, leaving Flyn and Marik alone.

'I thought my mistake at Larris' place was bad enough,' said the Urlun. 'I don't know how I could have been so stupid.'

He and the other three had already apologised several times. Rukka in particular was clearly ashamed at leading the others into a trap, even though the attackers had left him little choice.

Marik cleared his throat. 'Don't forget it's me they wanted. I'm just sorry you all got tangled up in this mess.'

'Not your fault. You were just trying to do the right thing.'

Marik was really beginning to wonder if doing so would ever get him anywhere. Gazing up at the ivy-covered tower once more, he was struck by a memory.

'The most popular spirit in Three Rivers is the Old Man of the Lake. They say you can only see him when mist lays on the surface. If you wait long enough he will appear. Upon seeing you, he will either drop below the waves or rise into the sky.'

Flyn listened carefully as Marik continued.

'If he descends, you will lead an evil life – bring pain to others. If he rises up you will do good – help others.'

'Did you go? Did you see the Old Man?'

'Eventually. Didn't summon up the courage until I was fifteen years old. I saw ... something. It might have been a figure. I was watching it, waiting for it to move. Then a wind came, and the mist cleared. The figure disappeared. But just before it did so, it seemed to move ... down.'

'No,' said Flyn.

'I know what I saw.'

'You believe it?'

'I don't know. But I have always tried to make sure it doesn't come true.'

An hour later, Magistrate Neryn emerged from the headquarters, accompanied by the sergeant. He addressed Flyn, Rukka and Karyl in Urlun, then Marik in Common.

'A nasty incident. You were unfortunate to cross paths with these criminals.'

Neryn placed both hands on the belt that gathered his voluminous robes. 'Marik, you do seem to attract trouble but the evidence suggests that you have again acted only in the interests of protecting others. I must commend you. With the three men dead, there is no possibility of matters reaching the court. On behalf of the city, I'd like to thank you for taking those three off the streets. If you work on your Urlun, we might even be able to find a post for you.'

Flyn smiled at this. Marik didn't have it in him.

A young guard came out, holding Marik's sword. The sergeant took it and offered it to him.

'We cleaned it up for you.'

Neryn rubbed his hands together. 'Well, there can be no doubt that the reputation of the warriors of the Nine Provinces remains intact.'

The others all nodded in agreement. Suddenly feeling the weight of the eyes upon him, Marik gave serious consideration to walking out of the courtyard empty-handed. But the blade had cost him a lot and served him well. He took it and hung the sheath from his belt.

Flyn said, 'Sir, can we go?'

'You three may,' replied the magistrate. 'But I would like to keep Marik for a while. Ah, he's here.'

Neryn was looking at the gate. A pair of guards on horseback made way for a familiar carriage.

'I thought Master Larris might want to see you. It appears I was correct.'

Marik sent the others on and spoke to Larris in a quiet section of the courtyard. All he really wanted to do was sleep but there was no avoiding this encounter. It did not start as he'd expected.

'I must apologise,' said Larris, who was already smoking his pipe, despite the early hour. 'That idiot Riddek is clearly not in your league.'

'No need, sir. I don't blame you. You have only known me for a few days.'

'Ironically, his failure actually told me what I need to know.'

Marik was trying to appear resolute though he felt anything but.

'Were you injured?' asked Larris.

'No.'

'You defeated three of them. Killed them?'

Marik nodded.

'There can be no further question about your ability. Nor it would seem your judgement. But I must ask – you do not have a propensity for violence? You act only when required? I ask because my daughters will attract attention and you will sometimes need to keep a cool head.'

'As you know, sir, I have worked as a bodyguard before. I've not had many complaints.'

'Good. Well, then I must say I am as sure of you as I can be. Will you accept my offer?'

Marik didn't have to think about it. He wanted to get out of Ralaska.

'I will.'

'Excellent. Because the timetable of the trip has altered somewhat. The golden easterlies have come earlier than expected. A captain I have dealt with before is leaving the day after tomorrow and I would rather the girls travel with him. If you are also present, I will feel a good deal happier.'

'I'll be ready, Master Larris.'

The moneylender offered his hand in the Southern manner; and Marik shook it.

There were only two days to wait but the hours passed slowly. He was summoned to the Larris residence only once: to meet the older daughter, Cara, and her husband. Both acted coldly towards him and the husband took Larris aside at one point, presumably to persuade his father-in-law not to trust this rough-looking Souther.

So, when Marik gathered his meagre possessions together and walked to the docks with Flyn, he was not entirely sure he would be joining the sisters. But Larris was waiting there and he immediately handed over the ten bronze coins in a fine leather pouch. The moneylender also promised to personally introduce Marik to the captain before departure. Lena seemed pleased to see him but Cara did not acknowledge him at all. Of her husband, there was no sign. The women were accompanied by a serving girl named Irikyl; and the trio looked on as their chests were loaded aboard.

'Well,' said Flyn, a hand upon his shoulder. 'You off across the Straits and me into the Long Marches.'

'Considering recent events, they both might be safer than Ralaska.'

'True.'

Marik remained grateful for all Flyn had done for him but there was now an awkwardness between them. Marik had not wanted to speak of those brief, horrible moments in the cellar but Flyn and his friends had done little else. They talked often in their own tongue but it seemed evident to Marik that this was their way of dealing with the experience. Each of them had taken the time to individually thank him and apologise yet again. Marik tried to assuage their feelings, tell them they could have done no more. But the truth was that a part of him almost hated them. Like so many Northers he had encountered, they lived a relatively easy existence but considered it difficult. They were often dismissive of the South but had little idea or interest in the horrors afflicting the lands beyond the King's Keep.

And for all Flyn's enthusiasm and good intentions, he was no warrior. Marik had considered giving the younger man a bit of straightforward advice; that another profession might suit him better. But he was not so old that he couldn't remember how twenty-year-olds thought. Flyn would not have listened to him. Still, he felt he had to say something.

'Watch yourself out there. Keep your sword with you at all times. Even when you're taking a piss – especially when you're taking a piss. Keep your eyes open, don't rely on what others tell you unless you trust them. And if you end up in a corner, come out fighting. Look your enemy in the eye and keep moving forward. You'd be surprised how many fights are won that way.'

'Thanks, Marik. I'll remember that. It's been good to know a Souther.'

'And for me to know a Norther. If we're ever back here at the same time-'

'-The Rampant Horse. I look forward to it.' Flyn glanced at Lena. 'Maybe you two will come back more than friends.'

'Unlikely.'

'I have some advice for you too. Watch the sailors. I know Larris is friends with the captain but most of them will be island folk. There are no better sailors … and no better thieves.'

Chapter Six

The ship was under way within an hour. Marik had already forgotten its name but the captain was called Eylirr: and he could have been nothing other than a sailor. Broad and brawny, he possessed a thick beard patched with grey. His head was utterly hairless but decorated by a dark green tattoo, part of which seemed to be a map. Like all the sailors, he wore a sleeveless tunic with voluminous trousers that did not seem at all practical. As captain, he also wore a dark blue jacket with patterned sleeves.

Marik had to admit that Eylirr and his crew seemed very capable. There was no question that Northern ships and sailors were far superior to their Southern counterparts. The largest vessel he had ever seen on the other side of the King's Keep was a twelve-oar coaster about sixty feet long.

This ship was more than a hundred feet in length, equipped with three masts and manned by a crew of thirty. Attached to the stern was a small tender that bobbed along in the larger vessel's wake. All three sails were full and the following wind propelled the ship west at what seemed to Marik great speed. He was dismayed to see that some of the sailors were slaves, identifiable by the iron collars around their necks. Queen Casarri of the First Empire still embraced the practice but Marik had seen few enslaved people in the north-east. Slavery had been outlawed in the Nine Provinces for decades but of late Baldar the Bold had resurrected it. Marik tried to shake off the thought by walking to the side-rail and looking out at the sea.

The water was wonderfully green and calm considering the strength of the breeze. Earlier, they had passed a small village built entirely on stilts, close to the mouth of the Kal river. Marik had watched the crew of a small boat unloading a seething mass of glittering fish. The women sang as they passed full baskets along a line, clearly celebrating their good fortune.

He now noted thick clusters of weed floating on the surface. Lying within one were the remnants of an oval wooden shield, its colours faded. Marik wondered what had happened to its owner. Was his corpse lying on the floor of the sea beneath them? Had he floated south into the Endless Sea? Washed up on some distant shore?

'Oh. Sorry.'

Marik had been so preoccupied that he'd failed to notice the young boy scrubbing the deck. He couldn't have been more than six or seven and was on his hands and knees, wielding a large pail and a hefty hand-brush. Marik sat up on the side-rail to make way. Pale by comparison with the older sailors, the boy was as grubby and ill-kempt as some of the homeless people Marik had seen in Ralaska.

'Looks like hard work.'

The boy – whose hair was also a shade lighter than most of the dark Urluns – stopped for a moment, then shrugged and grinned. At least his teeth were white.

'Ah, you don't speak Common?'

The lad shrugged again. Then he pointed at Marik's sword and grinned again. Marik wasn't entirely sure what to make of that.

One of the sailors wandered over and planted a boot on the boy's back. His kick was not hard, but sufficient to send the youngster sprawling forward. The youngster didn't even turn around; his only reaction was to continue scrubbing.

The sailor was a man of around Marik's age, lean and stringy with blue eyes that seemed unusually bright in his suntanned face. Hanging from his left ear was what looked like a fish tooth. The right half of his head was shaved to display another dark green tattoo – this one composed of some kind of writing. Like the captain, he wore a narrow jacket of some quality; this one black rather than blue.

Marik recalled Master Larris' remark about avoiding difficulties aboard the ship but he wasn't about to let the kick pass without comment.

'Nothing better to do?'

'Not at the moment.' The sailor nodded down at the boy. '*He* does though.'

Marik held the man's gaze long enough to make his point. But just then the ship rolled slightly and he had to grip the rail to stop himself sliding over the edge.

The sailor chuckled at this, along with a nearby pair who were repairing a section of deck. 'Souther on a ship – recipe for disaster.'

Marik felt his face reddening. He was about ready to tear that earring clean off.

'Where'd you get that blade?' asked the sailor. 'Looks cheap.'

He himself was armed with a long metal spike, presumably some nautical tool though it looked utterly lethal.

'Care for a closer look?' offered Marik as he slid down off the rail.

The sailor was about to reply when he was addressed in Urlun by the captain. Eylirr had just emerged from the cabin – the only structure built above the deck – where both he and his guests were accommodated. Marik was to sleep outside the door to Lena and Cara's quarters, which suited him fine.

The sailor turned, nodded respectfully to his superior and went on his way. Eylirr picked at something on his shaven head and walked over to Marik, who wasn't sure how much of the incident the captain had observed.

'What do you think of my ship then, young man?'

'Very fine,' Marik replied honestly.

'Would you believe that my first vessel was a little twenty-footer? I was a fisherman. This is the eighth vessel I have owned. She is thirty years old, originally built to take Urlun ambassadors all over the world.'

'Can you remind me of the name?'

'*White Cloud.*'

Eylirr looked towards the bow and bellowed some instructions. In seconds, a team of three took a rope from a cleat and began loosening the forward sail. Marik understood some of what occurred on a ship but the details were lost on him.

'So, we have a fair wind?'

'Very,' replied Eylirr. 'Gold usually gives us either fair easterlies or strong northerlies. We certainly don't want the latter. I was just telling the ladies – if this keeps up, we'll barely be at sea for two days.'

'About a hundred miles across the strait, isn't it?'

'A little more for us as we're heading south-west down the coast to Alkari.'

'Ah.' Marik watched a man cleaning the thick base of the mainmast. He was another slave; and at the back of the iron collar was a ring, presumably for a chain. 'I saw only a few slaves in the city – where do they come from?'

Eylirr raised a bushy eyebrow. 'You disapprove, I expect. But I should tell you that I know of captains now moving slaves by the hundreds down in the Nine Provinces. Unpleasant for your people, of course, but an opportunity for others.'

'*Unpleasant*'? Marik recalled Larris' instructions once more and did not pursue the matter.

Eylirr continued, undeterred. 'Most of this lot come from the western wastes – the land's unclaimed because there's nothing worth owning. A treaty settlement stretching back years broke apart – nobody seems sure why. Many small tribes, constantly changing alliances. They capture prisoners and sell them to slavers to pay for their weapons. The slavers bring them to the coast. You shouldn't feel too sorry for them – I only take men; and my slaves get the same amount of food and the same space to sleep as the rest of the crew. The only difference is that I own them.'

'Quite a difference.'

'I wouldn't expect a Souther to understand,' remarked Eylirr. 'We are so very different. Still, you seem to have landed on your feet. Larris tells me you're quite handy with that blade of yours. I understand that you're here to protect the ladies but if you have any problem of any kind with the crew, I suggest you refer it to me – not try and handle it yourself?'

'I'm sure there won't be a problem, captain.'

'As am I.' Eylirr leaned in close. 'You know Lena was really quite plain in her younger days. Not now, eh? Eh?'

Eylirr's lascivious grin was so broad that Marik couldn't help but smile. As the captain strode away, he couldn't decide if he liked him or not.

The *White Cloud* ploughed on across the sparkling sea. Some of the sailors struck up a song, led lustily by Eylirr. Marik noted that his friend with the tooth earring did not join in. He'd learned that the man was named Zyrin and that he possessed a senior rank.

Marik remained at the stern of the ship, only having to move when the sailors made some adjustment to the rearward mast and sails. Despite the breeze, it was a very hot day and he spent much of it in the shade – never far from the cabin. The structure was divided into three rooms. The one closest to the bow was the captain's, the sisters shared the middle one and the last was currently occupied by a young Urlun nobleman.

When the evening cool eventually arrived, the ladies emerged along with the serving girl, Irikyl. Lena and Cara were dressed in light, pale green gowns. Cara wore a pair of plain, flat shoes. When Eylirr saw that Lena was barefoot, he insisted that she wear something, warning her of splinters and the dangers of slipping. The captain was extremely attentive and escorted them from their cabin to the side-rail. Unfortunately, one of the crew choose that moment to relieve himself – thirty feet away but on the same side. When she saw the golden stream, Cara yelped and turned away in disgust. Eylirr bellowed an admonishment. The crewman hadn't finished and managed to splash a couple of his crew-mates as he dropped to the deck. The sailors roared at this until senior men – Zyrin included – cuffed several of them about the head. Lena ignored the incident; she was gazing at the setting sun.

Marik was back at the stern-rail, not far from the helmsman: a grey-haired fellow who whistled tunelessly. He was surprised to note that the man spent only about half his time facing forward: the rest was occupied with examining the sails and watching the sky. Marik would have liked to ask him about navigation but an early enquiry had been met only by another shrug.

Lena cried out. Marik was all set to move but swiftly realised she was merely pointing at something in the water. Eylirr gave a shout and suddenly a dozen sailors had gathered on the left side, many of them also pointing. Marik was stunned to see an enormous dark tail flick out of the water then slam downward, creating an explosion of water. The creature was quite far away so scale was difficult to judge but he could only imagine how large the rest of it might be. Equally disturbing were the expressions on the faces of the helmsman, the captain and the rest of the crew. At a word from Eylirr, two sailors darted down the main hatch.

Cara's mouth was hanging open and Irikyl looked terrified. Lena was transfixed, both hands planted on the side-rail. Marik watched as the creature's dark body eased into view for a moment before it dived and the tail flicked once more.

They all continued watching but when the leviathan did not reappear, the observers began to speak. The two crewmen sent below returned, each carrying a barrel. Once the lids were off, they used ladles to dump a chalky powder into the sea. Eylirr supervised this then continued to look for the creature with his senior men. When there were no further sightings, he spoke with them, brow furrowed.

Lena hurried back along the deck to Marik. 'You saw it?'

'Hard to miss. What a monster.'

'A kraal. I've never seen one that size.'

'I've never seen *anything* that size. Are they common around here?'

'Not usually at this time of year. Apparently, they head north for the mating season later on but not much sailing is done then. Where there's one there's usually more. They've been known to sink ships bigger than this.'

Marik affected his best steely look. This seemed like yet another reason for a Souther – or anyone, for that matter – to stay on dry land.

'What's that powder, miss?'

'It's made from the bones of the scaly runner – the only fish kraal don't eat. The sailors think it will keep the kraal away.'

'Let's hope that's the last we see of it. Good story to tell though.'

Lena smiled, though it seemed to Marik she was trying to fortify her own spirits. She turned to examine the sea for some time but there was no further sighting of the kraal. As she stood there, the wind blew her red locks around and she eventually plucked some twine from her belt and tied it back. Marik realised he was not the only one watching her; surely the crew had not often seen such a beauty aboard.

Lena had also noticed the attention. 'An interesting bunch – sailors.'

'Yes, miss, well – an interesting job. Are you looking forward to seeing your mother?'

Marik knew it was probably not his place to ask but he wanted to keep talking and it was the first thing that came into his head.

'Yes and no. It will be good to see her, of course, but she can be rather … demanding. You must miss your family, I suppose?'

Now Marik really regretted asking. 'I do.'

'You can't even send a letter. You really should learn to read and write. You could tell them about your adventures.' Lena leaned against the rail and moved a little closer. 'You didn't say much about them during the dinner. Is all well?'

Marik couldn't drag his gaze from those intoxicating green eyes and he felt a sudden, unfamiliar urge to answer honestly; to tell her everything. He couldn't do that; but he could tell her something of the truth.

'I don't really know. I hope my mother is still alive, perhaps my brother too. My father's gone.'

'I'm sorry, Marik.'

She put her hand on his arm, then removed it, perhaps realising how it might look to anyone watching. 'The war?'

'Yes.' That was all he wanted to say; and as much as he had ever said about his family to a Norther. 'There's not a lot left for me in the South, miss. I'm better off away from it.'

'I understand.'

'Lena!' Cara was on her way back the cabin. She looked upset about the appearance of the kraal and said something in Urlun before going inside.

Lena rolled her eyes. 'She's got something else to worry about now. I doubt I shall get *any* sleep tonight. Will you be all right out here?'

'Of course, miss.'

'I shall come out and see you, if there's time. And I'll make sure you get a good meal.'

'Much appreciated.'

*

As the sun slipped below the horizon, Marik felt a growing sense of unease. The wind had strengthened and he was not fond of the increased rolling of the ship, nor the white flurries of surf atop waves that now appeared black. Earlier, the forward sail had been changed; a job that required most of the crew. Marik had been thoroughly impressed by the courage and agility of the sailors – many of them no more than teenagers – who had scaled mast and nets to take down one sail and raise another. Now the deck was fairly quiet, illuminated only by the gritty glow of three lanterns. The closest was by the wheel just in front of the cabin, where a new man had taken over steering.

Marik had been furnished with two blankets and a cushion but was still unsure when – or if – his meal would turn up. He took out a tub of oil and some cloths he had bought in Ralaska, then unsheathed his sword and set about coating it with the oil before polishing. As he worked, one of the older sailors sauntered back to the stern. He walked with a slight limp and was puffing on a stubby pipe. In the gloom, Marik could make out little of his face.

'Free at last,' said the sailor. 'I've been meaning to come back and talk to you all day.'

'Is that so?'

'A chance to practise my Common.'

'Ah.'

'You're a long way from home, by all accounts.'

'True enough.' Marik was glad of the company but he didn't want to endure another interrogation about the South.

'Bodyguard. That always struck me as a difficult job.'

'Can be.' Marik began his polishing at the blade's base.

'All that waiting around, then the occasional moment of violence.'

'That pretty much sums it up. And what exactly do you do onboard?'

'Master of Sails.'

'Sounds grand.'

The old sailor chuckled. 'As I often say, it's as well I've risen to that rank – at my age, there's not a single other job I could do.'

'So, you decide when they come up and when they come down?'

'Yes, that – and which ones to use, how to set them and so on.'

'What do you know about those creatures – the kraal?'

'Not many of *those* down south, are there?' The man sounded almost proud. 'Well, I've seen a few in my time. Unfortunately, very close on a couple of occasions.'

'Really? I couldn't believe the size of it.'

'I've seen bigger. The males have an unfortunate habit of ramming ships. That one today was probably a female – no white band on the tail. They usually travel in groups so I would guess it was lost. I doubt we'll see another – not this early in the year.'

'You mariners see some strange sights.'

'True enough. Waterspouts, whirlpools, flying fish, sea-witches.'

'Sea-witches?'

'Oh yes. Beautiful they are – float above the water near the bow to tempt you on. Then they lead you to rocks and wreck you. Feed off your dying soul.'

'Have you seen one?'

'Not personally. But I know many who have.' The sailor crossed the deck to the cabin and offered his hand. 'Yerdek. Pleased to make your acquaintance.'

Marik reached up and shook his hand, enjoying the waft of pipe-smoke. 'Marik. Likewise.'

Yerdek pointed his pipe at the sword. 'The main tool of your trade, I suppose. I hope you don't have to use it anytime soon.'

Marik had no desire whatsoever to tell him that the blade had already taken three lives. 'I must compliment you on your Common.'

'My thanks. In my youth I sailed with the trade fleets. Down south as far as the Nine Provinces.'

'That's a long way.'

'Hard country down there. Tough people. But they were fair and friendly with us. I'm always sorry to hear of what's going on in the South.'

Marik was saved from a further enquiry by the cabin door opening. Lena came out bearing a lantern and was followed by Irikyl, who was holding a plate. The serving-girl stumbled as the ship moved but was steadied by Yerdek. Marik stood and took the plate.

'Sorry it's so late,' said Lena.

'Not at all.'

She smiled at the sailor. 'Have you made a friend?'

'Er, yes.'

'Yerdek, isn't it?'

'That's right, miss. Well, I shall leave young Marik to eat his dinner. Sleep well.'

'Thank you,' said Marik.

Lena smiled. 'I hope you enjoy it. Irikyl did her best. The rolls should be good – delivered by my favourite baker before we set off this morning.'

'Thank you, miss.'

'We shall also leave you to eat in peace.'

The dinner was most welcome and most tasty: spiced meat of some kind, a big lump of cheese, two large rolls and an apple. As he ate, Marik was struck – not for the first time – by all the strange turns his life had taken in recent years. He conceded to himself that he almost enjoyed not knowing where he would end up next; who he would meet; what would happen. He just hoped that things would quieten down for a bit. It was difficult not to think of that cellar; the slice of metal through flesh, the scent of blood in his nose-

Marik couldn't face any more food. He wrapped the remaining meat and bread in some cloth and put it in his pack. Just as he was about to return the plate to the cabin, the young boy wandered into view. He stopped right in front of Marik and grinned at him.

'Hello.'

'Hello there. Very good Common. What can I do for you?'

The lad scratched his face and said nothing more. When Marik gave him the apple he seemed delighted. Just then the cabin door opened and the lad scampered away with his prize.

Lena came out alone and picked up the plate.

'Please, miss.' Marik scrambled to his feet.

'It's all right, I can do some things for myself, you know. Nice dinner?'

'Very nice.'

'Good. And you're sure you'll-'

From inside the cabin came Cara's voice. She didn't sound happy.

'Gods,' whispered Lena. 'What is it now? Goodnight, Marik.'

'Night, miss.'

To his utter astonishment, Lena stretched up to her full height and kissed him on the cheek. Then, without another word, she hurried inside and shut the cabin door. Blushing, Marik looked around: fortunately, it was too dark for anyone to have noticed.

He was confused, unsure what it meant; if it meant anything at all. All he did know was how much he had enjoyed it. And that the black sea surrounding the ship now seemed just that little bit less threatening.

Chapter Seven

By noon of the following day, both wind and sea were calmer. Passengers and crew also seemed more relaxed, which Marik ascribed firstly to the fact that no kraal had been sighted and secondly to Captain Eylirr's prediction that they would reach Alkari the next morning. He had somehow achieved several hours of sleep despite the endless groans, squeaks and taps produced by the ship. Some of the sailors also slept on deck and when the wind died at dawn there were many snores to be heard too. Marik again donated part of his breakfast to the young lad and was engaged in conversation once more by Yerdek, who thankfully took the hints about what Marik was happy to discuss and what he was not.

As the deck grew almost unbearably hot, Marik again withdrew to a shady part of the stern. He had not been there long when he caught his first glimpse of the passenger staying in the third room of the cabin. He'd already heard about the nobleman and his servant but had not imagined the fellow would be quite so youthful. The passenger in fact looked no older than thirteen while his attendant was middle-aged. Marik thought it odd that the young man had not shown his face during the appearance of the kraal. He wore finely-tailored trousers and a white buttoned shirt that was only a shade paler than his face. Without the dark hair and narrow features, he would not have passed for Urlun at all. Upon noticing him, Captain Eylirr hurried back from the bow and made great efforts to ensure his guest was happy and comfortable.

Desperate to stretch his legs – and confident the ladies would not venture outside in the heat – Marik strode along the right side of the ship. This took him past numerous sailors, most of whom seemed fascinated by his fair hair. Marik had grown used to this in Ralaska but the glowers of the tattooed, sunburned mariners grew oppressive as he approached the bow.

He paused there to examine the horizon and was disappointed when he saw no trace of land. He heard movement behind him and, when he turned, found himself surrounded. Closest to him was a sailor with dark blue ink around both eyes.

'Trade?'

The man opened a worn leather case and showed Marik a selection of tiny instruments and finely carved figurines. There were also some cheap-looking gems and ancient-looking coins.

'No, thank you.'

'Trade?' repeated the man.

'No.'

There were now at least ten of them blocking his path. Over the shoulder of one, he spied Zyrin, who was leaning back against the side-rail, observing with interest.

'Play? Want to play?' Another man with a wart-covered face opened a grimy hand to reveal dice with too many sides for Marik to count.

'No, thank you. Excuse me.' He tried to force his way through but a big sailor suddenly barred his way. He was one of the few Urluns over six feet, a well-built man with several metal studs embedded in his head. From the vacant look in his narrow eyes, Marik doubted he was all that bright. The sailor flexed an arm, displaying a notable lump of muscle.

The gambler chipped in. 'Want to wrestle with him? With arm? For money?'

'No.' Marik caught Zyrin's eye. 'Can you tell them to move?'

Zyrin answered in Urlun, pretending to not understand.

Marik could not believe what happened next. Having closed his case, the would-be trader reached out and stroked Marik's hair.

Without a thought that this might be entirely innocent, Marik grabbed him by the wrist. 'Keep your bloody hands off me.'

He felt suddenly angry with all the staring sailors. What was wrong with them? Why didn't they realise what it felt like to be trapped like this?

'You. Tell them!'

Zyrin pushed himself casually off the side-rail and ordered the men away. They complied slowly; the big fellow and the gambler last to step away. Marik noted that the captain was watching from the stern but still attending to his wealthy passenger.

'Very helpful.'

'Why should I help you?' replied Zyrin, his blue eyes gleaming.

Marik considered some insult but reminded himself that he would be off the ship the following day. He walked past the Urlun, close enough to make his point.

But Zyrin wasn't finished. 'One more thing, Souther – don't give the lad any more food. The others don't like it. You're not helping him.'

Marik turned around. 'At least he knows not everyone in the world is an arsehole. I'd say that's a help.'

'You don't know us, you don't know this ship.'

'Problem?' Old Yerdek had appeared and now placed himself between them.

Zyrin said something to him in Urlun that did not sound complimentary.

'No problem.' Marik went on his way.

But it soon became evident that he did have a problem. Upon returning to the stern, he found Lena and Cara talking in serious tones to Captain Eylirr. Marik stayed out of the way and was disappointed when Lena followed her sister back inside without a word to him. Shortly after he was summoned by the servant, Irikyl. The expressions on the ladies' faces did not bode well. The cabin was very small, with narrow beds along two sides and a compact table with two chairs. Cara was sitting on one of the beds, hands clasped in her lap, sobbing.

Lena sighed before speaking. 'It appears we have been robbed.'

'Oh.' Marik then realised this was a fairly inadequate response. 'What's been taken?'

'Cara's jewellery case. She was showing me a new ring this morning and she forgot to put it back in the strongbox.' Lena gestured to the iron-ribbed timber chest on the floor beneath the table.

She and Marik had to steady themselves as the ship wallowed momentarily.

'We think she left it on her pillow. We've looked everywhere. It's not here. There were two other rings and a necklace. Hundreds' worth.'

Cara shot an accusing glare towards Marik then a burst of Urlun at her sister.

Lena spoke to him. 'You left your post for a while, correct?'

'I ... went for a walk. I was only away for ten minutes, no longer.'

'You should have told us.'

'Surely you saw I wasn't there?'

'Of course, we should have locked the cabin. But you've not moved from the stern – we thought you'd be watching the door.'

Once Marik admonished himself for this oversight, he considered whether anyone could really have sneaked inside the cabin without being noticed?

'The helmsman – he's stationed just in front of the cabin. He would have seen anyone going in.'

'He must be questioned,' said Lena. 'Would you fetch the captain, please?'

'Of course. Sorry, miss. And to you, Miss Cara. I would, however, mention that I am really here to guard you – not your belongings.'

Cara just glared at him.

Marik fetched Captain Eylirr, who cursed upon hearing of the theft but went immediately to his passengers, accompanied by the helmsman. Marik was the last to enter and shut the door behind him.

'Well?' snapped Cara, whose Common was clearly fine when she chose to use it.

Marik shrugged and gestured to the captain.

'Miss Larris, are you completely sure that the jewellery has been stolen?'

Cara threw up her hands. 'How many times?'

'Captain, we're sure,' said Lena.

Eylirr placed his hands on the back of a chair. 'I do not believe any of my crewman would steal from a passenger.'

The sisters exchanged a cynical look.

Marik considered saying something but – given his own culpability – it seemed wise to stay quiet for now.

Cara slumped down on the bed again, shaking her head.

Her sister remained standing. 'Captain, how many men are there in your crew?'

'Thirty-two including me and the three boys.'

'You're not seriously suggesting that none of those sailors is capable of theft?'

'I've not had many problems before, miss.'

'*Many?*'

'Well …' Eylirr scratched at his beard. 'Nothing involving passengers, you understand. The odd item has gone missing from the stores. And of course, the men sometimes accuse each other - but most of it's just talk.'

'Any known criminals among the current crew?'

Not for the first time, Marik was impressed by Lena's sharp mind and forceful nature.

'No, absolutely not. I let a man go last year. There are three or four that I've taken on recently – I cannot claim to know them as well as the others.'

'You will start the search? Do you have men you can trust to do that?'

'Of course, Miss Larris, I'll take charge myself. But I'll be very surprised if one of my lads is involved.'

Lena turned to the helmsman: a shaggy-haired fellow with the inevitable earring – this one made of several sea shells.

'You speak Common?'

'I do, miss.'

'Did anyone come past you – towards the stern - in the last hour?'

'Yes, miss. The stay-sail crew, Tola – and him.' The helmsman pointed at Marik.

Lena turned to Eylirr. 'How many in the stay-sail crew?'

'Six – they were sent back to heave it in when we changed course.'

'How long would that have taken?'

'No more than a couple of minutes.'

'You should perhaps begin your search with them?'

'Yes, miss.'

'Who's Tola?'

'One of the boys. He was cleaning the rear deck.'

Marik knew that was his young friend – the other boys were responsible for the front half of the ship and below decks. He couldn't help recalling the youth's interest in his sword; he hoped another object of value hadn't attracted him.

Cara stood up and pointed at Marik. 'We will search him too. Captain, you'll take care of it?'

When Lena glanced at Marik, he tried to swiftly overcome the awkwardness of the moment.

'Of course – that is only fair.'

'You're welcome to search my quarters also,' offered Eylirr.

'That won't be necessary,' replied Cara.

Marik observed a brief flare of annoyance from her sister, but Lena said nothing.

He felt the time had come to at least contribute to the discussion. 'There are the other passengers.'

'Baron Vo Kynell?' Cara glared up at him, her brow furrowed. 'What a ridiculous suggestion.'

'He has a servant,' countered Marik quietly.

Lena shook her head. 'We can't possibly even mention this to the baron.'

Marik guessed the young aristocrat had some powerful connections back in Ralaska yet it seemed stupid to ignore the two people closest to the site of the theft.

Cara turned her attention back to Eylirr. 'Could you please make a start, captain – we'll be in port by the morning.'

'Of course.' Eylirr and the helmsman left.

'I shall search the area outside,' said Marik, 'just in case.'

'Very well,' said Lena.

Marik was on his way out but Cara stood up beside her sister for one last comment.

'If the jewellery is lost, I will insist that you pay back every coin my father paid you. Understood?'

Marik's fruitless search of the deck made him feel even more ashamed by his failure. It was true that he was primarily present to guard the two ladies – not their belongings – but they clearly didn't see it that way and he imagined their father might not either. If he really did have to give up his earnings – and miss out on those to come – the whole trip would have been a waste of time. When Captain Eylirr returned, he too cast a venomous look Marik's way.

'Couldn't you have just watched the door?'

'Any developments?'

Eylirr ignored him and continued on to the cabin. The sisters were both standing outside, holding on to the doorway as the ship negotiated a slight swell.

'Ladies, my officers are conducting the searches and I have questioned the stay-sail crew. Five of them came back to attend to the lines, and they maintain that none of them went near the cabin. As soon as they were done, they returned below – I had them working the bilges. It's not possible that one of them might have got inside the cabin without the others noticing.'

Marik didn't make the point that they might all be in on the robbery; or that loyalty might prevent them from betraying their shipmates.

'I've also questioned young Tola. He's not been with us long and I'm afraid to report that some of the others believe he's taken food and other belongings from them. He denies it, of course, and we've not found the jewels, but he might easily have stashed them somewhere.'

'So could anyone else who took them,' said Marik.

'It must have been the boy,' said Cara. 'Do what you must to get the truth from him.'

'There's no evidence,' said Marik, stepping forward. 'And you haven't even spoken to the men next door.'

'Time to search *you*.' Cara pointed at Marik.

'As you wish.'

Marik fetched his pack and returned to find the others inside the cabin. He handed the pack to Eylirr who laid it on the table and opened it up. Having found nothing incriminating, he turned to Marik, who had some questions for him.

'Tell me, who mentioned the boy had stolen from them?'

'Three men.'

'Which three?'

'You don't know them.' Eylirr patted down Marik's shirt, then his trousers. From one of the deep pockets, he retrieved only the leather pouch containing the ten bronze coins paid by Larris. Having accounted for it, Marik persisted with another question for the captain.

'Are they friends of Zyrin?'

Eylirr didn't answer. He checked Marik's lower legs, even the loose tops of his boots.

'The jewellery could be at the bottom.'

Cara's suggestion was met by a glare from her sister.

Marik kept his attention on the captain. 'Well?'

'Why do you ask?'

'He and his friends seemed quite keen to keep me at the bow while the theft was carried out.'

'Zyrin is not a thief.'

'Are the men his friends?'

'Two are, yes. But – like him – loyal, long-serving men. Listen, I don't like to think ill of the boy but we took him straight off the streets. He might have picked up some bad habits.'

'How long has he been with you?' asked Lena.

'Two months or so.'

Ideally, Marik would not have weighed in but he felt he had to. 'I'll say it again, there's no evidence.'

Lena replied: 'Marik, there is the testimony of the other sailors. Captain, please bring the boy up here.'

'Of course.'

Marik followed the captain out and looked forward. Some of the crew were attending to the mainsail but about a dozen were gathered close to the bow, Zyrin among them. Marik knew he had only his dislike of the man and his affinity for the boy to guide him but he couldn't avoid the feeling that Tola was a convenient scapegoat.

He returned to the doorway and addressed the sisters. 'Would you at least let me speak to the baron and his man? I can be diplomatic when I need to be.'

'I doubt it,' said Cara.

Lena kept her voice down. 'We cannot even approach the baron regarding such a matter. Nor is there any need. Forget it.'

Marik was pretty sure the jewellery case had already gone over the side. There were countless places the rings and the necklace could be secreted aboard the ship. He felt sure that they would not appear; and that he would arrive in another strange land without a coin to his name.

The entire exchange between Tola, Eylirr and the sisters was conducted in Urlun. Marik could easily deduce that the boy was strongly denying any involvement; and that the sisters did not believe him. He managed to grab a word with the captain as he left with Tola.

'What did he say?'

'He didn't do it. What did you expect him to say?'

'But-'

'-Not now.'

Minutes later, the crew carried out a course change and Marik had to relocate several times. Once all the heaving and shouting and flapping of sails had subsided, the vessel seemed to pick up speed. Captain Eylirr was nowhere to be seen; Marik presumed he was still below deck, conducting the search.

Spirits as low as they'd been for a while, he gazed out at a small island no more than a mile across. Only one end featured any vegetation: a stand of skeletal trees covered by some plant that resembled a great green net. Below the trees were a few ramshackle buildings and between the island and the ship, a trio of boats. All the men within were wielding fishing rods and spared only brief glances for the passing ship.

'Don't turn. Don't look at me.'

Marik couldn't resist doing so – out of the corner of his eye. Old Yerdek was now standing at the side-rail about six feet away, ostensibly cleaning his pipe.

'Just listen.'

'Very well.'

The old sailor looked down at the pipe as he continued. To any observer, it might seem that he was mumbling to himself or reciting a song.

'Last night – Zyrin was seen talking to the men that have blamed the lad. I've never heard anything about Tola thieving before – it's nonsense. I'll do what I can but I can't take on Zyrin. He'll gut anyone that goes against him. He couldn't care less what happens to the lad. I don't know what you can do but …'

'Thank you.'

'You must not tell. I can prove nothing.'

'Understood.'

A few moments later, the old sailor walked away.

A shift in the cloud cast sunlight onto the waves, creating a glittering strip that cut across the sea behind the ship. Marik's eyes were drawn to it but his mind was busy. He doubted he would be able to do much while aboard the *White Cloud* but once they reached Alkari, he might be able to take matters into his own hands. Zyrin would probably try and sell the jewellery quickly. Expecting to be dismissed by the sisters, Marik would be free to keep an eye on him and exact his own form of justice. He wondered whether he would be able to help Tola. If he could prove to Eylirr that his officer was behind the theft, the lad might keep his job. Come to think of it, Marik might also be able to keep *his* if he acted swiftly.

He looked towards the bow. Zyrin was leaning casually against the mainmast, gazing forward, perhaps thinking about how to spend his ill-gotten gains. Marik's fingers twitched as he thought of marching forward; getting the truth *his* way. He let out a long breath and wished he could throw himself into the water; forget all this, cleanse himself of all the bad that seemed to follow him around like a black cloud. Was it him; or was it the world?

'Lovely day.'

He turned to see the young Ralaskan nobleman beside him. Baron Vo Kynell could have just stepped out of a mansion. His black hair was combed and oiled, his angular face as smooth and unblemished as a baby's. He wore blue trousers and a yellow shirt with black buttons. Upon his feet were a pair of soft shoes; the type a king might wear while relaxing in his chambers.

'Wouldn't you say?'

'I would, sir.'

Behind the baron was his attendant, a man whose clothing and manner seemed designed to render him almost invisible. Hands clasped behind him, he followed his young charge to the side-rail.

'You're the bodyguard – a Souther, I gather?'

'That's right, sir.' Marik would have preferred to avoid a conversation but his standing with the sisters would not be improved by snubbing the nobleman.

'Long way from home.'

'A fair weather for the crossing, at least.'

'Indeed. Any idea what all the fuss is about?'

'Sir?'

'The captain's been running around all morning and your ladies seem rather upset.'

Marik didn't think it sensible to lie. The baron would inevitably hear of the theft sooner or later: so he told him.

'Oh. How unpleasant.' Vo Kynell turned to his attendant and spoke to him in Ralaskan. With a brief nod, the man hurried back into the cabin.

'Taking precautions, sir?'

'Yes, just double-checking. But we've been very careful anyway. Captain Eylirr is a trustworthy fellow but we all know how sailors can be. We've seen a few of them hanging around the stern when they've no business doing so – especially at night.'

'Really, sir? Might I ask who?'

'The young cleaning boy, for one. And that very large fellow with the metal in his head. I believe it was the first night - he seemed overly interested in the cabins. I didn't wish to offend the captain by mentioning it. Then there's the old helmsman chap. Spends a lot of time back here, even when he's not on duty.'

The baron leaned closer to Marik. 'Between you and me, I wouldn't trust a single one of them.'

Chapter Eight

Night came; and with it a sense of inevitability. The winds were still fair and the *White Cloud* was expected to reach Alkari not long after dawn. The captain was out of ideas and Lena seemed to have resigned herself to the loss of the jewellery. Cara remained determined to recover her belongings. She asked Marik if he had anything more to contribute but he felt unable to pass on the information from Yerdek without any supporting evidence. And after what the baron had said, it even seemed possible that the old sailor might be trying to cover his own tracks. Yerdek appeared a decent fellow to Marik but perhaps winning him over had been part of his plan.

Just after the sun set, a tearful Cara informed the captain that she would not be leaving the vessel without her jewellery. Marik was surprised to see how upset the apologetic Eylirr was; he imagined that news of the theft would not be well received by his other wealthy customers.

With the deck quiet, Baron Vo Kynell and his attendant exited the cabin. Marik – who was sitting in his usual position – stood up and moved aside as the young nobleman approached the ladies' room and knocked on the door. Lena answered and was immediately presented with a small box and some brief pleasantries. She bowed and accepted the gift with a servile smile of the type Marik would have thought her incapable. Before shutting the door, she glanced at Marik, who believed he detected a second smile for him. Cara was lying on her bed, staring up at the cabin roof.

'A gift to raise their spirits,' the young baron told Marik before
glancing curiously down at the blanket laid out beside the cabin.
'Don't you get cold at night?'
'No, sir.'
'I have heard you Southers are hardy folk.'

With the unassuming attendant holding a lantern behind him, Vo Kynell patted down his hair. 'Most unfortunate for your mistresses. And for the captain. Very awkward.'

'I don't suppose they'll be my mistresses for much longer, sir – on account of the theft.'

'Ah, yes, I see. Also unfortunate. Goodnight then.'
'Goodnight, sir.'

Once the two had returned to their cabin, Marik walked forward. It was a calm, clear night and though the wind was not strong, it was sufficient to propel the ship eastward with full sails. Marik knew he should probably have stayed by the cabin but he would discover nothing by standing there and it seemed likely the morning would bring only unemployment. He also knew some of the other sailors spoke Common; perhaps there was a final chance to learn more.

The first of them he encountered were the helmsman and an officer. Marik knew Zyrin was one of three officers, all of whom were distinguished from the lower ranks by the fitted black jackets. Both men shrugged their shoulders when he tried to address them. A second attempt to converse with the officer resulted only in a brisk shake of the head. It seemed to Marik that the man didn't deem a lowly bodyguard worthy of conversation.

He continued along the deck. Close to the mainmast, three men were replacing a damaged plank by lamplight. One of them was a slave who didn't even look up. The other two did, and Marik recognised one from the incident at the bow. This man remained silent when he greeted them.

The third sailor muttered, 'Don't speak Common,' before picking up a plane to run over the new plank.

Marik didn't have far to go for his next conversation.

'You bothering my men, Souther?'

Zyrin emerged from the gloom, a bottle in his hand. Not far behind was his hulking friend; the metal studs in his head sparking orange from a nearby lantern. Marik was almost glad to see the abrasive officer; he didn't feel like he had much to lose.

'Aren't they the captain's men?' he countered. 'Aren't *you*?'

Zyrin shook his head in mock-despair. 'Wouldn't expect you to understand something like the chain of command. Bunch of barbarians, your lot. No understanding of organised warfare. Probably why you lost the only time you tried to fight Northers.'

Marik nodded at the bottle. 'Celebrating?'

'Maybe.' Zyrin seemed a little drunk.

'You heard about the theft, I suppose?'

'I did. Difficult. Especially for you.'

'Well, of course, I wouldn't have been away from the cabin for so long if your big friend and all the others hadn't surrounded me. Probably just a coincidence though.'

'If you've got something to say, Souther, say it.' Zyrin passed the bottle to his compatriot, who took it but did not drink.

'Your captain seems to think the young lad did it – I wonder who gave him that idea?'

Zyrin looked around and grinned. 'I did.'

'You admit it then?'

'Oh yes. I got the men to blame him. And – yes – I got the others to keep you at the bow. Thanks for giving us the opportunity, by the way. Good lads on that stay-sail crew. Reliable. Loyal. And one of them in particular has a useful set of skills.'

By the time he'd finished, Marik realised Zyrin wasn't taking much of a risk. Only his wordless friend was present to hear his confession and who would believe Marik's account?

'I guess you'll take the largest share of the earnings?'

'You guess right.' Zyrin chuckled.

'I'd spend the money quickly if I were you,' said Marik, barely able to resist the temptation to rip that earring out and shove it down the sailor's throat.

'Is that a threat?' Zyrin stepped forward, one hand now on the metal spike hanging from his belt. 'Because you won't last long enough to call for help.'

The big man didn't seem to have a weapon on him but judging by the size of his arms and hands, Marik doubted he needed one. This wasn't the moment to pick a fight.

'Be careful in Alkari, Zyrin. Watch your ba-'

Marik assumed he must have been blindsided – hit by one of Zyrin's friends – because he heard a loud crack and then found himself lying on the deck, staring at the big sailor's boots. A moment later, the nearby lamp crashed onto the timbers, spilling burning oil across those boots. Just as Marik scrabbled to his feet, the deck lurched under him and he fell again. Except this time he slid too because the ship was suddenly at an angle. He reached out and grabbed a cleat on the mainmast, then got his other hand on a nearby rope. A flailing Zyrin flew past him.

Trying to get his bearings, Marik looked forward and glimpsed the horizon. The line was faint but it showed him the angle of the deck to the water – at least forty-five degrees. He heard shouts; what sounded like the orders of Captain Eylirr. Most of the lamps had gone out.

Then the ship shifted again, falling back and hitting the water with a great shudder. Somebody bounced off Marik's shoulder as they careened past him. Once the deck was level again, he steadied himself against the mast. He had only just done so when a heavy object fell from the rigging and smashed through the timbers only a few yards away. Ducking instinctively, Marik looked around. He could hear a man screaming and another whimpering but the rest of the noise was a tumult of panicked Urlun. The mast was not far from the main hatch and he could hear sailors rushing up to the deck.

Lena.

Marik hurried towards the stern, alarmed to find that the helmsman had disappeared. He tripped twice on unseen obstacles and was almost to the cabin when the ship moved under him again. When it stopped, he realised he could hear timbers cracking. Already scared, he now felt his entire body tingle with fear. Was the *White Cloud* breaking up? Would it sink?

Suddenly a light appeared ahead of him. The lantern was in the hand of Captain Eylirr who reached the sisters' room and wrenched open the door. With him was one of his other officers. Marik arrived there to find Lena, Cara and the maid pulling shawls on over their nightdresses. The officer stayed with them, issuing instructions. Eylirr hurried past Marik to the left side of the ship. Marik grabbed his pack and sword then followed and looked on as the captain peered down into the darkness. The sound of creaking timber and rushing water was much louder here. Eylirr walked forward, silent and strangely calm. Over his shoulder, Marik saw the lantern's glow reach a damaged section of the hull. Fully ten feet of the side-rail had been smashed to pieces. The interior of the ship could be seen, now a broiling cauldron of water and wreckage.

Eylirr said two words to himself and repeated them several times.

'Captain?'

Eylirr spun around. 'We're going down. Some kraal has sunk us.'

Marik wondered why he hadn't realised sooner. What else could have done this to the ship?

The captain moved away. As the vessel tipped down to the left, Marik found himself lying against the side-rail, paralysed by fear. They were only hours from Alkari. How far was the land? Was there anyone close enough to help?

The ship tipped over another few degrees. Marik put his pack on and hung his sword belt from his shoulder. He retreated towards the stern but it was already a struggle to fight the angle on the smooth deck. He was astonished to find what seemed to be every person aboard gathered at the rear of the ship. Only two lamps were alight but they gave out enough to illuminate Eylirr. The captain was standing high, a hand on one of the stays that supported the rear mast, bellowing at the sailors. Close to him, the officer was helping Lena, Cara and Irikyl through a narrow gap at the stern.

Baron Vo Kynell and his attendant were waiting behind them, the servant laden with various bags and boxes.

Marik remembered the ship's tender but knew the small craft would accommodate no more than ten. For now, the sailors were allowing the passengers to get aboard. Marik wondered how long this forbearance would last; there was no other method of escape.

Two more sailors rushed past him and joined the back of the crowd. When the ship tipped further over, several of them slipped and one of the women screamed. Marik wanted to go and help Lena but he knew he had no chance of getting in that tender.

Fearful the left side would go under, he used the cabin to haul himself up the incline. A powerful run was required to cover the final few feet and reach the right-hand rail. Marik threw his hands over it just as a hulking figure came up through the hatch. Behind him, carrying a lantern, was Zyrin. Both men had one end of a large piece of timber which they then wedged between a cleat and the side-rail. Both also had large packs on, made of some shiny material that glistened under the lantern-light. Marik guessed they were waterproof; made of some animal skin.

Just then, he felt something grip his leg. Peering down, he saw a small, pale face and a pair of terrified eyes. Young Tola reached for his hand and gabbled to him in Urlun. Unsure what to say or do, Marik settled for patting his head but the grip on his leg remained vice-like. He hoped the boy understood that he knew less about surviving a shipwreck than probably any man aboard.

'Very sweet,' said Zyrin, holding the lantern up as he noticed the two of them. 'But you best worry about yourself.'

'What do you care?'

'I don't.'

Zyrin hung the lantern from a nearby cleat and helped his friend manoeuvre another great log up on deck. The big man also had a paddle hanging from his shoulder. Zyrin had a coil of rope which he tied around the centre of the log. He passed the end to his friend, who repeated the process with the first timber. The pair seemed utterly disinterested in the unfolding events at the stern.

Captain Eylirr could still be heard, his voice now shrill with panic.

Marik put a hand on Zyrin's shoulder. 'What do we do?'

Zyrin answered without turning around. 'Not very bright, are you, Southy? This thing will be under the waves in minutes.' He handed the lantern to Marik. 'Find something that floats and will take your weight.'

The officer spoke to his friend in Urlun. They rolled the two great logs over the side-rail then climbed up over it themselves. The big man jumped straight into the water. Zyrin took a single look back – not at Marik, but at the crowded stern. Then he jumped.

Tola grabbed Marik's hand and tried to drag him forward. Marik hesitated, thinking that the lad meant to go below. Even if it meant finding a float, Marik wouldn't risk being caught down there. When he refused to move, Tola went ahead alone, both hands on the rail, toes pressed against the sloping hull.

With no other plan or idea, Marik followed him, holding the handle of the lantern in his teeth. Zyrin's warning and the noise from the masts and rigging was enough to convince him that they had to get off the ship quickly. By the time he caught up with the agile Tola, the lad was beside four spars lashed to the side-rail. The beams were roped together and narrower than Zyrin's logs but there was no other alternative. While Tola started detaching the far end, Marik hung the lantern from a cleat. He pulled out his sword and hacked at the ties until the spars were free. Tola had to wait for Marik to sheathe the sword before they could lever the spars onto the side-rail.

'Ready, lad?'

Marik heard nothing and could see little of his face, so he simply tipped the spars over the side. He looked back at the stern. Beneath the glow of a lamp he could see several men struggling, perhaps even fighting.

'Come on, before they float away.' He gripped the lad's arm and hauled him up onto the side-rail. Tola climbed over and squatted on the hull. The *White Cloud* lurched over again, knocking him off balance. With a yelp, he slid down the timber and into the water.

Marik clambered after him, having to free his sword on the way. As he sat there, he could see nothing but darkness below. He moved to the right before jumping, to make sure he avoided the boy.

The water was colder than he could have imagined. He arrowed in deep and there was a horrible moment when he thought he would not float back up. Even when swimming in lakes, Marik had not liked putting his head under and he was weighed down by sword and pack. Remembering to kick, he propelled himself upward and eventually broke the surface.

A hand smacked him across the brow. Tola's little face suddenly appeared and the lad tried to grab him.

'Hey! What are you doing?'

The boy was panicking, his head dipping under the waves as he tried to attach himself to Marik.

When Tola's hand caught him on the nose, Marik decided on decisive action. He slapped the lad across the cheek, gripped his tunic and held him above the water – but at a distance. Knowing he wouldn't be able to keep that up for long, he looked around. The dark bulk of the *White Cloud* was to his left. To the right he saw and heard what could only be Zyrin and his friend, already manoeuvring themselves away from the foundering ship.

Thankfully the moonlight also picked up the polished surface of the floating spars. Dragging Tola with him, Marik pulled himself through the water and got a hand on the precious timbers. Once close enough, Tola put his arms over the spars and rested his head against one, dragging in deep breaths as he calmed down.

From behind them came a groan. The *White Cloud* levelled out but then began to sink with such speed that Marik could feel water tugging at his legs. The shouts from the stern multiplied and grew louder. Marik gripped the spars himself, kicked out hard and told Tola to do the same. The lad clearly understood because soon he had joined in the effort. Only when Marik could no longer feel the pull did he slow down.

Turning around, he was stunned to see only one of the vessel's masts still visible above the waves. Behind the stern he could also make out the tender, which seemed to be moving away from the sinking ship at speed. In the other direction he could see the churning water produced by Zyrin and his friend. Both they and those in the tender seemed keen to move quickly and it didn't take much imagination to work out why. Unless a considerable amount of wreckage was left behind, every last man in the water would be searching for something that floated.

'Kick, boy, kick.'

Marik didn't give much thought to direction and just hoped the beams remained lashed. Together, they were about three feet across and nine long, probably buoyant enough for he and the boy to clamber up and rest if they needed too.

'Marik!'

When his name was repeated, he and Tola stopped kicking.

'Marik, is that you?'

He didn't recognise the voice but calculated that there were not many aboard who both knew his name and spoke Common.

'Yerdek!' It was Tola who called out. And he continued to shout at the old sailor in Urlun.

'Shit,' whispered Marik.

The ship had disappeared completely now and only a few voices could be heard. As his night vision improved, Marik realised he could see dozens of heads and arms. Some seemed to still be following the tender but many were grouped where the stern had been. Yerdek was about forty feet from that point and twenty from Marik and Tola. Marik could also make out the odd bit of wreckage but nothing like enough for the whole crew. One man was already crying out, imploring others to save him.

'Quickly!' hissed Marik, trying to keep his voice down. He was relieved to see that Yerdek was at least a capable swimmer. Soon the old sailor was throwing his hands onto the spars on the other side of Tola. Between panting breaths, he spoke briefly to the lad then to Marik.

'Thank you. Thank you.'

'Forget it. We have to get away. For the lad, if not for ourselves.'

Without another word, Yerdek dropped lower into the water and began to kick. Marik tried to copy him in keeping his legs below the water to reduce noise. With trousers and boots on it was difficult but the three of them propelled the makeshift raft well enough. Yerdek spoke to Tola, clearly explaining to him that they should try to be quiet; the lad obeyed.

From behind them came many calls. At one stage, Marik thought he heard the voice of Captain Eylirr but he wasn't sure. He felt a certain degree of shame at their covert escape but could see no other choice. Nor did he feel a great deal of sympathy for the sailors, who should have surely had more foresight than he and a young boy.

They kept going for what might have been a quarter-hour but could have been double that for all Marik knew. The shouts continued – some seemingly directed at them – but became infrequent and faint. When they finally stopped, Marik pulled his boots off, which was no easy task. Tying the laces together, he placed them on the raft.

Young Tola was puffing; and now that they had stopped, Marik could actually hear his teeth chattering.

'Let's get him out of the water.'

The two men took a leg each and hoisted the boy upward. He rolled up tight and lay there, shivering. Marik did not yet dare consider their chances. It was not particularly cold but they would have no chance to dry out and there were many hours of darkness ahead.

He heard another shout and saw two men swimming in their direction, no more than fifty feet away.

'We must keep going.'

Yerdek did not reply but, like Marik, he sank back into the water, pushing the raft and the three of them on into nothing but darkness and cold. Marik eventually realised the old sailor had not replied because he was sobbing. He supposed there was a difference between abandoning strangers and abandoning shipmates.

They heard shouts only three times more. The third of them seemed so far away that they felt safe to stop again. Marik insisted that Yerdek get himself out of the water and the old sailor was so tired that he had to help him do so. Marik did not try to get up on the raft himself; it clearly would not support all three of them.

'You must take your turn soon,' said Yerdek.

Marik was trying to stop his own teeth chattering but he reckoned there was one advantage to the cold: it stopped him thinking of his legs just dangling there, waiting for whatever awful creatures dwelt below to take a bite. Surely the kraal was still around somewhere. Marik had been cold – horribly cold – more times than he could remember. Any man that travelled far in the South could not avoid that. And he had been cold and *wet*; traipsed through rain for days on end. But to be so cold and actually *in* the water – that was a new kind of unpleasantness.

Yerdek spoke to Tola, who insisted on keeping his hand on Marik's arm.

'Is he all right?'

Yerdek replied: 'He says he is but he's shivering even more than I.'

'How far are we from the coast?'

'Around twenty miles, I should say. If it stays clear, we might even be able to see it at dawn.'

'Yerdek, what are our chances?'

'Not good. I am praying. Are you?'

'I'm not that desperate yet. Will there be boats around in the day?'

'Not many – unless there's a ship bound for Alkari or Ralaska.'

'Fishermen? There was that island – with the strange weed in the trees.'

'Kokerra is a long way behind us now. Our best chance is the Three Shells.'

'What's that?'

'A group of islands south of Alkari – about fifteen miles off the coast. The current will take us that way but I've no idea if we'll strike them.'

'And if we don't?'

'I'd rather not think about that.'

'Open sea?'

'Worse. The-'

The shout was clear; and seemed to come from Marik's right. He was by now so disorientated that he had no idea where they were in relation to the sunken ship.

Another shout; Marik could not make out the meaning.

'I think that's Zyrin,' said Yerdek.

'What should we do?'

'Be silent.'

'He gave me a lantern and told me what to do. He helped us.'

'Marik, we three all know what he did. He'll be with Utiss – the big man. He'll have weapons.'

'I have my sword.'

'He's in no better position than us,' said Yerdek. 'We've more to lose than gain.'

Marik couldn't argue with that but it seemed to him that there was strength in numbers. It also seemed to him that Zyrin was a born survivor and – in truth – more likely to endure than the aged Yerdek.

But they heard nothing more and in fact Marik was not sure the voice had belonged to Zyrin. Tola was the next to speak; Yerdek translated.

'Do you have any food? He's hungry.'

Marik had earlier placed his pack and sword on the raft along with his boots. 'In there - some bread and a bit of pork. Probably very wet.'

'Any water?' asked Yerdek.

'No.'

'I have a flask here with me. Full.'

Marik let out a heartfelt sigh of relief. 'At least you were thinking clearly.'

'Not really. I can't believe she's gone.'

'She?'

'The *Cloud*. I've had a couple of near misses with kraal over the years. Thought I'd got away with it. The poor captain...'

'There was no place for you in his boat?'

'No.' Yerdek replied with less emotion than his previous statement. 'He had to take the guests. Then there's only room for him and his oarsmen – a nephew and a brother. Not his fault.'

A minute later, Yerdek was snoring; a bizarre turn that would have drawn a grin from Marik were he not utterly freezing. He locked his elbows over the spar he was holding and rubbed his hands together, which made no difference whatsoever. Tola was still shivering and Marik did not enjoy his complete inability to do anything about it. If the lad died, it would not be his fault; yet it seemed like something he would struggle to forget.

Marik did not particularly like children – they were always making noise or asking stupid questions – but this boy Tola had endured a life far harder than his. He deserved better than to die like this.

Marik wasn't sure if *he* deserved better but he wanted to live; he knew that much. He wasn't all that concerned about becoming rich or successful or making a name for himself. He definitely wanted to bed more women (though in fact he hadn't done badly over the years). And while he wasn't ready yet, he felt that at some point he would return to the South. If any of his family or friends were still alive, he wanted to see them – one last time, at least.

He looked up. There was still not even a trace of cloud in the sky. Hundreds of stars could be seen and several constellations were clear: the Trident, the Great Diamond, the North Flower.

Yerdek had stopped snoring. The only sound was the lapping of water against the raft and the sharp little breaths of young Tola. Marik was still not yet ready to utter a prayer.

An hour or two later, Yerdek offered to swap. Marik was barely able to haul himself up in the old sailor's place. He drank a little water from the flask and lay down beside the lad. He could not feel his toes nor his fingers and the cold had planted a pulsing ache above his eyes. He was about to remove his soaking shirt when sleep took him.

He awoke to dazzling sunlight and the sound of Tola crying. The boy was sitting cross-legged, hands covering his eyes. Only when Marik sat up did he realise that they had lost Yerdek during the night. The old man was gone.

Chapter Nine

The weather was perfect: bright, warm sun but enough cloud to ensure they didn't burn. Marik and Tola had stripped off all but their underclothes and laid their wet garments along the spars. They sat there together, gazing out at the dark green sea and the brilliant blue sky. Marik was glad the boy had stopped crying and wished he could keep him occupied with conversation. Tola at least knew his name now and he seemed to have enjoyed his breakfast: a handful of pork and a piece of bread.

Marik guessed it was around the third hour of the day. Given that visibility was good, he was surprised that they couldn't see either the tender or Zyrin and Utiss but then both had a means of propulsion; it was likely they had made some progress west. Marik shivered as he thought of poor Yerdek, perhaps drifting off into sleep before slipping quietly below the waves. He felt guilt; but also an equal degree of regret - regret that he and the lad no longer had the local knowledge and wisdom of the old sailor to guide them.

Tola started humming and kicking his feet in the water.

Marik put a hand out. 'Don't do that. Kraal. Understand, kraal?' He wasn't sure if the lad did comprehend but he at least stopped.

Marik licked salt from his dry lips and forced himself to form a plan of action. He had not made much progress when Tola nudged him and pointed. Marik imagined there must have been mist earlier, because now he could see land, in particular a headland higher than the surrounding area. He could make no guess of distance but at least they had something to aim for now. Regardless of the risk of attracting kraal or something equally as dangerous, they had to try.

Marik moved his gear and the clothing to the centre of the makeshift raft and positioned himself at the back on the right side, legs over the four spars. He sent Tola forward on the left side and when he started paddling, the lad swiftly got the message. Marik had to control his stroke carefully to compensate for the difference in strength but he couldn't fault Tola's enthusiasm. Over the next two hours, they kept at it, taking breaks when needed and only stopping when the sun was directly overhead. Marik clapped Tola on the back and smiled at him but he had no idea if their efforts had made much difference.

After they had eaten a little, Marik retrieved Yerdek's flask, which he had hung below the raft from a bootlace. The heat had grown throughout the day and every cold drop was delectable. With the sun now so hot, he put on his dry clothes and tried to make Tola do the same. The lad resisted. Though he was darker in colouring, Marik had no doubt he would burn and had to insist: an intense frown was sufficient. As the lad curled up and dozed, he got up on his knees and surveyed the seascape in every direction.

They were in what sailors called 'a swell' – long, low undulating waves that were generally not found close to the shore. Given the food and water and the fact that they could keep dry, Marik reckoned they could survive for a while, but he doubted there was any chance of reaching the land just by paddling. And then there was the southern current Yerdek had mentioned.

Marik spent some time tightening the ropes that held the spars together then lay out beside Tola. The lad stirred briefly when Marik put a hand over his arm; he didn't want him slipping over the side. It seemed strange to even try and sleep but his body needed to rest and he had several more hours of paddling planned.

After a few minutes he heard a squawk. Looking up, he spied two white birds heading for the shore. He was glad to see them; glad just to see two other living things. He didn't suppose a bird had the wit to appreciate its fortune in being able to fly but he imagined what it saw now: two small figures on a pile of wood and string, floating on the vast sea.

Marik shook his head as he thought of the misfortune that had struck him since arriving in the Urlun Empire: in particular, the robbery on the road and the two fights with Ralaskan criminals. In recent days, things seemed to be looking up; the possibility of a proper job, the kiss with Lena. The loss of the jewels had seemed such a blow but what did it matter now? He hoped the sisters made it to shore. Perhaps they and the captain would send someone to look for survivors.

His sleep was beset by dreams of a kraal rising up and smashing the raft to pieces. He was woken by Tola, whose face was rigid with fear. Marik sat up and looked around. He wondered what had alarmed the lad then realised it was him; he must have cried out while dreaming. He felt a surge of relief when he saw that the sea was now even calmer. Three more white birds were idling nearby.

'Sorry, lad. Right – time to paddle again.'

They worked on through the afternoon. As the sun began its descent, Marik weighed up the position of the headland. He could not tell if they had made significant progress towards land but it was without question now further to the north. The southerly current had taken effect. Knowing they needed to save their strength, he stopped the paddling in the evening and they ate a small meal. Tola asked for more but seemed to understand the need to ration. The three birds stayed with them for some time and one began swimming around the raft, which at least gave the youngster something to look at.

As the last of the light faded, Marik stood up. It took him some time to steady himself; there was a breeze and the sea was a little rougher. He reckoned he could see two low shapes away to the south-west. Could these be part of the Three Shells – the islands Yerdek had mentioned? Marik resolved to keep up with the paddling once dawn returned. He guessed they could have continued through the night but he did not like the idea of putting his hands into the dark water.

When he sat down he saw that Tola was gazing eastward, his eyes wet with tears. Marik guessed he was thinking of the *White Cloud.* From what he knew, the lad hadn't had much of a life onboard but then he didn't seem to have much of anything at all. Marik didn't like to see the lad cry. He ruffled his hair and smiled but it made no difference. He decided to try some Urlun and managed to say 'Ralaska – good city' and 'I like meat' and 'I like bread'. This was enough to get Tola going and soon he was talking at quite a rate, often using wild gesticulations. Marik nodded enthusiastically but understood not a single thing. In fact, he was relieved when the lad eventually quietened down and fell asleep. At least he seemed a little happier.

Marik checked the raft over again and used some spare rope to tie them both to the spars. He also made sure all the gear was secure before he stretched himself out. By the time the sun dipped below the horizon, the temperature had dropped considerably. Tola lay close beside him, head resting on his ribs.

When Marik took his last look to the west, the sky had turned dark.

It wasn't the type of weather that would have concerned anyone on a ship but the two occupants of the raft endured a horrible night. The waves became shorter and higher, throwing them around so much that they both almost slipped off several times. There was also a harsh chill to the wind that cut through their meagre clothing and seemed to leech into Marik's bones. He considered himself something of an expert in long nights but this was one of the very worst; and he would have gladly swapped it with any of those spent on dry land.

Dawn was an immense relief; a slow blossom of heartening colour. And though white cloud had replaced dark, those clouds betrayed them, dropping a light but persistent rain for the best part of the morning. They were both so cold and miserable that they didn't even eat. They simply lay there, shivering, waiting for some mercy from above.

It came after midday. The clouds were blown away to the south and, though the sun was watery and weak, the temperature rose. Marik and Tola again stripped off to dry their soaking clothes and at last ate a few mouthfuls. In the night they had drifted close to a collation of weed some ten feet across. Paddling over, they examined it and found several objects of use: two yards of thick rope, an old patch of fishing net and the remains of a large crab. The crab was far beyond edible but Tola entertained himself for some time by hollowing out the insides and manipulating it into different positions.

As Marik set about untangling the fishing net, the lad repeatedly thrust the dead creature towards him and unleashed what he clearly believed to be the noise an angry crab would make. Once again glad to see him with a smile on his face, Marik played along for a bit. After about the tenth occasion he told him to stop. After the twentieth occasion he shouted at him and threatened to throw the crab away. This had the desired effect.

Once untangled, the net was about ten feet long and four wide. There were numerous holes but Marik wondered about weighting it somehow and hanging it below the raft. It seemed unlikely he would catch anything but the food supply wouldn't last long: there was only a handful each of pork and bread.

Later in the afternoon, Marik stood to once more examine their position, Tola steadying his legs. He was fairly sure he could still see the coast to the west but he could not make out the headland. As the wind had also been pushing them south, he concluded that they must have travelled some way. He turned in that direction, hoping to spy some trace of the Three Shells but saw nothing.

Marik sat down and made a few calculations. They had been adrift for at least thirty-five hours. He knew that currents could run at one or two miles an hour and Yerdek had made it clear that this one was particularly strong. When he took account of the wind, he realised they might easily have travelled a hundred miles or more. This seemed almost impossible to comprehend but perhaps explained why the headland was nowhere to be seen. Without alerting Tola, Marik looked to the west again and decided he was really not sure he could see land at all. What truly alarmed him were the implications for any potential rescue. Even if anyone from the ship had reached land and sent help, what possible chance did they have of finding them if they were already so far from their original position?

Before the sun set, Marik gave the last of the food to Tola and they both drank a little water. Using the remaining light, he arranged the net to secure their belongings and the newly-acquired rope for them to lie under and give some semblance of security. Earlier, he had checked every piece of line again to ensure the spars were still well-bound.

Their clothes had not fully dried but at least the sea was comparatively calm as they settled down for the night. Above, the sky was clear. As the stars revealed themselves, Marik wished he'd paid attention to an old captain who'd tried to teach the younger soldiers about using the constellations to navigate. Marik could not remember a thing.

From somewhere behind him came a loud splash. He and Tola turned and scanned the water for whatever had made the noise. The disturbed area was visible, about twenty feet away. They watched for a minute or more but saw and heard nothing else. Marik told himself not to think about kraal, which only made him think about them all the more.

After a few minutes of silence, he lay back and gazed up at the sky once more. The specks of light in the firmament were quite beautiful but he was beginning to feel as if he and Tola were the only people alive; as if the rest of the world no longer existed.

The second noise sounded very similar but came from their right. Tola really took fright now and buried his head against Marik's flank. Marik put his arm over him and listened for the creature. He did not hear it again but Tola seemed unable to recover himself. He began sobbing and just could not stop. Marik tried his best in Urlun and in Common but nothing made any difference. After what must have been at least half an hour, he decided to sing a song. He could half-remember some his mother had sung but the only ones he could properly recall were marching songs. Many of the words weren't exactly appropriate for a youngster but as Tola couldn't understand, that hardly mattered. As he sang, Marik realised what a good rhythm they had and he delivered them with as much gusto as he could summon. At one point the lad gave a little laugh. Marik gradually reduced the volume until he was sure Tola was asleep.

Islands; and enough moonlight to see there were two of them. Without the sun as a reference, Marik had no idea which direction they were in but the humped shapes led him to believe they might be two of the Three Shells. He undid the thick rope and sat up. When Tola stirred, he pointed at the dark shapes and the lad was the first to spot that there were three lights on one of them. Distance was even harder to estimate in the dark but Marik reckoned the islands were no more than a mile or two away. With the sea calm and no wind to affect them, this was a chance they could not miss.

'We have to paddle, lad. We have to try and get there.'

He directed Tola forward and took up his familiar position at the back of the raft. The lad took a while to get going but was soon paddling as hard as he could. After half an hour they took a break for a mouthful of water then continued on. Another half hour passed but Marik could not be sure they had made any progress whatsoever towards the lights. Before long, he realised that the southern current had them in its grip once more; or perhaps they had never been out of it. He sung again to keep them going and Tola did his best to join in, reciting the words he was sure of at the top of his voice. They continued the pattern of intense paddling followed by a short break for another hour.

The island with the lights was the southernmost of the two. By the time Marik could be sure they were closer, the raft had been pushed so far sideways that he could make out the southern end. Not long after that he made the decision to stop. The pair were close to exhaustion and there was no chance of making landfall. The worst moment came when Tola tried to continue alone, apparently not understanding that their efforts were in vain. Marik had to physically stop him paddling and when he did so, the lad cursed at him and lashed out. Marik cuffed him across the head which caused Tola to seek refuge at the other end of the raft.

Marik sat alone, watching as hope slowly vanished once more.

He was woken by the lad shaking him. The first light of dawn had illuminated a third island, no more than a quarter-mile distant. With the landmark so close, Marik could see the current was still in effect. Nevertheless, the two of them set to paddling without a word; and with something so near to aim for, they worked harder than ever.

But with good fortune came bad. The island – or at least what could be seen of it – was little more than a bleak lump of dark rock perhaps a mile long. Marik and Tola were faced by sheer cliffs at least two hundred feet high. There were traces of green near the odd crevice or shelf but the only real signs of life were the large grey seabirds that had nested there.

Hundreds were visible and streaks of their waste had coloured much of the rock yellow.

They were soon within a hundred feet but Marik could see nowhere to land, let alone a route up the cliffs. He kept going largely because Tola was paddling so furiously. As they got closer, he began to spot outcrops poking out of the water. Some were round, others were sharp and Marik knew he could not risk the raft that had kept them alive for two days.

'Stop.'

Tola turned.

'Stop. There's nothing here for us. We might as well let the current take us.'

The lad frowned but ceased paddling. As the raft drifted south, neither of them could take their eyes off the island. There was something foreboding about the shadowy hollows at the base of the cliffs, where the water swilled over pockmarked slabs of rock and into cracks and caverns. There was also a bitter odour emanating from the place and Marik found himself almost glad when they approached the southern end. Just off the south-west corner was a rounded formation – about twenty feet across – where two birds sat, observing the approaching craft. Marik began to paddle, to ensure they avoided the rock.

Tola gave a shout and pointed up at the cliffs. At first Marik couldn't see what had caught his eye. Then he spotted an angular shape just below the top of the island. On a small, sheltered plateau, a dwelling had been constructed, the walls a multi-coloured jigsaw of rock. There were no signs of life but that did not stop Tola – then Marik – shouting. Marik guessed they were at least five hundred feet away. But it was a calm day and there was little other noise.

They kept shouting as they paddled the raft towards the formation, causing the two seabirds to flap away. Marik reckoned that if they could stop there, they could at least continue to try and hail the occupants of the dwelling – if there were any. He had begun to detest the accursed current and it took all their energy to adjust their course before it dragged them away.

As they neared the boulder-like formation, he realised there was nothing to get hold of. The rock was slick with water and weed and there was not even a crevice or knob to hang onto. When Tola also moved to the right side, the raft wobbled but both of them held on. Four hands touched the slippery surface but they could do nothing to arrest the raft's motion. Marik bellowed curses. Now alongside the rock, their view of the dwelling was obscured and their cries muffled.

Tola gave a little shout when he managed to get his hands on two limpets but he inadvertently pulled them free.

'It's no good,' said Marik, once again wary of wasting their limited energy. 'We can't stay here. It's no good.'

Tola seemed to understand and they both let go. Once the dwelling was again in view they continued shouting. Marik felt sure they would have been heard and concluded that the place was long-abandoned. He could not imagine why a dwelling might have been built in such a bleak, exposed location.

He looked all around but could see no other sign of land.

Tola moved back to the middle of the raft and showed Marik the creatures inside the shells, which were surprisingly large. With an eager grin, he passed one over and spoke in Urlun.

'Lunch.'

They drifted on through the third day towards the fourth night. Marik ached all over. He'd sustained various cuts and scrapes from rolling around on the wood and rope, none of which were made better by the salt water. They had no food left and – worse – only a quarter of the water remained in Yerdek's flask. The two of them just lay there, what little remained of their energy drained by the hot sun. Directly overhead and uninhibited by cloud, it became an enemy from which there was no hiding. Marik made Tola cover his head with his shirt and change position regularly to avoid sunburn.

In the middle of the afternoon, they dropped into the water to cool down. The sensation was wonderful – especially when Marik dunked his head – but his fear of the depths ensured he didn't tarry. Tola seemed to enjoy himself and swam around the raft a couple of times. Once back on the raft, they both lay out and fell asleep.

When Marik awoke, the sun had long begun its descent. He realised he had been asleep for some hours and cursed himself for not keeping an eye on Tola. Despite his Urlun complexion, the lad's exposed skin was red and he seemed dazed, almost feverish. Marik covered him as best he could and gave him some water. Over the next hour, the youngster rallied and in fact it was he who spied the land.

The shore seemed to be closer than at any previous point; they could actually make out a long, pale stretch that might well have been a beach. Marik considered paddling but the day had been a tiring one and he preferred to conserve their strength. He doubted they could survive another day in such blistering heat.

At dawn, he realised Tola was not well. The sunburn on his ankles and one side of his face was severe. Worse, he had vomited several times and seemed unable to stop shaking. Marik was grateful for the blanket of white cloud that covered the whole sky and hoped it would not burn away.

As he sat there with him, the lad spoke quietly in his own language. Marik pretended to understand and he felt guilt every time he looked at his reddened skin; he had let the child down. All he could do was scoop water onto the worst areas and keep them covered.

The coast was still in sight and certainly no farther away. Leaving Tola to doze, Marik set to paddling for most of the morning. At one point he heard a tremendous splash and looked up to see a dark shape slap the waves some way ahead. Thankfully, Tola slept through the incident but Marik froze and did not put his hand back in the water for some time. Later, he glimpsed the shape again – around fifty feet away – but could not identify what part of a creature it had been, let alone what creature.

Determined to continue while he could, he eventually returned his hand to the water. After only a minute, he saw a fish – clearly dead – floating on its side. He paddled over to it and plucked it out of the sea, surprised by the weight. He reckoned it had not been dead long and wondered if the mysterious creature had killed it. He placed it under some clothes to keep it cool and hoped Tola might have appetite enough to enjoy a fresh meal.

Marik kept paddling all afternoon, altering position often to save his aching limbs. He assumed they were still being pushed south but was also sure that a whole day's effort could not be a waste. He told himself that even a mile closer to land might make a difference. They might see a ship or a fishing boat; and would surely be more likely to strike another island.

It was hard not to think about water. Thankfully, the flask was hanging below the raft, out of sight. Marik began to imagine mountain streams. Cold mugs of beer. Fresh snow. Waterfalls. The South didn't have all that much to recommend it but you were never far from a source of fresh water. Towards the end of the day, he even became tempted to drink the brine but used it solely to cool himself.

Tola seemed no better; but no worse. When Marik ceased his efforts and roused him, the lad was still lethargic and feverish. Marik gave him some water and took a little himself. As the sun set once more, he used his sword to gut the fish, then ate several handfuls of flesh. He preferred it cooked but many in the South ate it raw. The taste confirmed to him that it was indeed very fresh. He offered some to Tola but the lad refused and the odour of it made him vomit again. Marik gave him more water and settled him under the thick rope for the night.

He sat at the other end of the raft, watching the sunset, feet in the water and too tired to care if some passing creature noticed them. The remaining streaks of cloud appeared to have been daubed across the sky by a giant brush. The sun illuminated them in many shades, from a burnished gold to a thin yellow and the deepest orange imaginable. It was what Marik's father would have called a *kind sky*; the type that made you sleep easy, feel thankful and look forward to the next day. He just wanted the weather to stay calm; give young Tola a chance to recover.

'Stay like this,' he whispered. 'Just like this.'

He was about to lay down when he noted something floating nearby. It turned out to be another collation of weed and among the detritus he found a broad, shallow wooden bowl. There was something rotten inside but once he'd cleaned it up, the bowl looked as good as new. And then he didn't feel so concerned about a change in the weather; because if it did rain, they now had something to catch it in.

As Marik settled down, the last of the sun's light vanished from the sky. He realised Tola had stopped shivering, which raised his spirits greatly. It might have been the exhaustion but he felt better than he had at any point since they'd escaped the *White Cloud*.

Chapter Ten

Three and a half days; approximately eighty hours on the raft. Marik reckoned that meant they were at least eighty miles south. But if the current was as strong as he suspected – twice or even three times that – they might have drifted two hundred miles; even further. The concept seemed barely credible. Yet it did not take a mathematician to appreciate that, if constantly in motion, great distances could be covered. And while Marik was sure this was the fourth day aboard the raft – he had marked them with his sword – if felt more like the fourth *week*.

Tola was certainly better – the shivering and fever had gone – but he hadn't yet regained his appetite. Knowing the fish wouldn't last much longer in the day's heat, Marik finished the rest for breakfast; a hearty portion that at first made him sleepy than gave him a surge of energy. He took a brief dip in the sea then set to paddling with an oar he had fashioned from his sword and the bowl. It was heavy and unwieldy but shifted a good deal more water than a hand.

Tola lay at the front – well covered this time – and at one point summoned the strength to dip his hand in and help. Marik was so moved by the sight that he felt a tear come.

'Weak-minded cretin,' he whispered to himself as he wiped it away.

Tola heard him and turned, his head covered by Marik's wet shirt.

'Nothing. Just ... thanks.'

Tola grinned for what seemed like the first time in a long time and continued his paddling. At midday Marik shared out some water. It was hard to tell by looking in the flask but he reckoned there was about an inch left at the bottom.

There could be no doubt that they were nearer the coast. Marik suspected some change in the current was responsible but he could discern a narrow beach and thick forest beyond. He reckoned they were between three and six miles offshore.

The weather was kind once again. Every time the sun threatened to burn them, the light breeze would bring a cloud or two and considerable relief. Tola began babbling again in Urlun and Marik eventually realised he wanted him to sing. They struck up the marching songs once more, which helped them get through another lengthy bout of paddling. In midafternoon, a dark grey cloud passed overhead and dropped some rain. The pair ceased their work and sat with their mouths open; ingesting every drop they could. By the time the cloud had passed, there was about half an inch in the bowl, which they decanted carefully into the flask.

In late evening, Marik stood and gained his clearest view of the coast yet. He could actually make out what he believed to be a large log lying on the beach; and variations in the heights of the trees beyond. He reckoned they could be no further than two miles distant. As darkness came, a fleck of orange appeared on the beach: a fire. Though he could know nothing of those who had lit it, Marik felt a little happier just to know other people were close.

Only an hour later, any semblance of optimism was long forgotten. Cloud settled in above, obscured the night sky and dumped an enormous amount of rain. The pair were soaked within minutes. All they could do was sit there, heads covered, as the downpour continued. There was of course a great benefit; before long the bowl was full and the contents in the flask. Marik drew considerable satisfaction from watching it fill again. In a way he was glad they had no food, because it would have been ruined. The water got absolutely everywhere and the sheer volume was such that they could hear nothing but rain hammering into sea. It was not an icy, winter rain but with no shelter or protection, Marik and Tola grew colder and colder. They sat on the raft together but after an hour or two, both were shaking.

At one point, Marik tried to look up to see if the cloud was moving or breaking up. The downpour was so strong that he couldn't see anything other than a barrage of water that had now settled into a relentless, pummelling rhythm. He tried to tell himself that it wasn't the gods or a punishment – it was just rain – but somehow this felt like an attack. Or a test. At what he guessed to be around the middle of the night, Tola gave a sudden cry. His face contorted, the youngster shook a fist at the sky and screamed what sounded like curses. Marik joined in and soon the two of them were shouting. After that they laughed long and hard. But five minutes later it was still pouring; and they were still miserable.

The rain stopped some time during the night. Marik had stayed awake long enough to fill the entire flask with water. This gave him another surge of optimism and he seemed to have waited so long to sleep that it came easily. At dawn, the sky was mostly clear, the last remnants of the rainclouds drifting away to the east.

Tola knew the drill by now. Though the sun was obscured by haze, he stripped off and laid his clothes out. Marik did the same, then they both enjoyed a long drink. Once he'd secured the flask in the water to keep it cool, he noted Tola looking around. Visibility had improved throughout the morning but Marik was concerned that he could no longer see the shore. It might have been due to the haze but he knew they could easily have drifted away somehow during the hours of darkness. Once again, they appeared to be utterly alone, with nothing visible to offer any guidance.

He was glad that Tola was dozing when he saw the dead man: a corpse floating on its back not far away. Marik knew there might be something useful to be found but he couldn't bring himself to investigate. He also wondered why the body hadn't been eaten by sea creatures. Perhaps it had gone into the water recently. Was it possible that it could be someone from the *White Cloud*? The haze had by now cleared sufficiently for him to make out a watery sun and orientate himself. He set to paddling westward once more and by the time Tola awoke again, they were well past the body.

They did not sight land again that day, but at dusk came an encouraging sign. For some hours, they had been nearing a triangular outcrop of rock. Even when they halted paddling, their progress towards it was clear. Only when they were close could Marik gauge its size: the rock was no more than thirty feet high, similar in width. Upon standing, he saw that there was a broader, shelf-like formation underneath. Waves were breaking on it here and there but the raft's path was clear. What Marik also noted was the direction of the water sluicing past the angular rock. The current was now taking them west at quite a pace.

Once he'd sat down, they both watched the rock, which receded into the distance as darkness returned. Marik tried to explain to Tola why he thought this was a good thing but he didn't have the words. Despite the lad's night-time rage at the elements, Marik was impressed by his resilience. He'd known many adults in his life – soldiers included – who would have already cracked. Marik marked off the fifth day. He didn't dare entertain much hope but they were at least moving quickly; and that meant things would look different in the morning.

At dawn, all became clear. For the first time since the sinking of the *White Cloud*, they could see two areas of land. Once again, the sky was hazy but the sun was visible and it seemed to Marik that they were still moving roughly westward. And to both the north and the south were low shorelines. There could be no doubt; they were within the mouth of a broad estuary.

'River. Big river, right?'

Tola was as preoccupied by the sight as he but they were unable to exchange anything meaningful on the matter. Marik continued to scour both shores for any landmark but spied nothing. It seemed that this current was at least as strong as the one that had taken them so far south. They had to make the most of it.

His stomach was grumbling at the lack of food and he was glad that there was something tangible for Tola to focus on.

'Let's paddle.'

Tola pointed to his mouth.

'Yes, drink first. You're right.'

Marik leaned across the raft and put his hand into the water. The flask wasn't there. Then he realised he must have made a mistake and checked the other side of the raft. But the flask wasn't there either. It had disappeared.

'Do you have it?' Surely that was the only explanation. But Tola had asked for the water.

'Where is it?'

The look on the boy's face sent a shiver down Marik's spine. They both frantically ran their hands across the underside of the raft, desperately searching for the precious flask. Tola threw himself in to the water and did a complete circuit. As sweat beaded on his forehead, Marik searched under their clothes and every other part of the raft, which did not take long.

Tola continued round the raft a second time. By that time, Marik had begun to accept that it was gone. Either he had failed to secure it properly or the line had snapped or some creature had taken it. His fault. He should have been more careful. They still had the bowl but unless it rained again they were in trouble. Marik grabbed the bowl and found there was still a little left in the bottom. He offered this to Tola as the lad clambered aboard. Tola licked up all the moisture he could then returned to his usual position and began to paddle.

'I'm sorry,' said Marik. 'Do you understand? I'm sorry.'

The guilt worsened; and the only thing worse than the guilt was the thirst. If he hadn't known about the loss of the water, Marik reckoned he could have worked all morning without a drink. But because he knew there was nothing, every breath seemed to leave his throat drier. After an hour or so, he stopped and told Tola to do the same. The youngster ignored him and Marik had to actually take his hand out of the water.

'I said I was sorry. What else can I do?'

Marik was not unused to making mistakes but this had to be one of the worst. He'd been over the events of the previous night countless times, trying to pinpoint where it had gone wrong; where he had made this fatal error. Eventually he stopped himself; it didn't matter – the flask was gone and that was that.

When they began paddling again, he could see they were now battling an ebb tide. Though the flood had clearly dragged the raft a long way into the estuary, would they now be pushed out? He tried to explain this to Tola – that paddling was a waste of energy – but was again forced to physically stop him.

Though there was no rain, there was – mercifully – enough cloud to shield them from the worst of the heat. Marik squeezed all of their garments out above the bowl and managed to produce a mouthful of water each. Once they'd drunk this, Tola tried to paddle again and Marik had to shout to make him conserve his energy. However, when the lad dozed off later on, Marik created his paddle once more and did what he could to counter the adverse current.

In the middle of the afternoon, the tide slackened then eventually began to pull them back into the estuary. Tola woke up and did his bit. Marik reckoned they completed a solid three hours and when evening came, they had clearly made progress. He thought they were marginally nearer to the northern shore; no more than five miles. He was considering whether to alter course towards it when Tola gave a shout.

The boy pointed to the south-east. There, some miles away, was a ship. Two great sails were full and the vessel was headed out to sea. Tola stood and began to wave. Marik could not see any hope of the sailors noticing them or their tiny craft but he let the youngster try. Although nothing came of it, he once again felt gladdened by this trace of humanity.

And less than an hour before sunset, they saw something else to raise their spirits. The sandbank was no more than two feet above the water but – upon sighting it – Marik and Tola paddled towards it at speed. Once there, Marik got off first and hauled the raft onto the sand. Tola jumped off but his legs went from under him and he collapsed in a heap. Once he'd checked he was fine, Marik helped him up. Dragging the raft further onto the bank, he waited for his legs to adjust to this unfamiliar sensation, then surveyed the bank. It was oval in shape, no more than fifty feet long and twenty across. He had no doubt that it was only visible at certain states of the tide and – with the flood well underway – knew it might disappear soon.

The two of them wandered around the bank, surrounded by the ever-darkening sky and sea. The novelty of walking on solid ground was pleasant and Tola made some gesticulations that suggested he understood they had to make the most of the tide. Having collected some sea weed and a handful of winkle-type creatures, he returned to the raft. The creatures were at least wet and provided a little moisture to their parched mouths. Tola was all set to eat the seaweed but Marik warned him off, knowing the saltiness would exacerbate his thirst. He did however spread some out on a beam, to show him they could dry it for emergency rations.

By now, there was only a little moonlight to guide them. With Tola back onboard, Marik pushed the raft back into the sea. With his last step, he could not help wondering when – and if – he would ever touch ground again.

At dawn, they were still closer to the northern bank. Marik took up his paddle but Tola could not rouse himself. As he lay there, Marik could not help looking at the boy's dry, cracked lips and sunburned skin. The guilt at least drove him on and he made the most of what seemed to be a slack tide. He was not sure how far the overnight ebb had taken them out but when the flood returned, he set his sights firmly on the shore. Stopping around midday, he could make out a beach once more, and guessed the distance at no more than two or three miles.

Overall, Marik reckoned they had been fortunate with the weather, but on this day that luck finally deserted them. The sun was brutally, pitilessly hot. Tola had a coughing fit that seemed interminable. The lad put a hand into the seawater and again, Marik had to stop him drinking. Later, Tola began to sob.

Though he seemed to have no energy left, Marik covered his head with a wet tunic and kept paddling. By now the tide was taking them out again but he knew he had shortened the distance to the shore. As afternoon turned to evening, the beach to the north had been replaced by an area of rocky inlets and coves. It did not look hospitable but Marik no longer cared; he was convinced the distance was now under a mile. He was determined to make landfall by night and redoubled his efforts. He continued on until darkness returned and he could simply not work his arms any longer.

Yet lying beside Tola was worse. Because he could hear the lad's dry rasping breaths and – once inactive – the thirst gripped him again. He himself had to fight the temptation to drink from the water that surrounded them. Marik had not prayed since travelling to the North but he did so now: to Hadarrak, Father of The World.

Save us. Please save us.

He was woken by Tola shaking him and the lad's expression told him something serious was afoot. Marik sat up to find that dawn had broken and the raft was no more than three hundred feet from land. When he looked closer, he saw that the shore was the end of a spit that reached far out into the estuary. And in only those few moments he could see that the tide was ebbing once more. Their luck had turned again but they did not have long.

Without a word, the pair began paddling and Marik scanned the shore. The spit seemed to stick out about half a mile and he could also see the remains of a boat on the beach. There might be people here.

Not for the first time, the elements seemed determined to foil their efforts. Time and again, Marik tried to adjust their course to account for the current but there was also a wind pushing them back out to sea. He estimated that they had cut the distance to around two hundred feet but they were already opposite the middle of the spit-head.

Deciding on a change of tactic, he put down his makeshift paddle, lay on his front just behind Tola, and used his arm as if swimming. Typically, the lad didn't even look at him or pass comment; he was as focused on reaching the spit as Marik, who guessed he understood they might not get this opportunity again. During the night, Marik had dreamed of the endless torture of being pulled in and out of the estuary without ever reaching land.

Now they were closer, he could see that the spit-head was quite large, rising at least twenty feet above the water at its highest, the banks of sand surprisingly steep. And he could see the water sluicing past at an alarming rate. Somewhere deep inside, he heard a voice telling him that they would not make it, that this was a waste of energy. He ignored it.

A hundred feet. A party of gulls were hopping around on the spit-head, their indifference to the struggling duo total. The raft was almost opposite the seaward end of the spit-head now. Marik had no idea how fast he and Tola could propel the craft but he doubted it was quicker than the powerful tide. The lad was breathing so rapidly that Marik feared for him. As his slender left arm ploughed through the water, his right hand gripped a rope, knuckles white. Marik's muscles were burning.

'Swap. We have to swap.'

As soon as he moved, Tola understood, crawling underneath Marik as they exchanged positions. With their rested arms now at work, they thrashed away with renewed vigour. But with the tempting yellow sand of the spit-head no more than fifty feet away, they were now past the seaward end. Marik was shocked by how tired he already was; the initial upsurge hadn't lasted long and he realised how much the recent days had tired him. Tola was staring down at the water ahead, teeth gritted, arm working. Thirty feet. But they were past the spit-head now, turned towards it, fighting the current. A minute passed, two; and Marik knew they hadn't moved any closer.

Just as he bellowed an invocation – to the gods or himself, he didn't know – the raft came apart. He hadn't possessed the energy to keep up his usual inspection of the rope and wood. Some of that rope had evidently rotted because suddenly they were in the water. Once sure that Tola had a hand on one of the spars, Marik saw that considerable effort would be required to put the raft back together. Too much.

It was a gamble – and not only with *his* life – but he made the decision.

'Tola, we have to swim for it. Come on!'

He pushed the raft away complete with bag and sword. Tola watched it drift off, eyes wide.

'Come on!'

Marik knew the lad could swim from the time he'd spent relaxing in the water. He set the example with a strong but steady pace and was pleased to see Tola next to him. But the waves broke in their faces and the wind blew them back. Marik got his head down, tried to ignore it; pulled with his arms, kicked with his legs. At every second breath he checked that Tola had kept pace; the lad was doing well.

He looked up. Twenty feet; no more. If the banks of the spit-head hadn't been so steep, their chances would have been better. Marik spat out brine and willed his limbs to fight on. The pain was not only there; but in his guts, his chest, his throat, his head. It felt as if some great hand was pulling him away from the spit, pulling him towards death.

He turned to check on Tola only to find that the boy had disappeared. Then he felt a hand grip his ankle. Reaching down, he grabbed Tola's arm and pulled him to the surface. Even though he was spluttering, Marik knew he couldn't waste time or energy. He had once seen a man save his son from a lake and he knew his best chance was to turn on his back and drag

Tola along with an arm around his chest. This he did and the lad remained still, though he continued to cough. Marik kicked and kicked and did what he could with his spare hand. He could not turn and look but he knew they had lost precious distance.

The sea seemed to quieten now he was on his back and Tola settled down, his little hands gripping Marik's right arm. Far above the sky was a warm blue that somehow made him want to stop fighting. Marik felt his strength fading.

He knew it was over. They wouldn't make the spit and the raft was already too far away. He had done it again; made a bad decision. He had let the boy down. He had failed him; condemned him to death. Killed him.

Was it real? The shout he'd heard. When he heard it again – carried to him by the wind – he knew he had to turn. Still keeping tight hold of Tola, he twisted his head and glimpsed a white-haired man making his way down the bank of the spit, swift steps kicking sand into the water. Looped over his shoulder was a coil of rope.

Though Tola panicked when Marik first let him go, he soon recovered when he saw the man. Dressed in baggy trousers and a long smock, the stranger had stopped several feet above the water and was calmly uncoiling the rope. Now renewed, Tola swam again alongside Marik, who saw that they were still least thirty feet away.

The man shouted something as he cast the rope into the sea. There was nothing on the end of it but the current pulled it towards them. By the time it was fully extended, the line was only a matter of feet away. Marik thrashed towards it but seemed unable to close the distance; merely hold his position. Worse, Tola was fading again.

He looked to the shore. The man dropped down another couple of feet and the rope came tantalisingly close. Marik glanced at Tola. The lad was no longer swimming properly, merely trying to keep himself up.

'My leg – hold my leg!'

He let it float up to the surface and Tola made a grab for it, clearly out of desperation as much as understanding.

'Hold on.'

Marik knew he couldn't do much with his other leg – and he had already lost more distance – but he buried his head in the water and thrashed forward, both arms slicing through the water. He did not look at the boy or the man. He took breath only when he needed it and concentrated purely on generating as much power as he could. Once he'd adjusted to the weight on his leg, the pain seemed to drift away and he found a rhythm. But then a wave sloshed its way into his mouth and he faltered.

Shaking his sodden hair out of his eyes, he looked up to see the end of the rope right in front of him. He also had time to glimpse the white-haired man waving frantically at him to seize it. Marik did just that, pulling himself closer so he could get both hands on it. Then he helped Tola get a hold of the line just behind him. Even with the rope in his hands, it seemed to be all the lad could do to keep his head above water.

Marik soon realised the struggle wasn't over. With the weight of them on the rope and the current and wind against him, the man was barely able to hold his ground. He was leaning back, almost sitting against the bank. His face showed the strain.

'We have to help him. Tola, we have to help.'

Despite the welcome moments of rest, Tola was clearly beyond doing much other than surviving. But Marik held the rope in one hand and swam with the other, checking on the boy every few seconds. Before long, the man was able to pull several yards of the rope in.

And then he was able to move up the bank and finally to haul them into the shelter of the spit's seaward side, where the rushing current was weaker. Here the banks were less steep and before long, their saviour was hauling Marik and Tola towards the shore with relative ease.

Now closer, Marik saw that the white hair belied his age. The man was no more than fifty, weathered and well-built. He dropped the rope and when Marik staggered out of the water and flopped onto the sand, the stranger went straight to Tola. The youngster could not even stand so the man picked him up and threw him over his shoulder. Marik was on his knees, water lapping around him, still unable to move. The man said something that Marik did not understand, though the words sounded a little like the language he had heard in Baron Zanzarri's lands. He shook his head as the man helped him to his feet.

It took a while for them to negotiate the bank and reach the flat area atop the spit. Marik had to put up a hand and drop to his knees again to catch his breath. While he knelt there, almost wanting to kiss the sand beneath, Tola seemed to recover. The man put him down and the boy ran to Marik, throwing his arms around him. Marik held him close.

When they were at last able to move, the stranger offered a friendly smile and the three of them walked along the spit towards the shore. For once Marik was grateful for the seawater, for it hid his tears.

Chapter Eleven

Marik awoke to the sound and smell of frying fish. But as soon as he opened his eyes, there was only one thing on his mind – and thankfully a mug on the table beside his bed. Without even checking the contents, he glugged down what turned out to be cool, sweet-tasting water. Emitting a groan of satisfaction, he eased his head back down onto a soft pillow. It took a moment for him to remember where he was but then he recalled arriving at the house after an exhausting walk from the spit. He'd collapsed through the doorway and been helped into the bed by the white-haired man and his wife. Marik couldn't recall either of their names.

A familiar face was watching him. Tola leaned against the doorway, arms folded, expression suggesting both contentment and nervousness. He gave a brief smile then ambled to the end of the bed. He'd clearly had a good wash and was now wearing a long sleeping tunic.

'Like flowers, do you?'

The lad frowned.

Marik pointed at his chest; the tunic had an image of blue flowers sewn into it. Tola looked down and shrugged.

'Well you look a good deal better than the last time I saw you.'

Tola mimed eating then pointed at the doorway.

'Breakfast time is it?'

'Lunch, actually.'

When the white-haired man walked in, Marik sat up, suddenly feeling guilty for lying in the bed. He noticed now that his host had a broad nose and large, prominent ears.

'Come and join us,' he said. 'You must be hungry.'

'You speak Common. I didn't realise.'

'I didn't realise *you* did until just now. You barely managed a word yesterday. At one point I thought I might have to leave you - you're too big to carry.'

'Wait, that was yesterday ... morning? I slept through an entire day and night?'

'You did.' The man pointed at Tola. 'This young fellow woke last night. We heard him rummaging in the cupboards.'

'Ah. Sorry.'

'Not at all. Only to be expected after what you two have been through. He told us all about it.'

The man noted the surprise on Marik's face and explained. 'My wife knows a little Urlun. He's quite a chatterbox once he gets going. He said the two of you are best friends.'

Marik didn't dare look at Tola when he heard that, for fear of embarrassing himself. Relief washed over him once more: he'd got him off that bloody raft and on to dry land. For the moment, that was all that seemed to matter.

'Quite right.' Marik pushed the blanket covering him aside. He was wearing only his exceptionally dirty underclothes so did not stand.

The man gestured to a nearby stool. 'We washed your tunic and trousers as best we could. I'm afraid I've nothing that would fit you.'

'Thank you.'

'The eggs are ready, so be quick.' With a smile, the man turned away and said something to his wife in their language.

Tola stayed and watched Marik dress, then walked with him into a spacious parlour. In the centre of the room was a worn but large table which the man was furnishing with plates and cutlery. His wife was squatting in front of a fire, mixing something into a pan of eggs upon a grill. Above was a well-made chimney which did an excellent job of keeping smoke out of the room. Unlike the rest of the timber house, this was constructed of brick.

'I forgot to introduce myself.' The man offered his hand and Marik shook it firmly.

'Orim Kersay. My wife, Tarikka.'

She placed the pan of eggs in the middle of the table, where there were already cooked cuts of meat, a loaf of bread and a jar of preserved vegetables. Like Orim, Tarikka looked to be around fifty and she greeted Marik with a kind smile. Her fine head of hair was a mix of black and grey.

'No speak Common. Sorry.'

'Nice to meet you.'

Orim caught Marik's eye. 'Between us we should just about be able to understand each other.'

With a grin, Marik took the seat offered to him – a stool opposite Tola. The lad's face showed the signs of exposure – patches of red, peeling skin and several sores. But his dark green eyes were as bright as Marik had seen them, especially when he weighed up the delights in front of him.

Tarikka was not slow to oblige. Once she had ladled a large dollop of eggs onto every plate, she added a cut of meat. Tola went for this first, gripping with both hands while he gnawed at it.

'Sorry,' remarked Marik. 'I don't think he's ever been taught any table manners.'

As Orim translated, Marik regretted his words. His family had not been wealthy and life had never been easy, but he had grown up with enough to eat; and with affection and guidance when he needed it. He could not know how much – or how little – Tola had been cared for.

Tarikka waved the comment away and offered Marik the bread board. He could easily have downed several slices and everything else on the table but took only one and reminded himself to eat slowly. He had often endured long periods without much food and knew the dangers of overeating. Tola clearly did not.

'Could you tell him to take it slowly?' He might be ill.'

Orim was pouring water into the mugs. 'We already have but a reminder won't go amiss.' He spoke to his wife who in turn warned Tola.

Marik had to slow himself down. The eggs and the bread were nice but the meat seemed even better than Ralaskan chicken.

'Pig?' he asked when he finally stopped shovelling it in.

'Boar,' replied Orim. 'Killed it last year – been smoking it through the winter. You have boar in the South?'

After the salty meat, Marik needed more water and had to mask a powerful belch afterward. 'We do. Some weigh as much as four men. Talking of the South, I suppose I'm a lot closer to it than I was? I don't know much of the area but how far are we from Alkari?'

'A long way,' said Orim. 'I believe a rich man owns those lands.'

'Zanzarri.'

'Could be. South of that is the Varrick Bight – a bleak stretch of coast. You're lucky you didn't come ashore there; I don't believe there's a single settlement for a hundred miles. It sounds as if you drifted past that, past the Yellow Sands and into Salka Reach. It was lucky that I saw you well before you reached the spit-head. I was on the beach collecting driftwood. I knew there was no chance without a rope so I ran to a friend's house. He wasn't there but I managed to find the line. Even when you had it in your hands, I wasn't sure you would make it. You're a strong fellow.'

'Not as strong as I was.'

Tarrika said something and Orim translated.

'She says you should keep eating. That will build you up.'

Marik answered her with a smile. When she spied Tola about to scoop egg into his mouth with his hand, she gave him a spoon and showed him how to use it.

Marik turned back to Orim. 'So, what's this place called?'

'Northcrest. Just a village. There are only six other houses here. About twenty of us.'

'Any towns nearby?'

'No.'

Marik noted a glance between husband and wife but was unsure what to deduce from it. Having finished the eggs, he turned his attention to the bread. To him it tasted fine, but it was roughly-made and gritty. He glanced around the kitchen. What the pair owned was of good quality but there wasn't much of it.

Marik suddenly remembered his ten bronze coins. He reached for his trouser pocket but then realised that he had put the leather pouch in his pack for safe-keeping. Given the fortune of their survival, the thought didn't trouble him for long but he wondered at the ease with which coins slipped through his fingers. Somebody somewhere didn't want him to ever accumulate any wealth.

'Are you still aiming to reach Alkari?' asked Orim.

Marik sat back, deciding he had already eaten enough. 'Not sure, to be honest. Long trip?'

'There is no coastal route. You'd have to head inland until you picked up the Crown's Road.'

Marik had heard of it while journeying through the lands north of the King's Keep.

'Much between here and there?'

'The road is more than a hundred miles away. Rough territory, most of it.'

Marik shook his head in disbelief. He really was in the middle of nowhere – not that it wasn't preferable to a raft floating out of sight of land.

'What will you do with the lad?' asked Orim.

Marik had no answer for that.

When breakfast finished, he noted that neither Orim nor Tarrika had eaten all that much and that the leftovers were carefully collected. And when Orim took he and Tola out for a walk around Northcrest, Marik soon realised that nobody here had much of anything.

The village occupied a clear area within a sparse forest of slender trees that somehow grew in the sandy soil. No more than a hundred feet from Orim's dwelling was a long, high berm of sand that shielded the village from the sea.

'That'll be the crest then,' observed Marik.

'Quite so,' said Orim.

His house was one of eight built around the edge of the cleared ground. Two of the dwellings had fallen into disrepair, the timber cannibalised for other houses. In the middle of the communal space were several wooden racks and lumps of stone.

'For fish?'

'That's right. Not that we catch much. Don't have a single seaworthy boat between us.'

Only two other villagers were in view: a woman brushing dust away from her door and a man repairing a fishing net. When Orim led his two guests across the central space, Tola alighted on the wooden racks and set to climbing on them.

'Hey.'

The lad stopped and glanced at Marik.

'Don't worry,' said Orim. 'We don't use them.'

Marik followed Orim towards the fisherman and realised he was being watched; not only by the woman with the broom, but also from behind several windows. As they approached, the local put his net aside and stood. He was somewhat older than Orim and missing two fingers on his right hand. He nodded politely to Marik as they were introduced.

'Good day,' was all he could say in Common.

'The only real fisherman among us,' explained Orim.

'How does he manage without a boat?'

'Knows a few tricks.' Orim spoke for a while to his friend then they moved on through the trees towards the sea. A whistle from Marik summoned the energetic Tola and the trio followed a path that led up to the lowest point of the berm, which was still twenty feet higher than the village.

'Nice spot with this shelter.'

Orim nodded as Tola sped past them, frantically ploughing through the sand to ensure he was first up the berm. Like Marik, he was barefoot. It was a warm day and when they reached the top, the onshore breeze was cool and refreshing. As Tola negotiated the far side with leaping steps, the men stopped.

Ahead was a broad stretch of sand that ran all the way to the shore. Away to the right was the spit; and Marik could make out the disturbed water near the head. He shivered as thoughts of that near-fatal struggle returned.

The oblivious Tola was already investigating a nearby pool.

Marik turned to the east. It was a clear day and both sides of the estuary were visible. 'So that's Salka Reach?'

'Yes. Ten miles upstream, the river divides. The True Salka continues on for a hundred miles but the delta is more like a marsh – a large stretch of shallow water and thousands of islands, most of them very small.'

'Have you been there?'

Orim tugged anxiously at his earlobe and looked at the ground for a moment before replying. 'I was born there. All of us were.'

Before Marik could ask anything else, Orim mumbled something and walked back down the crest. He stopped after a few strides.

'I'll see you back at the house.'

Marik nodded, then made his way down the slope. It seemed evident that all was not well with his host, nor this place, but he didn't feel ready or able to concern himself with that. For now, he just wanted to relax and enjoy a day without the fear of death hanging over him.

Tola had found a fish skeleton and was now poking it with a stick. Marik looked out at the waters of the Salka Reach, then glanced down and moved his toes. Though the sand gave way, the novelty of solid ground beneath his feet had not yet faded. It seemed that finding his way out of this remote, harsh land would be difficult and there was also the boy to think about. But Marik smiled; he had escaped the capricious grip of the elements and was his own master once more.

The day passed pleasantly. With Tola amusing himself on the sands, Marik laid out at the base of the crest and spent several hours dozing. The lad kept bringing him things to look at; a process that was rapidly becoming tiresome until he returned wearing a clump of seaweed as a wig. Marik at first refused to take his turn but eventually relented; and when he draped the soaking weed over his head, Tola collapsed into a fit of giggles that eventually became a raucous cough.

'Calm yourself,' said Marik before throwing the weed at him.

Tola picked it up, gave a shout, and threw it as far as he could. It occurred to Marik that - now he was safe - the boy was also happy to be free of his life aboard the ship. As Tola trotted off once more, Marik reminded himself not to be too friendly. Their moment of parting would come at some point; there was no reason to make it more difficult for the lad.

While journeying north, he had spent some time in the city of Whitehaven. He had never seen a place with so many kind folk. He'd had little money while there and had been accommodated and fed by a group who called themselves The Children. They were devoted to one of the Northern gods and believed that the only way to reach his paradise after death was to do good deeds. Marik had seen a hospital and an orphanage; all well-staffed and well-equipped. This – or somewhere like it – was the right place for the boy.

Having dozed off once more, he was roused by Tola, who pointed at his mouth.

'Hungry, eh? Me, I'm thirsty. Come on.'

They hurried back along the path and in the village found six locals standing together by the wooden racks. Judging by their clothing, none of them were any better off than Orim and Tarrika. As the new arrivals approached, the two women present beamed at the sight of Tola, who stayed close to Marik.

'Good day,' he said in Common as he passed them. One man replied but the others simply stared.

When Orim met them at the door, his previously cheerful demeanour seemed to have returned. 'I did come to fetch you earlier but you both seemed to be enjoying yourselves.'

'Very peaceful,' said Marik before nodding at the youngster. 'Well, most of the time.'

'Come, food's ready.'

Marik ushered Tola through the door and glanced back at the square. 'Village meeting?'

'They're curious about you. I told them your story.'

'Do you get many visitors here?'

As they stood on either side of the doorway, Orim avoided Marik's gaze. 'No.'

'Listen, you've been very kind but we can't impose on you like this. We'll leave soon.'

'You must leave only when you're ready to.' It sounded like something that had already been agreed.

'At least let me pay our way somehow. Is there much game in the forest? If you have a bow, I can hunt; or lay traps.'

'I'm going fishing in the morning. Perhaps you'll join me?'

'Of course.'

'Good. Go and sit.'

Marik did so and found Tola already tucking into some soup. With a kind smile, Tarrika gave Marik his own bowl. The soup was thin but satisfying, mainly some kind of root vegetable and a tasty mix of herbs. Orim arrived in time for the main course, which was similar to the lunch.

'Are the others all fishermen too?'

'Everyone has to be everything these days, I suppose. We work together when we can.'

Marik was trying to think of topics that wouldn't provoke a reaction from his host. 'Much else to hunt other than the boar?'

'Some rabbits. Ooka.'

'What's ooka?'

'Like a rat but with a broad tail – they live in the trees.'

'Ah. Taste good?'

Orim turned to his wife and repeated the question. Tarrika grimaced.

'Ah,' said Marik. 'Please tell her the soup was lovely.'

He was again taking his time with his food and even Tola seemed to be savouring every bite of bread and meat.

'We were lucky with the boar,' said Orim. 'We'd set traps but had nothing for weeks. I happened to be passing and I heard it struggling. Took three of us to carry it back here.'

'Not many traders coming through, I suppose?'

Orim shook his head. 'We aren't on the way to anywhere. One of the men out there is named Dotor. He is a carpenter – sometimes works in a town named Hindmarch. It's fifty miles but in the same direction as the Crown's Road. He's got a job starting soon and he said you're welcome to go with him.'

Though excited by this news, Marik did his best to hide it.

'When will he be leaving?'

'A few days, depending on the weather. How are you feeling now? I believe my wife has something for those sores.'

Marik had one on his cheek and several on both arms and legs. They were already drying out but were still itchy.

'Very kind.'

For a while nothing was said. Tola was offered second helpings by Tarrika but a brief glance from Marik deterred him from accepting them.

When Orim's wife then asked her husband a question, a long debate began and the atmosphere around the table became tense. After a while, Orim waved a hand at his wife and stood. Tarrika shook her head then began clearing the table.

'Excuse me,' said Orim as he headed for the main door.

'Listen,' said Marik, 'I'm happy to sleep anywhere – please use the bedroom tonight.'

Orim gestured to the room beside it. 'We have another. As long as you don't mind sharing with the lad.'

'Not at all.'

Orim left without a word to his wife.

Tarrika had opened a wooden chest and taken out a board game which she placed on the table in front of Tola. Marik began collecting the plates and, when Tarrika protested, pointed at the game. With a reluctant nod, she sat beside Tola and began showing him the pieces. Marik piled the plates and cutlery by a pail of water then sat on the floor and began cleaning them. As he worked, he listened and, though he understood only the odd word, it seemed to him that Tola was quite articulate. It was also clear that Tarrika was impressed by how swiftly the boy grasped the rules.

Once the plates were dry, Marik placed them on a shelf beside the chimney. In doing so, he passed the chest and noted the contents. There were other games but also two female dolls and some pictures drawn by a child's hand: pictures of birds, flowers and trees.

Chapter Twelve

The onshore wind grew through the night, creating a seascape of surging, white-tipped waves. The few seabirds that dared risk the skies soon found themselves blown inland. Sand and pebbles were thrown up the beach and dragged back with equal power.

Orim, Marik and Tola arrived an hour after dawn, equipped with two long rods. Orim had been out early to fetch worms for bait and – counter to Marik's expectations – claimed that the rough conditions would not worsen their chances. Having attached heavy weights, he cast both lines forty feet into the water then handed a rod to Marik. Tola was in charge of the pail but soon decided to weigh this down with a rock and explore the beach.

Not long afterward, Orim pointed out a sail far away to the south. Considering the conditions, he was concerned that they were too close to the coast, in danger of foundering on the sandbanks in that area. After a time, the distant vessel disappeared from view.

Marik had always preferred hunting to fishing but he found the cold wind invigorating. And he still felt immense relief that he was no longer out there, fighting for survival on that accursed raft. He thought of his few belongings, no doubt now scattered across the waves. The iron sword and the bronze coins would be resting on the bottom somewhere. Marik couldn't even summon much anger that his efforts in Ralaska had been in vain; that he once again had nothing. He and Tola were alive and in good health. Before departing that morning, they had applied more of Tarrika's ointment to their sores. Orim had also supplied Marik with a hooded cape like his own. Tola wore Tarrika's with the sleeves rolled up.

'At least the rain has stopped,' said Orim.

'Wind's worse though.'

They were standing twenty feet from each other to keep their lines apart and had to almost shout to be heard. The rod and line were moving so much that Marik wasn't even sure he'd notice if he got a bite. The fisherman they'd met the previous day was already on the beach. While Orim had chosen a spot a mile seaward of the spit, the villager was on the other side.

'Not for the impatient, fishing.' Orim seemed to have returned to his usual cheerful self, despite the incident on the berm and the argument with his wife.

'Hunting's no better. Though I must admit I like to be on the move.'

'What did you hunt in the South?'

'Anything we could. Boar, horners, sometimes even snow bear – doesn't taste good but if you kill one there's plenty of it.'

'Snow bear? You've seen one? It's true that they're completely white?'

'Apart from the snout and paws. Big bastards. One of our neighbours has a skin – fifteen feet from nose to tail. My father was a very good archer, my uncle even better. They once cornered a snow bear but had to put twelve arrows into it before they could get close enough to finish it off. Wish I'd seen it but I was only a boy – younger than Tola.'

'He's had his share of adventures by the sounds of it. A ship's no place for one so young.'

'Agreed.' Marik looked to check the boy was all right then told Orim about Zyrin and his plotting.

'Sounds like a very unpleasant character.'

'That's an understatement.' Marik noted that Orim never cursed. He had also seen a religious figurine in the house.

'Excuse me for asking, that carving you have – Sa Sarkan?'

'We call her the Goddess of Creation or the Great Maker, but yes.'

Marik had come across the deity all across the North. Though it seemed that no single people followed her, Sa Sarkan was popular where no other religion held sway.

'I wish we had more to give her on the days of offering,' said Orim. 'But we do not have much to spare.'

'I believe that's known as a vicious circle.'

Orim did not reply.

A moment later, Marik thought he had a bite but then realised he had simply allowed the rear of the rod to get stuck in the sand behind him.

'Marik, in your land, spirits are worshipped more than gods, correct?'

'Mostly. Where I lived, we honoured twelve different spirits. It's been like that for as long as anyone can remember. It was only when I left Lothlagen that I realised anyone believed any different.'

'Is that a city?'

'One of the nine provinces.'

'May I ask why you left?'

For once, Marik didn't feel so concerned about such a conversation. He owed Orim a great deal and the man had taken him into his home.

'I joined the People's Guard – a kind of army.'

'Who did you fight?'

It seemed obvious that Orim knew little of developments south of the King's Keep. After all, why would the people in such a remote spot know much of the outside world?

'No one to start with. Then war came.'

He expected Orim to press him but the man simply turned back towards the sea. Perhaps he'd belatedly realised that such a disclosure would oblige him to speak more of his own past. Marik was curious about why Orim, Tarrika and the other inhabitants of Northcrest had left the delta – and what had happened to their daughter – but he was not going to ask and it seemed Orim didn't want to tell. Despite his gratitude, Marik didn't want to get to drawn into whatever had befallen his host and the villagers. He and Tola would be leaving within days. Some stones were best left unturned.

Though they spent most of that time together, Marik and Orim continued to avoid talk of the past. The day of fishing yielded nothing other than two crabs Tola pulled from the surf. There was enough for four small portions and all agreed that the meat tasted excellent. Tola seemed more than a little satisfied that he had trumped the adults. That evening, he again played the board game with Tarrika, while the men plotted the next day's hunting trip.

When Tarrika ordered that Tola remain with her on account of his sores and sunburn, the lad complained but swiftly gave in. Marik suspected that he was enjoying the attention and – as they would shortly be stuck with each other for some time – he thought it healthy. The hunting party was bolstered by two villagers, neither of whom spoke much Common. Marik was armed with Orim's bow – which was not really long enough or strong enough – but he bagged a young deer and two of the ooka. He insisted that the other men have a haunch of deer and all the locals were full of admiration for his marksmanship. Marik had hit the deer in the neck from fifty feet: even with that bow, he would have been embarrassed to miss at such close range.

And so they ate well again that night, along with the carpenter who was to guide them to the Crown's Road. Orim later explained that Dotor was ready to leave and glad to have an ally to travel with – he had been robbed more than once. Marik wanted to leave his hosts with some food and went out hunting alone on the last day. He returned with nothing substantial but no less than six ooka. He knew from Tarrika that the meat was only edible when heavily seasoned but the eyes of both his hosts lit up when he walked through the door carrying so many pounds of meat.

The last evening was a warm one, and the four of them sat outside, the adults drinking from a flask of wine. Tarrika presented Tola with a new pair of trousers, a loose shirt and a cloak she had made for him. Marik was somewhat embarrassed to be handed two newly-made loin-cloths but was extremely grateful nonetheless. He would have to make do with his battered tunic and trousers but Orim had also fashioned some simple sandals from leather and driftwood for them both. Marik greatly enjoyed the last few hours with the kind hosts who had done so much for them; and he did what he could to include everyone in the conversation. He considered asking Tola if he wanted to stay with the couple but – if the thought had occurred to them – they would have surely offered by now.

The lad and Orim fell asleep around the same time. Tarrika poured Marik a little more wine then sat beside him. When she began talking quietly but earnestly in her broken Common, he thought perhaps that she did wish to discuss Tola. It soon became obvious that she was preoccupied by something else.

'Daughter.' Tarrika pointed at the house. 'Daughter.'

Marik kept his voice down, as she had. 'Yes. You had a daughter. I saw her sleeping tunic and the belongings in the box.'

'Men. Men here.'

'What happened?'

'Men ... they ...' Frustrated by her inability to say more, Tarrika kicked the ground. This woke her husband. She hurried over and knelt in front of him; and it seemed to Marik that she was pleading. Orim leaned forward and took his wife's hands in his. They spoke for some time; he composed and wilful, she desperate and tearful.

Embarrassed, Marik stood and picked up the sleeping Tola. He put the lad to bed and covered him with a blanket. When he went to shut the bedroom door, Orim arrived, a candle in his hand. Before either of them could say anything, the door of the other bedroom was shut with some force.

'Sorry.'

'Not at all. She was trying to tell me something about your daughter.'

Orim squeezed his eyes shut before answering. 'She was taken from us.'

'Taken? She's-'

'-She's alive but … well … Tarrika has wanted to tell you for several days. She always seems to want to tell people. I don't know why – what good does it do? I'll walk with you tomorrow – for the morning at least. I'll ask the women to come and sit with Tarrika. That will help. Goodnight.'

Marik couldn't sleep. After seeing Tarrika in such distress, he was no longer sure he could keep the silent agreement he had made with Orim. He could not know the man's reasons for hiding the truth but there was clearly more to it than Tarrika's need to share her burden. She hadn't simply been trying to tell him something; she had wanted to *ask* him something.
Stay out of trouble.
Sometimes you just couldn't do it.
Orim had saved two lives and he and his wife had shown generosity of a type Marik had rarely encountered.
Not only had they lost their daughter, there were evidently no children in Northcrest; in fact, there seemed to be no one under the age of forty. Something was terribly wrong.
Though he was supposed to be walking out of the place in hours, Marik got up, walked to the other bedroom and knocked on the door. Orim answered but in the darkness Marik could see almost nothing of his face.
'I think it's about time I heard the truth.'

Orim roused Tarrika, who lit a lamp and placed it on the table. The two of them spoke for a while and Tarrika began to cry. Orim fetched his wife a handkerchief and poured them all a small glass of wine. Marik waited patiently while he composed himself. Outside the wind was again strong, occasionally whistling through gaps in the timbers.
Orim began: 'Before everything went wrong, our lives were very different. Not easy but we had our daughter and a good community around us. The same goes for everyone else in Northcrest. You've seen Salka Reach – it's all connected to that. This whole area: the islands of the delta, the river, the land for many miles; it all belonged originally to the Yevgens – a family who have dominated the region for centuries. The last lord, Varentis, was the nineteenth son to inherit the title. His domain stretched for a hundred miles in one direction, two hundred in another. That all changed over a matter that at first seemed of little importance.'

As Orim drank his wine, the lamplight flickered. Tarrika sat beside him, her arms on the table, hands clasped together. Orim pulled anxiously on his earlobe before continuing.

'The Reach is – was – a possession of the Yevgens. For as long as anyone could remember they collected a tax from the League of Traders, an organisation made up of the wealthy merchants and ship-owners whose vessels passed through the Reach. A tax of five points in a hundred. In recent years, that volume of trade has reduced, so they wanted Lord Varentis to reduce the rate. But he refused to even negotiate.

'When the League decided to simply stop paying it, hostilities broke out. Varentis had several ships of his own which he used to blockade the river. The League hired mercenaries to take him on. There were several battles, and many dead, but it did not really affect us in the delta. Over time the war spread. Varentis lost a brother and son and refused to give in. The League decided they had no choice but to beat him and take his lands. When they won control of the Reach, trade slowly began again and their wealth increased. Finally, the League's mercenary army crossed the delta and attacked Hindmarch. Varentis had retreated to his manor with a few loyalists but he was defeated easily. They made every villager from miles around come and watch them dismember his body.'

'The League?'

'The mercenaries. They were led by a man named Essereti – he'd been a general in the First Empire. It was said that he'd fallen out of favour with Queen Casarri. The League rewarded him with control of Varentis' lands. In return, they received trading rights and taxes from every corner of what had been Yevgen possessions: Hindmarch is an area of good farmland and there are tin mines to the east. There were many fishing villages like this; and the islands of the delta.'

Orim paused to speak to his wife. Marik was surprised that so much could have happened in this remote area. He vaguely recalled some mention of the League but had never heard of this General Essereti, nor the Yevgen family.

'Essereti divided up the lands and placed his men in charge. But not long after he died – kicked in the head by a horse. Without him, there were soon power struggles between his underlings and the locals rebelled. Most areas won back their freedom. But not the delta. Our lands were under the control of a man named Reverrik, the most vicious of them all. There are more than thirty inhabited islands and the population is thinly spread. We could not easily organise ourselves to resist. Reverrik took Old Island, which is large and close to the centre of the delta. He fortified it and gathered his men there. He demanded tributes from all the islanders and anyone who didn't obey was killed.'

'These others who had rebelled – they didn't help?'

'They have always looked down on the marsh people. And after fighting for so long, they didn't have it in them. They are all free of the mercenaries now but they haven't the stomach to take on Reverrik. Nobody does.'

'Your daughter?'

Orim let out a long breath before answering. Tarikka clearly understood what was going on because she put her hand on his.

'They didn't take just money and goods. Reverrik has many men there and there is little to do. I suppose they require … entertaining. All the young women were rounded up and taken. I … we …'

Orim cleared his throat. 'We tried to stop them. Men were killed. I did not want to die and leave both my wife and daughter alone.'

Orim now had to use the handkerchief and it was several minutes before he could speak again. 'That was more than two years ago. We tried several times to find out what had happened to Korina but we learned nothing. Our town was once one of the largest in the islands but there are only a few dozen people there now. The islanders are isolated, divided, terrified. We and a few others decided to leave; far enough to have our freedom but still close if the situation changed. Most of the villages like Northcrest were abandoned during the battles with the League. It seemed like the safest place to go.'

'You've not returned?'

Orim shook his head. 'Sometimes someone will pick up a bit of news. It's never good.' Orim drained his mug of wine then looked Marik in the eye. 'Now you know.'

'We have a saying in the South: the truth never dies. I'm glad I know.'

'The last we heard, Reverrik has some giant Easterling with him, an enforcer. They say he's as big as two men; ten feet tall. Reverrik is stronger than ever.'

'Tarrika wants me to help.'

She seemed to understand and spoke briefly to her husband.

'Yes. But there's no sense in it. I know you were a soldier but there's nothing you can do. I don't want anyone else to die or suffer at their hands. And there's the boy to think of.'

Marik didn't feel the need to choose his words; weigh his options. Sometimes you just had to do what felt right. He had not always done it but this time he would. He nodded towards the sea.

'That boy would be a dead thing floating out there if not for you. As would I. Perhaps there is nothing that can be done, perhaps there is. I make no promises. But if I can help, I will.'

Chapter Thirteen

They didn't tell Tola the reason but he did not seem concerned about the delay. When Marik and Orim left the house, the lad was already helping Tarrika move some firewood. As Marik passed her, she briefly placed her hand on his arm and he nodded an acknowledgement. With the clarity common to early morning, he almost regretted demanding the truth from them. Now they – or certainly Tarrika – expected something; and from what he'd heard, doing anything to help their daughter would be very difficult.

He and Orim were on their way to Dotor, who knew more about the current situation in the islands. When they reached his home, the carpenter met them in the doorway, clearly ready to leave. He noted that Marik had nothing with him and questioned Orim. They spoke for some time and then Dotor gestured to a bench beside the door. The two locals sat down, Marik remained standing.

'He has heard nothing new since his last trip to Hindmarch but he will tell us all he knows.'

The carpenter began, halting every few sentences so that Orim could translate. While they talked, Marik heard a woman inside the house coughing. Whatever was afflicting her, it sounded bad.

'Reverrik hardly ever leaves Old Island. He has everything he needs there. During the fighting he amassed a considerable amount of wealth. They say he has a great pile of coins and a warehouse of rare spices looted from Lord Varentis. Anything he wants, he buys – including the giant, who is named Hammerhand. He leads the tribute parties, even though there's not much left to take now but food. All weapons have been confiscated. As for the girls, he has at least thirty there, some only thirteen or fourteen.' Orim stopped for a moment, and Dotor put a hand on his arm to comfort him. Marik knew that his daughter, Korina, was older – now seventeen.

Orim was ready to continue. 'There are some male prisoners there too – trouble-makers. Things are done to them; to make them an example to others. In Hindmarch there are a small group of former islanders who have appealed to the League; and even to Queen Casarri of the First Empire and King Elemer of the Urluns. But no help has been offered. Dotor here tries to stay away from the islands. Everyone is so hopeless there. The only reason they remain is to be close to their daughters and wives.'

'What else do we know about this island? Numbers? Defences?'

Again, Dotor explained what he knew and Orim translated.

'Old Island is quite large – half a mile long, a quarter at its widest. But it has clear water around it; easy to defend. They patrol the waters, not that there's much need these days. Reverrik has at least a hundred men, all well-armed and equipped. Almost everything in the islands is made of reeds but he's had timber brought in to reinforce the old buildings there: a barracks for his men, a house for himself and the women.'

Orim gazed blankly at the holed floorboards below. 'I don't know why I even ...'

'How many locals in the islands?'

Dotor took a while to answer. 'Hard to say. At one time, perhaps two thousand. Now, no more than three or four hundred.'

'Is there any form of organised resistance at all?'

'No. Most of those who fought them are dead.'

'Most?'

'There is young Parrs,' explained Orim. 'A basket-maker. He lost his father to them. Dotor saw him in Hindmarch in the spring and he was talking more openly than most would dare. Parrs lives alone so has no one to worry about. If anyone would help us, it's him. But what can we do?'

Marik didn't want to raise false hope but neither did he believe there was none. And after what he'd heard the previous night, he couldn't help imagining Orim and Tarrika living out the rest of their lives, unable to enjoy more than a moment, always waiting for the inevitable, terrible news. He had to try.

'Maybe we can get a look at the island - find out more about your daughter. Would this basket-maker help us?'

Orim translated again. 'Dotor thinks so. He lives just outside Ettwater – used to be the closest thing we had to a town. It's on Spring Island, only six miles from Old Island. We would have to be very careful. Reverrik has informers. He may even know that Parrs is someone to watch.'

'How far to Spring Island from here?'

'About thirty miles. For the second half of it we'll need a boat.'

Dotor spoke again.

'He would help but he has his wife to think of. She is not well.'

The two then spoke for some time and it seemed obvious they did not agree.

'What is it?' asked Marik.

'Nothing.'

'Orim, I need to know what you know.'

'It's not … there … there was a woman. A holy woman. When Reverrik and his men came to the delta, she said that he would bring tremendous suffering but would be dead in five hundred days. That time will pass within the next month. She also said that salvation would be delivered in the form of a stranger; a stranger who came by the sea.'

Marik reckoned that was all he needed; a prophecy that predicted success where failure seemed far more likely.

'Of course, I don't believe it,' said Orim.

Marik did not believe him.

They needed an excuse for Tola and – while he played outside with one of the villager's dogs – they decided on it. Tarrika called him in and explained that Orim and Marik were going to help a friend who was building a house. They would be gone no longer than a week. Tola accepted this explanation without a word but Marik noted his calculating looks at the three adults. Though clearly glad to be remaining at the house, Tola insisted that Marik promised to come back – in Urlun – before he was satisfied.

While Tarrika prepared some food for them to take, Orim quietly ushered Marik around to the back of the house. Upon sighting the men, the three chickens that lived there squawked and fled into their coop. Orim fetched a shovel and began digging at an apparently random spot. 'Reverrik's men came up here twice but the last time was many months ago. I took the precaution of burying some useful items.'

Marik was not surprised when Orim pulled an iron box out of the ground. Wrapped in cloth inside were a dagger and a hatchet. Both were weapons of war and very well made.

'Are you sure we should even take those?'

Orim frowned.

Marik explained: 'If we get caught with them, we have no chance of bluffing our way out.'

'You heard what Dotor said. We have to be able to defend ourselves.'

Marik walked over to him and took the hatchet. It was a light weapon but easily wielded, the wooden shaft engraved with swirling patterns. The blade was steel and honed to a murderous edge. He twirled it, allowing two revolutions before snatching it out of the air.

'Have you ever killed a man?'

Orim shook his head. 'These were my father's. He fought for the Yevgens.'

'I'll carry the weapons. If we're caught, you can say I forced you to guide me to the island. We can pretend I want to join this Reverrik. That way, there's still a chance they'll let you go free.'

'Not much.'

'That's better than none. At least one of us might make it back here.'

Orim looked down at the dagger. 'Should we even be doing this?'

'We don't know *what* we're doing yet. First, we need to find out as much as we can: about Reverrik, about the island and that base of his.'

Orim ran a hand through his soft white hair, his face tight with tension. 'I – we – have no right to ask this of you.'

'You didn't, remember?'

'You know what I mean, Marik.'

'I've said I'll help and that's it. We needn't discuss it again.'

'Very well. You've killed men?'

'I have.'

'How many?'

Marik was always surprised by how many people asked that question. He answered it honestly: 'I was a soldier. You lose count.'

They set off two hours later. Orim and Tarrika said their farewells in private so as not to upset Tola. Marik also kept the tone light when he said goodbye to the lad, having told him via Tarrika to behave well and listen to her at all times. Tola didn't seem too concerned but watched the men until they were out of sight. Marik brushed off a mild pang of sentiment, putting it down to the fact that the boy had been his sole responsibility since the shipwreck. Glancing at the man beside him, he noted the irony of replacing one such burden with another.

They walked all afternoon, stopping only once to eat some of the food Tarrika had packed. For the first few miles, they followed a broad, sandy track that took them through increasingly dense woodland. Orim then led the way onto a neglected path that the casual observer might easily have missed. Though skeletal and thinly covered, the trees here were so closely packed that little daylight reached the ground. It seemed to Marik a dry, lifeless place; a thought confirmed by how few animals they encountered. He was glad when they eventually emerged onto open ground where the path wove its way through low scrub and muddy pools.

As evening approached, they passed a high, grassy mound topped by an unusual object: a ball made of thousands of interwoven twigs and decorated with flowers and berries, their colours now faded. Orim explained that this was a holy site, where followers of Sa Sarkan gathered. Judging by the surrounding ground, no such gatherings had occurred for a while. Orim asked for a minute to pay his respects before they moved on.

He'd spoken of a good location to camp and they reached it as the sun edged the horizon. The site was at the top of a cliff, which provided a remarkable view of the Salka Delta. Marik and Orim dropped their packs and surveyed the territory below while there was still some light. To the south – Marik's left – was the higher ground that separated the delta from the river. Ahead, to the right, and as far as the eye could see lay the marshes. In total, perhaps half was water, two-sixths reedbeds and only the remaining sixth solid ground. Most of the islands were small and most of the reedbeds looked impenetrable. There was only a smattering of high trees. The piercing call of an unseen bird floated up to the watchers upon the cliff.

'Too dark to see Old Island or Spring,' said Orim. 'But that's where we're bound for tomorrow – Scarton.'

Following Orim's outstretched arm, Marik could just make out a cluster of buildings at the edge of an island almost surrounded by reed. Trying to plot a route from the base of the cliff, he could see no clear path to the settlement. It reminded him of a child's puzzle he had seen in the First Empire.

'We can get there from here without a boat?'

'Easier than it looks.'

'I've never seen territory like this.'

'There is nowhere like it.' Orim shook his head and turned away. 'Sorry, it's been a while since I've seen it. The delta looks so peaceful – you would never know.'

'Not much light left,' said Marik, aiming to keep his companion's attention on the task at hand. 'Let's eat and get some sleep.'

It was not a cold night and the blanket Tarrika had provided was more than sufficient. Orim didn't think there was any need to keep watch and Marik was surprised to find he slept through until dawn. He suspected his body was still recovering from the lack of food and – despite what lay ahead – he enjoyed their breakfast of bread and dried fish. Once packed up, they were soon following a stream that cut its way down the cliff face. It was a direct route but very steep and uneven in places. Marik was relieved to see that Orim moved well for a man in middle age but he stayed quiet to avoid distracting him until they reached the less hazardous ground at the base of the cliff.

'Scarton – anything to be wary of?'

'It's possible Reverrik might have a spy there but I doubt it – not this far out.'

'Have you come up with a story?'

'We'll say that you want to visit Ava in Ettwater. She's a healer, makes all kinds of concoctions. Perhaps you need help for your ill son. A fever that won't break.'

'That'll do. You sure she's still there?'

'We'll find out soon enough.'

'And we'll definitely be able to get a boat in Scarton?'

'We have a saying: in the delta, there are more boats than shoes.'

Once beyond a narrow strip of woodland, they walked through clinging mud until they reached a wall of reeds at least eight feet high. Without a word, Orim simply turned to the right and followed the edge of the wall for about a mile. Marik was about to ask how exactly they were going to make any progress towards Scarton when they reached a gap.

Grinning, Orim gestured towards it. Marik hurried forward and saw what could only be described as a bridge made entirely of reeds. Thick bunches of the plants had been bent over from either side of the path to form a thick, solid platform that extended out of sight.

'See the red tinge at the bottom of each plant?' said Orim. 'This type is incredibly strong and durable. They take a long time to grow but once mature can be bent into all sorts of shapes and they'll still live. The bridges need trimming now and again but they last for decades.'

A bank of soil at the end of the reed-bridge allowed access and, once on it, Marik realised just how sturdy the structure was. The surface was very uneven and springy but he was impressed by the technique.

Orim set off along the bridge. 'Just watch your step and if you hear a hissing noise, stop.'

'Snake?'

'We do have a few but most aren't poisonous. Yellow toads. If threatened, they'll spit. There's a substance in the saliva that will infect your skin. Won't kill you but it will drive you mad. People have been known to cut the affected areas out because they can't take it any more. Yellows sometimes make themselves at home in these bridges.'

Now it was Marik's turn to gesture forward. 'After you.'

*

To Marik's relief, he didn't see – or hear – a single yellow toad. The reed-bridge was at least a mile long and came to an end on a small island close to a large stack of timber, most of it rotten. The pair were then able to 'island hop' for the next two hours, traversing muddy stretches between solid ground. The entire area was strewn with one particular type of plant: a pale, spindly bush with unpleasantly sharp tips. The bushes were so neatly equidistant from one another that the arrangement appeared unnatural.

At one point, Marik and Orim were close to one of the wider waterways and saw a group of men in small boats. They were too far away for Orim to even guess their identity.

As he'd said, they then negotiated two more reed-bridges, neither of which was as long or well made as the first. The last one ended at Scarton, which had been built on an island much higher than most. As they came to the first dwellings, Marik saw that though timber was used for the frame, the walls and roofs were formed of various types of reed. In the South, stone was the essential building material. Here, this unusual natural resource seemed to be even more crucial to the people of the delta.

As they walked between the two rows of houses that constituted the village, people came into view: a woman washing clothes in a tub, two boys play-fighting and a man striding towards the newcomers. Clad in ragged, soiled clothing, he was bone-thin and had a slightly crazed look about him. Orim hailed him and the two conversed for some time in their own language. Marik had time to look around and observe the approach of several other men. He was relieved to see that none were armed and that they looked rather more civilised than their compatriot. All the villagers – women and children included – wore clothes coloured either dark green or brown. Upon their feet were home made sandals of varying types.

Orim greeted the villagers politely and the conversation continued. At one point, he nodded at Marik, who felt appraising eyes upon him until the group began to break up. After a few more exchanges, Orim led him past the houses towards a little dock area where the bank had been reinforced with timber.

'Sorry about that. I didn't want to say too much about you.'
'What did you learn?'
'Quite a bit. They don't even venture to Spring Island now if they can avoid it. Apparently, Reverrik orders patrols and tributes almost at random, making it very hard to predict where you might run into them. They

seldom get this far but he has quite a few boats and anyone that resists or even raises suspicion ends up dead or captured. No one's seen the man himself for months but Hammerhand has personally killed at least a dozen. He has a habit of throttling them in front of their family and friends – with one hand.'

Tied up at the waterfront were a number of small craft. A man was sitting close by, making rope from a thin species of reed.

Orim stopped before they reached him. 'This fellow will sell us a boat. I'm assuming you still want to go on to Spring Island?'

'Yes. Do you?'

'Of course. But even if we set off now, we won't reach it by nightfall.'

'Will we be able to find solid ground to camp overnight?'

'Yes.'

Marik gestured towards the man. 'I shall leave the boat-buying to you.'

Orim hailed the man, who ceased his rope-making and greeted him with a barely perceptible nod. Marik realised that all of the boats were in fact made of reed and the local was soon showing them one of the longer vessels. These reeds had a yellowish hue and had been roped into tight, stiff bunches that formed the hull and sides, even a little stern and prow. Marik estimated the two-man vessel to be about ten feet long, two and a half wide at its broadest. He was still admiring the ingenuity of the design when Orim handed him a paddle.

'That was quick.'

'I've not paid for it yet. This thing's got to get us twenty miles and they're not built for big Southers like you. We need to test it.'

'What if it sinks?'

'Then we're in trouble - it's the biggest he has.'

'There must be some wood in there somewhere,' Marik remarked as he eyed the craft.

'Just reed and black sap – that's what holds it all together and seals the holes. They need re-treating every year or so but we've been using canoes like this for centuries. Come.'

To Marik's considerable relief, the vessel not only took their weight but was surprisingly manoeuvrable; and he could not help thinking of those countless hours of paddling with Tola aboard the raft. Once back on dry land, Orim purchased the canoe and pronounced himself pleased with the price, suspecting that the boatman hadn't had a new customer in months. As they still had enough provisions to last them, they replenished only their water and set off at once: Marik at the front, Orim at the rear and their gear between them. Marik made sure the knife and the hatchet were within reach.

From Scarton they followed a broad waterway towards Ettwater. Marik learned that the occupants of the delta had once been so numerous and organised that they'd been able to keep these routes as clear and neat as a city's streets. Most were natural features that had been adapted but some had been cut straight through reed-beds and islets. As they paddled steadily though the murky, green water, Orim also pointed out different areas of reed, some that would make an ideal hiding place, some that were too dense to pass through without considerable effort.

It seemed to Marik that the delta was teeming with life: from the tiny – but apparently harmless – insects that attacked whenever they neared the shore, to a great variety of colourful birds and reptiles. This did not include a yellow toad but Marik was the first to spy a snake that seemed to slither across the water towards their prow. When he alerted Orim, the local told him to take his paddle out and thankfully the snake went on its way.

Marik asked if there were any larger creatures and Orim explained that there were some sizeable fish and also something called a srayl – a tentacled creature not unlike a squid. These were seldom seen but dwelt just beneath the surface near the edges of channels. Those that lived to a considerable age could grow to the size of a man, their tentacles ten feet long. Marik shivered when he heard that they kept their prey alive – just above the water – to ensure tender flesh as they consumed them slowly over many days. The srayls had no teeth, but an acid within their tentacle suckers allowed them to remove and ingest flesh.

As the sky darkened, the pair negotiated a series of much narrower routes, some of which were almost impassable due to encroaching reeds. By the time they'd pulled themselves through, Marik's elbows and arms were covered with scratches. From this point, however, they entered a broad lake broken only by a few islets.

'Those are too exposed,' said Orim. 'We'll find somewhere on the other side for the night.'

'Straight across?' asked Marik. He was weary and as they had not encountered a single person on the water it hardly seemed a risk. But Orim insisted that they stick close to the edge of the lake and Marik soon had cause to be thankful for his companion's caution. Hearing a whispered warning, he turned to his left but could not see the craft Orim had spotted.

'Paddle out, stay low,' instructed the local as Marik continued to scour the gloom.

Eventually, movement drew his eyes to the craft. It was not a canoe but a rowing boat, with one man at the oars and two others with him. The boat was heading directly across the lake and had just passed one of the islets. To Marik, their position felt vulnerable.

'Into the reeds?'

'No, just keep down. In this light, we'll blend in.'

Silent and hunched over, Orim and Marik watched the craft cross the lake. After a while, Marik realised he could actually hear the splash of the oars and the odd snippet of conversation.

'They're heading for the wider channel further up,' whispered Orim.

'For Scarton?'

'Possibly. There are other settlements in that direction.'

Dark was settling over the delta at some speed. As the craft reached the side of the lake, Marik lost sight of it.

'Must be gone by now,' said Orim eventually.

Marik straightened up, wincing at his stiff joints. 'Friend or foe?'

'It's traditional to carry a lantern, even if there's enough light to navigate by. Bearing in mind the craft - probably Reverrik's men.'

'Or someone who wishes to avoid them.'

'Either way, I'm glad *we* avoided *them*.' With that, Orim dipped his paddle and set them away once more.

Chapter Fourteen

They camped close to the water's edge. Having hauled the canoe up and out of sight, they laid their blankets beneath a tree with low-hanging branches that rendered them virtually invisible. While Orim prepared some food, Marik conducted a quick check of the surrounding area. He did not get far due to the thick vegetation and encountered nothing more alarming than a particularly aggressive bird. Back at the camp, he and Orim made swift work of some dried boar meat and pickled vegetables. They agreed that there was no need to post guard and – despite some unpleasant imaginings about srayls – Marik rested well.

At dawn they checked the lake, found it quiet, and immediately set off. The waterways Orim followed were similar to those of the previous day though Marik also noted several dwellings – all abandoned – and a number of signposts mounted on high wooden poles. The clammy morning mist did little to ease existing tensions but eventually disappeared. Later, they encountered another canoe that emerged from an adjoining channel with such speed that they couldn't have hidden even if they'd wanted to. Fortunately, the occupant was a friendly fisherman who confirmed they were only five miles from Ettwater. The fellow seemed keen to move on and Orim thought it unwise to enquire about Reverrik's men.

Upon reaching a signpost that announced they were within only two miles, they landed at a muddy beach. After downing some lunch, Marik transferred the hatchet and the knife to one of Orim's two packs. He wrapped the weapons in a blanket and put the pack on.

'You're sure?' asked Orim.

'I'm sure.'

'We should keep moving. There's Ava to visit and we want to reach Parrs' place in daylight.'

Spring Island came into view within less than an hour. The approach was a twenty-foot-wide waterway that carved through a sprawling expanse of floating plants. Each had a delicate purple bulb at its centre, surrounded by thick, dark green leaves, some of which were a foot long. The plants grew so closely together that no clear water was visible and Orim explained that young children could actually walk across them without getting wet. The purple bulbs bloomed for only the summer months but the plants were evergreen and virtually surrounded the island. As they neared a timber-built dock, Marik saw dozens of houses beyond.

Several canoes were tied up and two men were working on an upturned craft nearby. Both glanced at the new arrivals but wordlessly returned to their work. Orim and Marik moored the canoe then walked into Ettwater. There was a clear and well-worn path that led through the nearer dwellings toward an open space. Some of the houses were clearly unoccupied and derelict. Again, some timber had been used but the inevitable reed-bundles and compacted mud were the main building materials. Most of the dwellings had a fenced off yard at the front or rear. Upon the occupied houses were a few adornments – coloured doors, hanging lanterns, even some roof and chimney tiles – but for the most part it seemed a poor, neglected place. Several sets of eyes observed the pair from shadowy windows.

'So, this is the biggest settlement in the delta?'

'There was a time when every house was occupied. On market day you could hardly move in the square.'

The square was in fact circular, and now nothing more than a patch of dusty ground occupied by a pile of rotting reeds and three penned goats. Marik now understood more clearly why these people had been so unable to resist their occupiers. This remote, isolated, divided population had never had much of a chance. It was then that Marik realised Orim had said little about his own home.

'And your place was close?'

'Not far – just us and a few other families. There's nothing for us there now.'

Marik doubted his companion wanted to say more on that subject but there was in any case no opportunity; they were swiftly intercepted by three men. One knew Orim by name and shook hands with him enthusiastically. Another also greeted him while the third was more restrained. Marik was not surprised by the suspicious gazes he attracted. Apart from being half a foot taller and several shades paler than the local men, he was a foreigner in a place where foreigners had brought only suffering and death. With that in mind, he tried to appear friendly.

'This is Marik,' said Orim in Common. 'He washed up close to Northcrest and his son is very ill. I thought perhaps Ava could help.

Is she still here?'

'Aye,' said the friendly man, who Orim introduced as Yoritt. 'But I hope you've a few coins. She doesn't give away her concoctions cheaply.'

Marik knew that Orim had some money with him. The cover story was important but he hoped it wouldn't cost much; the man clearly didn't have any to spare.

More of the locals drifted over, including one who immediately approached Marik. He was long-haired fellow, his face thin and pitted.

'Where you from? South?'

'Yes.'

'How'd you get to Northcrest?'

'My ship sank. Orim here rescued us. But my son has a fever.'

Nodding vigorously, Orim turned and spoke to the new arrival in their own language. The long-haired man and the others listened keenly but at no point made it obvious that they accepted this version of events. When their discussion finished, Marik decided to speak again: slowly and with as much conviction as he could muster.

'Listen, Orim has told me what's happened here. I don't blame you for being concerned but I am only here to help my son.'

'And we should do just that,' added Orim. After a few brief comments to Yoritt, he bade farewell to the others then led the way back towards the boats.

'Ava's not in the village?' asked Marik.

'No. She moved to an abandoned house on the other side of the island – apparently to avoid entanglements with Reverrik's men. They were demanding medicines without payment.'

'Any news?

'A little – Hammerhand and his men turn up every few weeks or so. Their last visit was six days ago, so we should be clear. But there is talk – rumour only – of a few people banding together. They've not done anything yet but it's said they plan to build up their numbers before taking Reverrik on. Yoritt and the others want nothing to do with it; they believe it will only mean worse treatment for all. I didn't dare mention Parrs. Neither did they.'

Orim glanced back towards the town as they neared the dock.

'What about that long-haired man? Not very friendly.'

'I don't know him but I'd be surprised if there isn't at least one spy in Ettwater. Another reason why it's so difficult to get organised – nobody knows who they can trust. If only we'd known about Ava, we could have avoided showing our faces here at all. Sorry.'

'You couldn't have known,' replied Marik. 'But it's all the more reason for us to move quickly.'

*

Despite the fact that Orim had knocked on the door a minute earlier, there was still no sign of life. The house was a small one but solidly made of the reed and mud mixture. Nearby creeping plants had covered much of a side wall and reached almost to the stone chimney. The door was made of timber and equipped with a simple latch. When Marik moved towards it, Orim held up a hand.

'We shouldn't.'

'How long do we wait?'

Orim lowered his voice. 'Like most healers, she is a tad … eccentric. I remember calling on her before and disturbing her in the middle of some experiment. She refused to talk to me for a month.' Orim sighed. 'Then again, I suppose we don't really need to be here at all.'

Marik glanced at the thick undergrowth that separated the small area of clear land on this side of Spring Island from Ettwater. It was perfectly possible that some spy was observing them. 'We should see the cover story through. Someone might check with her later. How long to Parrs' place from here?'

'No more than an hour.' Orim warily knocked on the door once more.

Marik wandered along to the nearest window, which was barred by shutters. He was about to peer between them when a spear thudded into the wall two feet from his head. Marik was already reaching for his pack when a giggle halted him.

Walking towards them with a basket in her hand was a middle-aged woman. Marik had expected some strange hag but Ava was in fact rather striking; not pretty but even-featured and rather elegant in her own way. She wore a long, pale dress and flowing robes decorated with coloured thread. These threads had also been woven into her hair.

'Forgive me,' she said, still giggling. 'I just wanted to see your reaction. Orim, you've gone white. Who is this?'

Ava put her basket down and Marik was surprised to see it contained not only flowers and plants but also several dead animals, including a tiny snake.

'His name is Marik. A Souther who came ashore near Northcrest. His son is ill with a fever. We need help.'

Ava looked Marik up and down then walked up to the spear and levered it out of the dried mud. Lowering her grip, she proceeded to spin the weapon once then aim the tip at Marik's chin. The sharp end was not metal but some sharpened stone that would do the job well enough.

'Which province?'
'Lothlagen.'
'Capital?'
'Rookburg.'

When she gazed into his eyes, Marik felt a brief twinge of the type he had not experienced in a while.

'Reverrik has a few Southers with him.' Before either Marik or Orim could reply, Ava lowered the spear. 'None from Lothlagen though. And I see nothing malign in your eyes.'

'Even though I was about to take that spear off you?'

'I like a man with a sense of humour. Lovely hair too.' She lifted the basket off the ground using the end of the spear and turned to Orim. 'How's Tarrika?'

'Well, thank you.'

'Good. I always thought you were lucky to have her.'

'Quite so.'

Ava gestured to the door. 'You know how it works.'

With a nod, Orim reached into a pocket, took out a money bag and emptied the meagre contents into his palm.

'One copper for the consultation,' said Ava. 'Anything else depends on what I make for you.'

Orim handed over the small, worn coin featuring the familiar image of Queen Casarri. As far as Marik knew, the First Empire was the only body with the wealth and facilities to create coinage. The silver, bronze and copper coins produced by Queen Casarri's mint were used in most of the territory north of the King's Keep. In the South, only salt and gold were used in place of barter.

Ava slipped the coin into her robes and opened the door. 'Please.'

With the shutters open, the interior of the house was surprisingly bright. There was a small chamber to the rear but the front room was clearly where Ava conducted her work. Other than a bench close to the door – where Orim and Marik now sat – the floor was covered with woven baskets, wooden chests, iron cauldrons and numerous large bottles. Upon the shelves were dozens of smaller bottles and jars, none of which seemed to be labelled. Ava had listened carefully to Marik's generic description of a fever and was now sitting on a low stool, crushing several types of seeds.

'I have most of these dried but fresh is more effective – the sooner you get them back to the lad the better.' Ava clearly took her work very seriously and had already explained that she would give provide a tonic and a paste. Marik felt a little guilt at the deceit, especially as she seemed a rather intriguing character. Most of the healers in the South were crones whose treatments failed more often than they succeeded.

'Can I ask why you came to live over here?' asked Orim.

Ava kept at her crushing for some time before answering. 'Quieter. I can concentrate on my work.'

'Reverrik's men were bothering you?' asked Marik. When he shifted slightly, the bench groaned.

'Try not to break it,' said his host. 'I don't want my customers sitting on the floor.'

As the bench protested again, Marik decided to stand. He had to bend his head to avoid the ceiling.

'Six and a quarter-feet?' asked Ava.

'About that.'

'It's fascinating. The differences in the races of the world. And not only the physical ones. Southers are said to be stupid. Any observations so far, Orim?'

'Er …'

'Don't mind me,' said Marik.

With a wry smile, Ava finished crushing the seeds and put them in a wooden bowl. She then picked up a branch and began stripping some small berries.

'To answer your earlier question – yes, partly to avoid Reverrik's men. The villagers too, if I'm honest.'

'How so?' asked Marik.

'My mother called it the unwinnable game. She was a healer, like me. If our treatments don't work, we're charlatans; if they do, we're witches. I suppose if I had a husband, they might be more trusting.'

Marik was tempted to ask why she didn't but there were more pressing matters at hand. Without betraying his true purpose, he could perhaps gain some more useful information. 'What are they like, Reverrik's men?'

'Those I've seen – arrogant, violent, lazy.'

'Lazy? Why do you say that?'

'They don't even have to try now. The delta is theirs and they know it.'

Marik resisted the temptation to glance at Orim.

Ava now crushed the berries and added them to the bowl. 'The spirits are important to your people, correct?' From between those two arcs of greying hair, her keen gaze locked on him.

'That's right.'

'Always seemed sensible to me – worshipping something connected to the natural world around us rather than some random deity that's only sacred because people have been praying to it for so long. Ava grinned. 'Orim's thinking that's another reason why I wasn't popular in Ettwater. And he's right.'

Orim shrugged.

Marik said, 'In the South, healers invoke the spirits *and* the gods.'

'Why wouldn't they? I put my trust in nature and the knowledge of how to use it passed down to me. I don't possess the insight of my mother but I do my best. I learn something new every day. How many people can say that?'

She added a little water to the bowl, stirred it and poured the paste into a jar. Having sealed this with a stopper, she turned her attention to the tonic.

Marik looked around the room once more and noted a high shelf with a few small bottles upon it. The shelf was dusty, the bottles covered by cobwebs.

'Poisons?' He caught Ava's eye and nodded towards the high shelf.

'No. But some dangerous substances. There are several animals I need for certain ingredients. Those help me to temporarily disable them – with no harmful effects.'

That didn't sound to Marik like the whole truth but he didn't press the point.

Ava had already poured three separate ingredients into a second jar when she spoke up again. 'Your name – Marik – what does it mean?'

'Nothing, as far as I know.'

'Don't lie. All names have a meaning.'

Marik continued to lie, and for what he considered good reason. 'If there is, I wasn't told it.'

'I don't believe you.'

There was something about this woman that he couldn't help liking. She was not one to be deterred.

'All right, in old Southern it means 'fearless'.'

Ava stirred the tonic. 'Well, well. A lot to live up to. I expect that's why you don't share it.'

'I expect you're right.'

'Why the interest in Reverrik's men, Marik?'

He realised he had asked too many questions. Ava was clearly sharp and there was of course the slim possibility that she was somehow involved with the occupiers, especially given her lack of affection for her fellow locals.

'It's not right. The people here don't deserve it.'

Nodding neutrally, Ava finished stirring the tonic and put a stopper in the second jar. She turned her attention to Orim. 'I presume your daughter was taken with the others?'

Orim nodded and gazed down at the floor.

'Any news of her?'

'No.'

Ava let out a long breath and stood. 'You two *are* only on Spring to see me?'

For the moment, Orim seemed incapable of answering.

'Of course,' said Marik.

'I hope so,' Ava continued, 'because no matter how 'fearless' a man might be, he would be a fool to take Reverrik on. He would be throwing away his life and that of anyone who helped him. We in the delta enjoyed peace for centuries while much of the rest of the world fought and burned. As a Souther, you know what war is like. It is simply our time. But that time will pass.'

'I hope so,' replied Marik. 'I just want to get back to my son.'

Ava located a cloth and cleaned off both jars.

Orim wiped his eyes and stood. 'How much?'

Ava handed the jars to Marik. 'These are inexpensive, the copper will suffice. But I will need one more thing from you.' She reached over to a nearby shelf and picked up a small but well-honed knife. When she returned to Marik, the knife ended up roughly level with his groin.

'Now I'm getting nervous.'

'You'll have to bend over.'

'Make that *very* nervous.'

Ava smiled. 'Don't be foolish. I have never seen hair of such a beautiful hue. Even if I cannot find some use for it, I want it as a keepsake.'

He bent over and she cut off half a handful.

'Promise you won't use it to put a curse on me?'

'Curses are for witches.'

'Of course. My apologies.'

Chapter Fifteen

When both Marik and Orim were satisfied that no one could have followed them, they turned into the most confined waterway yet. There was barely enough space to pass, and on several occasions, Marik had to bend a branch back or pull the canoe past a thicket of reeds. Every time his hand was near the water, he half-expected a srayl tentacle to attach itself and pull him into the green depths. The opposing banks were so thick with vegetation that the low, broad trees almost connected over their heads. There was a fetid, almost sweet smell about the place and Marik soon found himself longing for the clean air and open spaces of Northcrest.

Thankfully, Orim's prediction that the tough going would last only a mile or so proved correct. Where the waterway met a break in the trees, they found an aged canoe and a small pile of stones covered with moss. The bank was slick with mud and by the time they'd pulled their own craft clear, both men were covered up to the knee.

'The house is this way,' said Orim, nodding towards a barely discernible path.

'How far?'

'Half a mile.'

'Are we going in quiet?'

'Normally, I would say we should approach openly, as friends. But nobody had much news of Parrs. It's possible they're watching the place; even that someone has taken his house. We must be cautious.'

Marik placed the sheathed knife in the wide pocket of his trousers and followed Orim. Within a few minutes they had reached a flooded section of the path where they had to slosh through dirty water and negotiate patches of thick, sticky mud. The area was strewn with many reeds that appeared dead: white, broken and as thin as paper. There was simply no way to move quietly across this terrain and Marik was glad when they finally reached higher, drier ground. Here, the path ran between dense, pale yellow bushes which reached to waist height. Orim stopped when they passed beyond them into a wood.

He pointed ahead. 'See there?'

It took Marik a while to identify the timber wall and window. 'Got it.'

'Should we split up, come in from different directions?'

'Only if you want to take the hatchet – and we agreed we weren't going to do that. Let's get a bit closer.'

They stopped again at a distance of around a hundred feet. Marik was surprised to see that Parrs' house was quite large and built of wooden planking. It was a long structure and though they couldn't see the entrance, there was no sign of activity. Arranged neatly against the rear wall were numerous piles of reeds. Beyond the house, no more than a quarter-mile distant, was an open waterway – a method of approach Orim had considered too exposed.

'Looks quiet,' he said.

'It'll be dark soon. We need to know.'

Keeping his hand close to his pocket, Marik continued along the path, eyes scanning left and right every step of the way. Soon they were walking along the side of the house, eyes probing the darkness beyond the windows. They arrived at the front door to find it ajar.

Marik reached into the pocket and had his fingers on the knife's hilt as he pushed the door open. Hinges squeaking, it swung back and clanked gently against the wall. The house was in fact one very large room: with a kitchen at the near end, two beds, then what looked like a storage area. Everything was covered with dust and there was no trace of any recent inhabitants.

Marik glanced towards the waterway and saw a small dock built at the edge of an inlet. There were depressions on the path that suggested activity but no obvious footprints. Halfway between the house and the dock was a clearing where more bundles of reeds had been stacked.

'Inside?' asked Orim.

With a nod, Marik entered first. It was soon evident that some of the house's contents had been taken. A good deal of cooking equipment remained, as did some clothes and bedding; but four wooden chests to the rear had been left open and empty.

'Looks like he hasn't been here for a while.'

'Someone's been through it though,' said Orim. 'Taken what they fancied.'

'Might have been Parrs himself.'

'And just leave it like this?'

'Maybe he had no choice. Keep looking. I'll check outside.'

As he stepped out into the twilight, Marik heard a noise from the direction of the dock. He crouched down, moved forward, and hid behind a tree while he scoured the area. He couldn't be sure of the sound but he remained there for some time, eyes and ears alert.

'Marik?'

He straightened up and walked back to Orim, who was now peering around warily himself.

'Probably nothing. Keep at it. I'll check out here.'

Marik began a circuit of the house. He'd seen no obvious sign of a confrontation inside but guessed a fight outside was as likely. However, spotting disturbed ground or drops of blood would be difficult in the fading light. In fact, he saw nothing of note until the second circuit. A shovel had been left standing against the side of the house furthest from the water. Nothing unusual in itself, except that Marik had earlier spotted a large basket of tools just inside the door. He picked the shovel up and saw that the scoop was covered with dried soil. It had been used recently, perhaps in the last few days. He turned and surveyed the terrain on that side.

Ahead of him was a section of muddy ground where only a few weeds grew, beyond that another tract of the low, yellow bushes. Marik moved that way, eyes fixed on the ground, but saw nothing of use. The bushes began around twenty feet from the house. The dense vegetation made passage difficult but, even in the evening gloom, he spied a few broken twigs where someone had forced their way through.

Marik didn't have to travel far to find what he was by then expecting: about fifty feet from the house – but entirely hidden from view – was a small area of open ground surrounded by the bushes. And in the middle of it, a mound of freshly dug earth.

Marik spun around but it was only Orim approaching. 'Nothing inside. Found anything?'

'I have. Bring the shovel.'

While Orim knelt and prayed to Sa Sarkan, Marik began digging. He didn't want to interrupt the man but if – as expected – they were about to exhume Parrs, he needed to know what they were going to do. They could still try and at least scout Old Island but without any local and/or current knowledge about what they might face, that seemed risky. And as he drove the shovel into the earth and flicked the soil onto the nearby bushes, Marik began to wonder if Orim's lengthy prayers might be for his daughter, not this stranger whose help they'd depended on.

When he finally stood, Orim volunteered to take over.

'It's all right. Could do with some light though.'

With a nod, Orim headed off into the gloom. The darkness had settled swiftly and Marik was not looking forward to the trip back to the canoe.

This macabre task was doing little for his nerves. He had buried plenty of men but he could not recall ever having to dig one up. In the South – he guessed in the North too – this was considered an ungodly act. Still, they needed to know.

Marik shook soil off his feet and continued digging. At the third drive into the earth, the shovel hit something solid. In fact, the clang sounded distinctly metallic. Marik wondered if he might have struck an object Parrs had been buried with, perhaps even bone. Yet it didn't seem likely that his murderers would have had any reason to dispose of anything other than the body. Using the edge of the shovel, he scraped soil away and soon realised that he had exposed the top of an iron chest. By the time Orim returned with a glowing lantern, Marik had removed enough to see exactly what he was dealing with: a container five feet long and two wide.

'Where's the body?' asked Orim.

'I'm not sure there is one.'

Marik squatted down and discovered that the clasp on one side was tied only with string. Once that was off, he heaved the top of the chest open. As it thumped into the pile of soil he had created, Orim lowered the lantern. Marik removed the cloth that covered the contents and found himself staring down at a dozen swords: iron-made but of reasonable quality.

'Thanks for saving us the effort.'

Marik cursed and berated himself for not listening to his instincts. He *had* heard something earlier.

Orim turned towards the bushes from where the voice had emanated. When three dark figures advanced, the lamp-light illuminated two arrow-heads, one aimed at Orim, one at Marik.

Orim asked something in his language but received no reply.

The swords were out of reach but Marik's right hand was hidden from the interlopers. He was considering going for the knife when the man spoke again in Common.

'Hands up. Both of you.'

'Who are you?' asked Orim.

He received no answer.

Whoever they were, they were in a hurry; and the digging wasn't the end of Marik's labours. He and Orim were instructed to carry the chest to another inlet beyond the dock. Here the three strangers had their own craft waiting; not a canoe but a fifteen-foot skiff. Bearing in mind what he'd previously heard, Marik was convinced that they were Reverrik's people. There was more light close to the water and he noticed that one of the three was a woman.

Once they had loaded the chest into the skiff, Marik and Orim had their hands tied behind their backs. The trio were very professional; they operated with minimal talk and an arrow-head was pressed against Marik's throat while he was bound. His knife had already been taken from him.

When one of the men moved Orim towards the skiff, he tried to speak. This resulted in an elbow between his shoulder blades that sent him to his knees, wheezing.

'Very impressive,' said Marik, though he knew it unwise. 'Hitting a bound man in the back.'

The man who had spoken first still had a bow and arrow cradled loosely in his hands. He took the arrow from the string and poked the tip into the underside of Marik's chin.

'Prefer to see it coming? That can be arranged.'

Marik did not reply. The glow of the nearby lamp illuminated nothing more than a grim face and a thick moustache. Marik could not see enough of this or the other two faces to establish how local they appeared. With a smug grin, the leader withdrew.

Once Orim was back on his feet, the prisoners were placed on either side of the chest in the middle of the boat. The woman went to the front (replacing her bow with a paddle) while the leader took up position close to the prisoners, now armed with a dagger. The lamp was put out and the last man pushed them off.

Marik took a little encouragement from the fact that they had not been killed immediately. But he had been captured twice before in his life and knew what a terrible thing it was to be at the mercy of those who mean harm. Given how he and Orim had been discovered, there was little chance of making the cover story stick, so he spent the ensuing hours developing several alternatives. He hoped at least to draw the attention on to him and ensure that Orim stayed alive.

The man did not seem to be doing well. Head bowed, he sat slumped beside the chest, apparently devoid of hope. Marik imagined he would be thinking of his daughter and his wife. If the pair of them simply never returned to Northcrest, Tarrika would have to suffer uncertainty about the fate of both husband and daughter. At one point, Orim could be heard whispering another prayer. It seemed unlikely to Marik that Sa Sarkan was now – or had ever – concerned herself with the wellbeing of this good man and his family.

He also tried to occupy himself by observing all he could of his captors. It was a clear night and the combined light of the Red Moon and the Grey Moon was sufficient for the trio to find their way in silence and allow Marik to gather some information. Of the man behind him, he was able to establish that he was small in stature and sharp in manner, his head and eyes constantly on the move. The woman appeared taller than average and had shaved off her hair. She said not a word; even her breathing was quiet. That left the leader, who too was tall, perhaps even close to six feet. He kept a close eye on their surroundings and occasionally hummed a tune. Marik guessed that his superiors might be pleased with his day's catch.

The three-hour trip took them past some solid land but he could not tell if they were close to Old Island. During the last hour, they followed a circuitous path around islets and tracts of reeds. Marik tried to memorise all the twists and turns but there were no landmarks to help him and he eventually gave up. The final stage took them to a particularly impenetrable wall of reeds that was at least ten feet high, the individual plants two inches thick.

When the leader gave a fairly convincing bird call, a similar response came. A minute later, Marik was stunned to see an entire section of the reed wall separate from the surrounding plants and shift forward. As the trio guided the boat out of the way, he realised the false reed-wall was built upon a floating platform perhaps twelve feet across. Sitting in a canoe was the man who had pushed it out. With only a few words of greeting, the trio manoeuvred their skiff behind the wall and into a waterway that led into the heart of the sprawling reed-bed. Similarly intrigued, Orim also looked on as the fourth man pulled the fake wall back into position. Conversation continued as the sentry followed the skiff along the waterway. Not far ahead, three smudges of light defied the darkness.

Instead of an arrow-head, it was now the tip of the leader's knife under Marik's chin.

'Talk.'

Marik was kneeling beside Orim, hands still bound. Once hauled out of the boat, he'd found himself on another floating structure apparently made entirely from reeds and reed-rope. It was impressively large and clearly home to at least a dozen people. As they heard of the new arrivals, more gathered beyond the glow of the lantern held over the prisoners by the woman.

'Talk,' said the leader between gritted teeth, his blade now almost piercing Marik's skin.

Marik's problem was that he didn't know what to say. Given the secrecy of this base, he could not now be sure that these men were affiliated to Reverrik – why the need to hide? – but neither could he be sure that they were not. Still, saying anything was preferable to having that blade stuck in him.

'What do you want to know?' Though he would have preferred to head butt the bastard, he tried to sound polite. The man possessed only a few wisps of hair on his head but the bushy moustache extended down to his jaw. Marik had not seen any other locals with such an affectation.

'Start with your name and what you were doing at Parrs' place.'

He couldn't see any harm in disclosing that and was keen to keep the attention on himself. 'My name is Marik. I got this old fool to take me there. Wanted to see if there was anything worth stealing.'

The leader turned his attention to Orim. Marik squinted, trying to examine the others present but the nearby lantern made this impossible.

'Do I know you?' the leader asked Orim.

'I don't believe so.'

The leader moved the knife away and straightened up. 'How did you know where the weapons were?'

'He didn't,' interjected Marik. 'I saw the spade, found the pile of earth.'

The leader's eyes were still on Orim. 'Do you know Parrs?'

Marik and Orim turned to each other. Marik wanted to help but who knew what the right answer was?

'I – I –'

'He knows me.'

The leader turned, as did everyone else. Several stood aside as a man emerged from the gloom, one hand over the shoulder of another who was supporting him. Even in the dim light, he did not look well.

'Parrs,' said Orim. 'Thank the Great Maker.'

'You're awake,' said the leader.

'Just about.' Parrs halted close to Orim. He looked to be in his twenties and was broad-chested and muscular. He was also barefoot and dressed in a sleeping tunic, his face clammy and pale.

'They said you were at my house. What do you want, Orim?'

'To ask for your help. I want to get my daughter back.' Orim nodded at Marik. 'This man is going to help me.'

Clearly still suspicious, the leader exchanged several comments with Parrs in the local tongue. They spoke for some time until he suddenly lifted Orim up and gripped him tightly by the shoulders. Marik was about to issue a threat but the man only wanted to speak, his voice now quiet but intense. Orim nodded and answered in some detail. The leader had several more questions for him but Marik was impressed by how calm his companion remained. The tension gradually lessened until finally the leader untied the ropes binding Orim's wrists.

Marik was glad to see Parrs summon a smile for his old acquaintance and shake his hand. The young man introduced Orim to the others and he seemed to recognise several of them. Marik was left standing with the woman, who had kept her fierce gaze on him throughout.

'Any chance you could untie me?'

Having consulted the leader, she did so but Marik subsequently found himself ignored. The sentry had already returned to his post but the remaining inhabitants of the hideout gathered and a lengthy discussion ensued. Marik sat at the only table – also made of reed bundles – with Orim and Parrs and was eventually given some water to drink. He therefore had more time to admire the base, which was square in shape, at least thirty feet across and with one half covered by a roof. Other than the waterway, it was surrounded by the reedbed, which reached fractionally higher than the roof. The whole design was quite ingenious and Marik reckoned the construction must have taken place over many months, if not years. Though he was still very much in the dark, the existence of this small group was the first encouraging development since he and Orim had entered the delta.

'Sorry,' offered Parrs after an hour or more. 'There is much to say.'

'Clearly.'

Parrs offered his hand across the table.

Marik hesitated.

'Don't worry, you won't catch what I have. I passed through an area of bad water and picked up a fever. I'm through the worst of it.'

Marik shook his hand. 'Is that why you didn't come to reclaim the weapons?'

Parrs nodded. He now had a blanket over his shoulders which he pulled tighter around him. 'We stole the chest right out of one of their boats but we had only a canoe. Damn thing was slowing us down so much we had to dump it. My place was close by.'

'You don't use your house anymore?'

'Not for about three months. I knew they were starting to suspect me.'

'Reverrik's men?'

'Yes, though no one's seen him in a while. It's the giant we have to worry about.'

'And what exactly were you doing?'

'Spying for this lot.' Parrs gave a proud grin. 'With my work, I had a good excuse to travel all over. I'm glad to be here though I think Slicer wishes I was still his eyes and ears.'

'Slicer – the fellow with the moustache? He's in charge?'

'He and Garrun – see the older fellow standing there?'

Garrun was indeed quite old: a bearded man with a pronounced stoop. Like the others, he was currently listening to Slicer. Marik had now had time to examine the faces surrounding him and saw that they indeed shared the dark colouring and black hair of the delta's other inhabitants. This small group reflected the appearance of the wider population, some narrow-featured like the Ralaskans, others with broader, flatter faces.

Despite his current affliction, Parrs seemed a friendly, cheerful fellow. 'We'd be nothing without those two.'

'We?'

'We rebels.'

'How many of you are there?'

'Those you see here and a few others. But there are many who will fight with us when the time comes.'

'Slicer doesn't know Orim?'

Parrs wiped his sweaty brow. 'He and Garrun and several others are from the north of the delta. When the group began, it was Garrun that suggested the hideout. This is an ideal position – out of the way but only two hours from Old Island.'

'What about her? asked Marik quietly, nodding towards the archer, the only woman present.

'Nasreen. The Rats made her leave Old Island a few months back and she took up with us.'

'Rats?'

'That's what we call them. Vicious and hard to get rid of.'

'Seems apt.'

Parrs was still looking at Nasreen. 'Doesn't say much. Spends all her time practising with that bow. She's almost as good as Slicer.'

Nasreen was leaning against one of the roof supports, arms crossed. Like the others, she wore green tunic and trousers; presumably for camouflage. Though the shaven head caught the attention, when she had untied him Marik had seen that her entire face and hands were covered by some kind of scarring. The lurid circular marks resembled burns and had afflicted even her mouth, ears and eyelids.

Parrs whispered: 'They got rid of her because of it. Some kind of disease that she caught from one of the mercenaries. It doesn't harm you but the scarring is permanent. Every last inch of the body. I suppose she wasn't pretty enough for them anymore.'

Chapter Sixteen

Given the late hour, it was decided that nothing more be discussed until morning. The two guests were allocated a space to sleep under the roof. Marik spoke briefly to Orim but realised that the older man was even more exhausted than he was. As he reflected on the course of events since their arrival at Ettwater, he was grateful that such a trying day had ended well. The noise from the insects within the sprawling sea of reeds was distracting but – once warm under his blanket – he drifted off to sleep and didn't wake until dawn.

Due to the surroundings, not much light reached the interior of the hideout, even though the morning sky was clear. Marik was greeted by Orim and a mug of water. Upon the table were two large plates, one containing dried meat, the other a collection of berries. Already sitting there were Garrun and Slicer. Marik was surprised to see that only Parrs and one other were present.

'Where is everyone?'

'Patrols,' explained Orim. 'They're worried that our appearance in Ettwater might have attracted some interest.' He cleared his throat before speaking again. 'Marik, my daughter is alive and well. The girl Nasreen told me.'

Marik clapped his companion on the arm. No words seemed adequate.

Orim gestured towards the table. 'Come, they want to talk to us.'

'Very well.' Marik wiped his tired eyes and took his mug with him. He and Orim sat opposite the two leaders.

'Sorry about the water and the food,' said Garrun. 'Obtaining both is a constant difficulty.'

'Worth trading that for the security though, I suppose.'

Marik was so hungry that he didn't wait to be asked. The dried meat did not taste pleasant but he was grateful for it nonetheless.

Slicer took a handful of berries, the juice of which had already stained his greying moustache. Marik was surprised at how wrinkled the man's skin was; he had to be close to fifty. Garrun was at least ten years older and it was he that kept talking.

'I wish we had more news of young Korina; and all the others held on Old Island.'

Orim added: 'They imprison those considered dangerous and make them fight – to the death. The mercenaries wager on the outcome.'

'How close can you get?' asked Marik.

Garrun turned to Slicer. The bow was not in evidence today but he had two throwing knives sheathed in a leather cuirass across his chest.

'Tell me how you came to Northcrest.'

Marik considered it entirely reasonable of the man to want to check if his story matched Orim's. He told it in as much detail as he could, starting with the wrecking of the *White Cloud*. Unsurprisingly, Slicer wanted him to go back even further, and Marik obliged, up to a point. Slicer stopped him on several occasions but by the end seemed satisfied that any discrepancies were minor. Yet his questions hadn't finished.

'An unlikely tale but that doesn't mean it didn't happen. You need to understand that the only Southers I've ever met are fighting with Reverrik. Give me one good reason why I shouldn't assume that you're a spy sent to infiltrate our group.'

'With respect, why would Reverrik go to all that bother? From the sounds of it, you cause him little more than the occasional inconvenience.'

Slicer glared across the table.

'No offence,' added Marik.

'It is true that we have not been able to do much damage yet,' admitted Garrun. 'But that will change.'

Slicer smoothed his moustache with finger and thumb. 'You a good fighter?'

'Depends on the opposition. Listen, can we get down to the matter at hand? Can you help us?'

'What do you imagine you're going to do?'

'Scout Old Island, replied Marik. 'Try to establish exactly where Korina is. Maybe even get her out.'

'Just like that.' Slicer waved a dismissive hand then stood and walked away.

'Of course not. But we have to try something.'

Garrun sighed. 'All the people that have tried something are either captive or dead.'

'I asked how close you can get.'

Slicer shook his head and stared along the waterway. When Orim said something conciliatory in their language, the joint leader eventually turned around.

'It's a long way to the observation point but there is a decent view of the north and east side.'

'When were the swords stolen?' asked Marik.

'Several weeks ago,' replied Garrun. 'They put out a few search parties out but in general they patrol less these days. Hammerhand still goes out for the tributes but we know they've grown complacent. As you said, not much of a threat to worry about.'

'So, you can get us there?'

'Yes,' replied Slicer, taking a step towards Marik. 'But you need to understand how it is. There are over a hundred well-armed men. Even if – by some miracle – you got the girl off the island, they'd hunt you down.'

Marik moved his mug aside and laid his arms across the table. 'Parrs told me that you don't have many sources of information. Isn't this an opportunity to look for routines, weaknesses? If it's impossible to even consider a move, then we won't try.'

Slicer turned to Garrun and they spoke again briefly in the local tongue.

'I will take you,' he said after some time. 'Nasreen can come too. She can tell you more about the island itself.' Slicer paused. 'Garrun isn't sure. He thinks it's a risk. In case you betray us.'

The older man seemed annoyed at the disclosure but added nothing.

Marik stood up and faced Slicer. 'That's not going to happen. Anyway, no need to worry about me. I have no blade. You've got two.'

They travelled in two canoes, one crewed by Orim and Nasreen, the other by Marik and Slicer. As the better paddler, it was obvious that Slicer should take the rear but Marik also felt sure it was so the veteran could keep an eye on him. All four wore light, hooded cloaks. Slicer had insisted that this was necessary; to hide their identities should they encounter the Rats. Before they departed, the morning patrols returned, announcing that there were no signs of enemy movement to concern them. With that in mind, Garrun despatched a crew to reclaim Orim and Marik's boat and gear from Spring Island.

Once beyond the secret entrance, they turned in the opposite direction from their approach. The waterway ranged between five and ten yards in width and not a trace of soil or grass could be seen on either side. The reeds here were if anything even thicker than those surrounding the base and many were taller than two men. The stems were varying shades of green and each was topped by a frail frond of light brown.

Though this was clearly a seldom-used area, the hooded Nasreen kept the lead boat very close to the edge of the meandering channel and occasionally stopped to listen for any activity. With two experienced paddlers aboard, their movements were more efficient than Marik's boat and he soon became annoyed by Slicer's constant admonishments.

He was also annoyed to still be unarmed though there was a long leather bag in their canoe that clearly contained at least one sword. Marik didn't like Slicer – he felt sure that his overconfidence masked some deficiency – but he had to admit it was reassuring not to be the only one who knew his way around a blade.

After two hours or so, they crossed an open area then entered another waterway. They hadn't gone far when they passed a smaller channel blockaded by a barrier of rotting wood. Atop the barrier was a painted sign with something scrawled in white paint. Marik was about to ask what it was when Slicer told him to paddle harder. Eventually they turned left into another very narrow channel, this one obstructed in several places by dead or dying reeds which had to be pushed aside. On each occasion, either Nasreen or Slicer would ensure that they left no trace of their passage behind. Despite this measure, when they finally stopped and hauled the canoes out onto solid ground, Slicer insisted that they drag the vessels into a thicket of bushes and again cover their trail. Only then did he allow the others a few minutes' rest.

Nasreen spend some time checking her bow. To Marik, it looked rather short but he could see it was well-made, equipped with a layer of sinew to generate additional bend and power.

'Nice weapon. Where'd you get it?'

She didn't even look at him.

'From a dead Rat,' said Slicer.

Nasreen put the bow over her right shoulder, her quiver on the left. The bolts also looked short to Marik's eye but the condition of the flights demonstrated how well the woman cared for her equipment.

Nasreen kept her gaze downward. Marik imagined it was difficult to look at others when it brought attention to you. Even though she wore the hood, the unforgiving daylight showed how awful the scarring really was. It was impossible to imagine how she might have looked before.

'Fortunate that we didn't see anyone,' said Orim.

'Normal,' replied Slicer. 'There's nothing but reeds at the end of that waterway – no way through. Part of the reason why we placed the hideout where it is.'

'And nothing but this stuff in here.' Orim wearily regarded yet another type of dense undergrowth that reached up to around chest height. This stuff boasted no flower or bright colours and seemed to be made up entirely of thick, intertwining shoots. Gaps were few and far between.

'Bindroot,' said Slicer. 'It's well named and it only gets worse from here.'

He took the leather bag from his shoulder and placed it on the ground. Once it was open, he took out a hatchet and handed it to Marik.

'In the hope that you chop better than you paddle.'

'I was expecting a sword.'

'Maybe later.'

'They won't hear us?'

Slicer grinned. 'We've got miles to go yet, Souther, and a marsh to cross. We'll be lucky if we get anywhere close before nightfall – so, if you don't mind?'

Slicer pointed in a direction roughly opposite to the channel they had taken to reach the land. 'That way. And try to go straight. Any deviation will cost us time.'

Marik couldn't help recalling the grinding, relentless work at the demolition site in Ralaska. He had seen nothing in the South to compare to the obstructive properties of bindroot and was sweating within minutes as he hacked, chopped, wrenched and tore his way through the vegetation. He kept at it for what he estimated to be an hour before stopping for a water break. Slicer had no comment to offer so Marik knew he was doing well and had kept a steady course. Orim offered to take over but Marik persisted through a particularly difficult area where there was also a low-lying weed to complicate matters. He only gave up the hatchet when he was through this section and they reached a small clearing. With an appreciative nod, Slicer took the hatchet and led the way. His expertise was evident in the efficient manner he cleared the bindroot with the minimum of effort. Marik was glad to be at the rear of the little column, where he had time to recover.

Despite Slicer's skill, he too was drenched in sweat by the time they left the bindroot behind. It was a hot day and the fetid, penetrative odours of the delta seemed even worse than usual. Marik could appreciate Orim's affection for the place – certainly the waterways – but it was not somewhere he would want to live. Though he did not like to admit it to himself, few weeks passed without him experiencing a degree of longing for the clean air and high places of the South.

The marsh was similar to the territory they had crossed on the way to Scarton. There was as yet no clear sight of Old Island, merely another reed-bed on the far side of the marsh. At an order from Slicer, Nasreen began navigating an efficient path around muddy pools and exploiting patches of grass when possible. Marik would have enjoyed the open ground were it not for the winged insects that shot up from the soil to attack. Though again apparently harmless, the clouds of the tiny creatures grew so thick that Slicer called a halt and handed round a jar of unguent. This also smelled unpleasant – like rotting meat – but even the small amount they smeared on their clothing had the desired effect.

From the sun's position, Marik guessed they had only an hour of light left by the time they reached the reeds. Orim offered to take up the hatchet but Slicer explained that they were now close to Old Island. This was the cover that would enable them to observe Reverrik's headquarters.

'Just enough time to get a look before dusk,' explained the rebel leader. 'We should be safe. There's no reason for them to be on this side of the water. They have a guard tower but it's in the middle of the island, some way away. One more thing – it's nesting season. Watch out for birds. They could easily give us away. We'll leave our gear here.'

He put his pack down, as did Orim and Nasreen. Marik had no pack so spent a moment surveying the marsh behind them. He saw no sign of a pursuer or that anyone else had been here recently. As Slicer entered the reed-bed, Marik noted that this type was thinner and less dense than most. Though high enough to provide cover, they also shifted easily, the fronds announcing movement to any watching eyes. The result was incredibly slow progress but they did not have far to go.

A whispered warning from Slicer stopped them short of the bank and from there they crawled forward. There were still some reeds obstructing their view but as low as they were – and in the fading light – there was no chance of being seen. Slicer ordered them close together so that they could communicate. Marik lay to his right, with Orim to the left and Nasreen beyond him. Their position was roughly opposite one end of the island, which extended away for some distance.

It was easy to see why this piece of land had been exploited. It rose unusually high out of the water and was surrounded on all sides by a deep channel. At no point was Old Island less than two hundred feet from the nearest reedbeds or solid ground, making an assault difficult. Built close to the near end was a large timber structure and others could be seen behind it. The only visible people were a small group clustered around a fire. Judging by the smell, they were cooking meat. Occasionally, their voices would drift across the water to reach the hidden observers. In the twilight, Marik could discern only the fact that they were men. None seemed large enough to be the infamous Hammerhand.

'The building nearest to us is their barracks,' said Slicer. 'Behind that – not visible from here – is the armoury. According to Nasreen, the men keep their personal weapons with them but there they store spares plus arrows, spears and suchlike – plus all the weapons they've taken from us. You can just see the edge of another building to the left of the barracks.'

Marik nodded, though he couldn't be sure in the gloom.

'Reverrik's place. Used to be where our elders met. He's enlarged it. There's a kitchen downstairs and rooms for the women. Hammerhand and a few others have quarters there also. Past the house is the warehouse, where Reverrik keeps his spoils. You can see the guard tower for yourself.'

This was not hard to spot and seemed to be situated in the middle of the island. A lantern had just been lit, one of several now visible.

'There are a few trees at the other end,' added Slicer, 'but he's had most of them cut down so it's even harder to infiltrate the place. You can't see the dock but it's to the left of the guard tower. The island is shaped like a kidney, forming a cove on that side. They've got dozens of boats, including a twelve-oar coaster that was brought in last year. Any questions?'

'None that can't wait. Can't see much now anyway.'

'We'll return at first light.'

The four did what they could to clean the mud off themselves then settled down for the night on a grassy area close to the reeds. Slicer handed out more of the unguent which continued to do a good job of keeping the insects at bay. Despite the smell, Marik was glad of the stuff. He recalled an episode during his time with the Guard when an entire offensive had been called off due to the effects of woodfly bites.

Once they had eaten, Slicer arranged a sentry rota that would see them each do two stints before dawn. He even had a little hourglass in his pack to count the hours. Since dusk, clouds had slid in from the west and Marik could barely see the others' faces as they lay out on their blankets.

'Well then, Souther - questions?'

It seemed to Marik that, having done what he'd agreed to do, Slicer now drew satisfaction from showing him what they faced. In fact, the island itself did not offer insurmountable difficulty. Marik reckoned he could have taken it with around sixty well-trained men. But as they had only a dozen – plus whatever willing locals could be rounded up – that appeared near-impossible. As for extracting Orim's daughter, he could not yet make an informed judgement.

'The women – how carefully are they watched?'

Nasreen answered, her voice quiet but steady. 'At night, Reverrik or one of the others comes upstairs and takes his pick. There are thirty or so girls there now. During the day, they all have duties – cleaning, fetching water, cooking, repairing clothes.'

'There's no contact from outside?'

'None. Nor are they allowed off the island.'

'How are they treated?'

'Reverrik treats some of them almost like daughters, though he's not shy of taking any of them into his bed. The men know not to abuse them because it makes him angry. He … controls the women. He controls everyone.'

'Forgive me for asking but what about children? Surely some of them must have been made pregnant?'

'He has a potion brought in from Hindmarch,' said Slicer. 'The girls have to take it. Our people don't use it because of the side effects – if taken over time, it will make them barren. Nasreen and two others were sent away when they caught the disease, the man who brought it too.'

'Would it be possible for one of the girls to get out of the house unseen?'

Nasreen answered. 'Very difficult. Both doors are locked at night. If they're not with one of the men, the girls sleep in two big rooms.'

'I'm sure a few would fight back if they could,' added Slicer. 'But some are so afraid that they might even alert the guards. You must remember that many have been there for years now. They don't expect to ever leave unless Reverrik dies. And he's a paranoid old bastard – has someone else taste his food before he'll eat it, posts a guard at his own door. And he sets Hammerhand on any of the men he suspects of plotting against him. They go in the pit with the prisoners.'

'The pit?'

'We can't see it from the bank. A big hole dug out close to the barracks. The prisoners are given just enough to survive. Used for labour now and again but they usually only come out when Reverrik wants to see a fight. Entertainment. He keeps his warriors busy – they've just finished extending the warehouse. Hammerhand drills them and keeps them out on patrol. Reverrik knows he's bled the delta almost dry so he doesn't pay them much but keeps them well fed. He keeps them scared too.'

'What do you mean?'

'He comes from the East and was born into some sect devoted to the Red Moon and a spirit that dwells within it. He believes that's where his power comes from. He offers the dead prisoners as sacrifices.'

There was quiet for some time. Eventually Nasreen spoke up again. 'When the Red Moon is full, he has the blood from the fights collected in a special urn, sometimes the monthly blood of the women too. He drinks it then prays to his moon-god.'

When Marik started his shift, the Red Moon was shrouded by cloud. The Grey Moon – smaller and less luminous – was clear and gave enough light for him to see some way across the marsh. Standing a few yards from the camp, he saw nothing to concern him. The only sounds to be heard were the occasional chirruping of birds and the whooshes of the windblown reeds.

He had already devoted considerable thought to how he might extricate Korina from Old Island. He had some ideas but they were yet to coalesce into a plan with much chance of success. He resolved to see what else could be learned when he observed the island and its inhabitants in daylight. Having seen only a few of the Rats, Reverrik and Hammerhand seemed almost mythical figures, especially after Nasreen's colourful description of the foreign mercenary who had carved out a fiefdom for himself.

Some time later, Orim got up and walked over to Marik. They moved further away so as not to disturb the others.

'Can't sleep?'

'We're so close,' whispered Orim. '*She*'s so close. If I can't sleep, I must pray. We don't have much of a chance, do we?'

'We'll learn more tomorrow. It changes nothing, I know, but I'm glad to hear that the girls are not simply abandoned to the men. At least they have each other.'

'I suppose you're right. I asked Nasreen about my daughter but she couldn't tell me much. I wonder if she's hiding the truth from me.'

'What's she like – Korina?'

'A good girl. Not perfect – she sides with her mother too much for my liking and she has to be told everything twice. But a good girl. When she was young, she would follow me all round all day, wanting to help with everything. She's curious, always wanting to know more of the world. I took her to Hindmarch once and she was fascinated by the place. I was hoping to take her back there just before … well … before. I hope she still says her prayers.'

Chapter Seventeen

The morning of observation yielded more useful information. Marik and the others were back in their hide before dawn and they witnessed a good deal of activity. The coaster departed in the first hour but their low position prevented the watchers from seeing who was aboard. According to Slicer, the single approach waterway was on the far side of Old Island. From there it was connected to other main routes, one leading in the direction of Ettwater, one towards Averthorp, a village connected by road to Hindmarch.

Marik also got his first look at Reverrik. The leader of the Rats was sighted outside the barracks, issuing orders. At that distance, it was hard to make out much but Slicer and Nasreen easily identified him by his naked chest and heavy beard. Apparently, he never wore anything other than a mail-shirt on his top half. Marik detected a slight limp and saw that his followers obeyed his every direction with great speed.

When Reverrik moved on, the watchers' attention shifted to the pit. A ladder had been put down by the Rats and prisoners appeared one at a time until ten had emerged. Even at that distance, their lethargic movements and lolling heads betrayed their poor condition. Reverrik's men swiftly doled out food and got their charges moving. Apparently, there was a fighting circle marked out between the pit and the barracks.

'Looks like he's planning one of his 'celebrations',' said Slicer.

'Always when the Red Moon is full,' added Nasreen. 'Four nights to go.'

Marik watched as wooden swords were placed in the hands of two prisoners and they were made to fight. Despite the men's condition, they put in plenty of effort and the heavy impacts echoed across the water.

'What happens during these celebrations?' asked Marik.

The other two listened in as Nasreen answered.

'It all begins when darkness falls. Usually he makes a speech. Sometimes the girls have to dance and sing. But the main event is the fights. There are always at least three, sometimes more. As long as they're conscious, the prisoners have to keep fighting – until someone dies. The men make wagers. And on this night, they are given the best food and as much ale as they can drink, which Reverrik usually controls carefully.'

Slicer said, 'That might be where the coaster is going – to get fresh food and ale from Averthorp.'

Nasreen nodded.

Slicer caught Marik's eye. 'I know what you're thinking, but the men take it in turns to miss out. Hammerhand selects about thirty who don't drink.'

'It's still an opportunity. Especially if we're able to tip the balance in our favour elsewhere.'

'How?'

'I have some ideas. But it's all irrelevant unless you can gather a group of decent size: all with weapons, all prepared to use them. Is that possible?'

Slicer frowned. 'You're not suggesting that we strike in three days? We have to talk to Garrun, we have to-'

'-Fair enough. But how many can you get? I'm talking about men who are prepared to kill.'

Slicer let out a long breath and stared at Old Island for sometime before answering. 'Fifty. Maybe.'

They were halfway back through the reeds when the cry went up. To Marik, the man's voice sounded close: to his right and – crucially – on *their* side of the channel. Like the other three crawling ahead of him, he froze. The man shouted again. At first, Marik thought it was some foreign tongue, then he realised it was Common.

'- here! Tracks. Fresh tracks!'

They were too deep into the reeds to see the man – or what was happening on the island. Slicer got up and set off in a crouching run. As the others followed, the slender reeds betrayed them and Marik knew that if they hadn't been seen already, they would be soon. Despite their pace, it took them at least two minutes to reach the packs, which they had secreted at the edge of the reed-bed. While the other three put them on, Marik ventured warily towards the marsh and looked to the right.

No more than eighty feet away, a young man stood beside the reeds. His gaze alternated between the rebels' position and Old Island. More shouts went up; clearly help was on its way. There was no mystery about what the lone mercenary was doing there: over one shoulder was a bow, over the other a fishing rod.

Marik held his hand up to keep the other three in cover. Feeling cold metal against his fingers, he gripped the sword offered to him by Slicer.

'What are you waiting for?'

'He has a bow.'

'Others are coming,' said Slicer. 'We have to move now.'

He and the other two had raised hoods to cover their faces. Marik did the same. 'He'll have a clear shot.'

'No, he won't.' Nasreen plucked an arrow from her quiver and nocked it, then took two steps forward and turned towards the mercenary. Once down on one knee, she drew back and took aim. Marik moved forward in time to see the fisherman throw himself to the ground as the projectile whizzed overhead.

'Go,' she said, already nocking the next arrow.

Slicer ran past, dragging Orim along with him. 'You too, Souther!'

Wishing he had a bow instead of the sword, Marik reluctantly followed. Only a few seconds later, an arrow flew close to the others, causing both to duck. When another whistled past, Marik knew one man could not have fired in such quick succession. He stopped, turned and saw another archer with the fisherman. Before they could shoot again, two mercenaries burst out of the reeds some way behind them. The first was a squat fellow wielding an axe. The second Marik had already spotted because he was taller than the reeds.

It could only be Hammerhand. Even at that distance, Marik could see that this was not simply a large man: he was at least nine feet tall, his body and limbs incomparable to his compatriots. Marik had heard the tales, of course, but it was still remarkable to see that they were true. In the Eastern lands beyond the Sky Mountains, giants still lived. And one of them was right here in the delta.

Two arrows struck flesh at the same time. Orim went down first, a bolt embedded in his upper arm. Slicer stopped and tried to help him up. The fisherman would not ever get up again: Nasreen's third arrow had hit him in the throat and he toppled back, arms flailing. To his credit, the other archer kept his nerve, unleashing a shot that missed Nasreen's head by inches. Distracted by some order from Hammerhand, the archer was still reaching for another arrow when her fourth shot tore through his palm. He dropped the bow, stared down at his ruined hand, and lurched towards the reeds.

Hammerhand and his companion charged on towards the rebels.

Marik realised that Nasreen had been hit around the same time she did. Running back to her, he saw that the shot had grazed her head, scraping away skin and a hair. As it began to bleed, she staggered.

'You're all right,' said Marik, an arm over her shoulder as he helped her to the others. By now Slicer had Orim up on his feet.

Hammerhand and the axe-man were still charging towards them, the giant's stride cutting the distance swiftly.

'Go on.' Slicer shoved Orim towards the marsh then raised his sword. Marik knew he had misjudged the veteran when he strode directly towards the onrushing pair.

Nasreen was trying to take another arrow from her quiver but was clearly distracted by the blood dripping down her forehead onto her face.

'Stop,' said Marik.

Though Orim's face was ashen and he had an arrow lodged in his arm, he could clearly still move. Marik ushered the wounded pair together. 'Go. As fast as you can. Don't look back. We'll be behind you. Go!'

Thankfully, they did his bidding and Marik was able to turn and join Slicer.

'You should go too, Souther.'

'And leave you to take all the glory? No chance.'

'Glory? Have you seen the size of this bastard?'

'Well, the bigger they are-'

'-the harder they hit?'

'Probably true.'

When the axe-man and Hammerhand came to halt, Marik had a chance to appraise the giant in detail. He wore huge hide and leather boots and a sleeveless black tunic that extended down to his knees in the Eastern style. Around his waist was a thick, elaborate belt of interlocking metal rings. Around his chest was a harness of some kind that clearly held a weapon upon his back. His face resembled a rock carving, his brow an overhanging cliff.

The axe-man was literally half his size, a beady-eyed fellow with long, greasy hair. 'Bad move, lads – should have run like your mates.'

Marik felt a tremor of fear but kept his gaze on Hammerhand. 'What about you – nothing to say?'

The enormous mercenary reached over his shoulder and a shackle clicked. He slowly retrieved the weapon then lowered it to his side. It was a mace, but one unlike any Marik had seen. The handle was of ridged, dark wood and attached to a sturdy chain. At the end of it – enclosed within a net of lighter steel chain – was a solid ball of rock at least eight inches wide. Marik did not want to imagine what it weighed, or what kind of damage it might do.

'Sort of says it all, don't it?' added the axe-man.

'Sort of does,' conceded Marik.

'Who you?' grunted Hammerhand, in a voice somehow even deeper and more ominous than could be imagined.

'Enough talk.' Slicer plucked one of the throwing knives from his cuirass and threw it with casual grace. The axe-man had just about registered that it was sticking out of his chest when Slicer nipped forward and launched a long swing of his sword. Despite a belated attempt at evasion, the axe-man was too slow. Slicer's blade cut him just below the chin; not deep, but deep enough. He went down gurgling, eyes rolling back in his head.

Hammerhand was quicker. With surprising agility, he closed on Marik and Slicer and whipped the mace into a deadly arc. The rock cracked against Slicer's blade, knocking it from his grasp; and Marik only avoided the same fate by ducking low. The rock missed his head by at least a foot but he knew already that this was not a fight they could win. He supposed they could have run but judging by the speed at which he'd pursued them, the huge bastard would easily keep up. They also could not leave Orim and Nasreen defenceless.

Slicer made no attempt to recover his sword. Instead, he took out his second throwing knife and flicked it at Hammerhand. The giant got his free hand up quickly and made no discernible reaction when the blade lodged itself in his immense forearm.

'Small knife.'

As the dying axe-man finally became still, blood from his throat swirled into a muddy puddle.

Hammerhand then seemed to make a decision about who to kill first. Moving to his right to isolate Slicer, he offered a token swing of the mace that nonetheless sent the veteran diving away. Marik took the opportunity to claim the rebel's sword. Armed with two blades, he circled around behind Hammerhand, trying to at least occupy his attention. Once he had it, he lobbed the second sword into the air. The blade flew over the giant and landed close to Slicer, tip down in the mud.

Marik had no time to admire his throw. With a nimble flick of his wrist and a jangle of chains, Hammerhand unleashed the rock once more. Arm extended, the reach was even further than Marik had anticipated. He felt sure the rock was going to hit him, even as he threw himself backward. Tripping over his own feet, he slammed into the ground.

He didn't actually see what happened next but the noise gave him a sense of it. Hammerhand continued both his turn and his swing. Marik later guessed that Slicer might have still been recovering his sword but he clearly didn't – or couldn't – defend himself.

The rock struck his head with sickening power and a horrible finality. Marik got up and saw Slicer lying in the mud, body limp. His already lifeless eyes seemed to be staring straight at Marik, who had never seen death come so quickly. Hammerhand had snuffed the veteran out with the ease of wet fingers on a candle.

Marik gave serious thought to running at the Easterling but the mercenary didn't give him a chance. Arm out high, Hammerhand swung his arm in a tight circle, keeping the rock moving.

'You next.'

Marik crabbed to his left and held his sword up in the hope that it might at least take a blow instead of his head. Hammerhand kept his pale grey eyes on his foe as the smaller man circled him. Marik did not see much in those eyes other than the faintest suggestion of enjoyment.

He kept moving and, half-way through the next circuit, passed close to the dead axe-man. The thought had barely come to him before he acted. Two yards past the corpse, Marik halted and shifted back the other way. As he'd expected, Hammerhand saw this as an opportunity. A neat flick sent the rock hurtling towards Marik, who stepped forward, held the sword up and ducked down onto his haunches. Forcing himself not to close his eyes, he waited until the chain had swung once around the sword. He was about to let go when the blade was wrenched out of his hands. He glimpsed Hammerhand frowning at the sword now entangled in his weapon.

Marik dropped beside the dead axe-man. He pulled the throwing knife out of his chest and turned back towards Hammerhand. Marik didn't remember the last time he'd thrown a knife but as a young warrior he'd spent hours doing just that. The range was no more than ten feet; the result far better than he'd expected.

With several inches of steel now buried in his left eye-socket, Hammerhand roared with pain. He fell to his knees, sending up enough muddy water to splash Marik's face. The giant reached for the knife then changed his mind and roared again, teeth grinding as slobber dripped from his mouth. Despite the evident agony, he continued to swing his mace back and forth, complete with entangled sword. Even if he'd still had a weapon, Marik wouldn't have risked trying to finish him off. Hammerhand was down and he wasn't about to waste this chance at escape.

As he ran past Slicer, he briefly placed a hand upon the dead man's shoulder.

Marik had made the decision long before they reached the bindroot. Once they were in cover, he let go of Orim and turned to Nasreen.

'I need your bow.'

Her forehead was slick with blood from her head wound but the flow had already lessened. 'Why?'

'Getting back through the bindroot with you two injured will take an age. We have to slow them down.'

As the trio had crossed the marsh, Marik looked back regularly. Hammerhand eventually stood and lumbered back towards the reeds. Reinforcements appeared not long after. There were now four men sprinting across the marsh, currently around a quarter-mile away.

To Marik's relief, Nasreen handed him her bow and quiver.

'Get as far as you can,' he said. 'I won't be long.'

Orim was pale, and the wound was bleeding badly. Marik hurried over to him and examined the injury. The arrow had gone at least halfway through his upper arm.

'I can't take it out now but I'll snap the end off.' He knew the arrow would inevitably catch as they struggled through the bindroot, causing Orim more pain and slowing them even further.

'It will hurt.'

'I know.'

Marik gripped the shaft with both hands and broke it as swiftly as he could. Orim somehow did not cry out but he sagged backwards and might have fallen had Nasreen not grabbed him. He took a moment to recover himself.

'All right. Go.'

As they set off, Marik returned to the end of the path. There was a patch of undergrowth more accessible than the bindroot and here he set himself, down on one knee. The Rats were around two hundred feet away, running towards him. Some of Nasreen's arrows had been knocked around but Marik found three in good condition. He moved a couple of reeds aside, nocked an arrow and took aim. He wanted to be sure of hitting the lead man first time so waited until he was within a hundred feet.

It was not an accurate shot. Marik had been aiming at the centre of his chest but caught him in the groin. The man went face-first into the mud and did not get up. He was still shrieking when one of his compatriots was struck in the chest, the impact knocking him off his feet. Though he knew what kind of men these were, Marik did not enjoy seeing the results of his actions.

They were, however, effective. The two remaining Rats withdrew some distance before stopping to consider their wounded fellows, both of whom were clearly in a lot of pain.

Marik waited. It took a minute for one of them to summon the courage to advance towards the injured. Marik let him get halfway there before firing again. The shot missed by several feet but sent the mercenary scurrying away once more. Shouldering quiver and bow, Marik moved carefully back to the path, staying low so they had no clue he had retreated. Once there, he sprinted after the others.

Even though they had cleared a path the previous day, the trio did not move as quickly as Marik would have liked. Orim was doing his best but he continued to lose blood and grew weaker with every passing mile. For the first hour, fear drove them on. After that, all three began to trip and stumble and flag. It was Nasreen who realised they were at last approaching the channel and Marik went ahead, sword in hand. He half-expected a party of Rats to be there waiting for them but the area was quiet.

While the others recovered themselves, he listened intently but heard no suggestion that their pursuers were close. He pulled one canoe out of the bushes and dragged it down into the channel. Nasreen loaded the packs.

'We must assume they'll send people around by water, yes?'

She nodded. 'If they left quickly, they'll be at the Lake before us.'

'The Lake?'

'The open area of water we passed though. About an hour from here.'

'So, we're likely to run into them if we go back the way we came?'

'Yes.'

'And the other route runs into a dead end. Any suggestions?'

Still breathing heavily, Nasreen shook her head.

Orim placed a hand on Marik's arm. 'We won't make the Lake but we might make the Pool.'

'What's that?' Marik helped Orim into the canoe.

'An area of water where cobees live – birds. They can't fly so they have to build their nests low down.'

Marik wasn't sure this was the moment for a nature lesson but he listened as he and Nasreen climbed into the canoe. This end of the channel was so narrow that they could propel it along simply by levering the paddles against the bank.

'The nests attract srayls,' continued Orim, his voice strained. '*Lots* of srayls. Everybody avoids the area, including Reverrik's men.'

'How long to get there?'

'No more than half an hour. It's closed off but I'm sure we can find a way through.'

'Wait, I saw it on the way here. Barricaded by timber? Marked by a sign?'

'That's it. What do you think?'

'I think we have no choice.'

Once out of the channel, Marik and Nasreen powered the canoe along the waterway; silent as they poured every ounce of effort into reaching the Pool. Orim lay between them, initially keeping the bow at the ready but later unable to do so. Marik knew that every upward tilt of his head was due to a pulse of pain from his arm. He had no doubt that the arrow had struck veins and ligaments. Even assuming they could clean the wound out and bandage it quickly, poisoning was possible. Marik reckoned he would be lucky to keep the arm.

Every turn of the waterway threatened discovery but it was as empty as the previous day. At one point, a sudden disturbance from the reeds startled all three of them but turned out to be no more than a pair of warring birds. A few minutes later, Orim directed them towards an area of thin, flexible reads just short of the Pool's barricaded entrance. Marik and Nasreen were able to guide the canoe through without leaving an obvious trail and then paddle through to the open area behind the ramshackle wooden barrier.

The trees were unlike any Marik had previously seen in the delta. They grew directly out of the water and the fan-like growths just above the surface looked more like fungus than branches. Though they moved deeper into the Pool with great care, the trio disturbed several birds, some of which Orim identified as cobees. They were plump little creatures with dark plumage and orange beaks. Marik didn't waste any time looking for their nests; he was preoccupied by the water and half-expected to see a tentacle wrapped around his paddle every time he pulled it clear. Much of the surface was topped by clingy, green weed which offered further cover for any submerged predator.

They halted in open water about three hundred feet from the barrier and turned the canoe towards it. There was no question of approaching any of the trees for cover; Orim and Nasreen reacted with horror when Marik even suggested it.

With Nasreen keeping watch, he decided to deal with Orim's wound. It was immediately obvious to him that the arrow had taken some cloth in with it – another danger. The tip had not gone in far enough for him to push it all the way through. Removing it would be slow and incalculably painful. Though Nasreen had bandages, needle and thread in her pack, there was no wine or other alcohol to ease Orim's suffering. The poor man was lying at Marik's feet, eyes squeezed shut.

'Just do what you have to. I don't suppose you can knock me out?'

'I might hit you too hard, or not hard enough. Chances are, you'll faint anyway.'

Marik was not looking forward to the operation but blood and gore had never bothered him all that much – unless it was his. He had been taught how to tend wounds in the Guards, and though he lacked the skill and patience to be a surgeon, men in his troop had often asked for him to treat them if no professional was available. He'd been told it was because he was not overly rough but decisive and quick.

'I have coldthyme in my pack,' said Nasreen. 'It will help keep the wound clean.'

'Good. Can I borrow your knife? Mine's too wide.'

She took it from the sheath, cleaned it and handed it over.

'See anything?'

'No,' she replied. 'Shall we make for the hideout when it gets dark?'

'I reckon.'

Marik explained to Orim what he was about to do then set to it. Turning the arrow was the best way to check if the head was caught and, if possible, free it. As he began, Orim bit down on one of the pack straps to stop himself crying out. Ignoring the shaking and whimpering, Marik continued to twist the shaft and attempt to retract it. Orim lasted no more than a minute and Marik was glad when he fell unconscious.

He soon got the arrow to a position where it would move then widened the wound with Nasreen's knife. Inflicting more damage with the barbs was inevitable but he avoided slicing any more veins open and eventually managed to retract the whole arrow. Relieved to see that the head was intact, he threw the bloodied projectile over the side and inspected the wound. It was a deep hole, not too wide but not yet ready to stitch. Thankfully the piece of cloth was visible and though tweezers would have made the task easier, Marik was eventually able to extract it with the knife. He cleaned the wound as best he could with water then added the coldthyme – a dry, reddish substance – and bandaged it.

'Good work,' said Nasreen.

'Time will tell.' Marik cleaned her blade off then returned it to her.

Orim woke up not long after. As he was thanking Marik, Nasreen put up a hand. From that distance, they could not see a great deal through the barricade but Marik spotted a canoe on the move, heading towards where they had landed. Shortly after he saw another.

'Two?'

'Three,' said Nasreen.

Though the Rats were soon out of sight, it took some time for the tension to fade. Marik glanced around at the weed-covered water and the trees, convinced that numerous srayls were watching their little vessel, ready to fly up from the depths and strike.

Orim let out a long breath, then propped himself up against the side of the canoe. 'You weren't wounded?'

'No,' replied Marik.

'You said Hammerhand killed Slicer. What exactly happened?'

'It was all over very quickly. He wouldn't have suffered.'

Orim turned to Nasreen. 'I wonder if Garrun will blame us. What do you think he'll do?'

She shrugged and kept her eyes on the barricade.

'I misjudged Slicer,' said Marik. 'He was a skilled warrior. Brave too.'

With a last wary look at the water, he leant back against the stern of the canoe and folded his arms across his chest.

'Are you going to sleep?' asked a clearly surprised Orim.

Marik's eyes were already shut. 'I'm going to try.'

Chapter Eighteen

If daytime in the Pool was unsettling, night was nothing less than horrible. The srayls were more active in the hours of darkness and more than once Marik heard the dying cries of a cobee as it was dragged into the water. He also embarrassed himself by reporting an impact on the canoe that turned out to be the rope tied to the bow. He'd hoped and expected that they would be able to leave as soon as night fell but three more times the Rats passed, lanterns alight. The trio took the canoe close to the barricades and spied the grim, determined faces of their foes. One group was in a skiff, the others in several canoes of their own. Only when two hours elapsed without a sighting did they feel safe to leave the Pool. But any sense of relief was immediately forgotten during the tense journey to the Lake; and here they saw another patrol, this one fortunately moving away from them. With so many hours of rest, Marik and Nasreen were at least able to move the canoe along quickly and Orim complimented Marik on the progress he'd made with the paddle. Marik in turn praised Nasreen's navigational skills; she guided them back to the hidden entrance with ease. Even so, dawn was close when they finally dragged their aching bodies into the reed-house. Realising that the strain of the last day was swiftly catching up with him, Marik said nothing to Garrun and the other rebels. Leaving Nasreen and Orim to explain what had happened, he took himself off to a corner and lay down to sleep.

'You! Hey, you. Wake up!'
This last instruction was accompanied by a kick to Marik's shin. He always slept with one hand on whatever weapon he had with him – in this case Orim's knife. Within seconds he was on his feet, blade aimed at his assailant. The burly, sneering man before him wore the same green as the other rebels but was not familiar to Marik. He was thick-necked and stocky, his lumpen face made uglier by a blunt nose.
'Well at least you're up now.' The man didn't seem all that concerned that Marik was about a foot taller than him. With the knife aimed at him, his hand was now upon his sword-hilt.
Marik told himself to stay calm. 'You could have tried 'good morning'.'

'It's not though, is it? It's the worst we've had in a long time.'

Marik looked around. Orim, Nasreen, Parrs and Garrun were watching, as were about fifteen others, several of them also new faces.

'That's not my fault.'

'Seems to me it is.' The man nodded at Orim. 'Yours and *his*.' The voluble rebel stepped forward, so that there were no more than a few inches between them.

'Get out of my face,' said Marik, already considering the non-lethal alternatives for dealing with this idiot.

'Or?'

'Or I'll embarrass you in front of your friends then throw you in the water.'

The man held his stare and muttered bitter curses in his own language before turning away.

Young Parrs spoke up. 'You'll have to forgive Dalkus. We … it's hard to believe Slicer's dead. It's true, you fought Hammerhand?'

'Didn't just fight him,' said Nasreen. 'Put him down.'

Marik hadn't realised she had seen that. Her comment drew the attention of all those present, even Dalkus.

'He will be angry,' said Garrun. The white-haired leader appeared even more hunched than usual, as if Slicer's death had added to his burden.

'Oh, he's angry,' replied Marik. 'Then again, I would be too if someone stuck a knife in my eye.'

Dalkus stalked back towards him. Despite his dark colouring, his face was growing red. 'You think this is funny?'

Marik shrugged. He hadn't anticipated having to have this discussion so soon but it was quite clear to him that the best – possibly only – chance of freeing Orim's daughter was a full-scale attack on the island. He didn't particularly want to take charge but he was sure the rebels would stand a better chance with his help than without.

'Reverrik will be angry too,' added Garrun.

'Also true,' said Marik. 'All the more reason to strike quickly.'

'Slicer was the best of us,' said Dalkus. 'Now he's gone. And for what?'

As the man was now at least sounding reasonable, Marik decided he could too. 'Your friend had his doubts, but it seemed to me that he thought an attack might work, that defeating the Rats *is* possible.' He looked to his two companions. 'Am I right?'

Nasreen and Orim both nodded.

Marik continued: 'It was just bad bloody luck that we ran into Hammerhand. But when it came to it, Slicer didn't hesitate. The odds were against him, as they are against you. That didn't stop him. If he was the best of you, maybe you'll honour him. Maybe you'll follow his example.'

Noble words; but an hour later, Marik wasn't sure he should have said them. Despite the evident doubts of Garrun and Dalkus, the rebels had suggested a formal meeting and they clearly expected him to contribute. Once Orim's wound had been re-bandaged by Nasreen, he came and sat by Marik, who was currently occupied with breakfast: stale bread, dried fruit and some very weak wine.

'How are you doing?'

'Sore. She said the wound still looks clean at least.'

Nasreen had also added a sling to immobilise the arm.

'That's what counts,' said Marik. 'Don't get your hopes up. You won't be able to use it for weeks, maybe months.'

'I know. Marik, you spoke well. And they are not only upset about Slicer's death, but *angry*.' Orim lowered his voice. 'We can use that.'

Marik just chewed his bread.

'What's wrong? You seemed so sure of yourself earlier.'

'I must remind myself not to make speeches when I've just woken up.' Marik also kept his voice low. 'Orim, I said I would help you, and I believe this is probably the only way to get Korina out, but what if it all goes wrong? What if they do agree to attack but it fails? Reverrik will still be in charge and this lot will have died for nothing.'

'Then we have to make sure it doesn't fail.'

Marik looked down at the green water below his feet.

'Right is on our side,' added Orim.

'That doesn't mean we'll win.'

The table had been moved aside and the rebels stood in a circle. While Garrun first spoke in the local language, Marik counted the rebels: twenty-one. There were precious few with the experience and presence of Slicer and even the aggressive Dalkus looked more like a farmer than a warrior. Marik had already resolved to ask several questions before he offered any answers. For the sake of his own conscience and the rebels' sense of themselves, the decision had to be theirs.

'Well then,' said Dalkus, turning to Marik, 'what exactly do you propose?'

'Nothing yet. I need certain guarantees before I propose anything.'

Garrun ran his fingers through his snowy beard. 'Such as?'

'Fifty fighting men. That is a minimum.'

Nasreen cleared her throat and tapped her bow against the floor.

'Sorry,' added Marik. 'Fifty fighting men or any woman that can fight like Nasreen. They will need to follow orders without hesitation and kill without mercy. Without this, any further discussion is a waste of time.'

Garrun translated for those who did not speak Common. A protracted discussion ensued, in which just about everyone was consulted. The leader himself didn't contribute much and it was Dalkus who finally addressed Marik.

'We believe that's possible.'

'You will have to *make* it possible.'

'If you tell us what exactly you're planning, we might be able to persuade people that it has a chance of success.'

'If I tell you *exactly* what I'm planning, everyone here knows. As soon as you start to try and recruit people, all *those* people know. By the following day, half the population of the delta will know.'

'Including Reverrik,' added Parrs.

'Exactly,' said Marik. 'If what I say now convinces you, I will share the specific details with Garrun.'

'And Dalkus,' said Garrun. 'He has been elected to lead with me.'

'Very well. You must understand the importance of security – who knows what. I can assure you that when the moment comes, every one will know what they need to.'

Parrs spoke up again. 'Marik was a soldier. He fought with the People's Guard in the Southern Province of …'

'Lothlagen,' said Marik. 'For ten years.'

'A *professional* soldier,' added Orim.

'What *can* you tell us now?' demanded Dalkus.

'I learned a lot from what I observed and what I was told by Nasreen. I have a basic plan for assaulting Old Island.' This wasn't entirely true but it seemed like the sort of thing his audience wanted to hear.

'There are certain occasions when Reverrik and his forces are vulnerable. That is when we will strike. I believe I might also have a method for disabling a majority of his mercenaries *before* we have to fight them.'

'*Might?*' repeated Dalkus.

'There are very few certainties in battle. And things rarely go to plan. That is why we must also rely on surprise and speed.' Marik thought it wise to add at least one specific suggestion. 'Reverrik's prisoners are kept in a pit near one end of the island. If we can free these men and arm them, they can add to our force.'

Garrun weighed in: 'We barely have enough arms for ourselves.'

'I rely on you to round up every single weapon you can. Another point to consider is targeting Reverrik's armoury.'

Several hushed discussions broke out.

'And what about Hammerhand?' said Dalkus.

Marik reckoned he had been fortunate to survive one encounter with the Easterling and he was not planning to risk another but he knew when the time was right for a bit of fighting talk. In the minds of these people, the giant had become a symbol of Reverrik's invulnerability; and the impossibility of their struggle.

'Well, I've already blinded the bastard,' he said with a grin. 'Looking forward to finishing him off.'

Even Dalkus seemed to like that one.

Everyone at the reed-house seemed to have a job. Some were preparing a newly-caught haul of fish; others – Garrun and Dalkus included – were discussing who they might recruit and how best to approach them. Several were working on bows and arrows and Marik was glad to see baskets full of well-made bolts. There was a lack of melee weapons, however: other than the stolen swords, most were hatchets. Neither metal nor suitable wood was in abundance within the delta and there was now little time to find new arms.

Upon asking to see all their weaponry, Marik was shown a supply of rudimentary spears. Strong, sharpened flints were bound to the shafts but without glue to reinforce the lashings. They were more than adequate for spearing fish but wouldn't last long against a shield or a blade. After a long discussion with Orim and Parrs, Marik established that they had some appropriate ingredients and after a bit of experimentation he came up with a glue-like mixture that would do the job. Despite the odd coughing fit, young Parrs seemed to have recovered himself and listened attentively as Marik showed he and some others how best to use the spears against their foes. Parrs was considerably bigger than most of the others and favoured a sleeveless tunic that showed off a powerful pair of arms.

At one point, Marik found himself alone with a small man who had barely uttered a word. The rebel was barefoot and clad in threadbare green, his thick fringe almost covering his eyes. 'You blinded him? Really?'

Marik nodded as he wrapped rope around the shaft of a spear to improve grip.

'He killed my brother.'

Marik stopped working but the man continued sharpening a flint.

'We had nothing to give them. An example to others. His men held me back while they did it. Strangled him with one hand – Hammerhand seemed proud of that.' The rebel didn't look up once as he continued speaking. 'My brother – the look in his eyes. Always with me. Can't forget it. Maybe if we win. Maybe if Hammerhand dies. Maybe then.'

Later, Marik made another useful discovery in a box full of random supplies. The locals favoured their homemade sandals but here were several pairs of leather boots, one just large enough to accommodate his sizeable feet. He also located some mismatched socks and – once again dressed like a Souther – knew he would move and fight better.

Marik's doubts resurfaced regularly and he wondered if Garrun had been right in what he said during their first discussion; that the rebels should wait to gather strength before attacking. But Parrs and many of the others seemed glad that decisive action was to come. They felt that there was no sense in waiting; those prepared to fight were few in number but as willing as the rebels. It was only their families that had prevented them joining the others at their hidden base.

As arranged, Marik later met with Garrun and Dalkus alone. Here he outlined the details of his plan, including the timing. Garrun suggested that Reverrik might cancel the celebration in light of the incident with Hammerhand but Dalkus was not convinced.

'Nothing we've done has worried him so far.' The man seemed quick-tempered but Marik was glad to see he had overcome his initial anger at Slicer's death.

'Nobody hurt Hammerhand before,' countered Garrun. 'We know there are more patrols out. The Easterling won't rest until he's had his revenge.'

Marik said, 'Let's see what we can learn but it seems this ceremony is important to the man. If he's as complacent as he appears, I believe he'll go ahead.'

They had already agreed that no one would be sent out in daylight hours. Once darkness came, small, specially-selected teams would be despatched to communicate with their allies and return with responses before dawn. Dalkus already had a suggestion regarding a location for the attacking force to gather: he and Slicer had previously identified a channel that emerged close to the main approach to Old Island. It could be accessed by carrying canoes overland. This would require clearing and another team would be despatched the night before to ensure the larger force could use the route.

The three then discussed how they would take care of the waterborne sentries. Marik intended to be on Old Island long before that and the next step involved the coordination of several elements. Timing would be crucial.

By the end of the discussion, he was glad that both leaders had contributed. Garrun clearly still had his doubts while Dalkus seemed determined to wreak revenge. Marik felt it important to reiterate one particular point.

'You may be tempted to pass some or all of this on to your people. I beg you not to. We are not asking most of them to do anything that requires a lot of preparation. They will get their orders on the night. It's actually better that they don't know exactly what they must do. They will worry less.'

Garrun shook his head. 'Worry? I should prefer to call it fear.'

Dalkus drew in a long breath. 'We will spill their blood as they have spilled ours. They will be the ones to suffer now.'

'That's the spirit,' said Marik. 'And, Garrun, you must show it too - whether you believe it or not.'

Garrun looked across at the hard-working rebels.

Dalkus turned to Marik. 'Need anything else?'

'Not from you.'

Four canoes left at dusk. Having been giving the all-clear by sentries watching the waterway, they set off in the same direction but split up soon after. While the others carried out their recruitment missions, Marik and Nasreen were headed for Spring Island, a journey that would take at least three hours. Marik planned to use the following day to achieve what he needed to before they returned to the hideout.

He had asked Nasreen to accompany him for two reasons. Firstly, she had proven herself calm under pressure and an excellent shot. Secondly – and as importantly – the pair of them had a better chance of bluffing their way past any Rats than Marik and one of the male rebels. Nasreen had immediately agreed to help and seemed to take a certain pride in her contention that her former captors would not believe she was now fighting against them. Her head wound had been stitched and she seemed as keen as Marik to get out of the crowded hideout.

The pair worked well together in the canoe. Marik concentrated on providing the power while Nasreen would steer and keep lookout. They communicated only when necessary. For his part, Marik admired not only the woman's strength of character but her concentration. He had not met many men who could have guided the way with such composure and calm.

They sighted the Rats twice. On the first occasion, it was a large rowing boat with lanterns at the stern and bow. Marik and Nasreen simply reversed course and she found another way past them. Later they almost rowed straight into a pair of the mercenaries. The Rats were in a canoe themselves, also with no light. It was Nasreen who saw them coming and only a last-minute diversion towards the bank saved them. An overheard conversation confirmed they were Reverrik's men.

'Well spotted,' breathed Marik when he was sure they were clear.

Nasreen laid down her bow and continued paddling without a word.

She did not speak until they reached Spring Island. It was not an area she knew well but between them they located a quiet cove in which to land. From there, they carried the canoe into a nearby copse to see out the night.

'Is it far from here?'

'No,' replied Marik as he laid out his blanket. In fact, he couldn't be entirely sure until he saw this side of the island in daylight. He hadn't explained to Nasreen exactly what they were doing, only that it was an essential task ahead of the attack. He was grateful for her trust, and he reckoned a good part of that was due to what she'd seen of the fight with Hammerhand.

Orim had provided them both with some food before they left and they ate it in silence. Nasreen had made her bed on the other side of the canoe and could soon be heard settling down.

'How's the head?'

'Can't feel it.'

Marik doubted that was true. Moonlight penetrated the copse and he could see Nasreen lying against her pack, looking up at the sky.

'Where are your family? Will any of them fight?'

She didn't reply.

With a shrug, Marik lay down on the blanket, wrapping the spare material around him. Above, the Red Moon was vivid and almost full, the near-circle divided by the branches of the trees above. Marik's eyes drifted from one black line to the other and he was almost asleep when Nasreen finally answered.

'I've not been home. I don't know.'

Marik could think of at least two reasons why she might not wish to seek out her loved ones.

'What will you do afterward? If we defeat them?'

'I don't think past it,' she said quietly. 'What about you? What are you doing so far from home anyway?'

'Long story.'

'I'm not going anywhere.'

'Long story I don't want to tell.'

Again, a long pause, then Nasreen spoke once more. 'Reverrik won't cancel the celebration. He enjoys it too much.'

'That's what I'm counting on.'

'Marik, if it comes to it, if you get him - leave him alive. Leave him for me.'

Chapter Nineteen

With the canoe well hidden, they rose before dawn and made their way along the shore. Marik soon recognised the area and hurried to Ava's door. He was glad to see no one else around and hoped it was too early for her to have left. There was a long delay after he knocked but he was relieved when the door finally opened.

Ava eyed him suspiciously before speaking. 'Didn't expect to see you again.'

Marik did his best to be charming. 'Well, it's a pleasure to see you, Ava. This is Nasreen, a friend. We're here about an important matter. *Very* important. May we come in?'

Ava opened the door fully but did not move aside. 'Forgive me, Nasreen, but I must ask if your affliction is roundflesh or-'

'-It's round*mark*. It can only be caught through-'

'-Through close contact. I understand. Please, come in.'

Five minutes later, Marik was back sitting on Ava's bench, this time alongside Nasreen. Both of them had been given a mug of leaf-tea to drink. Marik wasn't all that fond of the smell but found the liquid quite refreshing. Ava had remained quiet while preparing the tea but now sat opposite them with her own mug.

'This 'important matter'. Is it to do with the Rats?'

'It is.'

Ava turned to the younger woman. 'You were on the island?'

Nasreen was sitting stiffly on the bench, both hands on the bow between her legs. She didn't answer.

'One of them infected you so they cast you out.'

Nasreen nodded.

'I'm told it's very painful, especially around the mouth and nose. I can give you something for it.'

Nasreen looked away. It seemed to Marik that the woman was so used to cruelty and loneliness that it was now kindness that upset her. He thought it best to move the conversation on.

'I must apologise,' he told Ava, 'for lying to you. I – we – are going to try to rescue not only Orim's daughter but all the others held by Reverrik. I know you may think the idea foolish but I am here to ask for your help.'

Marik felt he'd learned enough about Ava to know that money wouldn't persuade her. His job was to convince her to do her part for the delta.

'Is that why you brought Nasreen? To appeal to my better instincts.'

It was in fact only one reason. 'No. Nasreen is here to protect me. She's very handy with that bow.'

Ava glanced towards the window. 'I saw two patrols yesterday – more than the entire previous week. You should be very careful.'

'We won't be here any longer than necessary.'

Ava ran a finger along one of the many coloured threads in her hair. 'What do you need?'

'Poison. It needn't be lethal but something quick-acting that can be put into kegs of ale. Is that possible?'

She shook her head. 'I should have sent you on your way. What if your attack fails? It won't take them long to work out who made the poison. They'll string me up.'

'It *won't* fail,' said Nasreen. 'Marik blinded Hammerhand. He's a good leader.'

'I'm afraid I don't share your confidence in his abilities. You do know there are more than a hundred of them?'

'There are many of us,' countered Nasreen, causing Marik to hold up his hand. He didn't want her mentioning the hideout to anyone.

'You spend your life helping others,' he told Ava. 'I don't believe you'll ignore your own people now. At least tell me if it's possible.'

'How many kegs?'

'I don't know. Five, ten.'

'Liquids are very unpredictable. I can guarantee nothing.'

'I am not depending solely on this. But I am taking several measures to try and tip the balance in our favour. This is one.'

'I do not have any poisons in sufficient volume. What we do have here on Spring are akiva trees.'

'The berries,' said Nasreen with a knowing nod.

'Yes. If concentrated, the syrup causes nausea and vomiting. It is not long-lasting but those who ingest it will be weak for several hours. Also, there is no strong taste. But in order for it to be powerful enough, we will need a lot. Two baskets of berries at least, I should think.'

'There's nothing more powerful?' asked Marik. 'I don't care if it cripples the bastards.'

'Nothing I can prepare quickly and in sufficient volume. Assuming the ale doesn't negate its properties, it should do the job. They will barely be able to stand, let alone fight.'

'I take it that means you'll do it?'

Ava walked over to a corner and fetched two baskets. She handed them to Nasreen. 'You know what they look like? The twisted trunk and the dotted leaves? Follow the shore for a quarter-mile then turn inland at the third stream. You'll find them. Take only those that have more orange upon them than green.'

Nasreen looked at Marik, who shrugged.

'What am I doing?'

'Whatever I tell you to.'

Ten minutes later, Marik found himself in the second room at the rear of the house. Ava closed the door behind her and walked over to him.

'I suppose I am no better than the Rats – taking what I want because I have power over you.'

By now, Marik understood what she expected of him in return for her help. 'You're assuming I'm unwilling.'

She smiled and ran her hands over his chest and shoulders. Marik still could not say she was pretty but there was a warmth to her and his body was already responding to her touch. He kissed her on the cheek, then the mouth. Ava pulled herself against him, running her hands inside his tunic and up his back. She sighed. It had been so long that Marik would have been quite happy to just keep kissing but she led him over to the bed. Ava took her dress off over her head and lay down, naked. Marik had not been with a middle-aged woman before and he had to admire her brazen courage. Her body was lined and a little heavy but generously proportioned and undeniably appealing. He removed his boots, trousers and tunic.

She examined him for some time before speaking. 'Even more impressive in the flesh. But even big, handsome men sometimes disappoint. You won't disappoint me, will you, Marik? A successful transaction depends on two satisfied parties.'

'I've not had many complaints.'

Bold talk – but in fact he was out of practise and knew he would have to take this slowly to avoid a swift conclusion. He lay down on the bed beside her. His kisses moved from her mouth to her neck to her chest and she sighed again.

By the time Nasreen returned, Marik was dressed and awaiting her outside. A few minutes earlier, Ava had washed them both down from a barrel of scented water. If she was dissatisfied with the transaction she hadn't said so. As for Marik, he had not enjoyed himself so much in months. Before leaving the back room, they had kissed again and embraced for some time.

If the attack went badly, Marik was glad to have experienced such a pleasure. He told Ava that – in other circumstances – he would quite happily have stayed with her a good while longer. She laughed this off but her tone changed abruptly when she warned him once again about underestimating Reverrik. She did not know of Marik's debt to Orim and told him that he should not throw his life away for a fight that was not his.

Nasreen had filled both baskets with berries and Ava instantly set them to work. Marik's job was to remove any remaining leaves and stems and then pass them on to Nasreen. Her task was to crush the berries, sieve the liquid and pass the juice on to Ava. The last stage involved adding two more herbs, one that would help preserve the mixture, another that would augment the poison. After a solid two hours of labour, Ava filled two clay flasks and informed Marik that the poison would be useless within a week.

It was almost midday when she moved on to creating the treatment for Nasreen's skin. The girl protested that it was not necessary but Ava insisted and Marik reminded her that they could not in any case leave Spring Island before nightfall. As the two discussed the condition, he felt a new degree of sympathy. Nasreen was only twenty-one and had arguably suffered even more than the girls still stuck on Old Island. By this point, Marik was not in need of motivation to take on the Rats but if ridding the delta of them gave Nasreen some comfort, all the better.

He took himself outside to get some air and was halfway to the shore when he heard voices. Easing himself into the cover offered by a nearby tree, he turned and saw two men approaching from the path that led to Ettwater. Thankful that he had thought to hang his sword from his belt before leaving, Marik appraised the pair. They did not look like locals: in fact, they had the solid frames and round features of Easterlings. But they couldn't be Rats because they were unarmed. In fact, one was barefoot and – as they got closer – Marik saw that their clothes were dirty and torn. They appeared to have nothing.

As they neared the house, Marik stayed low and crept around to the back. By the time he'd slid up to the corner to listen in, Ava had opened the door. Marik hoped Nasreen would stay hidden and not get involved.

'Morning,' said one of the men in Common. 'We heard you're a healer?'
'Yes.'

'We've got a couple of friends who've picked up some kind of pox – scabs on the inside of their noses. The itching's driving them mad and their complaining is driving us *all* mad.'

'Have you been near the mudflats?' asked Ava politely.

'Walked right through them. That's the cause then?'

'Almost certainly. There are mites in the mud that carry the pox.'

'Have you got anything for it?'

'Yes. It won't cure it but it'll ease the itching. If the men stay clean, the scabs will disappear after a few weeks. One copper and I'll give you enough for both of them.'

The same man continued talking: 'Thing is, we haven't got any money on account of some recent bad luck. Don't suppose you could just give it to us?'

'If I start giving everything away, I won't have any money to live.'

The second man spoke up. 'One little thing we're asking for. And you must admit we've asked nicely. We can always take it, you know.'

Concerned that Nasreen might step in, Marik walked around the corner. He leaned against the wall but made sure they could see his sword.

'Morning, gentlemen.'

The two turned to him and moved slightly apart, clearly ready to fight if need be. One was a bald fellow with thick hair sprouting from his grimy shirt. The other was younger, sleeves rolled up to show prominent muscles. Now closer, Marik could see that both had tattoos upon their heads and necks. He spied maps and other images that reminded him of the crew from the *White Cloud*.

Sailors. Marik thought instantly of the vessel he and Orim had seen from Northcrest beach.

'Fortunately for you, I have a little credit here.'

Ava rolled her eyes at this but Marik pressed on.

'I'll happily fund the treatment in return for some information.'

The pair looked at each other and shrugged.

'How did you end up here?'

'Long story,' said the bald man.

'I saw a ship close in to the shore nine days ago. Did you come from there?'

'We did. She's called *Blue Trident*.'

'You were wrecked?'

'I wish,' said the bald man. 'We were carrying a cargo of slaves down South. The bastards revolted.'

The other man spat.

'Killed half the crew. Only thirteen of us made it to shore. We've been heading inland ever since. Isn't much of anything around here, is there?'

'You're Easterlings – heading that way?'

'Not sure. We've got nothing, not a single coin between us. If not for the villagers we would have gone hungry again last night.'

'Thirteen men, you say?'

'Well, twelve men and the captain.'

'Ah.'

'Captain Vasvarro,' added the younger man. 'You've probably heard of him.'

'Can't say I have. But perhaps we should meet.'

Ava soon prepared a jar of ointment for the sailors and then returned to work on Nasreen's treatment. Marik reminded Nasreen to stay hidden if anyone else came to visit, then set off for Ettwater with the sailors. It was without doubt another risk but he felt it worthwhile. Largely to avoid revealing too much about himself, he fired questions at the pair, both of whom seemed utterly dejected and angry at their fate. Marik also didn't share his view; that as slavers they were entirely deserving of that fate.

They arrived in Ettwater to find a scene of chaos that at least distracted attention from Marik's return. It seemed that one of the sailors had stolen something and now most of his compatriots and half the village were involved. While the argument raged in the muddy centre, Marik observed two other sailors calmly working on a roof nearby. They were being supervised by a local woman and Marik learned that they had exchanged their labour and expertise for provisions. He did not see Yorrit, Orim's friend, but did recognise some other faces. The argument showed no signs of dying down but at least no blows had been struck.

'Where's the captain then?'

'Right there,' said one of the sailors.

A man wearing only trousers marched across the mud towards the fray. He was not large but carried himself with the confident air of a leader. He had a great hook of a nose and dark, deep-set eyes. Upon his head were no tattoos, just a thin covering of fine, grey hair. He burrowed his way straight through the crowd and dragged out the man at the centre of it all, even though the sailor was loudly proclaiming his innocence. The villagers tried to approach but a hand from the captain was sufficient to halt them.

'*Did* you take the wine?'

'No, captain. I swear it – on my daughter's life.'

'Do you offer the truth before the ever-watchful eyes of Azreyel?'

The man hesitated then looked at the sky. 'I cannot. It is true. I took the wine. I-'

The captain turned to the villagers.

'Whose wine was it?'

A middle-aged woman raised her hand.

'I apologise. This is no way to repay those who have shown us kindness. We have nothing to offer for you but this man will work for you until we leave. Give him any task you wish and do not worry that he will steal anything else – if he does, I will cut his throat.'

The woman didn't seem entirely happy with this resolution. A few others voiced their complaints.

'We will be leaving tomorrow,' added the captain.

His words seemed to appease some of the locals.

The thief obediently followed his victim towards her dwelling, head bowed.

The captain noticed the three watchers and walked over. Now he was closer, Marik saw the green colouring on his hands. He knew that many Easterlings – slavers, in particular – were followers of Azreyel. Their religion held that he had become a god by conquering the entire world in an earlier age. Among his many possessions had been slaves, and so his followers also believed slavery to be an acceptable practice. They did not conduct war or conquest but every moment of their lives was devoted to the enrichment of themselves, their families and fellow believers. Green was the colour associated with Azreyel and the ink upon their hands was a permanent reminder of his presence and their obligations to him.

Vasvarro looked Marik over. 'I'd take a guess you're not from around here.'

'True. Do you have a moment? I have a proposal for you.'

'You'll have to forgive my appearance, I have only one shirt and it is currently drying.' At Marik's request, Captain Vasvarro had followed him to the rear of a disused house so that they might speak in private. Vasvarro leaned back against a wall and flicked a hand at an insect. He was short and slender with not an ounce of fat upon his body.

'Not at all,' said Marik. 'I hear you've had some bad luck of late.'

'Something of an understatement. I have lost my ship, most of my crew and a hundred head of slaves.' Vasvarro scratched one of his protruding ribs. 'I was too soft, you see. There was very little wind so I allowed them on deck for some air. Somehow, one crafty swine picked the lock on the chain connecting them. They ignored the rest of us, went straight for my key-master. Cost them a few lives but once they had the keys and freed the others, we didn't have a chance.'

'I'm surprised they left you alive.'

'They didn't. While we were fighting, no one was in control of the ship so we drifted towards shore. My men held them off as long as they could. When we were close enough to jump, we did.'

'You're heading back east?'

'No. Once I have … once I am able to, I will reclaim my ship and have my vengeance. It might take months, it might take years but I will not stop until I am at the wheel of the *Blue Trident* again, preferably with those thieving dogs hanging from my yards.'

'I don't doubt it.'

'Anyway, this offer of yours?'

'I need fighting men. It will not be an easy fight but, if victorious, there are great prizes to be had.'

'Such as?'

'Slaves.'

'How many?'

'As many as you want.'

'You work for the mercenary? The one they call Reverrik?'

'No.'

'Against him then?'

Marik raised an eyebrow. It was of course possible that Vasvarro might turn traitor and sell him out to Reverrik. But in a scrap, each of the sailors might be worth two of the inexperienced rebels. They were tough, desperate men with nothing to lose. They might make the difference.

'What exactly would we have to do?' asked Vasvarro.

'Be ready. Be ready when I come to get you. One night. One fight.'

'When?'

'Soon.'

Vasvarro made fists with his hands and bumped them together. 'Weapons?'

'Will be provided.'

'I don't know. My men have been through a lot.'

'There's something else. A ship – a twelve-oar coaster. All yours.'

Vasvarro now looked considerably more interested. 'Let's … assume that we're talking about Reverrik. I'm led to believe he's taken money off the locals too.'

'I believe so, though I'm not sure there was ever that much here to start with.'

Vasvarro scratched another rib. 'I want the ship and thirty slaves – any more is too many for us to handle. And I want half of any treasure. In return for that, my men and I will fight for you. By Azreyel, I pledge it.'

'The ship, thirty slaves and a *quarter* of the treasure.'

'Can we settle on one third?' Captain Vasvarro offered his hand.

Marik shook it. 'All I ask is that you be ready. Day or night. It won't be long.'

'Understood. Might I ask, Marik, what your interest is in all of this?'

'I wish to see justice done.'

'A noble sentiment. I thought perhaps it was just because you wanted to fight. That is what you Southers love above all else, isn't it?'

Marik did not intend rising to the provocation. 'One last thing, captain. It would not surprise me if a man in your position were tempted to go to Reverrik. We both know he might reward you for useful information.'

'The thought had never even entered my mind,' replied Vasvarro with a lop-sided smile.

'I would make two points for you to consider: one, if you side with him, you won't get the ship.'

The Easterling conceded with a nod.

'Two – remember how you told me you will hunt down your enemies and take revenge – even if it takes years?'

'Point taken.'

The first half of the return journey went well. Though Nasreen clearly did not approve of Marik's deal with Vasvarro – and told him that none of the other rebels would – she retained her usual concentration to guide them back across the darkened delta. Before the Lake they spied only a pair of fishermen who they gave a wide berth. But once across the open water and approaching the route that led to the hideout, they found their path blocked.

As soon as Nasreen stopped paddling, Marik knew to do the same. They drifted slowly on and he studied the gloom ahead. Between the high banks of reed on either side of the channel were several dim silhouettes: a large rowing boat and at least three manned canoes. The Rats had no lanterns lit and were waiting in silence.

Marik and Nasreen were close to the middle of the Lake, perhaps a hundred feet from the blockade. As there was no channel behind them, they would not be silhouetted like their enemy, or so Marik hoped. He had already hunched down low and pulled up his hood. At this distance, only their eyes might give them away.

'Back,' whispered Nasreen.

Using gentle strokes, they reversed the canoe across the Lake. Constantly aware of their background, Nasreen guided them to a nearby islet, where they found adequate cover beside a bank of malodorous mud. Marik had learned to wait for her to survey every new area with eyes and ears before talking to her.

'Not good.'

'I've seen this before. They used to do it quite often.'

'Probably looking for me.'

'What if they stay there all night? Do you think they know about the hideout? They might have found it already.' Nasreen sounded unusually anxious.

'How many waterways lead off the Lake?'

'Four main ones.'

'So, it could simply be guesswork? A coincidence?'

'They used to change the location, hope to catch someone unawares.'

'Then there's no need to panic. Probably only the fourth or fifth hour of night. Let's wait and see.'

An hour passed. Two. Marik's eyes became so tired and sore from staring into the darkness that he could no longer make out the blockade. They heard the occasional snatch of conversation but the Rats seemed determined to guard the waterway and see out the night. Marik reached into his pack and took out the last of his food, some dried fish.

'Nasreen, you hungry?'

'No.'

Like Marik, she was lying low in the canoe, hood over her face. She had tied the bow-rope to a nearby root, which was sufficient to hold them in place.

'Is there anyway to get around them? On land?'

'It would take hours.'

'We may not have any choice.'

'They've clearly been told to guard it. What if they've found the hideout?'

'Calm down.'

But Marik knew Nasreen could be right. He also knew that he had already been away too long. Dalkus seemed to have been won over but if the reluctant Garrun had the inclination and time to work on his compatriots, he might easily persuade them to take a different course.

'I think they're moving.'

Marik put the piece of fish down and sat up higher, trying to blink away the tiredness. 'All of them?'

'Not sure. But I can hear the oars from the boat.'

Only now did Marik see the traces of movement against the paler background of the channel. Then he too could hear the splashes of the oars.

'Marik, they're coming towards us.'

'Directly?'

'Not sure. Close.'

He was unsure what to do: move and they risked exposing themselves; stay and the Rats might row right into them.

'Would they come to the islet?'

'I don't see why.'

'We sit tight.'

'Looks like they're heading for the Ett Channel. It will be close.'

Marik didn't answer because something had just brushed against his leg. That something was wet and heavy and behaved in an extremely odd way. It seemed to have come from his left and was now moving over his knee. And the strange feeling was not just due to the weight or the cold of the water; it felt as if dozens of little fingers were poking at his skin. His pulled his knife from the sheath on his belt.

By now the weight of the tentacle was tilting the canoe towards the shore.

'What are you doing?' hissed Nasreen.

'Srayl.'

She spun with such speed that the canoe rocked. This seemed to have no effect on the tentacle which now slid onto Marik's right thigh and encircled it. Even though it seemed to be exploring rather than attacking, Marik could feel the strength of the creature.

'I have my knife.'

'Don't. It will fight back.'

The rhythmic splashes of the rowing-boat oars were now quite loud and Marik could see one man standing up at the stern. They were not heading for the islet but they would indeed pass close.

'Do you have any food?' suggested Nasreen.

'I think it's already taken it.'

'Try to stay calm. They don't always attack.'

She turned towards the boat, watching from beneath her hood as it approached.

Marik almost screamed when a second tentacle slid over his left shoulder and under his arm pit. He shivered; and both tentacles stiffened, as if ready to drag him into the water. Marik tightened his grip on the dagger hilt. If it took him down, he wouldn't go without a fight.

Whistling. Someone – perhaps the helmsman – was whistling. The boat drew level with the canoe, no more than thirty feet away, oars squeaking in their mountings. In trying not to shiver again, Marik did exactly that. Again, the creature gripped harder and this time it tried to pull him. But Marik had wedged his feet against the sides of the canoe and he did not move.

The second tentacle came up over his chest, the suckers pulling at his tunic. Certain that he was being sized up, Marik raised his arm to keep it free. Regardless of the nearby enemy, he was ready to stab the thing.

He could smell it; a rotten, bitter smell that only added to the revulsion. *Don't move. Do not move.*

He heard one of the Rats shout something. The sound seemed a long way away.

'We're clear,' said Nasreen. 'Are you all right?'

'Are you *serious*?'

'I've undone the rope so we can move clear,' she said, her voice determined. 'I can hit this tentacle. Can you hit that one?'

'You said it will fight back.'

'Not if we both hit it and get away quickly. Don't cut. Stab. Ready?'

Marik shifted so that he could strike the tentacle where it came over the side of the canoe. 'Ready. Don't stab me.'

'I won't. On three. One, two, three.'

Marik came down hard enough to send the blade right through the tentacle. It whipped away with such force that the knife was torn from his grasp. Suddenly all the weight was off him and Nasreen had pushed the canoe away from the shore.

Marik grabbed the sword and pulled it from the scabbard, ready to strike again. They heard water bubbling and a light splash then nothing more.

The canoe drifted silently away from the islet. Marik lowered the sword, then turned to confirm that the Rats were still moving away from them. He rubbed his brow and let out a long breath. Of the countless ways there was to die, he did not want to go like that.

'How can you live here with those things?'

Leaving Marik to recover himself, Nasreen retrieved her paddle and guided them towards the channel. 'People are worse.'

Chapter Twenty

Once safely back at the hideout, Marik intended to tell Garrun about Vasvarro but the leader had other concerns. There was only an hour or two of darkness left and everyone had returned except Dalkus. He had been part of the group sent to clear their route of attack close to Old Island. Though they'd done so successfully, the arrival of a mercenary patrol had forced the group to spilt up. The four others were present but of Dalkus there was no sign.

Marik listened to the latest from Parrs and Orim. It seemed that the recruitment effort had been only partially successful. There were only twenty new volunteers they could be sure of. Hearing that the rebels could muster a total of forty at most reinforced Marik's notion that the slavers' contribution might be essential. Orim was keen to also take part but Marik and Parrs insisted that he not even consider it. Somebody would have to man the hideout, in any case.

As dawn approached, all those who had been sleeping roused themselves when they heard Dalkus was still missing. The concern from Garrun and the others was that he had been captured. Marik knew this was the likely scenario but there was also another.

He took Parrs to one side. 'How well do you know him – Dalkus?'

'Not all that well. Don't forget I've only been here a few weeks.'

'How long has he been with the rebels?'

'I'm not sure. Slicer trusted him, I know that much. Marik, what if they have him? Reverrik has tortured men before. What if he knows we're coming?'

'We were held up. Perhaps Dalkus has been too. He may yet return.'

But time was running short. When he looked to the east, Marik saw a thin bank of cloud already coloured gold by the unseen sun.

Dawn came and Dalkus had still not returned. An hour later, Marik decided he had to talk to Garrun. The aged leader listened carefully as Marik spoke, concluding with his belief that the tough sailors could make a decisive difference to the attack. Preoccupied by Dalkus' absence, Garrun was clearly taken aback but he did not argue.

'I will collect them myself tonight,' said Marik. 'They will fight well, I'm sure of it.' As he said this, he could see the doubt in Garrun's eyes. 'You *will* attack? Even if Dalkus doesn't return?'

Lost in thought, Garrun put a hand on one of the house's supports to steady himself.

'Listen to me,' continued Marik. 'Even if they have him, we have to trust him to hold out – not tell them anything. And we have a decent chance of him still being alive when we get there.'

Marik wasn't surprised by Garrun's reservations. The man had lost one – possibly two – of his fellow leaders; and he was clearly not a natural fighter.

'Look around you,' he added. 'Your people are ready. It has to be now.'

'The decision is mine,' replied Garrun, for once looking Marik straight in the eye. '*Mine.*'

With that he walked away.

Orim picked his way past several people continuing their preparations on the floor of the reed-house. 'Trouble?'

'Could be. You've had more time to watch them than me. Is there anyone else? Another they will follow?'

Orim looked at the rebels. 'Not that I've seen. Garrun started it all. He's old, I know, and indecisive perhaps, but he hates the Rats as much as anyone. Why?'

'He might use this as an excuse to stop the attack going ahead. We can't let that happen.'

'I will pray to Sa Sarkan for Dalkus' return.'

The sun reached its zenith and still the missing leader did not appear. The rebels kept at that their preparations. Marik moved amongst them, giving encouragement and advice, and he persuaded Orim, Parrs and Nasreen to do the same. If he saw someone inactive, he found them a job to do. Canoes could be taken out of the water and checked for holes or damage. Paddles could be cleaned to minimise sound. Blades could be sharpened, bindings reinforced, handles sanded to improve grip. Marik lost count of the times he recounted the brief battle with Hammerhand. He told the would-be warriors that they faced only men; that he had no doubt they could win.

The intention had been to deliver a final briefing that afternoon. With the rebels about as ready as they could ever be, some began demanding that Marik and Garrun disclose the precise details of the attack. It was impossible to hide anything within the confines of the reed-house and Marik had seen Garrun watching him; drawn confidence from the fact that the leader did not intervene. He had the rebels where he wanted them – worked up and ready to fight – and it seemed to him that Garrun would now struggle to hold them back. If Marik had to lead them himself, so be it.

But before he could approach the leader about the briefing, Garrun called the rebels together. He stood there with his hands clasped solemnly in front of him and waited for absolute quiet.

'I see that you are all ready. Ready to fight our enemies. I admit, I was not convinced that the time was right. For so long we have waited and watched. Perhaps I had lost sight of our true goal. But Slicer was right, Dalkus too. And we have much to thank you for, Marik.' When Garrun gestured to him, many of those listening nodded enthusiastically.

'We *can* strike. We must. But, friends, it *cannot* be tonight.'

Dissent broke out immediately but Garrun raised his hands. 'Hear me out, please.'

Again, he waited, and eventually the rebels quietened down. Marik could feel Orim and Nasreen's eyes on him.

Garrun continued: 'We must assume that either Dalkus is dead or that the enemy have him. In either case, given where he was and what he was doing, they will know that something is afoot. The incident with Hammerhand was only days ago. The likelihood is that they will be expecting us; that they know we are coming. I can tell you now that Marik has won a few more allies for us but we are still outnumbered two to one. With surprise on our side, we had a chance. But now?'

Parrs spoke up. 'The full moon is tonight. The celebration.'

'It *has* to be now,' added Orim.

'Even if they know we're coming?' said another man.

'Exactly,' replied Garrun. 'They might even make it appear that all is normal but we could be walking into a trap. If surprise is to be our weapon, let's wait until we can be sure we have it. We are armed, ready, we can still pick our moment. We will have our time. But this is not it.'

'I'm sorry, Garrun,' said Parrs, 'but you're wrong.'

'Let us vote,' suggested a man sitting close to him.

Marik could see that many were on his side, but others were clearly with Garrun or unsure.

'Let me be clear,' said the rebel leader. 'I believe we must strike. But with our numbers we will only ever have *one* chance. Let us not waste it.'

Parrs spun around. 'Marik, say something!'

Marik was still not sure of Garrun's motives. Was he simply taking advantage of Dalkus' absence? Were his concerns genuine? Did he intend to forestall the attack permanently?

'The decision is not mine to make. If you still wish to attack, I will lead you.'

'Then let us vote,' said Garrun. 'And if the decision goes against me, I will fight alongside you, tonight.'

Marik rolled his eyes. The wily leader knew his well-chosen words would have changed a few minds.

Parrs went and stood beside Garrun. 'Raise your hand if you believe we should attack tonight.'

Nasreen was the quickest to follow Parrs in doing so and also pulled up Orim's arm. 'They have his daughter and he's one of us now. He should have a say.'

Nobody disagreed.

Garrun turned to Marik. 'As an objective party, perhaps you could count up for us?'

Marik had to credit him; his acting skills were impressive. He briefly considered throwing the old bastard into the water. But that would not help.

He made the count. 'Nine.'

Despite the pleas of Parrs and several others, no one else could be persuaded to join them.

'And those who believe we should wait?' Garrun raised his hand slowly, almost reluctantly. Though her ravaged face was as ever hidden beneath her hood, Nasreen glared at him.

Other arms had already gone up when Orim spoke: 'Wait, look there!'

At the other end of the channel, the sentry had just moved the platform aside. Word spread quickly and soon all the rebels – Garrun included – had moved to watch who would enter.

Even at that distance, the broad figure was distinctive. Dalkus calmly guided his canoe along the channel as the sentry hurriedly replaced the camouflage behind him.

Orim offered a prayer of thanks and many of the rebels raised a hand in greeting. Dalkus returned the gesture. But his expression was grave and as he neared the reed-house, a number of discussions broke out.

'What is it?' asked Orim.

'Can't see,' said Nasreen.

The three of them were at the back of the group and only Marik could see over the top. 'There's something in the front ... someone. Tied up. A boy.'

He looked to be about twelve, possibly a little older. Once the canoe was tied up, an exhausted-looking Dalkus dragged the boy into the reed-house and threw him down onto his knees. The new arrival was bony and slight and his tunic was several sizes too big. Instantly assailed by questions, Dalkus put up a hand and went to fetch himself some water. As he drank, several of the rebels questioned the boy. But he remained silent, staring blankly downward. Upon his cheek was a welt where he had been struck.

Orim and Nasreen had no idea who he was so Marik questioned Parrs. 'You know him?'

'Amars. Second cousin of mine. Lives with his parents over in Ettwater. Garrun's nephew.'

The leader had not yet approached his relative but it was the mention of Ettwater that concerned Marik.

Dalkus looked as if he could barely walk but he stood behind the boy and addressed his fellow rebels. 'Good to see everyone else made it back. I got stuck between two patrols – had to drag my canoe out of the water and sit tight. It wasn't until a couple of hours ago that my path was clear.'

Dalkus kneed young Amars gently in the back. 'Saw this one coming towards me. When I asked him what he was doing heading for Old Island, he tried to get away. Just as I caught up, he threw this into the water.' Dalkus reached into a pocket and pulled out a sodden piece of paper. 'Ink had run by the time I fished it out. Can't read a word. I asked him again what he was doing. He refused to answer. When I said he had to come with me, he swung his paddle at my head.'

'Speak up, lad,' said one of the rebels crowded around him.

'He won't,' said Dalkus. 'Either he's spying for them or he's working for someone who spies for them. Perhaps his uncle might have some luck?'

Garrun came forward. 'Amars? You can talk to me. What were you doing?'

The lad looked up at his uncle briefly then returned his gaze to the floor.

Dalkus turned to Garrun. 'When did you last speak to your brother?'

'It's been a while.' Garrun took the piece of paper from Dalkus. It was so saturated that he couldn't even unfold it. 'Marik.'

The others moved aside so that Marik could approach the leaders.

'Ettwater. You were there yesterday. I think it's time you told everyone what you told me.'

Marik couldn't really argue with that request, though the timing was unfortunate. 'A slaver captain is passing through with a dozen crew. The slaves revolted and they were thrown off their ship. They have nothing. I persuaded them to fight for us.'

'I meant to ask,' said Garrun. 'What did you offer in return?'

'A share of the spoils.'

Dalkus frowned. The other rebels exchanged glances and murmurs.

'It was the right thing to do,' added Marik. 'We need their help.'

'But at what cost?' Dalkus glared at him, his unappealing face growing red once again. 'You should have asked us.'

'There was no time.'

Dalkus put a hand on Amars' shoulder. 'Was it these slavers? Did they send you to Reverrik, to sell us out?' He bent close to the lad's ear. 'It doesn't matter now because you didn't get there. I expect they threatened you – I understand why you might have done it. But we must know the truth.'

'There are spies in Ettwater,' said Parrs. 'We all know it. Could have been anyone sent the lad.'

Another man spoke up: 'On the day after the Souther makes a deal? Quite a coincidence.'

'His name's Marik,' stated Parrs.

Marik stepped forward and knelt in front of Amars. 'These people are being very reasonable with you. I won't. So I suggest you tell us who sent you and what was in that note.'

Amars seemed even younger when he spoke. 'I don't know what was in the note. I was told not to read it and I didn't.'

'Very well. But who sent you? Speak up, lad, or I'll give you cause to regret it.'

'Don't threaten him,' warned Garrun.

'He's not leaving us much choice,' said Dalkus.

'Last chance,' said Marik.

The lad just kept looking at the floor.

'All right then.' Marik grabbed his tunic, pulled him to his feet and hauled him over to the side of the reed-house. He then held one arm, flipped Amars over and grabbed his right ankle. Swapping his other hand to his left ankle, he held him with his head just above the water.

'No, please, no-'

Marik dunked him in up to his neck. He felt a hand on his shoulder and was surprised to find it belonged to Nasreen.

'Don't,' she said.

'I have to.'

Marik could hear Garrun protesting but it seemed that Dalkus and some of the others were holding him back. Marik waited another few seconds then pulled Amars up. The lad was coughing and spluttering.

'Who sent you? All we need is the name. Was it Vasvarro, the slaver? The grey-haired man? Was it him?'

Marik was glad that he didn't say yes, less glad that he had to dunk him again. This time the lad struggled and Marik was forced to push downward.

'Stop it!' said Nasreen. Parrs pulled her away and she responded with an angry shove. Even Orim looked unsure.

But as the lad was still moving, Marik held him under. He had no intention of doing serious harm and was now pretty sure who had sent him.

He lifted Amars clear of the water once more. The lad sucked in breath and lashed a weak punch at Marik.

'Give me the name or you go under again.'

'Enough. That's enough.'

Marik was relieved but not surprised. He gently set Amars on the floor as all eyes turned to Garrun.

'*I* sent him.'

Amars was coughing. Marik squatted beside him and slapped his back to help him get all the water out. It was the only sound within the reed-house.

'What did you offer the Rats?' said Marik. 'Me?'

Garrun nodded and knelt beside his nephew. 'In return for ten male prisoners, ten female. I know-'

'-Traitor.' Parrs pulled Garrun to his feet. Dalkus marched over and gripped his other arm.

'What do we do with him?' asked Parrs.

'That's up to you,' said Marik.

As they dragged Garrun away, Marik helped Amars up.

The shivering lad pulled free of his tormentor. Nasreen put a blanket over his shoulders and escorted him to a quiet corner of the reed-house.

Chapter Twenty-One

The rebels gathered for a final time. There were no more debates or stirring speeches: simply a detailed briefing by Marik and Dalkus. They repeated the plan twice and answered several questions before all were satisfied.

First, Marik and Nasreen would collect Vasvarro and the sailors and guide them through the newly-cut path to the channel close to Old Island. By the time they arrived, Dalkus would be in place with the main force. Marik would then leave, alone, to infiltrate the island and poison the ale. Two hours later, Nasreen would lead an advance party, using bows to eliminate the sentries that habitually guarded the approach. The main force would then land at the dock and attack; all except Parrs and three others – they were tasked with freeing and arming the prisoners.

By the time the meeting broke up, the sun was setting. While Nasreen prepared the canoes they would be towing for the sailors, Dalkus spoke quietly to Marik.

'The poison – what if you can't get to the ale or it doesn't work?'

'Then I'll do whatever else I can. If you see fire, attack. Otherwise, wait the two hours. But no longer – I might not make it. If the poison hasn't taken effect by then, it's not going to.'

From their discussions to date, Marik adjudged that Dalkus wasn't the sharpest sword in the rack and he would've much preferred to have Slicer leading the rebels. But in the short time he'd known him, the man had shown himself to be totally committed to the cause. Wiping sweat away from above his top lip, Dalkus looked around at the rebels, most of whom were checking their weapons and equipment.

'Some helmets and armour wouldn't go amiss.'

'If we do this right, the Rats will be a lot less prepared than us. I'll instruct Vasvarro to hold the armoury but the rest of you must attack the celebration. Easy targets. Hopefully we'll also have some of the prisoners out and fighting by then.'

Dalkus gulped anxiously.

Marik continued: 'There can be no mercy. If there's an unarmed Rat – you kill him; drunk – kill him; on the ground – kill him. Surprise gives us five minutes, maybe ten. If we give them a chance to regroup, we lose.'

'I understand.'

'See you later.'

Marik shook his hand and crossed to the other side of the reed-house. Here, Orim stood guard over Garrun and young Amars, both of whom had been bound at the wrists and ankles. Marik reckoned the former leader was lucky to be alive. In the South, such treachery was usually punished by execution.

After admitting his guilt, Garrun had disclosed that he met with his nephew while supposedly recruiting fighters. He had paid the lad no less than two bronzes to undertake the risky mission to Old Island. Marik could understand that Garrun thought exchanging him for twenty of Reverrik's captives was a good deal. But he still wondered about the leader's true motivation: to free the prisoners? Or to rid himself of the troublesome Marik? It hardly mattered now.

Garrun sat in silence with his head bowed but Amars looked up as Marik approached. Orim was standing nearby, one hand on a spear. Marik squatted in front of the youngster, who had also been given some food by Nasreen.

'You're a tough lad. Loyal too. Probably waiting for me to say sorry but I'm not going to – I had no choice.'

'Should have told you straight away,' answered Amars, casting a hateful glance at his uncle. 'I swear I didn't know what was in the note. I can fight. Tell them, they'll listen to you. Free me and I can join the fight. I hate the Rats as much as anyone.'

'They wouldn't let you. Not this time. But they're good people. They'll give you a second chance.'

Marik stood. Before the briefing he had checked Orim's arm. The coldthyme and constant washing seemed to have kept the wound clean and Orim reported the pain was no worse.

'You'll be all right?'

Orim was to stay behind with a woman who was too ill to fight. He nodded, jaw trembling as he fought to control his emotions. For all that he hoped it happened, Marik didn't dare promise the man that he would return with his daughter.

'I'll see you tomorrow.' He gripped Orim's shoulder then walked over to where he'd left his pack. It contained a wooden float, the two flasks of poison and a fire-starting kit. He was armed only with a dagger – a sword would be too heavy for the swim. Even though the flasks were wrapped in several layers of leaves, Marik was careful as he hoisted the pack onto his shoulder.

Knowing many eyes were on him, he strode towards the pontoon with as much calm and confidence as he could muster. He took a moment to shake hands with Parrs and wished good luck to those who wished it to him. Nasreen was already in the canoe. Behind it, tied together in two pairs were the four canoes for Vasvarro and his men. Hidden under blankets were the best weapons the rebels had: eight swords and five axes.

Nasreen had not said a word to Marik since the incident with Amars.

'Forgiven me yet?' he asked as he climbed in behind her and grabbed his paddle.

Instead of replying, she pushed them off and got under way.

Of the trips taken to Spring Island, this was to be the easiest. The pair heard distant shouts while crossing the Lake but never identified the source. Nasreen seemed sure that the lack of patrols was due to the celebration. If that were true, it reinforced Marik's belief that – despite the encounter with Hammerhand – Reverrik truly thought himself untouchable. Yet he couldn't shake one particular fear: that they might be discovered before they could even land a significant blow on the Rats.

They landed not far from Ava's place and Marik set off at a run towards Ettwater. The Red Moon was partially veiled by cloud but there was sufficient light for him to find his way. He found the village silent but for the grunts of the few penned pigs. The slavers were still gathered in their camp in the middle of the settlement. A fire was alight but only two men seemed to be awake. Marik made sure they heard him coming and was glad to find that one of them was Vasvarro.

'I thought it might be tonight,' he said as his men set about waking the others.

'Why's that?'

'Several reasons.'

Marik was concerned by the noise the sailors were making. 'Can you ask them to keep quiet? It's better if none in the village hear you departing.'

'Of course.'

At a quiet whistle from Vasvarro, a man hurried over to him. He was a tall fellow with long hair tied in a tail.

'Quieten them down. Five minutes and we leave.'

With a nod, the tall man did his captain's bidding.

'Kaykirru,' explained Vasvarro. 'Was my third in command, now second. Not much of a sailor but as hard as they come.'

'Perhaps he can watch the rear for us. Will you travel with me? I'd like to tell you more about the island; and what we'd like you to do.'

'As you wish. Tell me, Marik, do your allies approve of our involvement? Have they agreed to my conditions?'

'They have. And they understand your worth to our cause.'

'Good, good.' Vasvarro gestured to the sky. The cloud had shifted, leaving the Red Moon clear and full. The familiar hollows and lines upon the surface were all visible, the blotches of colour ranging between scarlet and near-black. The glow gave a pinkish tinge to everything, including the faces of the men around him.

'I would believe this a portent,' added Vasvarro, 'but from what I've gleaned from the villagers, I know there's a more logical reason why you strike now.'

Marik didn't reply.

Vasvarro continued: 'Whatever this cultist may think the full moon means for him, it actually works in our favour – for Azreyel considers it to be a time of triumph for his *chosen* people.'

'Reverrrik believes that too.'

'No matter. He has devoted himself to an obscure sect beloved only by barbarians. Even if he exists, his god is no match for Azreyel. We will prevail.'

It seemed to Marik that some divine force *was* watching over them, for the second journey also went well. Perhaps it was solely because the Rats were more interested in their celebration. Marik was less concerned with the cause than the result, though there were at least now enough of them to defeat any mercenaries they did encounter. Vasvarro listened to the plan and was happy with the role of seizing and defending Reverrrik's armoury.

Unsurprisingly, the sailors were very capable at manoeuvring the canoes and there were only a few occasions when Nasreen had to slow down or send back an instruction. They sighted moving lights on the far side of the Lake as they crossed it but still made good time. Even so, four hours of darkness had already elapsed and Marik was keen to infiltrate the island as soon as possible. Then again, as the celebrations apparently went on until dawn, there was little harm in allowing the Rats to let their guard down even further. Marik could not help thinking of Hammerhand; who had not been spotted by any of the rebels. It was possible that the knife had done more damage than simply blinding him. Perhaps the giant was incapacitated; out of the fight.

Marik would never have found the meeting point, which was subtly marked by three reeds artificially raised high by the rebels. As Nasreen led the canoes close to the bank, they heard a familiar voice and Parrs appeared from the undergrowth. Under his direction, the occupants carefully climbed out and the canoes were pulled ashore. Though there was solid ground beneath, the reeds were very thick and the work took time. The entire operation was carried out without lanterns but under the glow of the Red Moon. Parrs asked them to pick up their vessels and they set off along the newly-created path.

Nasreen dropped back to watch the rear with Kaykirru while Marik and Vasvarro carried their canoe. They walked for half an hour without any delay and arrived at a small open area packed with rebels and their vessels. They were now less than half a mile from Old Island and another path had been cleared that led directly to the approach.

It was difficult to work out who was who but Dalkus swiftly found Marik. After he'd briefly introduced the rebel leader to Vasvarro, the two spoke.

'Patrols?'

'The usual,' replied Dalkus. 'Two men in a skiff anchored in the middle of the channel with a lantern alight. We should be able to take them out quietly.'

'You *have* to,' answered Marik. 'Three arrows each at least. If they shout out-'

'-They won't get the chance.' Dalkus collared a nearby rebel. 'Ellors here will take you most of the way. There's no path but he knows the quickest route. You'll end up right at the rear, behind the buildings. You should be clear.'

Marik peered closely at Ellors and saw enough to realise he at least knew his face; a young man who often seemed to be on sentry duty at the hideout.

'How long to get there?'

'About an hour,' said Dalkus.

'So, three in total. After that, you attack whatever.'

'I know.'

'Seen anything of the island?'

'We got a scout quite close earlier. Good news – they have a fire going and were already watching a fight.'

'I'd call that *very* good news. Ellors, we must leave now.'

'Yes, sir.'

Marik opened his pack and checked the contents once more. Nasreen approached him, holding a cloak.

'I won't need that. I have to swim.'

Then he noticed that Ellors was also donning a cloak.

'You'll be passing through an area of bitereed,' explained Dalkus – very sharp.'

'Ah. Thank you.'

As Nasreen hung the cloak over his shoulders, Marik was wondering what he should say to her but she swiftly withdrew before he had the chance.

Vasvarro emerged from the darkness and sidled up to him. 'Souther, I own cutlery that cost more than this sword.'

'*Owned*, you mean.'

The slaver emitted a dramatic sigh. 'Have any of these peasants even drawn blood before?' Vasvarro kept his voice low but not low enough for Marik's liking.

'These people are fighting for their loved ones and their freedom. They'll do what they have to.'

With another sigh, Vasvarro returned to his men.

'Ready, sir,' said Ellors.

'Right.'

'Good luck, Marik,' said Dalkus.

'You too. Dalkus, remember – no mercy.'

'No mercy.'

Marik soon had good cause to be thankful for the cloak. Ellors wisely kept them away from the channel and they passed first through a muddy area where Marik almost lost a boot, then a patch of thick but pliable reed. The bitereed that followed, however, was indeed vicious and he'd already cut his arms twice when he elected to keep them under the cloak. Despite the moonlight, it was impossible to see the murky ground and even the nimble young guide fell several times. He quietly apologised on the first few occasions but ceased when he realised Marik was stumbling with even more frequency.

As they circled around behind Old Island, the flush of the fire grew more visible, the roars and shouts more audible. The last stretch involved crossing a waist-deep stream which at least prepared Marik for the cold. They halted around twenty feet from the channel.

Marik led the way forward until they could see the water. Crouching low, he looked out at the island. From this side, he could better appreciate how long it was – seven or eight hundred feet. They were closer to the right side and beyond that the approach channel was visible, as was the faint light of the sentry boat. At the right-hand end of Old Island was a small copse of trees. Marik was also grateful to see some scrub and undergrowth on the near side though he also noted that the bank was quite high. Looking to the left, the first building was the largest.

'That's the warehouse, yes?'

'Yes,' replied Ellors.

'Next to that the armoury, then Reverrik's house, then the barracks.'

'Yes.'

The rear walls of the buildings were about fifty feet from the near bank. There were no lights in this unused area but several within Reverrik's house and the barracks. Between the two buildings, the fire illuminated dozens of dark figures. The fire itself wasn't actually that large, presumably because there wasn't all that much to burn.

Marik saw that if he swam straight forward, he would come ashore not far from the warehouse, where there was no light and no trace of activity. It was possible to discern silhouetted individuals walking between buildings with nothing behind them to mask their form. But where there were structures and trees, guards might easily be lurking. He would just have to hope that Reverrik believed he didn't need them.

Ellors had clearly been thinking about something else. 'The moonlight on the water. The sentry in the tower might see the canoes coming.'

There was no lantern visible up in the tower. 'They always post a man there?'

'Every time I've been here in the day. It's hard to tell at night.'

'We can't take the chance. Without a light up there the archers will never hit him. I'll deal with it.'

He handed Ellors the cloak then took off his boots, trousers and shirt. Once they were all in the pack, he used the straps to fix it to the wooden float.

'I suppose this cold water is nothing to a Souther,' remarked Ellors.

'Good reason to swim quickly, at least.'

'Your friend worships Sa Sarkan, doesn't he?'

'Orim? Yes.'

'I too. I have prayed to her – to watch over you this night. To watch over all of us.'

'Appreciated. You'd best head back.'

'Yes, sir.' With that, Ellors disappeared into the reeds.

Marik stood there, shivering, in water up to his knees, holding the float and the pack. It occurred to him that he could still get dressed, turn around and walk away. It would take some time – and he would certainly get lost – but if he kept going he would escape the delta eventually. Everything seemed to make sense when he was with Orim and the other rebels, but standing there – almost naked, facing more than a hundred men alone – nothing much made sense.

Was this to be another test like the one he had failed? When he had betrayed himself and those who depended on him? Even here, even when he was alone and so very far from the South in space and time, the very thought of it shamed him. Once had been enough and a repetition would be more than he could bear. In the immediate aftermath, he had thought several times about killing himself.

But this was a different time and place and though he would never be the same man, Marik felt he had rebuilt something of himself in the North; especially since meeting Tola and Orim.

Was this to be a victory; something to restore his pride, tip the scales of his life in favour of good? The fact remained that the rebels would strike. And unless he could seriously affect the odds before that happened, they would certainly lose. There wasn't really much choice at all.

Marik let out a long breath and recalled the words of his first captain in the People's Guard. The short speech never changed and was all the more effective for it.

Forget everything else. All that matters now is what's in front of you. Be quick in thought, quicker in deed. Move and fight until there is no enemy left to kill.

Other than the cold, there was a strangely relaxing calm to the crossing. Thoughts of the creatures that might be below and around him struck Marik only briefly and he concentrated on gripping the float and kicking rhythmically. He ensured his feet didn't break the surface which meant that progress was slow but there was no current nor weed to affect him. Halfway across, he paused to let the stiffness in his legs subside. His fingers and toes were beginning to lose feeling but he had known it a lot worse. The first week of Guard training involved a swim along a sixty-foot channel chopped out of a frozen lake. Candidates were roped and the majority had to be dragged most of the way. Marik had swum the entire length and pulled himself out.

From the island came a great roar; the sound of many voices combined. Guessing another fight was in progress, Marik continued at a quicker pace; coming ashore with the mercenaries preoccupied was something worth aiming for. When he did encounter weed, the first feel of it was unpleasant but he pushed through. About ten feet from the shore, his feet touched mud but it was so slick that he couldn't find purchase. Propelling himself forward, nostrils full of the now familiar mud-odour, he soon found himself below a steep section of bank. Quickly realising he would never be able to climb it, he kept one hand on the raft and the other close to the shore as he moved to his right. He covered forty feet but the bank was still too high and steep.

Pulling himself along using a dense network of root-like growth that didn't seem to be connected to any vegetation above, he eventually came to a miniature gully where a trickling stream reached the water. He lifted the raft and pack out and climbed slowly upward until the ground grew drier. Peeling clumps of weed from his shoulders, he took a moment to slow his breathing and calm down. Well hidden by the gully, he left the gear and climbed up until his head was level with the surrounding ground.

Marik found himself about thirty feet from the rear of the warehouse. Away to his right was the copse of trees. To the right of that, he could still see the lantern of the sentry boat in the channel. Reverrik's house was less than a hundred feet away: a broad, two-storey structure, with eight windows on both levels. At the rear was a door with a lantern alight above it. Several other rooms were illuminated.

Sliding back down into the gully, Marik swiftly removed the pack from the raft and got dressed. Leaving the raft there, he placed his sheathed knife on his belt, checked it was secure, then put on the pack. He reckoned it had taken him no longer than an hour and a half to reach this point. Assuming he could avoid capture, he had ninety minutes to cause absolute havoc.

Chapter Twenty-Two

The Rats were enjoying themselves. Most – sixty or seventy at least – were gathered around the fire. Not a single one was without a wooden mug and a few looked unsteady on their feet. The firelight revealed a variety of races: dark, narrow-faced men like the people of the delta and the Urlun empire; round-faced Easterlings similar to Vasvarro's men; and even a few tall, rangy Southers. Hammerhand was not present; Reverrik impossible to miss.

He was slouched on a huge chair like some tribal king, naked from the waist up. The mercenary didn't have much hair on his head but his bushy beard reached halfway down his chest. Sitting on his lap with a bored, blank expression on her face was a girl of no more than fifteen. Her tunic had ridden up and Reverrik was stroking her thigh. In his other hand was a mug, this one metal.

A fight had just finished. Cheered on and poked at with staves, one man had just beaten another about the face until he lost consciousness. The exhausted victor had been sitting atop his foe and now slid off, crying, as the Rats settled up their wagers. Reverrik seemed deeply unimpressed by the contest; and shortly after both fighters were dragged off to the pit, six women appeared. One of them had a drum and the five others were now dancing in front of their master. Their tunics were high at the leg and cut low to expose their breasts. The Rats lined up on either side of their leader to watch. One woman halted when she realised she had stepped in blood, which caused a great deal of laughter.

Marik was lying in long grass, no more than fifty feet from Reverrik himself. The prisoner's pit was directly ahead of him, the soldiers' barracks to his right. It had taken him some time to crawl around to this position and he was now also very close to the ale kegs. The one currently in use was on its side and housed in a timber frame. The two others behind it were upright and easily accessible. Unfortunately, a pair of mercenaries were leaning against them, deep in conversation.

Marik was considering his options when another group came into view: about a dozen mercenaries accompanied by some women. They had emerged from the barracks and Marik noticed that none of the men were drinking. Presumably these were the guards Slicer had mentioned; taking their turn to remain sober and ready to fight if need be. Perhaps time with the women was their reward? Like the others, they were now watching the dancing. The routine was quite athletic and elaborate; Reverrik and his followers were clapping along to the drum beat.

The two talkative men decided that they also needed to see the show. Seconds after they moved away, Marik began crawling towards the upright kegs. They – and he – were too far from the fire to be seen. But knowing one of the Rats might arrive for a re-fill at any moment, he wasted no time. With the flask of poison in his hand, he was all set to pour it into the upright keg when he realised he could go for the one currently in use. It was ten feet further forward but without question worth the risk.

Crawling forward once more, he hunched behind the frame and only then did he see his mistake. With the keg on its side – and a tap fitted – there was no easy way to administer the poison. Before he could work out how to overcome this, Marik heard movement close by. He looked up to see a man walking towards him, heading for a re-fill.

Marik crawled back to the line of upright kegs and placed the flask on top of his pack. Whistling merrily, the mercenary opened the tap. Marik could hear the ale sloshing into his mug. Then he heard a laugh – from behind him. Peering over his shoulder, he saw figures coming his way.

'Over here,' said a man's voice, 'where it's nice and quiet.'

'We better not.' The woman with him sounded scared.

'Just five minutes, sweetie. While everyone's busy.'

They were headed straight for him but Marik dared not move with the other mercenary only feet away. He bowed his head and pressed himself against the nearest keg but the pair kept coming. He could make out their faces now and see that the man was actually dragging the woman. Marik drew his knife. He heard the drinker close the keg-tap and move off, still whistling.

'Come on!' hissed the man.

'I don't-'

Suddenly the Rat stumbled towards the kegs and tripped.

'You stupid-'

His head struck Marik's knee as he came down; unfortunately, not hard enough to knock him out.

'What? Who-'

Marik's left hand went over the Rat's mouth. His right hand held the knife but by then the man had begun to fight back. He must have seen the blade coming because he threw up his arms and got both hands on Marik's wrist. The mercenary was smaller and weaker but Marik soon realised that one arm was not going to beat his enemy's two. Still struggling to keep his hand clamped over the writhing Rat's mouth, Marik abandoned the knife and pulled his free hand away. His aim was to punch the bastard in the gut but a flailing finger caught him in the eye. Unable to see what the Rat was doing, he kept the hand on his mouth and tried the punch again. But his foe had brought up his knees and Marik hit only bony shin.

The mercenary pulled his head away. Marik had no idea what the woman was doing but he knew he had to silence his foe quickly. Knocking his arms aside, he went straight for his throat, circling the neck and tightening his grip. The man fought back but Marik also had an elbow on his chest to pin him. The mercenary didn't have the reach to attack his face but his fingernails raked Marik's chest. Still squeezing, Marik smacked the Rat's head against the ground but the soil was too soft to do any damage.

Leaving his left hand on his neck, he reached back with his right, ready to smash him in the face. But the resilient mercenary twisted free and kicked out, his heavy boot catching Marik in the flank. When he hit the ground, he knew it was over; the mercenary would shout, help would come and the attack would fail before it had started.

The shout never came. All he heard was a low thump and then the mercenary fell face first onto the ground beside him, the knife between his shoulder blades.

The woman stood there, one arm still outstretched, her breath coming in panicked gasps.

'You all right?' Marik asked.

'Who … who are you?'

'A friend. Here to get you off this island. Come here, stay low or you'll be seen.'

As she walked warily around the fallen mercenary, Marik put a finger to his neck. The pulse was slowing and he wasn't moving at all. He would soon be dead.

Marik took the woman's arm and pulled her down next to him. 'Thank you. What's your name?'

'Ordi.'

Marik felt around for his pack but it wasn't within reach. When he moved towards the mercenary, he located a strap and realised the man had fallen on it. Marik levered him off and pulled out the pack. As he did so, he heard the sound of broken clay and felt liquid on his fingers. He was not surprised to find that both the flasks were broken.

'Shit, shit, shit.'

'What is it?' asked Ordi.

'Nothing. Listen, you should go.'
'What will you-'
'-I'll get rid of the body.'
'What ... what are you doing here?'

Though he couldn't see much of her face, Marik got an impression of a young woman with broad shoulders and long hair. He wasn't sure how to answer her.

'Just ... don't tell anyone you saw me.'
'Is something happening tonight? Maybe I can help?'

The fear in her voice had already lessened. Without the poison, Marik knew he was in dire need of alternatives.

He took a quick look over the top of the kegs. Fortunately, the dance was still in full flow and all the mercenaries were watching. He ducked back down.

'Maybe. Tell me why you killed him.'
'I hate him,' said Ordi, as if it was the most obvious thing in the world. 'I hate them all. Anyone who fights them is a friend of mine.'

'All right. Maybe you *can* help. I need a distraction. Would you be able to start a fire – in the kitchen at the house?'

'Yes, I ... yes.'
'A large fire – one that the men will need to put out.'
'I can do it. When?'

'About an hour. It needn't be exact. I'll wait for you. But listen, you must not tell anyone, even the other women. Understand?'

'Yes.'
'The trees on the other side of the warehouse – when things start to happen, you go there and hide.'

'I will. Listen, the guards – the ones not allowed to drink – they pass the time by gambling. They're in one of the barrack rooms, twenty or more.'

'Got it. What about Hammerhand?'
'The house. His eye pains him.'
'You best go now. I suggest going around the back of the barracks so you're not seen.'

Marik took another look over the kegs. None of the mercenaries were close.

'Go now, Ordi. And thank you.'
Keeping her head low, she scuttled away into the shadows.

Marik pulled his knife out of the mercenary's back and wiped it clean on his shirt. He turned the man over, placed the pack on his stomach and dragged him away.

Though he didn't have far to go, shifting the body was not easy. When he finally reached the water, Marik checked again for a pulse and felt nothing. There was still a lot of noise so he simply rolled the body off the bank and into the water. Once that was done, he opened the pack and checked his gear. Not only was all the poison gone but his fire-starting kit of striker, stone, cloth and tinder was wet through. Cloth and tinder he could find easily enough so he set about drying the striker and stone on his trousers. As he sat there in the darkness, he considered his next move. The kitchen fire would work well as the logical place for a blaze but if for some reason Ordi was foiled, he might have to cause the distraction himself. In any case, a second fire could only add to the confusion. The barracks seemed like the obvious choice, especially if he could trap the men gambling inside. Then there was the guard tower.

Once the striker and stone were dry, Marik placed them in a pocket and was soon squatting in the long grass just behind the barracks. The single rear door was to the right; the ideal place to set the fire. Marik scanned the area but could see no sign of firewood. There was, however, another source of fuel. The grass was very dry and quite thick. He drew his knife and began chopping.

Ignoring the shouts from the other side of the barracks, Marik formed the fistfuls of grass into bundles and placed them in a line. He glanced regularly in every direction but the only interruption was from a mercenary who came to the rear corner of the barracks to relieve himself. By the time he'd made ten bundles, Marik reckoned three quarters of an hour had passed since Ordi left him. Gathering up several bundles, he walked to the barracks and placed the grass beside the timber wall. He paused at a cry from above but swiftly returned with the second and third loads. The mound of grass was four feet high and four across. He felt sure it would be sufficient to set the timbers ablaze.

Marik then retreated until he could see Reverrik's house. He didn't know where the kitchen was situated but there were as yet no sign of flames. Keen to keep an eye on the celebrations, he moved back to his previous observation position to the left of the barracks.

The dancing was over and the Rats had now divided into small groups. There were too many of them in front of Reverrik for Marik to see much but he did spy several walking away from the pit. Two male prisoners were being hauled along by the mercenaries on either side of them. Like the others, they seemed barely able to walk, let alone fight.

Suddenly the noise lessened and Marik heard one voice rise above the others. Then he saw the distinctive Reverrik and realised the mercenary was standing upon his throne.

'Quiet there, lads.'

He didn't have to repeat himself. Even the men escorting the prisoners stood still as Reverrik addressed his private army.

'A feast and a dance and now another fight. Is it a good night?'

The men answered with a cheer. All had a mug in their hands and many had their arms over the shoulders of their compatriots. Marik did not like what he saw. They were drunk but not too drunk; and evidently a unified group.

'Of course, it is,' continued Reverrik. 'And merriment is all very well. But we must not forget – this is not only a good night but a sacred one. The Blood God has given us all we asked for and in turn we must honour him. On your knees.'

Reverrik was the only one not to do so; even the women and the prisoners prostrated themselves. The mercenary turned and raised his hands to the Red Moon. He began a chant, and the men repeated each line in turn.

'From the dark above, the eternal eye,
From the vessels within, the stream of life,
From sword and axe, the sweetest bite,
From sea to mountain, hear our cry,
'Creator, destroyer ... for you we fight!'

Seemingly impressed by the volume and vigour of his subjects' responses, Reverrik nodded to himself as he continued. 'To the Blood God Mefistrel – Breaker, Crusher, Shatterer, Tormentor, Maker of Worlds, Taker of Life, we pledge ourselves ...'

'Once, twice, thrice!' came the response.

Marik felt an icy chill run across his back. If he'd observed such a scene before, he wouldn't have ever dared try the attack. He had seen such togetherness and devotion in the South. Men with leaders like this fought well.

Reverrik began his rhythmic nodding once more and lowered his hands. 'Rise, my warriors. We honour him in everything we do. Later, we offer blood. And now, more sacrifices. Bring forward the prisoners.'

With his followers now standing again, Marik could see little. He thought of Dalkus and Parrs and Vasvarro; tried to imagine where they might be. Still on the bank? On the water? Had they already taken out the sentries? Were they already approaching the island?

The very notion sent him speeding back to the barracks. He was close to the pile of grass when the shout of 'fire' went up. Though he could not yet see any flames from the house, more shouts immediately followed. The cries continued along with the pounding of feet as the Rats ran towards the house.

Good girl.

Marik waited to see if anyone was going to emerge from the rear of the barracks. When no one did, he took out the fire-striker and flint. He knelt beside the pile of grass, where he had already placed a collation of twigs and tree-bark. He held the flint in his left hand with a piece of cloth from his shirt upon it, then chopped the metal striker downward. At the third attempt, he lit a spark on the cloth. Cradling it in his hands, he blew gently until he had a flame. Once he placed the cloth on the twigs and bark, the flames spread quickly. Replacing the kit in his pack, he stood and walked to the rear right corner of the barracks.

Mercenaries were still running towards the house. Staying deep in the shadows of the wall, Marik advanced and crouched down at the front corner. Only a dozen or so Rats remained beside the pit and Reverrik was not among them. Though Marik could see numerous torches and lanterns beside the house, there were no flames yet visible. But if the barracks also burned, it wouldn't matter if they were able to extinguish the kitchen blaze.

He waited for two more mercenaries to run past, then calmly walked towards the guard tower, safe in the darkness. The well-trodden area in front of the buildings was compacted mud and, unlike the rest of the island, even underfoot. No one came near him and he did not look back until he reached the guard tower. It was another timber construction, no more than ten feet wide. Marik found the ladder rungs with his hands before looking back at the house. He could smell burning and hear many shouts but was concerned by the absence of flames. He climbed swiftly up the ladder and heard the sentry before he saw him.

'What's going on?'

Knowing there were other Southers among the Rats, Marik didn't attempt to cover his accent. 'Fire. Watch the river! It might be part of an attack.'

He climbed up into the cramped confines of the tower to find the sentry facing away from him. 'See anything?'

'Not yet.'

There was a moment of quiet in which Marik almost froze. This wasn't the first time he'd had to kill a man who didn't know what was coming but that didn't make it any easier. He drew his knife, reached over the man's left shoulder with his free hand, pulled his chin up and slit his throat. Blood splattered the floor of the tower. Revolted by the smell and sound of the dying mercenary, Marik lowered him to the floor. Shaking the horribly warm liquid off his hand, he stepped up to the surround and accidentally knocked something over. Reaching down, he found that it was a bow and quiver.

Marik placed them in a corner and gazed downward. Directly below was the cove and the dock. Only the coaster was clearly visible though he knew there would be smaller vessels there too. He looked beyond the dock, towards the channel. The lantern was still alight. Of the rebels there was no sign.

He waited and he watched. Smoke was now issuing from three of the windows at the end of the house closest to the warehouse but Reverrik was throwing all his manpower at the problem. He seemed to have organised a human chain and pail after pail of water was being carried inside. The women were outside, gathered around Reverrik as he bellowed orders at the men.

Marik turned back towards the channel. Calculating that the rebels might have left the lantern alight to avoid arousing suspicion, he instead peered down at the water below. Noting that everything suddenly seemed darker, he looked up to see that a cloud had partially obscured the Red Moon. He hoped it was a portent of things to come but could still see no movement on the water. Surely the two hours had passed.

Where are they?

Just as he crossed the tower once more and looked down at the house, a familiar hulking figure appeared. Illuminated by several lanterns, Hammerhand had a patch covering his eye. As he approached Reverrik, Marik realised the giant was towing someone along behind him. A woman. Marik had not seen much of her in the moonlight but he knew instantly that it was Ordi. She was broad-shouldered; tall and long-limbed too. Hammerhand flung her to the ground at Reverrik's feet.

'No.'

The mercenary leader gripped a handful of Ordi's hair and yelled something. Marik could not hear it over the shouts of the men fighting the fire. Ordi didn't even try to resist him and kept her mouth shut. Reverrik back-handed her across the face.

Marik returned to the other side of the tower. But the cloud above covered more of the moon now and he could see nothing save the hull and mast of the coaster. He found the quiver and put it over his left shoulder then took the bow with him as he returned to the inland side.

'No, no, no.'

Hammerhand had one great paw around the back of Ordi's neck. Reverrik had a dagger in his hand which he now waved in front of the young woman's face.

'Just tell them,' breathed Marik. 'Tell them the truth.'

But she kept her mouth shut and her eyes on the ground. Reverrik drew the tip of the knife across one cheek, then the other. Even though they were surrounded by the other women, not one of them intervened.

Marik nocked an arrow and planted his legs against the surround. He drew loosely and took aim, even though he reckoned a shot was too risky. From his position, Hammerhand was to the left of Ordi, Reverrik to the right. If he aimed at either of them, he might easily hit her. The range was at least a hundred and twenty feet and he didn't particularly like the feel of this bow.

Reverrik closed in and shifted the knife to Ordi's neck.

Marik knew he had to shoot. But if he did, the mercenaries would know what was coming. They would have time to prepare. Surprise would be lost.

Reverrik shouted some final threat at Ordi.

The cloud shifted, revealing the Red Moon once more, improving visibility.

Hammerhand was slightly further away and the bigger target. Marik drew back and aimed at the giant's head.

Then a shout went up; not from the house but from the barracks. A thick pall of smoke was rising behind the building. Though he couldn't see the flames, Marik could see their glow and had no doubt the structure was well alight.

Reverrik and Hammerhand were both now looking towards the barracks, listening as the man kept shouting.

Marik leaped back across the tower and peered downward once more. With the moon clear, the entire scene was different. The water seemed to sparkle and he saw flashes of movement below. He could not see the canoes but he could make out several figures moving swiftly away from the dock. It could only be the rebels. Clearly Dalkus had realised the celebration had been interrupted and was heading straight for the preoccupied mercenaries at the house.

With a grim smile, Marik returned to the inland side of the tower. Hammerhand had disappeared but Reverrik still had hold of Ordi. Then the leader turned towards the dock. The women suddenly scattered, fleeing towards the house. Reverrik let go of Ordi and also retreated.

Shouldering the bow and quiver, Marik climbed down onto the ladder. He heard the rebels below as they sped past the tower and into battle.

Chapter Twenty-Three

Halfway to the ground, Marik paused to let them all rush past. With the lack of light under the tower, the rebels might easily take him for one of the Rats. He was tempted to join the main force but with the area surrounding the pit now deserted, freeing the prisoners was more important. The defenders would not expect a second attack from that direction. They still had the numbers and from what Marik had seen of the mercenaries so far, they would rally and organise themselves quickly. Piling shock upon shock was the best way to defeat them.

He bolted through thick grass, holding bow and quiver steady. Away to his left, the first tongues of flame were now visible at the rear of the barracks. Cursing as he stumbled on the uneven ground, Marik slowed as he neared the pit. Looking out at the water to his right, he could not see any of the second group's canoes.

Not a single mercenary was anywhere near the pit. Two men had just appeared from the barracks doorway but they immediately sped around to the rear. Even so, Marik kept low as he edged around the inky darkness of the pit. With only the moonlight to guide him, it took him a few moments to find the ladder. He had picked it up and was about to lower it into the pit when he heard movement behind him.

Turning, he saw several dim figures coming his way. Moonlight sparked off a blade.

'Parrs?'

The figures stopped. Then another hurried past them, halting only when he was close. 'Marik?'

'Yes.'

'Thank the gods.'

Marik recognised the young rebel's voice. 'Quickly, help me. The rest of you, ready the weapons.'

They took one side each and lowered the ladder. Marik could see eyes peering up from the gloom below but not one of the prisoners said anything.

'We're friends,' announced Parrs. 'Here to help.'

The prisoners must have heard him but none of them replied.

'Let's go down,' said Marik. 'I suggest you first.'

He followed the young man down the ladder and soon found himself standing on soft mud.

'Gather round,' said Parrs. Some of the prisoners moved in but others kept their distance.

'I am Parrs of Ettwater and we're here with Dalkus of Northolt and many others. This man is Marik. He's helping us. The fire is a diversion. Our main force is attacking the Rats over by the house. We have weapons for you. Will you fight?'

The man standing closest to them walked away without a word.

'Parrs.' Another came forward and threw his arms around the young man. 'It's me.'

'Kedrim?'

'You *must* fight,' Marik told the others. 'If you can, you must.'

'I will,' offered Kedrim, still embracing Parrs.

'I too,' added another as several of the prisoners came closer.

'Come then,' said Marik. 'Quickly.'

He hurried up the ladder and found the other three rebels waiting there, watching the barracks burn. Kedrim was the first of the prisoners out of the pit. Once he'd been given a spear, Marik ushered him to one side.

'How many of you?'

'About ten, I should say. The others will be of no use to you. It's not their fault.'

'Wait here.'

Marik ran past the ale kegs and almost to his previous observation post. Behind the barracks, another line had been formed by the mercenaries to fight the second fire. It seemed obvious that they had little chance of success but the thirty or so men present were busy and clearly still unaware of the attack. Marik knew he didn't have long.

He sprinted back to the pit and was dismayed to find men still climbing the ladder. 'Quicker, damn you, or this will all be over! Give me a blade.'

One of the rebels offered him the hilt of a sword.

'Anyone with a weapon, follow me.'

When he reached the kegs once more, Marik placed the bow and quiver on top of one. As the rebels and prisoners gathered around him, he counted them up. The last to arrive was Parrs – the fifteenth.

'Stay quiet until I charge. Be right behind me and make your first blow count. No mercy.'

Knowing he would now kill in cold blood again, Marik reminded himself that the girl Ordi had also done just that. As he led his meagre force towards the mercenaries, every last one of the Rats was transfixed by the fire. The closest man was standing with an empty pail in his hand, forlornly shaking his head, face illuminated by the flames. Marik bellowed as he swung from left to right, chopping straight into the side of his neck. As the mercenary crumpled, Marik darted around him. He was already seeking his next target when one of the rebels burst past him and hacked at another Rat, blade ripping through tunic and flesh.

Marik was grateful for the firelight and the ease of distinguishing friend from foe: the rebels wore the habitual green and the prisoners were barefoot. One of the captives – a skinny man of some age – thrust his spear towards a Rat. The tip delivered only a glancing blow and the mercenary had the presence of mind to grab the weapon with one hand while drawing his dagger with the other. Marik waited for him to raise his arm, then swept at it, slicing across the elbow. As the mercenary shrieked, the prisoner pulled the spear free and jabbed it into his chest. Confident it was a mortal blow, Marik pressed onward.

He came to a mercenary who had wisely retreated in order to draw his own sword and get a measure of the battle. The Rat saw Marik coming and raised his blade. He was tall and fair-skinned and his eyes narrowed as he realised he faced a fellow Souther.

'Who the hell are you?' rasped the warrior.

Marik feinted a two-handed thrust, then cut up towards his chin. The Souther spun away from the attack and covered his retreat with a full sweep. As the blade moved away from him, Marik leaped forward, his own sword positioned to block. His first punch caught the Souther square on his heavy jaw but did no more than knock him off balance. Marik followed up with a boot into his groin that doubled him over. With his enemy disabled, Marik bought his sword-hilt down on his head. Knocked cold, the mercenary fell at his feet.

Wary that he'd been unable to check his surroundings for the brief duration of the fight, he spun around, sword up. Having driven his way straight through he was now in open space, the other mercenaries too occupied to notice him. Caught unawares, there were more Rats on the ground than rebels but they were into the fight now, the numbers roughly even. Marik saw one mercenary lurch out of the melee, apparently unharmed, and run towards the house. He considered pursuing but didn't want to leave with the battle undecided. He had to improve the odds.

His chance came before he could pick his next target. He sensed more than heard a charge from the right and saw a powerfully-built mercenary armed with a weighty axe. Coloured orange by the flames, the blade flew at Marik, who only avoided it by lifting his arms high. He retaliated with an opportunistic lash that caught the Rat on the bridge of his nose. Eyes raging as blood poured, the man charged forward with surprising speed. As he swiftly retreated, the mercenary swung back and forth. Knowing the iron blade wouldn't last long against such a heavy weapon, Marik concentrated on avoiding contact.

But he had already backtracked ten paces. If he didn't do something soon, his foe would force him into the water. After the next sweep, the man stopped. Marik wondered if it was due to the blood loss from his nose but then the mercenary's head dropped. A moment later, his arms dropped too and the axe hit the ground. Marik was all set to attack when he heard a thump. The mercenary's head jerked up and he fell to his knees, two arrows sticking out of his back.

A lithe, familiar figure emerged from the darkness. As well as the bow, Nasreen had a sword hanging from her belt. 'Marik, you must come. The armoury – they're surrounded.'

'All right. This way first.'

Marik had no doubt about their best chance of affecting the main clash. With Nasreen close behind, he skirted the battle – which still looked in the balance – and ran back to the ale kegs. He sheathed his sword and recovered the bow and quiver.

'What did you see?' he asked as they ran along the side of the barracks.

'The sailors made it to the armoury but a group of Rats countered quickly. Dalkus' force went to help but the other Rats followed.'

'How many arrows do you have?'

'Sixteen.'

'I have ten. We must make every one count.'

Marik checked at the corner that their path was clear then made for the pit before turning right into the unlit area. He and Nasreen covered the distance at a run and soon reached the guard tower.

The fire in the house had been put out. The small armoury situated between it and the warehouse was indeed surrounded by several ranks of mercenaries.

'Seen Hammerhand?' asked Marik.

'No. Nor Reverrik. Are you sure they're here?'

'They're here. All right, this position will do.'

Backs turned, closely packed and less than fifty feet away, the Rats were easy targets. Nasreen's first victim was hit dead centre and he staggered away from the fight, unnoticed by his comrades. Marik's first shot somehow passed between two of the first rank and seemingly did no damage. Both of them struck with their second shots and as two more men lurched away and fell, others started to turn and prepare to defend themselves. Nasreen's third shot caught one of those men in the shoulder, Marik's hit one in the thigh. But they were out of the fight.

'Now we move.'

Staying low, they scuttled away from the tower. Marik only halted when they were opposite the house.

'The front ranks are almost to the door,' said Nasreen. 'What if they're all gone?'

'They're still fighting. Let's give these bastards something else to worry about.' Despite these words, Marik could see at least four ranks of mercenaries at the armoury – probably fifty men.

Those they had wounded with the arrows were too preoccupied with their own injuries to warn others. Only when Marik and Nasreen had taken out four more did the mass of warriors realise they were being attacked from the rear. When word spread, it spread quickly; and one tall man near the back barked orders at those close by. Marik sent an arrow his way, missing his nose by an inch and striking another unfortunate in the neck.

'Move again.' Marik led Nasreen towards the warehouse but they barely kept ahead of the first dozen warriors despatched by the tall man. He pulled Nasreen down and they crouched together in the grass. Dead ahead, women were fleeing the house, the left side of which was still smoking. Seeing that many were headed towards the warehouse, Marik hoped they were following the directions he had given Ordi. He was momentarily tempted to enter the house to try and find Reverrik; turn the battle that way. But he couldn't let the mercenaries claim control of the armoury.

'The roof,' said Nasreen.

'What?'

'The armoury roof. If we get up there, we can take out plenty more out. Give Dalkus and Vasvarro a chance.'

Marik knew instantly that this was the best course of action, especially as the mercenary hunting party was now spreading their way. Staying low, the pair sprinted forward then slowed to creep past the battling warriors and into the narrow space between house and armoury. The roof was sloped, the closest beams only eight feet above ground. But there was an overhang and – in the darkness – no obvious method of climbing up.

'Round to the back.'

Marik slowed briefly at the corner and was relieved to find the area unoccupied. Armouries usually had only one entrance and this was no exception. There were, however, several big barrels. Two were full and too heavy to move but the third seemed empty. Once they had dragged it under the lower part of the roof, Marik was able to grab a beam and haul himself up.

'Go on,' urged Nasreen.

'No. Two bows are better than one.'

Marik steadied himself with one hand and helped Nasreen up with the other. The roof was thatched with slippery and unstable reed so Marik clambered up to the twin beams that ran along the peak. Once Nasreen was behind him, he continued forward as quickly as he dared.

At the far end, he pulled the bow from his shoulder. From below came the familiar sounds of metal on metal, metal on flesh and the grunts and cries of men fighting for their lives. Without a word, Marik and Nasreen took up positions on either side of the central beams and aimed downward. Directly below was a morass of warriors, one side indistinguishable from another. But the mercenaries further back were easily seen.

Marik's first shot from the roof took the tall man in the chest. His hands went instantly to the bolt and he backed away from his compatriots, strangely silent. As Marik took another arrow and nocked it, he could not help feeling it was a terrible thing to kill so many in such a fashion but he had said it himself: *no mercy*.

Nasreen seemed to be enjoying herself. Like him, she stayed low and remained as quiet as possible. They took turns in order to avoid aiming at the same target. Reverrik's men were so caught up in the battle that they seemed incapable of identifying this new threat. Between them, Marik and Nasreen took out ten more before the first shout went up.

'Archers!'

'Where?'

'Must be the roof!'

Marik and Nasreen laid flat. A spear was launched vainly in their direction but then came a shout from the defenders that gave Marik great encouragement.

'We've got them on the run! Push them back.'

The distinctive Eastern accent of Vasvarro. Once he was sure no more spears were coming their way, Marik crawled forward and ventured a look over roof-edge. The defenders had at last gained some ground and were now arranged in a tight semi-circle. Some had shields and lances: clearly, they had been able to break into the armoury before the counter-attack. This was all the encouragement Marik needed. They were almost out of arrows and would now be of more use on the ground.

He considered whether to call out to his allies below. He and Nasreen wouldn't be much use to anyone if they surprised the defenders and took a blade in the arse for their trouble. Then again, if they announced themselves, they would be at their enemies' mercy as they negotiated the drop.

Thankfully, the decision was made for him.

'Look,' whispered Nasreen.

The mercenaries no longer had such a numerical advantage and were being pushed further away by the shields and lances. Their lines were broken and they were fighting on in isolated groups.

'No further!' ordered Vasvarro. 'Keep those shields together.'

'Come on.' Nasreen was already moving towards the edge. Marik grabbed her arm. 'No. Me first.'

Leaving the bow behind, Marik moved up to the edge. 'Vasvarro, it's Marik – coming down.'

He twisted around, gripped the overhang with both hands then lowered himself.

Somebody tapped him on the leg.

'You're clear!' shouted Vasvarro.

Marik dropped to the ground. He was surprised to find no one close by but reached up to help Nasreen. As she let go of the roof, he caught her under the arms and she too made it down safely.

The slight figure of Vasvarro was ahead of them, bodily shifting the defenders around to retain the shield wall. Marik was trying to count their numbers but a step backwards caused him to trip on some unseen object and land on something soft. Putting his hands out to push himself up he touched flesh. And blood.

Nasreen cried out in revulsion. 'They're ... they're everywhere.'

Marik struggled to his feet and realised that they were surrounded by corpses.

'Marik, where are you?' yelled Vasvarro.

'Here.' The answer was no more than a whisper.

Marik turned and saw that Nasreen had opened the armoury door and picked up the lantern inside. Beyond were many racks holding weapons, shields and other equipment. Closer lay several rebels; only one of whom was moving. Nasreen knelt beside him and opened the lantern shutter wide.

Marik recognised young Ellors, the lad who had guided him to the island just a few hours earlier. Across his chest was a deep, seeping wound. He put his hand on Nasreen's arm and stared wide-eyed around him at the many dead. Nasreen froze when she spied a figure lying across the doorway, his entire face and head matted with blood. One of Dalkus' lifeless hands was still on the wound that had caved in his forehead.

'Marik!' cried Vasvarro angrily.

Forcing himself to put aside the awful cost of the rebel attack, Marik stepped over Ellors and grabbed a large rectangular shield and a six-foot lance.

'Are there arrows?' asked Nasreen.

There were full quivers hanging from hooks and an open box containing dozens of bolts.

'There are. But stay here for now.'

She did not reply as he stepped back past her. Marik could not face the thought of losing even one more of the locals to this bloody night. Pushing his left hand through the two handles of the heavy shield, he held the equally heavy lance and went outside. Wincing as he stepped on the dead twice more, he came up behind Vasvarro.

The barracks was now well ablaze, and the orange light blanketed much of the island. It was obvious from the reduced movement and noise that the combatants on both sides were tiring. The defenders' shield wall was still in place and – though they hadn't retreated – the mercenaries were not trying to advance.

'Captain.'

'About bloody time,' spat Vasvarro. 'Is this all of them?'

'Not sure.'

'Anyone else on our side?'

'Not many if there are.'

'There are scarcely a dozen of us. We have to finish this now while we still have the armoury; while we still have the upper hand.'

He came from the direction of the house: a towering, lurching, inhuman figure, firelight dancing on the myriad rings of his mail shirt. Reinvigorated by the sight, the mercenaries gave a roar and several more emerged from the darkness to join their ranks. Hammerhand lifted the great mace, drawing another cheer from those who might have previously thought themselves close to defeat.

'That'll be the giant then,' stated Vasvarro with admirable calm. A tall figure beside him stepped forward, like Marik armed with a lance. Marik noted the long tail of hair and realised this was Kaykirru, the captain's best warrior. He seemed to be readying himself for Hammerhand.

Marik felt someone behind him and turned to see Nasreen, bow in hand and two quivers of arrows over her shoulder. In the orange glow, her ravaged face appeared even stranger than usual but Marik only really saw the determined expression that he now knew so well.

'Stay behind the shields.'

She was about to protest but his glancing touch on her hand dissuaded her.

Marik moved on to Vasvarro. 'I'll deal with him. Hold the line.'

'Very well,' said the captain, directing Kaykirru back into the shield wall. 'Rather you than me.'

Marik hurried over to the defender closest to the right corner of the armoury. 'Let me through.'

The man moved aside and Marik recognised another familiar face from the reed-house. He couldn't remember his name but they had worked on the spears together the previous day. The rebel gripped Marik's arm – fingers digging in – and spoke into his ear.

'Avenge our dead. *Avenge them.*'

Chapter Twenty-Four

Marik did not have a chance to even consider those words. As soon as he slipped between the shields, one of the mercenaries was on him. Marik kept his own shield low and waited for the swordsman to swing. The first upward drive of the shield-edge disarmed him, the second chopped into his jaw, the third sent him careening back into his compatriots.

'Hammerhand!'

The defenders and mercenaries all turned towards Marik, as did the giant. Hammerhand had also donned an angular helmet that covered all but eyes and mouth.

'I'm surprised they could find a helm big enough for your head. Oh, and how's the eye?'

Shield up, lance at the ready, Marik moved beyond the rear of the mercenaries to draw Hammerhand away. Vasvarro sensibly chose that moment to order another attack and Reverrik's men soon had jabbing spears to contend with. Hammerhand watched as Marik backed towards the guard tower, firstly to move farther from the light of the burning barracks, secondly to lessen the chance of a surprise attack from behind. Keeping the giant occupied – in fact, simply surviving – would require every ounce of concentration.

Marik halted, not wanting his strategy to appear overly obvious. Hammerhand followed him. From the sharp gleam of the mail shirt (which reached down to his knees), Marik adjudged it to be steel. The lance he had liberated from the armoury was of iron but well-made. Only a close-range, powerful strike stood much chance of getting through the mail and even that might not be a disabling blow.

Up came the mace and soon it was swinging in a diagonal arc above the giant's shoulder. Now only dimly aware of the battle beyond his foe and the inferno away to his right, Marik angled his body to present the shield and held the spear loosely in his hand. If he had to throw it, he still had his sword. Hammerhand had clearly not forgotten losing his own weapon during their previous encounter. He too had a blade at his belt – an enormous broadsword at least four feet long.

Marik let the first close swing of the chained rock whizz past; there was no point risking damage to the shield if he could avoid it. This too was well-made – timber planks with an iron boss – but he wasn't sure how well it would stand up to the mace.

Hammerhand took a long step forward, his swing accelerating. Marik misjudged his side-step and the next pass of the rock cracked the corner of his shield, almost loosening his grip. Sensing that the guard tower was directly behind him, he took a few more steps to his left, wary of limiting his manoeuvring space. Even if he didn't survive the encounter, he knew that every moment Hammerhand was occupied gave the rebels more of a chance.

That brief distracting thought cost him. Showing remarkable dexterity, Hammerhand bowed low and brought the mace over his head, stretching his great arm out to extend his reach. Marik had barely enough time to cower below the shield as the rock plunged towards him. It struck with bone-shaking power and if he hadn't already been crouching, he would have fallen. Looking up to find he was now holding half a shield, he felt dozens of pinpricks of pain in his head.

There was no time to consider their origin. Flinging the ruined shield away, Marik got both hands on the lance and drove straight at Hammerhand. Leaving his mace by his side, the giant simply kicked out. His boot struck close to the tip and again Marik almost lost his grip. To deter an opportunistic strike, he waved the lance towards the mercenary's face and skipped away to find more space. Almost tripping as he stood on an ill-placed stone, he realised the pain in his head had faded. Nothing serious.

'Not long now, little man,' uttered Hammerhand.

'You didn't answer me earlier. How *is* the eye?'

Marik had no doubt that the mercenary had survived more fights than him – probably a lot more – but he was clearly vulnerable to provocation. His earlier restraint was forgotten as he swirled the mace once more.

'Will cut out both of yours,' he growled between gritted teeth.

'I'd say the same,' countered Marik, though he kept his gaze on the weapon. 'But, of course, you've only got the *one* now.'

Unsure why he hadn't thought of it before, he altered direction, side-stepping to a position where he could better exploit Hammerhand's limited vision.

'You die soon,' said the mercenary, before demonstrating that he had in fact learned a great deal from their previous encounter.

He threw the mace. Marik tried to block it with the lance but the darkness impeded him and Hammerhand's aim was true. The rock caught Marik on the side of the head, a glancing blow but sufficient to trigger an explosion of white light and send him staggering away. Blind and unsure what had happened to the lance, he fumbled his way to the sword and pulled it free. Hearing Hammerhand's charge, he elected to do the one thing his opponent might not expect.

'Yah!' Two hands on the sword, he heaved the blade across a wide arc. The dull clink told him that he had struck the mail-shirt. Good to know he'd hit him; not so good to realise he was close. As his vision began to clear, Marik backed away, now swinging one-handed to cover his retreat. A dark shape materialised in front of him, following him into a patch of high, thick grass. A glance to his right told Marik that they were well past the guard tower; in fact, he wasn't that far from the water. At least he'd taken the giant out of the battle for however long he'd been fighting him.

Shaking his head to clear the fog, he saw the great figure blot out the flames and launch a horizontal blade. Though Marik got his own sword up into a parry, the steel sliced straight through the iron and suddenly the sword felt a lot lighter. Now virtually defenceless, he retreated once more.

'You die *very* soon.'

Though it didn't seem particularly heroic, Marik was giving serious thought to running and leaping into the water. But then Hammerhand was free to rejoin the battle and Marik was in no doubt that he could turn it single-handed.

'I cut out eyes with sword. Worse than knife.'

Marik didn't bother replying to that; he had plenty else to concern him. He was armed with half a sword, the water was only a few yards away and his foe was close enough to block any attempt to flee. Marik checked the blade. It had shattered unevenly, leaving a small but sharp tip that would at least cut through flesh.

From what he had seen, Hammerhand was vulnerable only below the knee. That was where he would have to strike. And this far from the fire, with only his one eye, his vision remained a weakness. If he could get close enough, Marik knew he could do some damage.

He moved to the right to get on that weaker side but Hammerhand was too quick. He blocked the move, sword out wide, and three of his long strides pressed Marik back towards the bank. Marik could feel the ground angling downwards. He didn't dare take another step, in case he fell and gave his enemy the chance to kill him.

'Hammerhand!'

Nasreen. Some distance away.

'I'm talking to you!' she yelled, sounding as bold as any man Marik had heard.

An arrow pinged off the back of the mail-shirt. Hammerhand emitted a sigh of annoyance.

But when another bolt struck him, he twitched. Marik reckoned the arrow had caused enough pain to concern him.

'Turn around,' said Nasreen. 'Show me that doltish face.'

Marik didn't like the edge of arrogance in her voice. If she got too close to him ...

Hammerhand had evidently decided to deal with his nearer enemy first. Marik heard the blade scything towards him before he saw it. There was nowhere to go but back and both feet slipped off the lip of the bank. His elbow struck it on the way down and he lost the broken sword. Just as his boots hit the muddy slope, he reached out with both hands and grabbed enough of the root-like plants and undergrowth to halt his fall. Half-expecting the vegetation to come free and send him tumbling into the water, he somehow braced himself. From above, the thumping impacts of Hammerhand on the move.

Knowing that Nasreen now faced the giant alone was sufficient motivation to send him scrambling back upwards. Though much of the undergrowth came away in his hands, the roots were solid enough. However, the mud was soft and the angle severe. He could gain no traction at all until he wedged his boot on a particularly thick clump of root. From there he was able to get his hands up onto the bank.

Marik heard a shriek from Nasreen and a rumble of laughter from Hammerhand. By kicking repeatedly at the same place, he made enough of a second foot-hold to throw himself upward. And once he had his elbows over the lip of the bank, he was able to pull his legs up and roll onto the grass.

Wishing there was enough light to find the lost lance, he loped towards the great figure now pursuing the smaller one towards the dock. Nasreen cried out again as she fell and Marik accelerated into a sprint. When she didn't get up, he realised she'd been wounded. Hammerhand wasn't wasting any time: he loomed over her, altering his grip to deliver a downward stab with his broadsword.

Marik launched himself at the giant's back. The fingers of his left hand slid up the mail and onto his shoulder. Throwing his other hand over the right shoulder, Marik felt his feet slipping. But the belt that held in the mail coat was large and the toe of his boot caught. Hammerhand was already reacting so Marik hurried to finish what he had started. Even a man so heavily armoured has vulnerable spots – if you get close enough.

Jamming both hands under the lower rim of the helmet, he wrenched it up and hoped that Nasreen could still use her sword.

'Throat! His throat!'

Marik turned his head away as Hammerhand's great left paw flailed at him.

'Nasreen – now!'

Digging his knees into Hammerhand's back he hung there, his whole body shaking with the effort.

The giant's left hand encircled Marik's left arm. Marik had set himself and his grip was good but even when reaching back and at an awkward angle, the strength in that hand was immense.

'Now!'

Then the right arm moved and he knew the blade would be coming at him. His forearms were against the giant's neck and he could feel the veins pulse. He saw the long blade raised high, ready to sweep down at him.

Something warm splashed his hands. The huge body on which he was perched spasmed and then became still. He heard the blood glugging from Hammerhand's throat. The grip on his arm weakened. Then came a hissing breath and a wet gurgle.

As the giant lost his sword, Marik let go and dropped to the ground. He narrowly avoided being crushed as Hammerhand took two stiff steps backwards then toppled over, thumping into the grass with arms outstretched. Another wet gurgle and then he was quiet.

Marik stood there, breathing hard, barely able to believe that the giant had actually been felled. Nasreen still had her blade at the ready. She staggered forward and hacked down at the body. The mail turned her blade and she stumbled, almost falling into Marik.

He grabbed her shoulder. 'Stop. He's dead.'

Nasreen sucked in breath and emitted a strange little laugh.

'You're hurt?'

'Leg.'

Marik reached down and checked for the injury.

'Stop feeling me up, Souther. Other leg.'

'Can't be that bad if you're cracking jokes.'

In fact, it was fairly bad: a long rent across the back of her thigh. Her trousers and the whole leg were sticky with blood though Marik was relieved to find the cut was not deep.

'How did he get you *here*?'

'I was running at the time. How can anyone be that big and that quick? What now?'

Marik looked up. The only movement he could see was at the armoury, where the battle still raged.

'I'm going to need your sword.'

The shield wall was long gone. The clash had broken up into isolated scraps between twos and threes and fours. Vasvarro had no more than ten on his side, the mercenaries perhaps double that. At the edges of the fight lay the dead, dying and injured.

Like the battle, the fire was past its peak and now cast a weak light upon weak men.

Marik approached with Nasreen limping along behind him. In his left hand was a lantern he had nabbed from outside the house. All seemed quiet there and he was beginning to wonder if Reverrik had escaped. If his force had been defeated, that would not matter.

'It's over!'

Marik had bellowed with all the strength he could summon. Men fighting for their lives were not easily distracted but before long they were all looking his way.

'You can see that. So, if you're one of Reverrik's, lay down your weapon now and I give my word you will live.'

'Ha!' Thankfully it was Vasvarro. Several of his sailors also gave a cheer.

Marik moved the lantern close to the dripping head of Hammerhand, which was quite remarkably heavy. He did not look at it himself: this was a gruesome, barbaric thing that he would not have done, given the choice. But he had seen such tactics before and knew them to be effective.

'By all the gods, you did it,' said another man whose voice Marik did not recognise.

'Weapons down and you live. I won't say it again.'

Nasreen had recovered her bow and stepped up beside him, an arrow already nocked.

A sword hit the ground, then an axe, then many more of the Rats' weapons.

A warrior whose tunic had been ripped apart walked over to Marik. He looked like a Souther and was carrying both a shield and an axe.

'You give your word?'

'I give my word. You will be spared.'

'Except Reverrik,' added Nasreen.

'Except Reverrik,' repeated Marik.

'Talks a good fight, that one,' said the mercenary. 'Don't see him down here in the shit, though, do you?'
He dropped his shield and his axe and walked back to his comrades.

Vasvarro took charge of the defeated Rats and soon had them bound and on their knees in a line outside the armoury. There were around thirty, some of whom had emerged from various quarters to give themselves up. Despite her injury, Nasreen was leading the efforts to gather the rebels, even the wounded. There were only a handful on their feet but Marik was glad to see the former prisoner Kedrim among them. He was even more relieved when young Parrs appeared. The lad was covered in blood, mud and sweat and didn't say a word. He simply stood with a hand on Marik's shoulder, gazing down at his sword.

Vasvarro approached. 'There are many wounded beyond help. We should finish them off.'

'The mercenaries, yes. Any rebels with breath still in them will be helped. Understood?'

Vasvarro didn't reply at first. And despite the difference in height, he was not concerned about stepping forward so that he was very close. 'I have only seven men left. Until I see the contents of that warehouse, I'll not be taking any more orders from you.'

Marik didn't have the energy to argue.

Parrs spoke up at last. 'Marik, the house.'

'Yes. It's time.'

There were lights at three of the upper windows and Marik spied the silhouette of a woman behind one of them. He moved warily, staying close to the front wall. He still had Nasreen's sword and had told Parrs to be ready for a fight. Reaching the front door, he found it locked. He addressed the woman and whoever else was inside.

'The battle is over! You're free. You can come out.'

No reply.

Marik turned to Parrs. 'Might be better coming from you.'

But Parrs didn't seem in a state to say much at all.

'It's you.'

As he heard these words, Marik watched a group of women emerge from the gloom, walking past the end of the house still issuing smoke. The tall woman leading them was holding a lantern and her smile seemed utterly out of place. Though he had seen little of her during their first meeting, Marik knew instantly who it was. Upon both cheeks were the cuts made by Reverrik's knife.

'Ordi.'

'Are they beaten?' she asked. 'Are they truly beaten?'

'Hammerhand is dead. What about Reverrik?'

Ordi turned towards the door. 'All that I could persuade came with me. Some are still with him.'

Suddenly the door opened. A single woman stood there; older than the others – not far off forty. Her gaze moved from Ordi to Marik.

'Are you the leader?'

'I suppose so.'

'He's waiting for you.'

Before Marik entered the house, more women came from the direction of the wood; the rest of Ordi's group. They were keen to help and he sent them in the direction of the armoury to aid the wounded. He asked Ordi and Parrs to accompany him and they were led silently through the house by the woman. The acrid smell of smoke seemed to have reached every corner of the building. Much of the interior was unlit but Marik saw enough to suggest that Reverrik had lived in considerable comfort. He noted well-crafted tables and chairs, tapestries and paintings on the walls, animal hides and rugs upon the floors.

'What's her name?' he asked as they followed the woman along the long corridor of the second floor, heading away from the end damaged by fire.

'Coroli,' said Ordi, apparently not concerned if the older woman overheard. 'She has always done his bidding.'

Coroli reached the end of the corridor, glanced through an open doorway and strode inside. Marik hesitated.

'Come, please.' Reverrik's cordial tone was difficult to reconcile with the bellowing chieftain Marik had earlier observed.

Marik peered around the doorway before entering. What he saw shocked him more than anything he had seen in the previous hours.

The room was spacious, equipped with a large bed, several tables and an oval, wall-mounted mirror. Above the bed was a painting of naked female figures arranged at all angles, hair and limbs intertwined. Reverrik was slouched on another large chair, bare-chested as usual, his hands at rest on his paunch. Above the curls of his beard, his bronzed face seemed surprisingly youthful. His eyes were pale blue; bright and fearless. Seated around him on stools were four women – two of them no more than girls. They were well-attired in clean, elegant dresses, their hair adorned with ribbons and bows.

Each of them was holding a knife against their own throat.

'Who else is there?' enquired Reverrik, as if he was hosting some social event. 'Do come in. All of you.'

Marik made way for Parrs and Ordi, sword still in his hand. He found himself standing opposite Coroli, who was clearly not easily unnerved. When Parrs saw the women, he whispered something to himself. Reverrik ignored him but sat up slightly when he saw Ordi.

He tutted regretfully. 'You always were a spirited one. I must say I'm a little disappointed though.'

'It's over,' she said, her voice trembling. 'But we can all live.'

'Unlikely.' Reverrik's face had been patched by soot, presumably while fighting the fire. He turned to Marik.

'And you must be the Souther. You really killed Hammerhand?'

'No, I just helped. Nasreen killed him. Remember her?'

That at least seemed to shake the man a little, though he recovered quickly. 'Well, well. Ugly bitches often make good fighters.'

Marik tapped the tip of his sword against a floorboard. 'See all the blood on my hands and arms? That's because a few minutes ago, I chopped off Hammerhand's head. Speak of Nasreen again, and I'll do the same to you. You must know you'll never get off this island.'

'Cut.'

He said it so casually that Marik did not immediately respond, even when he saw that all four women were moving the knives towards their throats.

'No!' yelled Ordi.

'Stop.'

They did so at Reverrik's order.

He grinned.

'Why?' breathed Parrs.

'They can't help it,' said Ordi. 'They've forgotten their mothers and fathers. He's everything to them now.'

'Couldn't have said it better myself.' Reverrik aimed a finger at Marik. 'But you should be careful, big fellow. You might have beaten my men but you'll not find it as easy to best me. I am, however, a pragmatist. You can have the island and all the rest but I will be leaving with Coroli and the girls. You will also give me eight of my men to handle the coaster. I will depart within the hour. I don't think I need to explain the consequences if these instructions are not followed.'

'Don't you see it's over?' said Parrs.

Ordi put a hand on his arm.

Parrs gazed at the youngest of the women. 'Sarina, you know me. It's Parrs. Our mothers knew each other. We used to go with them when they picked whitepetal near Ettwater. Don't you remember?'

Reverrik snorted. 'Very touching.'

'Sarina, you're free now. All you have to do is put the knife down and join us.'

Reverrik leaned forward, expression now serious. 'That's enough.'

'You're free,' repeated Parrs.

Reverrik turned to Marik. 'If you don't shut him-'

It wasn't Sarina who moved but one of the older women.

She turned and jabbed the knife straight into Reverrik's neck. It was not a stabbing weapon but nonetheless stuck fast. No blood flowed. Reverrik looked at the woman, his pale eyes bulging as the pain struck. She fell from her stool and scrambled towards the doorway. Sarina was just behind her.

The other two girls watched as Reverrik stood and reeled backwards, face contorting.

'Cut!'

Marik was already moving by then and he snatched the knife from the nearest woman. The last woman drew blood but the attempt was half-hearted and she was disarmed by Parrs before she could do any more damage. Coroli tried to join her master but was dissuaded by the tip of Marik's sword. He threw the little knife aside and was relieved to see others arriving in the corridor, including Nasreen.

'Get them out,' he said. 'Check for hidden weapons then get them all out.'

Two male rebels assisted Parrs and Ordi. Coroli spat at Marik, earning herself a heavy slap from Ordi, who dragged the older woman out by her hair.

Marik wiped his face and followed Reverrik, who had staggered to the far wall. Now beside the oval mirror, the mercenary hesitantly placed both hands on the knife, wincing instantly at his own touch. Blood had begun to seep from below the weapon's handle.

'I'd leave it in if I were you. It'll be less painful than what they'll do to you outside.'

Chapter Twenty-Five

Dawn brought a brilliant, pitiless light. The barracks had burnt almost to the ground, suffusing the air with smoke; and most of Old Island was now a muddy mess strewn with abandoned weapons and pools of blood. The enemy dead – including Hammerhand and Reverrik – had been thrown into the pit, the fallen rebels placed in a line behind the house. The remaining mercenaries were still beside the armoury, watched over by Kaykirru and another of the sailors. Two more had died of their injuries during the night and another six were with the rebel wounded. Of them there were ten; all now accommodated within the house and being cared for by the women. Ordi had already proved herself an able leader and was now organising the treatment. While some like her had grasped their new life, many of the others appeared hesitant and dazed; unable to understand what had occurred.

Marik had been occupied with collecting the dead; a job he was glad to have finished by dawn. He wasn't sure why he'd avoided trying to find Orim's daughter. It was as almost as if he didn't want to know the truth; in case something had happened to her or she was one of those who had remained loyal to Reverrik. In the event, she came to him, Parrs leading her by the hand.

'This is Korina.'

Marik detected some of her mother in her and was glad to see little trace of the distant gaze he had observed in others. She had the same kind face as Tarrika, the same long, dark hair. They both stood there staring and it was while before anything was said.

'I prayed to Sa Sarkan every day.'

'You father hoped you would. He and your mother did the same.'

'Parrs says you know them.'

'A little.'

'My father is injured.'

'Yes, but healing well.'

'When will he be here?'

'Soon, very soon, I'm sure.'

She reached out and took Marik's hand in both of hers. 'Thank you. From all of us, thank you.'

Marik looked up and saw that several of the women were watching from the windows.

'Are you all right?' Korina was looking up at his head, which had been struck by numerous large splinters when Hammerhand destroyed the shield.

'Fine.'

In fact, he felt as if he could drop where he stood and sleep for a week. But there was much to take care of before he dared rest.

'Is there anything we can do for you?' asked Korina.

Even though she had been on Old Island for so long, her presence amongst all this killing and death seemed wrong. But she was alive.

'Believe me, just seeing you is more than enough.'

Korina smiled. 'You must be hungry.'

'Not now. Maybe later.'

'*I'm* hungry,' said Parrs.

'Come with me then,' said Korina; and the two of them walked back to the house.

Including the former prisoners, there were only nine rebels on their feet. The oldest of them was Kedrim who, despite his weakened state, was evidently a courageous and capable man. It was he Marik went to before meeting Vasvarro. The Easterlings had two injured in the house but had already cremated their dead and conducted a ceremony honouring their comrades. Marik had allowed Vasvarro to take charge of the coaster but the warehouse remained untouched. The captain could currently be seen inspecting the vessel.

As Marik, Kedrim, Parrs and Nasreen gathered beneath the guard tower, four of the rebels were departing in canoes. Their task was to spread word of the victory and invite everyone to Old Island. Marik thought it crucial that the delta people see their dead enemies before they began a new existence free from fear. He also knew it would be easier to ensure Vasvarro stuck to the agreement if the sailors were heavily outnumbered by locals.

'Some of the women want to leave,' said Parrs. 'They don't want to stay here a moment longer.'

Marik answered him: 'Apart from the fact that we don't have the transport, I suggest keeping everyone together. In fact, I also suggest that someone address all those present. You will need to organise yourselves, ensure that nothing like this can happen again.'

'They just want to see their families,' added Parrs.

'Of course. But their families will come here.'

'I agree,' said Kedrim. 'We have weapons, hopefully we will have more people willing to fight – to replace those lost. We will need our own army.'

Nasreen was nodding keenly. Marik hoped she hadn't already forgotten his words about killing.

Kedrim gestured towards the ship. 'The Easterling is angry. He has barely enough men to handle the coaster.'

'I'm hoping his mood will improve when he takes his share from the warehouse,' said Marik. 'Don't forget he also has his slaves.'

'Good riddance,' said Parrs.

Kedrim was still looking at Vasvarro. 'Without the sailors, we would have lost. Good fighters, every man.'

Marik reached into his pocket and took out the fob of keys he had liberated from Reverrik's corpse.

'I'm assuming one of these opens the padlock on the warehouse. I'm going to tell Vasvarro that we'll divide the contents this afternoon. I'll need all of you there. Just in case.'

Marik did not want to go into the house. He imagined the women might fuss over him and he had no desire to see the injured rebels, especially when he heard that young Ellors had succumbed to his wounds. By midday, many of the delta people had reached the island. The power of Reverrik's rule was such that some stayed in their vessels or close to the dock until assured it was safe. Parrs and Kedrim guided the new arrivals to the pit, where they could see the bodies of Hammerhand and Reverrik for themselves. Those related to the women ran straight for the house and Marik observed several families reunite. Though he watched from a distance, it was good to know the sacrifice had been worthwhile. As there was, however, no sign of Orim, he took himself off to the copse and laid down by a tree, close to the warehouse in case anybody got curious.

He was awoken by a shadow falling across him. Vasvarro stood there, forearm now bandaged. Behind him was Kaykirru. The tall sailor's nose had been broken, the surrounding skin now coloured with faint yellows and purples.

'Time's getting on,' said the captain. 'Let's see what we've got.'

'What's the hurry?'

'I have a ship to reclaim, remember? I want what we're owed. We're leaving at dawn tomorrow.'

Vasvarro stared down at Marik without blinking, his face grim.

Marik got to his feet. 'As you wish. Let me fetch the others and we'll get started.'

Vasvarro and his man walked towards the warehouse door.

'Captain.'

The Easterling stopped but did not turn around.

'You and your men fought with great skill and bravery. I am grateful; as are the rebels. I am truly sorry that you lost so many.'

Vasvarro gave an almost imperceptible nod.

'There is also this.' Marik reached inside his tunic and took out a bag of coins. 'I found a chest in Reverrik's room. Here is a third of the coins. Solid silver; First Empire standard. The rest will go to the locals to divide as they see fit.'

Marik didn't mention the second chest he had found: it contained dozens of gems and pieces of jewellery that Nasreen confirmed had been plundered from the women and their families. He hoped every piece could be returned to its rightful owners.

Vasvarro took the bag. 'And for yourself?'

'Nothing. Yet.'

The warehouse was very well stocked and Vasvarro nearly filled the hold of his newly-acquired ship. With Kedrim, Parrs and Nasreen there to witness that all was done fairly, the sailors removed a third of the contents. For unwanted bulky materials such as timber and metal, Vasvarro insisted on being compensated with portable items. This meant that the sailors ended up with a considerable stash of spices, dried fruit, dried fish, dried meat, ale, wine, cutlery, crockery, hides and bronzeware. Once all this had been doled out and the warehouse locked, Marik handed the keys over to Kedrim. He had spent some time asking the other prisoners their view of the man and they confirmed what Marik had observed; Kedrim was methodical, calm and fair. In time, the locals could sort their affairs out but Marik reckoned the man would make a good temporary leader

Knowing that Vasvarro would insist, he then led the way over to the armoury and ensured the sailors got their share. He had already claimed Hammerhand's broadsword but only for its monetary value. Once the Easterlings had their booty, the weapons from the battle were also collected up and placed inside. Marik needed a weapon for himself and found several fine steel blades. After a few minutes spent testing them, he discovered an excellent piece with an exquisitely honed blade and a steel hand-guard. The engraved handle identified it as the work of Siletar of Utiro, the premier swordmaker of the First Empire. Marik had only ever seen a few of the blades.

'Anything else?' suggested Kedrim. 'A bow? A shield? Something from the house perhaps? You deserve it.'

'No, no. That's all yours. This will do me fine.'

With every hour that passed, Marik grew more anxious that Orim had not arrived. He was not the only one. Korina sat on the grass not far from the dock, clearly hoping her father would be on the next canoe that entered the channel. At least two hundred locals had arrived during the day and a strange, febrile atmosphere had gripped the place. The sight of the sailors loading up the coaster with their haul had caused a few enquires and Vasvarro's terse responses did little to ease the tension.

As the sun began to set, Kedrim took the initiative and called a meeting. He and Parrs gathered the people together and stood directly in front of the house to address them. Marik was pleased to see that the locals were respectfully quiet. Many were now reunited with daughters and sisters and they held each other close. He saw the uneasy expressions on the faces of some of the men. They had not been part of the revolt; perhaps they believed history would not judge them well for it.

As Kedrim began by describing all that had occurred during the night, Marik stood beside Nasreen at the back of the crowd.

'Are your family here?'

She shook her head. 'It's far. Word might not reach them for a while.'

'Will you go home then?'

She turned away and listened to Kedrim.

He started hesitantly – and at points seemed overwhelmed by the occasion – but the people listened, rapt, to every word. Marik observed a family nearby. Both mother and father had an arm around their daughter. She was in turn holding her parents so tightly that her fingers had turned white.

Nasreen nudged him and pointed to the dock. Korina was standing up and gazing intently at the channel. By the time Marik reached her, he could see her father.

Orim was at the back of the canoe; and even though his injured arm was in a sling, he was paddling with the other. In front of him was the ill woman who had also remained behind at the hideout. When he saw his daughter walking towards the dock, tears already streaming down her face,

Orim put his paddle in the boat and his hand over his face, apparently unable to believe what he was seeing. It was left to the woman to guide their vessel the last few feet. Marik hurried down and held the canoe against the wooden pontoon.

'We couldn't leave Garrun and the boy,' she explained. 'No one came to the reed-house until the afternoon.'

Korina fell to her knees on the dock. Her father at last took his hand away and beheld his daughter. When she leaned across, he first cradled her face, then kissed her half a dozen times and embraced her. As Marik and the female rebel held the canoe steady, they exchanged a smile.

Once Orim was on the dock, father and daughter began to talk, hesitantly at first, then at great speed. The woman was guided towards the meeting by Nasreen, who had come down to the dock.

'And you,' said Orim, gripping Marik's upper arm. 'I know you don't believe it but I am sure Sa Sarkan sent you to us. To all of us. How can I ever thank you?'

Marik could offer no more than an awkward shrug and was glad when Korina begged her father for news of Tarrika and Northcrest.

He walked over to Nasreen. 'How's the leg?'

'Ordi stitched it. Hurts. That's why I have this.' She took a flask from under the cloak she was wearing. 'Quite a store in the cellar. Want some? Maybe you'll let me pick some of those splinters out of your forehead. You look a right mess.'

'I'd appreciate that.'

'We'll need some good light. The house?'

'I'll see you there. I just need to speak to Vasvarro.'

Reverrik's room was not being used so they went there. Marik sat on the floor just below a lantern. Nasreen sat beside him in a chair with a hefty pair of iron tweezers provided by Ordi. She seemed quite happy to work away in silence and placed all the bloody shards of wood in a little pile. The flask – which turned out to contain a very strong red wine – was between her feet.

'May I?'

'Please. Plenty more where that came from.'

Marik took several long sips. He guessed Nasreen was a little drunk because she had for once lowered her hood. She was very close to him and he felt ashamed at his own revulsion. The affliction was the worst he had ever seen, leaving almost no part of her face untouched. He wondered at the cruelty of the gods, or the spirits, or whatever had created the disease.

'Don't,' she said.

'What?'

'Don't look at me.'

'Sorry. I don't mind, you know.'

'Maybe I do.' A pause, then: 'Anyway, don't get any ideas.'

Marik grinned.

'Oh, I forgot,' she added. 'You prefer older women.'

'Honestly, I'm not all that picky.'

'Maybe you should be. You're not bad looking – for a Souther.'

'I know compliments from you are rare so I'll just enjoy that one.'

She kept at her work. They both kept downing the wine.

'How many do you think we killed?' said Nasreen after a time. 'I reckon it must be-'

'-I don't keep count,' said Marik.

'Why not?'

'Maybe I'm worried someone else is.'

A minute later, Ordi appeared at the doorway, holding a lantern. 'All right?'

'Fine,' said Marik.

She stood there for a moment, then shook her head. 'There are so many happy people on the island now. Even here in the house. It hardly seems real.' She didn't wait for a reply but simply went on her way.

Nasreen took a moment to clean blood and wood off the tweezers. 'You're going to leave, aren't you?'

'Yes,' replied Marik, who had already made up his mind. 'With Vasvarro, in the morning. I don't think they particularly want me aboard but he needs help watching the Rats. As soon as they get to anywhere near a decent road, I'll be on my way.'

'I wish you'd stay.'

Marik winced as Nasreen wrenched a particularly deep splinter from his skull.

'Not for me,' she added. 'For everyone. For the delta. At least for a while.'

'I ... I've done what I said I would do. It's time. Nasreen, bearing in mind that we defeated the Rats and you got Reverrik, would you agree that maybe you owe me one?'

'Maybe.'

'Good. Because I have a proposition for you.'

'About what?'

'About you. About what you do now.'

Not for the first time, her mood changed abruptly. 'What business is that of yours?'

'Will you just hear me out?'

'Nobody tells me what to do. Or even *proposes* it.'

She stood up and put the tweezers on a nearby table.

'You're finished?' he asked.

'Yes.'

Nasreen pulled her hood up and headed for the door. But she never quite got there. 'I'll hear you out, Marik – *if* you tell me what you're doing so far from home. I asked Parrs, Orim – no one seems to know. And on Spring Island you refused to tell me.'

'You really care that much?'

'You know my story. I want to know yours.'

Of all the people he might have told, he didn't mind if it was her; especially in a good cause.

'All right.'

She returned to the chair. Marik put out his hand and she passed him the wine. He took a very long swig.

'You know I was in the People's Guard. Five years ago, a man named Baldar took command of the Guard in the province of Torvaris. In the Nine Provinces, most run their affairs through a council but in Torvaris it has always been weak – riven by tribal differences. So, the Guard there has always been powerful.

'A century ago, Torvaris was the dominant, most wealthy province. Baldar wanted to restore that dominance. He enlarged his army to double the size of any other – all illegal under our treaties, by the way. It was only a matter of time before he struck out. First to fall was Dramark – very isolated, though the other provinces tried to help. Baldar then forced his own treaty on the council of Ornsvall, bringing their Guard under his command. From there they took Naasa and Stenanger. That was when they started calling him Baldar the Bold. He has no respect for tradition, for the old ways, for anything decent. The man is a tyrant, a conqueror, everything the South used to favour before the Treaty of Councils.'

'I've heard of it.'

'It kept the peace for eight decades. I am from Lothlagen. To try and stop Baldar we formed an alliance with Farheim, Storholm and Harnovik – the province where the two armies first met. There were several battles, thousands died, only winter storms stopped the fighting. When it began again, we met Baldar's forces in a forest so remote it didn't even have a name.

'I was a sergeant – more experienced than most. The fighting was the worst I'd ever seen – relentless, vicious. I ... was not doing well. I kept up appearances in front of the men but my mind was weak. I couldn't sleep and when I did it was nothing but nightmares. It was as if I had been born in that forest and I fully expected to die there. We had lost so many. When it all started I'd been surrounded by friends and not one of them was left. One morning we were ordered to defend a gully, an important position.

'There were three attacks. We lost most of our men in the first, more in the second - including our captain. When the third attack came, there was only a handful of us. I was the senior man but ... I just ... gave up. I walked away. Left the line. Left my men. Couldn't do it anymore. We lost the gully and we lost the battle – in no small part because of me. My commander wanted me hanged but our general had known me for years. He sent me home. I started walking but ... I couldn't face my mother, my brother. I couldn't face anyone. Close to the border of Harnovik and Lothlagen, I turned north and headed for the King's Keep. I've not been south of it ever since. From what I've heard, there's even fighting in Lothlagen now.'

It might have been the hollowness of the hours after the battle but even after recounting his sorry tale, Marik felt little emotion. Perhaps it was because his trials did not seem so terrible in comparison with what Nasreen had been through. Even so, he appreciated being able to speak of it rather than just think of it.

She put a hand on his shoulder. 'Will you go back?'

'Not yet. I'll head north to Khard. There's an old friend up there – said I'd always be welcome.'

They drank until the flask was empty.

'What's this proposition then?' asked Nasreen.

'Come with me.'

Outside, the locals were enjoying themselves. A fire was alight and a considerable amount of food and drink had been distributed. Marik received many words of thanks and pats on the back as he searched for Orim. Once he'd found him and Korina, he introduced Nasreen and told Korina how important her contribution had been. Though Nasreen of course had her hood back up, she did speak to Korina, who was clearly as warm and friendly as her mother.

Marik took Orim aside, to a quiet area not far from the still-smouldering barracks. 'You asked how you could repay me.'

'Yes?'

'Nasreen – if she'll agree to it, I'd like you and Tarrika to take her in.'

Orim looked surprised but said nothing.

Marik continued: 'She has her own family, I know, but she won't return to them – not yet. You can imagine why. With you, perhaps she could get used to family life, a normal life. She's as good a shot as me – she'd pay her way. And maybe in time she'll be ready to return to her own kin. It would mean a lot to me.'

By the time he finished, Orim's expression had changed so much that he knew what the answer would be.

'Of course. She shall be made very welcome.'

'I thank you.'

'You're not coming back, are you? To Northcrest?'

Marik shook his head.

'You promised the boy. What shall I tell him?'

'He's already done without me for a while. If I return, it will only be more difficult for him.'

'And for you.'

'There's no one in the world I would rather entrust him too.'

'And we will be happy to care for him. By the Great Maker, Tarrika and I have been alone for so long. Now we will have five in our house. But what do I tell him, Marik?'

'I don't know.'

Orim looked toward the water for a moment before replying. 'Tola told me several times that the two of you were best friends. He was very proud of that. I could tell him that you said the pair of you will always be best friends – forever.'

'Yes. Tell him that.'

Marik said his farewells that night and joined Vasvarro and the sailors at dawn. A low morning mist hung over the island and the water but they had recruited a local guide who was confident he could get them out of the delta. The enslaved mercenaries were all tied to a chain that ran along the centre of the ship. On either side of them, six of the sailors manned the oars while Kaykirru watched the captives, a club in his hand. Vasvarro took the tiller himself and steered the coaster away from the island with the local guide beside him.

Marik sat alone at the stern. He had liberated a large pack from the house and filled it with two flasks of fresh water, dried fish, dried fruit and a flask of wine. In his pocket were the handful of silver coins that Kedrim had insisted on giving him. Lying beside him on the deck were the two blades he had claimed: Hammerhand's huge broadsword and the Siletar blade. He would sell the broadsword and keep the Siletar for his own use. He had never before owned a weapon with such a combination of workmanship, lightness, strength and durability.

Marik closed his eyes for a moment and saw a chaos of faces – the living and the dead. It seemed strange that he was now leaving them all behind but the sensation was not a new one. He had slept only for a few hours but felt all the better for it. Despite the dubious company aboard the ship, it also felt good to be on the water; on the move.

At an order from Vasvarro, the oarsmen settled into a steady, powerful rhythm. As the coaster picked up speed, Marik looked back over the stern. Old Island had already disappeared from view, lost in wreathes of thick, white mist.

ACKNOWLEDGEMENTS

Marik's Way is my first fantasy novel and was written over the last two years. There are some people to thank: firstly, my editors, and they're all Browns – Milena, Neil and Sarah. This whole process has been made easier by two very wise and generous fellow novelists: Simon Turney and Gordon Doherty, self-publishing gurus at the top of their games. Technical advice and assistance were provided by the very patient Leila Summers. Last but not least, thanks to my colleague and friend, Joseph Davies, who produced the map. Joe is also a writer; look out for news of our upcoming project.

My hope is that *Marik's Way* will become the start of a series but that depends very much on how many people buy it – so thank you for doing so!

Also by Nick Brown

Agent of Rome Series
The Siege
The Imperial Banner
The Far Shore
The Black Stone
The Emperor's Silver
The Earthly Gods

Short Story eBooks
Death This Day
The Eleventh Hour
The Flames of Cyzicus
Dead Eyes

Printed in Great Britain
by Amazon